I0571684

Gorgon Times

Roderick Robinson

We are in the hands of that brass-headed gorgon

Basil Greetham, editor, Real Production

ISBN 978-1-84327-941-9
Cover design: Patrick T Coyne

The Racing House Press
20 Cambridge Drive
London SE12 8AJ, UK

Printed and bound by Lightning Source

Gorgon Times
A working brief

The chances are you have a job; the chances are it isn't the sort of job that figures in novels. Unless, of course, you're a policeman, an art gallery employee, an academic, or – Lord help us – a writer. Book jobs are a tight little world.

I believe we are defined by our jobs but since most of us don't chase rapists, moon about Lucian Freud, deconstruct Derrida or overcome authorial block we rarely see our lives mirrored in fiction. Gorgon Times was written with most of us in mind.

Gorgon Times was also written in parallel with a blog, Works Well, which attempted to enliven what I call technology. Works Well took the line that a gearbox, described intelligently, can match a Brancusi. Occasionally I posted details about my progress with the MS and several readers responded with encouragement and help.

I owe special thanks to:

Plutarch *http://bestofnow.blogspot.co.uk/*
Read/re-read the MS; saved my bacon many times over.

Eleanor *http://eleanorfromthecommentbox.blogspot.co.uk/*
Created Kylie to the last scissor-snip; handed her to me on a plate.

The Crow *http://sofieonecrow.blogspot.co.uk/*
Discussed the nature of being a woman.

Julia *http://kolokolo.blogspot.co.uk/*
Taught me verse-writing.

Veronica Bore the absences, prepared the meals, shared the music.

Gorgon Times

Background noise

- I came to office with one deliberate intent: to change Britain from a dependent to a self-reliant society — from a give-it-to-me, to a do-it-yourself nation. A get-up-and-go, instead of a sit-back-and-wait-for-it Britain.

- Don't you think that's the way to persuade more companies to come to this region and get more jobs - because I want them - for the people who are unemployed. Not always standing there as moaning minnies. Now stop it!

- Successful entrepreneurship is ultimately a matter of flair. But there is also a fund of practical knowledge to be acquired and, of course, the right legal and financial framework has to be provided for productive enterprise to develop

- What is success? I think it is a mixture of having a flair for the thing that you are doing; knowing that it is not enough, that you have got to have hard work and a certain sense of purpose

- I do not know anyone who has got to the top without hard work. That is the recipe. It will not always get you to the top, but should get you pretty near.

- The desire to win is (inborn). The will to win is a matter of training. The manner of winning is a matter of honour.

- One only gets to the top rung of the ladder by steadily climbing up one at a time, and suddenly all sorts of powers, all sorts of abilities which you thought never belonged to you suddenly become within your own possibility.

- Whether manufactured by black, white, brown or yellow hands, a widget remains a widget - and it will be bought anywhere if the price and quality are right. The market is a more powerful and more reliable liberating force than government can ever be.

POLITICIAN TALK IN THE EIGHTIES

1. HATCH

French disconnection

HE'D noticed the building on three previous visits and each time he'd found himself pausing and staring.

The jutting angles said it was architect-designed, that it hadn't arrived as kit on a lorry. But what kind of architect specified buttresses – supposedly emblems of strength and security - in paper-thin aluminium pierced with wide circular holes? Or a central gazebo fashioned in clumsy square tubing?

And why ape the colours of the Swedish flag? Blue roofs that arched up like the prow of a ship supported by ribbed walls in dayglo yellow. The whole thing as insubstantial as a child's playhouse, too tinny to withstand even a mythical sea.

Hatch knew his limitations, knew his Britishness was out of step with the French desire to be different. But he was born into industry. He'd visited companies in France housed in similar buildings and this wilful fragility clearly represented a policy which other PDGs shared. Yet this one contained five units and must have been financed speculatively. What developer could be so certain of finding five tenants willing to accept this expression of commerce?

Hatch opened the door of the tiny Peugeot and for the first time noticed the surrounding car park was empty - offices and workshops unmistakably muffled and inert. Lemazaire's unit was on the right but there was no sign of life behind the glass frontage.

On Lemazaire's door hung an *horaires d'ouverture*: a plastic plaque with four clock faces and rotatable hands. Signs of presence and absence. On the Saturday clock both hands stood at twelve: the equivalent of nothing o'clock, no business. Hands on the weekday clocks had been positioned carelessly but he guessed that visitors arriving after twelve-thirty would kick their heels for two hours. Frustration that had subsided since Cherbourg rose again. Hatch tried the door, found it locked and banged at his sturdy-armed reflection. A shadow in *bleu de travail* appeared in reception, pointed to the clock faces and retired. Using fist and car keys Hatch banged away but to no avail.

There was however a sheet of paper – a letter – Sellotaped inside the door. Perhaps that offered something relevant. The text was short enough to encourage Hatch to make sense of the few lines of French. Then he noticed the date, 1988. The letter was two years old.

Hatch leant against the car, stuffed his hands into the pockets of his unsuitably thick corduroy trousers and looked again at the blue and yellow building. Saw the irony. A super-modernist shape combined with in/out clocks dating back decades. In the meantime where was Lemazaire?

He'd come too far and spent too much money to retreat in the face of all this Frenchness; to give in to these surrounding facades and their unhelpful acronyms - SNIC and FANECMA. But where and how? Lemazaire, he knew, drove a Mercedes which would stand out among parked French cars in the nearby small town. Hatch couldn't recall the colour but it would come to him.

Seized with determination he drove towards the town and pulled in at the waggishly named Relais des Noës. Inside the open doorway sweating waiters carrying full trays of aperitifs brushed past him but they were the ones at risk. He stepped abruptly into the flow and barked *Patron* at a startled young face. The lad directed him to the bar where a short man wearing a Harris tweed jacket lolled, apparently impervious to the heat. Too impatient to express what he wanted Hatch misused the word *affaire* and the man looked blank.

"*Affaire? Quelle affaire?*" he asked, comically scanning the bar for delinquent wives.

"Pardon. It is a matter of commerce."

Business, it seemed, was business. The man switched to circuitous but recognisable English. "This monsieur, you believe he is a client here? His name, please."

"Lemazaire. His office is near."

This brought no response. Hatch guessed Lemazaire did not eat at the Relais des Noës but the restaurateur wasn't prepared to admit it. There was a delay as the restaurateur reached down a bottle of scotch and poured himself a drink. Curious about the label, Hatch noted the brand: McClaggart, unknown in Britain, christened aggressively to appeal to the French.

"This monsieur, his *métier* is…"

Factor in welding consumables was way beyond Hatch's capacity but he responded in kind, indeed found it difficult to avoid doing so: "He interests himself in welding, er, *la soudure.*"

The restaurateur looked grandly out over the dining room and lied, "He does not take lunch today."

"He lives some miles – some kilometres – away. Too far away for lunch. Are there other restaurants?"

"Of course." This was, after all, France.

"Could you suggest…? It is vital I see him."

"Vital?"

"Important."

"And yet it is lunch time." He noted Hatch's perspiring forehead. "Perhaps you are not comfortable. Why not take a table, command a beer and eat here? In the afternoon you will meet your famous monsieur Lemazaire in his office."

"I would like to eat here. This is the sort of restaurant I like," said Hatch, lying with the same ease as the restaurateur. "Monsieur Lemazaire and I have a customer who needs our service. A customer, monsieur." Hatch gestured at the pastis-swilling crowd. "One must serve a customer."

This touched on a sense of professionalism and Hatch left with precise instructions about two other restaurants in the Place de l'Eglise ("Simple places, monsieur. The *plat du jour*."). In the second Lemazaire was immediately visible, looking up, a frond of radicchie hanging from his mouth, beside him a carafe of rosé a third consumed.

"Andrew you are here at last."

"And you… are there."

"*Bien sur.* You are hot. Some wine? Why don't you sit down."

Lemazaire, sitting, was forced to lean back to speak to Hatch. Hatch straightened up making it even more difficult. "You go to lunch early."

"The normal time."

"I was at your place soon after twelve-thirty. We would have passed each other." He looked significantly at the carafe. "You left early."

"It was lunchtime."

"An elastic concept."

Lemazaire's English was fluent but not complete. "I do not… Andrew, please sit down."

On the wall was a mirror on which *art nouveau* script advertised a drink called Suze. The words fragmented their reflection: he, the Anglo, with close-cropped brown hair, rolled-up sleeves, golden fuzz on his forearms, facing Lemazaire's delicate Mediterranean bones, artfully styled black hair and generously cut shirt. "You were supposed to wait. We were to go to Sofimam together."

"But it would have… lacked point."

"It was what we agreed."

"Andrew, please sit down." The urgency had increased and Hatch now understood why. Other diners, possibly business acquaintances, were watching Lemazaire with interest.

"Why pointless?"

"Because Baudinière would have left the plant."

"Our meeting…?" But Hatch knew the answer.

"He would have been at lunch himself." Lemazaire's concern was audible. He gabbled. "Today is Friday; he eats at Le Chêne Doré. Always." The dark liquid eyes engaged Hatch's. "Close to the Nantes – Brest canal."

That last detail – that non-sequitur - persuaded Hatch that Lemazaire had suffered enough. Saying nothing, he waited until the silence became unnatural then lowered himself on to a nearby chair. A sigh ran round the other diners.

Lemazaire's relief was palpable. "We did say ten-thirty this morning," He glanced at his wristwatch with its heavy expandable bracelet. "That was nearly three hours ago. He will have contacted another source of rutiles."

"Portsmouth had a bomb scare," said Hatch. "But surely Baudinière has a problem. He needs to weld up those pressure vessels. It's a defence contract with penalties. I have the first batch of wire in the car."

"Your… our delay will have let in our biggest competitor Toutsoudure. They will make the formulation very quickly. Andrew, you did your best."

"My best, Jean-Claude?" The midnight start had caught up with him and he was suddenly tired. "That isn't how Tamworth will see it."

"They will understand. It's a beautiful day. You may try an *andouillette* for the first time." Lemazaire tapped the carafe. "First a drink."

But the rosé reminded Hatch of the missed rendezvous. "Not that. Some of that," indicating the Suze advertisement. Lemazaire's eyebrows rose as did those of the waiter who took the order but neither said anything. Both watched interestedly as Hatch sipped. "What the hell's this?" Hatch asked incredulously.

"An *apéritif á la gentiane*. Made from flowers of the Alps. Rather bitter I would say. It calms the stomach. Did it calm your stomach?"

"Not exactly," said Hatch leaning back in his chair. Then he laughed and it was a relief to do so.

Forewarned by the Suze he asked Lemazaire to explain the *andouillette*, teetered, then shrugged his shoulders. After which the meal followed a leisurely course.

As they drank coffee Hatch's mind turned, as it often did, to the crux in his own professional life. "At university, Jean-Claude, what subject?"

"Political philosophy."

That sounded like two subjects. "And yet you sell for a living?"

"I think the English is: it's a stepping stone. I will move on. My uncle runs the holding company."

"And yet you are a good salesman. Friends recommended you."

"Except, perhaps, today," said Jean-Claude, demurely lowering his long eyelashes. "Yes, I am successful. But you, Andrew, were not always a salesman?"

"No," said Hatch heavily. "That's true."

AS OF OLD, Baudinière received him with heartless courtesy. The missed delivery? Such things happened. The communication failures by Lemazaire? (Hatch had come alone.) Jean-Claude was young and had yet to learn the exigencies of manufacturing industry. And the future? There was no reason why Hatch might not try again once this current *ennui* had been forgotten.

But Hatch, present only to apologise, had other things on his mind. They were sitting in an office on a mezzanine overlooking Sofimam's production area. Final assembly lay below and when Baudinière took an incoming phone call, Hatch swung round in his chair to inspect things more closely. It didn't make sense.

Behind him, Baudinière put down the phone and said genially, "Ah the war-horse smells the gunpowder. You notice our little changes. A production line that is not a production line."

"It looks - might one say - a little messy?"

"Exactly what my managers said. Engineers, all of them. They shouted about the aesthetics. Such nonsense."

Hatch waited but Baudinière, still smiling, still expansive, wanted him to ask the obvious question. As a way of substantiating his apology. "Why the changes, Luc?"

"Cellular manufacture."

Hatch gritted his teeth. "I thought it was still experimental. Only the Japs had tackled it."

"We are not the first, even in Loire-Atlantique. As you know Sofimam looked at just-in-time even when we were friendly competitors with Tempest. But in those days we lacked the technology."

Not wishing to waste his act of contrition Hatch ignored "friendly competitors". Back then Sofimam hadn't merely lacked the technology they'd lacked the cash and the professional daring. Tempest, Hatch's former employer in Britain, had been more profitable, more advanced and more commercially adventurous. Only an unforeseeable liability case by a litigious French retailer and a xenophobic court judgment about what constituted a safe wall plug had laid Tempest low. Sofimam's subsequent growth was mainly because Tempest had disappeared from the European market.

"And you designed the system down there yourself, Luc?"

"I am a genius at production, but not that kind of genius. After the age of forty one uses consultants. Our plant was analysed by an American - young enough to be my son yet he'd worked for Boeing and Intel. I paid his huge fee from the departmental budget to prevent argument. Then I told the board. They recognised the value of the changes more quickly than my engineers."

"And so..."

"One discards the central conveyor and learns much new jargon. We are now - " Baudinière pronounced the English phrases with relish, "demand-driven. We react to pull instead of push. There are, I believe, French translations but no one uses them. Instead, we stand everything on its head and see inventory cut to twenty percent. But you know the theory."

Hatch did know the theory. What he lacked was the experience. Baudinière resumed his unctuousness. "My dear Andrew, I am sure if Tempest had been more fortunate you would have told me what I have just told you. And I am convinced you would have got there first."

Fulsome, but nevertheless a compliment. "I envy you the exhilaration, Luc. Production is normally so gradual: a few mods here, a few there." Hatch gestured. "We spend quarter-of-a-million on a machine tool but the gains are small and so predictable. You re-ordered the universe."

"In the end it is company politics. One learns, one calculates the benefits, one influences those who control the *caisse*. But... what about you, at this moment? This company you work for, Weldworth..."

"Terrible name. Engineers are no good at christening companies. Welding and Tamworth. A sort of..."

"A *jeu de mots*. Ah, I see. Welding consumables are surely only a minor – and temporary - consolation?"

"It's selling, Luc. Something neither you nor I were trained for. And it's taking responsibility for others with imperfect skills."

"Selling is different, Andrew. Jean-Claude Lemazaire has no conception of critical path and we both do. But he knows how to - what do the Americans say? - put a foot in the door. He discovered you and I had professional links and he approached Sofimam. That is how selling works."

"Then wrecked the sale by misinforming us, forgetting to pass on a crucial date, and being unreachable for three days. He lacks discipline."

"His is a different discipline, Andrew."

Hatch switched from an unprofitable subject. "You used to have a drawing table in your office. Wasn't it your father's?"

"Indeed. He bought it for two hundred and seventeen francs in 1932. A colossal sum then. I discarded it several years ago, once I'd installed CAD."

"CAD?"

Baudinière frowned. "Computer-aided design."

Hatch knew about CAD but the pronunciation had foxed him. "I misheard. I'm not that out of touch." Yet it probably seemed all of piece to Baudinière.

"These days the drawings are on the network. The Sun over there has the CAD; the spreadsheets and word-processing are on the PC, here." Hatch had deliberately continued to keep up with computers since leaving Tempest. But it was one thing to spot trends and quite another to deduce why Baudinière needed two computer monitors.

Hatch drew himself up. "It was good of you to see me Luc. I needed to explain."

"Not for a moment were they your errors. I know you. I have been to your factory and you have been to mine. I have heard you give papers. It wasn't you."

Hatch said, "Once we were competitors, we both made washing machines. But we still got on. Nice to know that still happens."

"Washing machines are irrelevant. What matters is professionalism. The cell scheme lets us diversify. As you know, Jean-Claude's MIG wire -" Baudinière waved sympathetically. "was needed for pressure vessels. I refuse to concentrate eternally on stabilising the fast spin cycle. Yet, it is all production. By the way, you would be welcome to stay with us tonight if you can delay your return."

A gruesome thought. "Thanks Luc, but I do have a ferry to catch." Which was true but unimportant.

Driving north on the Rennes road, sweating as Sofimam's air conditioning became a memory, Hatch held Baudinière at arm's length. At Tempest Hatch had worked to a budget, a set of financial rules, an industrial necessity. Nothing to get sentimental about. Yet Baudinière's casual allusion to budgets gave the word a mild poignancy. It was of course a reminder of Hatch's lost office, that sales were a step down and a step away . This afternoon he had watched the show again, but from the wings.

ON THE Southampton ferry he bought The Daily Telegraph, throwing away everything but the classifieds. The newspaper would shortly become a new regime, something of a barometer of his affairs. Two years ago he'd been startled when his local newsagent, a visibly prospering Pakistani, had handed over his copy with a remark that assumed Hatch supported the Conservatives.

"It's the newspaper for engineers," Hatch had protested.

"Indeed. I trained as a systems analyst myself and I too read the dear old Bellylaugh. Now I find it consonant with my politics."

"And yet you.... " Hatch gestured at Mars Bars and Silk Cut.

"My dear fellow, mere economic pragmatism. I could have spent forty years with ICL and retired on a modest pension. Instead I shall sell this gold mine in four years and put my principles into practice. I shall stand for a constituency in the Conservative interest."

Hatch left the shop shocked at hard science traded for rolls of gift wrapping. He pretended the fellow hadn't been a good systems analyst but something about the newsagent suggested otherwise. And then there was also that damnable matter of politics.

At university Hatch had disdained politics on the grounds that it defied quantification. To the few leftists he met - and there weren't many at Loughborough - he pooh-poohed Gramsci and quoted instead Lord Kelvin's "To measure is to know" as the firmer rock on which to build a faith. He had neither the time nor the cash for newspapers at Loughborough but once he started work he noticed that mech-engs favoured the Telegraph, tried it, decided it was "factual" and willy-nilly became a Telegraph reader. At that point he'd have been hard put to say what the paper's political slant was since he only read the news stories and ignored the comment.

Here on the ferry he'd reduced the paper to a bunch of cards in a Job Centre. Appalled by the waste he picked a discarded editorial page from the rubbish bin. The major story described a government crisis but couldn't be taken at face value. It was a crisis that *might* happen *when,* or *if,* something else happened. In Brussels. Hatch hated this: looking for definition and finding only speculation.

He turned over the page and found a headline about the poll tax. Here at least he was on firmer ground. He knew that the government had declared local rates to be unfair and was intent on replacing them with a new system, said to be fairer. Moved by self-interest he had studied the poll tax in the early days when articles still explained rather than interpreted. He'd even pursued it in the weeks that followed since he was never able to see how the new tax was fairer or why it was worth the flak the government was attracting. Something of a political mystery.

By now he recognised a note of desperation as journalists scratched around to say something new about poll tax and to avoid repetition. Only a small part of the article he was reading could be termed news and even that was hardly current, dealing with the aftermath of anti-government riots in Brixton a month before. The rest speculated apocalyptically about the prime minister's future. Did this matter?

Presumably it did if one was a Conservative. And that for Hatch had never been truly established. During his time with Tempest, across management meeting tables, at professional conferences and on first-class train journeys down to London, the consensus was that the present government was "good for business". Since Tempest's profits had grown during the same period Hatch had nodded his head and had left it at that. Tempest's chairman had received an OBE in the New Year's honours and invited senior staff to agree that his gong "could only benefit washing machine manufacture". Shamefaced now, Hatch had nodded at this too. This made him Conservative by default.

Another strand in his life also supported this rather rickety stance. At Loughborough the tiny Socialist Workers Party, tickled by his Lord Kelvin quote, had taken a shine to Hatch after he'd led a group of self-conscious mech-eng students in a campaign to reinstate a canteen employee, fired for uncleanliness. The SWP met Hatch convivially in the student bar and bought him a beer to show solidarity. In the interests of equality the four of them allowed him to return the favour.

But the gesture foundered on the rock of their rhetoric. Hatch was alarmed by an avalanche of avowals about nationalising the means of production, disbanding the police and forming local militia.

Firing the woman was a typical capitalist power-play, he was told. The crushing of a vulnerable member of society. On a trumped-up charge.

"But it wasn't trumped-up," Hatch pointed out.

"Of course it was. Pure exploitation. Do you know what her hourly rate is?"

"That's irrelevant. She was seen regularly moving garbage bins and returning to the servery without washing her hands."

"A rumour cooked up by management."

"Not so. I've seen her do it myself – several times."

"But you campaigned…"

"It's an open and shut case."

"Oh look, come on"

"Incorrect procedures. Firing's a last resort. And only after informal and formal warnings."

Hatch found himself surrounded by angry, frustrated faces. The members of the SWP had either not taken Basic Management (Industrial Relations) or had done so and rejected its philosophy. In unison they stood up, condemned Hatch as a Tory wanker and made for the door. Two even underlined their feelings by leaving partially full glasses.

Hatch had mixed feelings. His views remained ill-defined but he had no enthusiasm for state-run manufacturing. Part of him at least must surely be Conservative.

If working for Tempest didn't exactly nourish a right-wing tendency it provided a marinade, preserving it and adding flavour. Tempest was flourishing and Hatch flourished with it. When the status quo brings bonuses and promotion there's less temptation to look elsewhere. Hatch continued to absorb the Telegraph's "facts" while remaining ignorant of its politics, sliding ineluctably towards the template that fitted a typical reader.

But failure breeds doubt. When Tempest lost out in the courts Hatch's ladder disappeared and with it his default Conservatism. Finding himself thrashing about in the world of selling brought doubts aplenty. And now even that unsatisfying job would be lost on Monday, turning him into an activist, tackling the establishment from outside. Work - desirable work - lay within a walled city which presently excluded him.

As the ferry ploughed the early evening sea, and the legions of the damned clinked their duty-frees round C Deck, Hatch turned his attention to the classifieds, analysing an invitation to join a noted engineering company as production manager. Degree, OK. Experience, OK. Even age seemed negotiable (Or did the law force advertisers to lie about this requirement?). Location in the West Midlands, fine. But how about: "Capable of supervising tightly-defined supplier partnerships"?

For Hatch, job descriptions were clear or cloudy mirrors of his competence. Supplier partnerships - where buyer and vendor open their books to each other - were outside his experience. He turned the page to read about opportunities in Indonesia but imagined being a non-smoker would tell against him as he asked to be allowed to commission a tobacco-products plant.

His heart wasn't in it. Job ads were depressing because they assumed a need to read them. A signpost between those tucked into comforting employment and those lacking that comfort. But the language of comfort itself was depressing, a collection of pebbles with all distinguishing features worn away. Could "hard working" ever hope to separate out the drones? And was "join a dynamic team" anything other than an invitation to enlist in the human race? Why was it that the companies all sounded fictitious?

But once, at least, he must have succumbed to such unreal language.

The ad that had drawn him into Tempest was now forgotten but it could hardly have been witty or out of the ordinary. Tempest was a traditional manufacturer through and through. Certainly

Hatch's initial months hadn't matched any grandiose promises and a less energetic trainee could have whiled away a decade as part of the company's residue. Moving on had forced him to be sly and ruthless, neither of them qualities mentioned in job ads.

While labouring in quality control – repetitive work, almost at apprentice level - he got wind of an unpaid vacancy liaising between the drawing office and Tempest's senior management. The role had never previously existed and lack of extra cash had discouraged applications. But the board had somehow identified the need and the senior manager charged with the appointment explained things quite simply: drawing offices cost money and, at the very least, deserved scrutiny.

"Basically, you want a spy." Hatch suggested.

The manager laughed in affirmation.

"How quickly is the board looking for results?"

The manager shifted slightly. "Quite quickly. Look, I could probably get you something ex gratia if you're interested."

"I'd rather be responsible for upping efficiency."

"What do you know about running a drawing office?"

"Very little. But ours gives poor service and I have a couple of ideas."

"Tell me about them." They went down well and Hatch was free to try his arm.

Elwyn, fat and disappointed, allowed his huge angled board to act as protection against Hatch, the new menace. He waited, mouth formed in protest, as Hatch said, "I intend to ride a personal hobby-horse here."

"So what? Drawing's fucking drawing. Simplest thing in the company. Nothing changes." Then came his well-honed masterstroke. "Thinking of saving a penny or two by watering the ink?"

"No. But I have been thinking about paper."

Elwyn's eyebrows shrank. "Paper! What the hell does that mean?"

"Any idea how much paper we waste?"

"None at all."

"None?"

"A few sheets. A piddling amount. No savings there."

"There are different ways of wasting paper."

"Don't know what the fuck you're talking about."

"That's because you do the drawings, you don't use them. You aren't bent over a lathe sorting through piles of detail sheets for the main specs."

Thinking he'd spotted a weakness Elwyn waded in. "So you'll do away with detail drawings? You'd better buy a shit-proof umbrella."

"Elwyn old chap, give me credit. That isn't the plan. But surely you can guess what the plan is. Do so and it's your idea rather than mine."

Elwyn dated back to washing machines with fitted mangles and his reflexes had long since slowed down. He stared at Hatch but the light-bulb failed to switch on. Devotion to routine had betrayed him and Hatch handed him a signed memo. "It's no big thing Elwyn. Here's a schedule of scale changes. We'll win sufficient space on the main specs to accommodate the detail drawings."

Elwyn glanced at the sheet of paper but the numerical data offered nothing he could absorb in the seconds he had available. A final glimmer from his porcine eyes: "The numbering system doesn't cover it. One drawing, one number."

Hatch passed over another memo. "I've rejigged the sequence. It's explained here."

Initial recognition came from the shopfloor. Tool operators tied to the multi-sheet system insisted on "Hatch" drawings. The senior manager, having answered the board's request without spending a penny, passed Hatch's name upwards – notably to the production manager who was planning for retirement and saw a bright candidate for his deputy.

One other Tempest employee was a gainer. Given time to examine Hatch's scheme more closely, Elwyn noted it didn't work with two export models; the obvious answer was to group the detail drawings. On his own initiative he drafted examples, made an appointment and laid them in front of the newly appointed deputy production manager.

Hatch grinned at Elwyn. "You'd never believe me if I told you I was aware of these two exceptions. They don't matter; my system holds true for the majority and I got acceptance for that. But you're due your bit"

Elwyn received £150 in W. H. Smith gift vouchers and his photograph appeared under the headline "Best idea of 1979" in the company magazine. His wife said the photo flattered him and he was encouraged to submit two other suggestions which were not adopted but gained him £10 vouchers on each occasion. On the rare occasions he and Hatch met in the company corridors a furtive look passed over his convex face.

Chilled now by the sea air Hatch folded up the newspaper and dropped it in the bin. In urgent need of coffee he nevertheless remained seated, idly drafting a job ad intended for the real world. "Young engineer wanted - probably maddened by routine work Willing to chance himself to escape drudgery. Some ingenuity desirable. Forceful enough to override entrenched opinion. Driven to get his own way. Skilled in hiding his own shortcomings and in seeing the benefits of compromise. Able to withstand peer hatred."

2. HATCH

Light to the suburbs

"IT'S simple enough. You cut out a floorboard in the small bedroom. That way you hide the take-off from the rose in your hallway. Link the take-off to another rose under the floorboards. Run one line to your new outdoor light and another, down the wall, to a switch inside the porch."

"Good God, I didn't think it would be so radical. There's fitted carpet in the small bedroom. Would we have to...?" Makings' voice faded as he imagined Hatch violating the house's interior, presently tidy and final.

"It'll take two hours," said Hatch.. "We'll be having a G and T at six, waiting for it to get dark so we can test it."

"I'm not sure Hester will approve."

"We'll be finished by the time she's back."

"Well.... "

Hatch worked quickly and surely to purge yesterday's disappointments in France. When Makings winced as carpet was torn noisily from the floor battens, Hatch sent him to B&Q to buy a number ten drill bit "which may be necessary". That way Makings would not suffer the greater trauma of hearing the floorboard sawn. Afterwards Makings was made to hand over tools, screws and cable as Hatch's acolyte.

By the time Hester's Renault turned into driveway the system was not only working but - to Makings' greater relief - the carpet had been relaid. Hester solemnly operated the burglar light switch in the porch. "You've been having fun," she said. "At least, one of you has."

Makings said, "Andrew worked as if he were driven."

"Nice to see something go right," said Hatch looking at his watch. "Isn't it about G and T time?"

They sat in wicker chairs overlooking the long manicured garden at the back of the house. As Hester stretched her generous body the basketwork creaked. She said to Hatch: "Thank you for the light. Tom seemed dubious. He told me what was involved and the word 'rose' cropped up non-horticulturally."

Makings rattled ice in his tall glass. "That turned out to be a minor matter. Like suturing after a heart-bypass. I won't go into details, my dear. You needn't share my fears - even retrospectively. Andrew was confident. I surrendered."

"Masterful Andrew," Hester said.

Hatch tried to shrug but was unconvincing from a sitting position. "It's the sort of thing I do. It's why I'm such a brilliant guest."

Hester said, "Tom and I are agreed about artisan work. If he explains every stage, and I can envisage the project, I may approve. Any woolliness and I put my foot down. Solicitors have only one skill - putting a fine gloss on delay. I can't abide his boasting about *bricolage*. I want him to talk about fees and case law, not Rawlplugs."

"Female chauvinism," said Makings. "DIY is for men yet here in my own home I'm discouraged. Cut off from my peers."

"For your own good, darling. You're not terribly good at screwdrivers. Mind you, I'd be just as harsh if you took up something chic - like bookbinding. Remember, only literary types can turn failure into something valuable. In your case it plays hell with the wallpaper."

"You're simply snobbish about DIY."

"Not at all. I would never, for instance, discourage Andrew."

"Sounds ambiguous," said Makings, grinning.

"Does my ambiguity disturb you, Andrew?"

"I'd repair anything for you, Hester. You know that."

"There, Tom. Andrew's not put out and you're free to apply your mind to other - higher - things."

A familiar battleground. Makings stood up, bent over his wife and kissed her affectionately on the mouth. "We need some more tonic. Be polite to Andrew while I'm gone."

As the door closed, Hester put down her glass. "Why did you make such a thing about this burglar light?"

"I needed to be useful."

"Oh," said Hester, disappointed.

"To do something Tom couldn't do, that he felt afraid of."

"That's better. Catharsis, then. This has to do with Weldworth?"

"I'm just back from France. Things didn't go well."

"Let's discuss it when Tom gets back. You know how he cares about that side of you. In the meantime let's look for tonic water options." She got out of the low chair with coordinated grace, knees and ankles together, a minimum of visible effort. Over the last decade she'd had put on a stone, which she disguised with one-piece dresses that clung to her shoulders and spilled vertically from her breasts. As a result her bodylines were columnar, the extra weight showing as majesty rather than bulk.

In the grandly appointed kitchen Hester retrieved a lime from the fridge and placed it on the monster slab of polished granite. "It becomes a grasshopper when added to gin," she said, refilling Hatch's glass and frowning at the amounts. The two of them stood quite close together.

"I didn't ask whether you would like a grasshopper."

"You didn't."

"People might imagine I dictate to you." It was a familiar game, no rules and a goal that remained obscure. Hester smiled without affection; a social expression. Not waiting for a response she went out through the French windows. Hatch followed.

Despite the straight lines of his profession he hated the severe lawn and flower beds.

"Your projects never included the soil," Hester said.

"The garden was a duty not a pleasure. Living over Mister Wee's shop has its disadvantages but at least I don't have to pot out. If that's correct; some gardeners pot on."

"Poor Andrew. Did Prudence force you to love nature?"

Hatch sighed. "I doubt she would have cared if the garden had reverted to a building site. Me, I took up the white man's burden, the white middle-class man's burden. I mowed the lawn just as I used a car and not a motorbike. It went with the territory."

"Dear Prudence," said Hester vaguely, ignoring the suburban rule-book. "Is she well?"

"Well enough. Febrile."

"If you don't want to talk about her, we won't."

"Do you really want to know, or - "

" – am I teasing?" Hester laughed, wriggling her shoulders in a way Hatch believed to be unique. "Andrew, you're a family friend. You come round for meals because we enjoy your company. Because you interest us. No more single-word replies."

"She's got a bee in her bonnet about the tenants. Wants them out. Wants the house back."

"Didn't she move heaven and earth to get them into the place?"

"She did. But now there's dirty work and she wants me to do it. We can't evict them of course, they've got a lease. I'm supposed to negotiate."

"Wasn't she pathological about the house. Bad memories, sense of the past."

"She refuses to explain." The irritation he'd suppressed was starting to show. "As if she had a cock-eyed notion of proving herself superior. As if my problems at work were a sign of weakness."

"Would you have split up if there'd been a child?"

The history between Hatch and Hester allowed her to ride rough-shod over him when they were alone. That was how Hatch saw things. But this was surely a foul blow. He stared.

"No offence. Just asking," she said casually, turning away.

"How do you mean, no offence?"

She half-turned and he saw her vulnerability. Knew he'd been too sharp.

They walked slowly down the garden and reached a trellised arch round which climbing roses had been trained. Hatch noticed the sinuous, almost random, routes the branches had taken and recalled the squareness of the flowerbeds. Framed by the arch, Hester turned to face him. Her face was calm now and thus ambiguous.

He, however, was concerned that the off-licence was less than half a mile away.

"Don't worry," she said, noticing his nervousness. "Tom likes you."

"I like him," said Hatch impulsively.

"That always surprised me. But after all he solved a problem for you."

"He's generous and charitable. He likes you and cares for you."

Hester looked startled. She resumed walking along the path that divided the vegetable patch. Hatch didn't care to be so far from the house, obscured by pampas grass and A-frames supporting the bean plants. He felt the two of them might appear covert if viewed from the French windows. Angling his shoulder towards the house he showed his unease.

"For goodness sake, stop fussing," Hester said. "I do the garden. Quite natural I should show it off to you."

"So that's what we're doing? Looking at the garden?"

"We're behaving as we always do. Avoiding questions that matter. Picking a scab, seeing whether it can be lifted, eager to see fresh skin."

"Do you see fresh skin?"

"I do not." Irritated, Hester swooped down on a strawberry plant and flicked a slug sideways towards the compost heap. Practised grace.

"And Tom?"

"Tom continues to be Tom, seeing good in everyone. Not that he has any reason to think otherwise. When you became a divorcé you became his obligation, albeit a pleasant one. The invitations come from him, every time."

"I assumed so. I thought of turning them down, phasing myself out. But he'd never leave it there. He'd be round to practise his forensic skills. He's a difficult person to lie to."

"Very difficult."

Makings, as thin as Hester was generous, saw meals as a back-drop to wine, his major interest. Since the bottles were plentiful and part of an agenda, the accompanying dishes had to be equally varied and numerous. Sancerre rosé matched tiny crab cakes and a more substantial Pouilly Vinzelle the sole. Now the first of the reds - Makings' true passion - was being poured as Hester laid down plates on which a single lamb noisette cuddled a teaspoonful of spinach. Because Hatch now cooked for himself, the Makings dinners had taken on added significance. Slightly tipsy, he admitted the logistics astonished him

Makings only entered the kitchen to wash champagne flutes and pooh-poohed the idea. "Hester says it's a matter of organisation. We needn't go this far; dry bread or crackers would be satisfactory."

"Oh no they wouldn't." said Hester.

Makings laughed. "No reflection, dear. But with this Pichon Longueville food's almost a distraction."

Under Makings' guidance the married Hatch had kept a modest cellar. Betsitterdom, a reduced income and a perverse enthusiasm for austerity had swept all that away. Opening a bottle of wine, alone, in a room where his bed was visible, would be close to self-abuse.

Makings was constantly sensitive to Hatch's changed situation. "I say, Andrew, I hope you don't see our evenings as Louis Seize. Hester and I only bring out the gold-plated corkscrew for people we like. Otherwise it's Languedoc-Roussillon." He invited Hester's support.

"Tom hates untutored gullets."

"It's more than that. Andrew, you're not here as a charitable ex-ercise. Not even because you're better than me with joists. We invite you - "

"I wasn't sighing because second-growth claret is financially be-yond me." Hatch sat up. "Look, the wine is fantastic and could run for another twenty years. And to hell with water biscuits, it needs the lamb. There, that's the diplomacy out of the way. Now it's time to blow my own trumpet. While we sit here boozing darkness has fallen. I insist Hester throws the light switch for real. Take your glasses: the better the deed the better the drink."

They gazed at the illuminated drive. "Contours I'd never known before," said Hester.

"It could cut the insurance," Makings responded.

"Needs a more powerful bulb; three hundred watts at least," said Hatch.

Only after the cognac did Makings return to the collective consciousness. "Are things tight?" he asked Hatch. "Surely there's some way we can help."

Hatch welcomed this approach. "Money isn't an immediate concern. I live on twenty-five per cent of what I used to think was the absolute minimum. And I'm like a fatty on a diet: proud of my economies. How about this: at seven-thirty the supermarket marks down unsold confectionery by a half. Bet you didn't know that. But if you're browsing at that unfashionable hour watch the faces. First the eager response; second that very English preoccupation - hiding the guilt. I'm not just surviving on short commons, I'm prospering. But thanks truly for the offer."

"If it isn't money then...?" said Makings.

"It's his wretched status."

"Not quite," said Hatch. "Oh what the hell, Hester's right. She stopped me from being more pompous. But let's say - *earned* status. That's the major distinction. I look back on the mech-eng, the shopfloor, the sub-manager jobs, the ten years before I had my own desk. Status for me, perhaps, but it meant nothing in the suburbs. I wasn't a doctor, a marketing prat or - " A gesture towards Makings. "a solicitor. People at dinner parties thought I wore a boiler suit at the plant."

He sipped cognac. "Personal status, as I say. Manufacturing never attracts lay applause. When I took three pee cost out of a front-loader door nobody clapped. Same thing when I bought polystyrene to cut packaging time by thirty percent."

"I clapped," said Makings. "Your job at Tempest was real world. Washing machines are real; county court judgements are ephemeral. You managed people. I manage paper - and opinions."

Hatch laughed harshly. "Pichon Longueville talking, Tom. Your view of manufacturing is a teensy bit suspect. I'm rather in love with that American phrase: a working stiff. I like the self-deprecation, the honesty. It's all I've ever wanted to be – a working stiff. Your working day is spent with articulate peers; your clients may be monosyllabic but they're just raw material. You mould them; it's clean and it's nicely theoretical. My working day was often spent in an ill-lit shed, persuading an eighteen-year-old press-brake operator to wear ear muffs. Fat chance. Ear muffs are for sissies - something that affected *his* status."

"But you're not outside industry, even now."

"Tom, I'm a salesman with Weldworth for Christ's sake. Selling welding consumables doesn't mean a rat's arse. What's hard to bear is I'm not a terrifically good salesman. I'm no huckster, no good at choosing other hucksters. In any case - " Hatch broke off.

"In any case, what?"

"Post-claret tristesse."

Makings was not equipped to break the silence. Hester said: "Andrew's had a bad day. This trip to France."

"France," said Makings. "You had high hopes. No, never mind. Let's have another cognac."

Makings' decency appalled Hatch. "Arggh," he said, rising out of the easy chair to hold out his glass. "High hopes are right. Were right. I was going to show a little Weldworth hustle. A customer in Brittany had an emergency, needed a special formulation of MIG wire. He set a deadline and we didn't make it. Result: no regular contract. End of story."

"Didn't make the deadline? That isn't like you, Andrew."

"You're the second person to say that. The other, for God's sake, was my customer, a French guy I've known for years. But it makes no difference. I had other responsibilities. I worked through a distributor, someone I appointed. He let me down – more than once - and I ended up in the last chance saloon, catching a ferry to reach the customer with an hour to spare. But the ferry left three hours late."

"Hardly your fault."

"It's my fault we flirted so close. I was all prepared last week until I got a call from my bastard distributor - who I appointed, remember. He wanted to check all was well. Ha ha. As we spoke he casually repeated the formulation and of course it differed from what he'd faxed. No time to argue. On my own authority I had Weldworth make up a new batch. That made me lots of enemies; incurred huge cost."

"You acted in good faith."

"This isn't the legal world, Tom. This is selling, selling for a Midlands company that's struggling in the cruel world of metal fabrication."

"You're pessimistic about what will happen?"

"No, I'm certain. I'll be out of a job the day after tomorrow."

Throughout, he'd been aware of Hester. Watching lazily, speculatively. Not surprising, of course. Unemployment would change him, make him more vulnerable, arguably more interesting.

For Makings, unemployment was remote like assuming a state of grace or catching leprosy. A partner of Tamworth's most dominant solicitors' practice, he had viewed boom and bust as profitable sides of the same coin. He swilled cognac round the balloon glass: "The Employees Protection Act - "

"only applies after two consecutive years work with one company. But we're talking about selling. Even if I'd worked with this lot for a decade I couldn't bring up the EPA. Selling is the shortest line between cause and effect; between expectation and achievement. Even a bad manager can make a case for retaining or firing a salesman. What's worse, the salesman himself - if he's honest - will usually agree."

The habit of advocacy died hard and Makings leant forward. "But you're a professional, Andrew. Put together a dossier about how the French fellow let you down. Don't accept traditional philosophies. Take the fight to your manager."

"Stop it you two," said Hester briskly. "I can't decide who's the more pathetic. Andrew lying and dying or Tom whiffling about a world he is only dimly aware of. Listen to me."

Both turned. She sat upright in a chair which would have encouraged most people to lounge. The extra pounds added authority. "Let's assume Andrew is right. The job ends and he has to look for work. What interests me is whether Andrew feels he must resolve this alone or whether he'll accept help?"

"From you?" blurted Hatch crassly.

"From both of us."

Makings looked at his wife, baffled. "I'm sure we'd both be prepared to help. But, Hester, did you have anything specific? I'm not sure... "

"A vague idea. It will take time. Are you going to be silly about this, Andrew?"

"Silly?"

"Would you accept outside help?"

"I'd be very grateful."

"Good." And Hester gestured with her brandy glass.

There was a need to move on. Makings chuckled, "You're ideal company, Andrew. You and I are perpetually at loggerheads. Is it anything to do with going to the same school?"

Hatch said, "It was a good school. If that's why we argue it proves the quality was evenly spread throughout the boys. There was only two years between us and yet we passed like ships in the night. I doubt I'd have noticed if you hadn't been a prefect."

"I never knew you were a prefect," Hester said in mild outrage.

"Oh come on," said Hatch. "Tom's a natural prefect."

"What about you? A lad dominated by straight-edge rules?"

Tom shook his head. "That was one of the school's failings. A touch of snobbism. Andrew did well in chemistry and physics but it wasn't enough. I did classics and history. Gravitas and all that."

"It was slightly more complicated," said Hatch. "More ironic. I might have become a prefect but for the opposite reason: working class tokenism. That is if it hadn't been for my mother."

"Your mother!" said Hester. "Didn't you fall out with her or something?"

"Let's say I disappointed her."

"How on earth did you manage that? Scholarship boy. Straight As."

"She felt my efforts could have been better directed." Hatch sat up. "I haven't mentioned this before, seemed like bad taste. My mother was a Catholic, my dad a pagan born and bred in Lozells, and they came together in a marriage of convenience. At first neither of them had time or energy for beliefs. She escaped a huge Anglo-Irish family and he gained a long-haired Molly Malone. She went to Mass on a Sunday and that was that. He dozed over News of the Screws. The rest was pure hard work. Ten years passed before my mother had time for an attack of guilt about my godless life."

Tom, like Hester, was seized by this revelation. "Still godless, even now."

"Not for the want of her trying," said Hatch. "Jesuits take 'em young but my mother missed out on that with me. So she latched on to my report cards. Flattery at first, blackmail to follow. I was clever enough to tackle any subject, she said, so why didn't I do something worthwhile."

"Like... theology," said Hester. "She wanted you to become a priest?"

Hatch nodded. "It sounds like a joke doesn't it? But not at the time. I had an isolated life. Scholarship boys often do. My classmates lived in bigger houses a long way away and I'd cut myself off from the kids I'd known at junior school. The pressure was relentless. I was lucky in one sense. She could never make a satisfactory case against engineering. Even with help from her parish priest her charges about worshipping Mammon were never persuasive."

Hatch smiled reflectively. "She couldn't convince me manufacturing was inherently evil. Which was what I clung to. Finally she made a desperate attempt and appealed to my headmaster. I didn't know at the time, thank God. Somehow he stonewalled, didn't even raise the subject with me afterwards. I got the A-levels I expected and the grant came through."

"But didn't your mother and father separate?"

"The final irony. After giving up on me she started on my father. She was far better arguer and she made his life a misery, tying him up in polemical knots. But the chances of conversion were virtually zero. He was born when miners returned home rather than go down the pit if they met a nun. Catholicism was bubonic plague. But she never let up. Nagging, insidious, artfully indirect assaults over the remains of the evening meal. Emotionally she could afford all this because her reason for marrying him – to escape sharing a bed with two of her sisters – now meant nothing. He was no longer a husband, he was a cause. Stubbornly, silently he resisted everything she threw at him until her own logical mind allowed her to leave home. Working for an unmarried mothers' charity was better for her soul than remaining in an irrevocably unchristian household."

Tom said, "So that's why you were never a prefect? Mother a zealot."

"I can't say it was my greatest setback. But it left me with an abiding gratitude towards the school. Without that turmoil I doubt I'd have attended the 1971 old boys' dinner."

"And…?" asked Hester, her eyebrows arched.

The men smiled. Tom said, "I would never have been asked about the conveyancing fees for a terrace house in – where was it?"

"Spark Hill."

A mini-cab waited to take Hatch from Lichfield's detached houses to the terraces in Leyfield, near the industrial park. The three of them said their goodbyes on the severely lit driveway. Soon after marrying Hester Makings had insisted Hatch put aside his stiffness when embracing his new wife. Brushing cheeks was deemed too

English. So Hatch, as instructed, took her upper arms, smelt her perfume and knew, if he looked hard, he would see individual particles of face powder at the outer corners of her eyes. Knew too that those eyes had depth. A faint movement of her head brought his mouth slightly closer to hers. Large firm breasts touched his chest briefly.

He got into the minicab – as always – with a sense of relief.

3. HATCH

Slipping the painter

A CON-ROD with a bent shaft gave Hatch's desk its only touch of individuality. In his absence someone had used it as a paperweight to hold down three of the company's derided message forms.

The message forms had local history. Infuriated by his secretary's ill-written notes, Weldworth's accountant had come up with a grid which included a dozen labelled spaces to cover every option. But he hadn't allowed for human instinct. During a brief period when staff were charmed by the novelty the forms were used correctly. After that information claimed to be "already known" was omitted. Then message-takers made notes *outside the designated spaces!* Recriminations grew. Hatch, who had traditional views about accountants, was grimly pleased to see the form's begetter shouting in the corridors.

Hatch noticed one message concerned his ex-wife. There was no honorific – simply Prudence Carolson. Had she any views about her status? He couldn't be sure. Certainly she had never liked her married name, finding it too abrupt, too utilitarian.

The space for Subject was also blank. Probably she wanted to talk about the house. Since the divorce he had met all obligations stoically including requests for extra cash. But the house was different. Ousting the occupiers would be irrational, likely to be embarrassing and complicated. Prudence was not typically irrational and Hatch wondered if her reasons lay outside his experience. Was age a factor? Not a subject he cared to explore.

The other two messages referred to meetings which customers had postponed - as if his future were already common knowledge in the wider world. Making sales calls was pointless and he assembled a sheaf of receipts on his desk so he could at least fill in his expenses. Totting up fuel expenditure he heard secretive whispering elsewhere in the office. Then he recalled no one had bid him good morning, nor offered to get coffee.

His firing took place mid-morning and resembled a profit-and-loss exercise. When the costs of the wire formulation were added to the ferry ticket and car hire Hatch was seen to have frittered away three thousand pounds for no tangible return. None of this could truly be defended nor had he any intention of doing so. But before the final words were spelled out he had to sit through a five-minute summary of his indifferent career with Weldworth.

"You'll remember I authorised the order on your guarantee," said Alnwick, the sales director, finally getting to the point and heavily emphasising "your".

Hatch shrugged, preferring to look out over the corrugated roofs of nearby factory units.

"They re-scheduled the machine."

Hatch shrugged again.

"Which led to knock-on costs when we delayed another order."

Hatch said nothing, having just discovered the effect his silence was having on Alnwick.

Alnwick shifted in his seat. "Do you imagine we're treating you unfairly?"

This sounded querulous. "Unfairly?"

"You know, unfairly."

"Do you mean am I going to take you to an industrial tribunal?"

Alnwick stared, knowing he had blundered

"I hadn't really thought," said Hatch casually.

Minutes later, in exchange for three months' salary, he signed a waiver which had lain – prepared - in Alnwick's desk drawer. As they stood up Hatch wondered whether one shook hands on these occasions but from Alnwick's deflated expression it seemed unlikely. The waiver must have been a last resort.

With a payroll of eighty-five Weldworth didn't merit a human resources department which would, in any case, have been called personnel. It was that kind of company. Linda, the managing director's secretary covered these functions and Hatch watched, amazed, as she gathered up the mound of paper that signalled his departure. But bumf wasn't his primary interest. Sitting close he practised a private indulgence, revelling in her upper lip which overhung at the centre in pendulous invitation, soft and grape-like.

"Is all this stuff necessary?" he asked.

Linda sighed, the sound of fatigue rather than irritation. "Social services pamphlets, Job Centre advice, and more." A light went off on her phone and she stood up hurriedly. "I'll dash in and get his lordship's signature."

For my cheque, Hatch concluded. In a valedictory mood he glanced round Linda's office for the last time. Or rather for the first time. Seeing a mahogany side-table mounted on a plinth shaped like a pineapple, the heavy woodwork scuffed and chipped. Four pale grey filing cabinets of institutional origin. Most significant, the desk, clearly a pre-war dining table bought for its huge surface. This was a shabby ante-chamber to managerial power. But then the managing director, who had also founded the company, was a former engineer made redundant by British Leyland many years ago. He would have laughed at the idea of spending money on matching furniture with stainless steel legs.

Typical, thought Hatch, recalling the Scandinavian feel of Baudinière's minimalist shell. Then honesty prevailed. Weldworth was linked to metal fabrication, an obscure activity to many, a meritocracy based on weld integrity, a service providing the unfamiliar, often hidden skeletons of structures. One wouldn't expect atriums or courtyard fountains. Wit, such as it existed, lay, perhaps, in a mild-steel lattice where several braces had been ingeniously designed out, maintaining strength yet cutting assembly costs. Asked to improve the room's décor Hatch too would have shrugged, as he had shrugged at Alnwick.

Seated again at her table-desk Linda dropped the cheque on a superfluous blotter pad. "I could put this in an envelope but I suspect you're going to stick it straight into your wallet." Laying her hand flat on the cheque she slid it towards Hatch.

Still pondering the room's lack of ostentation, Hatch noticed the hand – like the furniture – for the first time. Recognised the fragility of the wrist. How long since he had been alone with a woman? Last Saturday in Hester's garden: true, but not by choice. Here the outstretched wrist, white against the dark wood, echoed a life almost wholly forgotten. As he reached forward the pale hand slowly withdrew.

He read the cheque's satisfying symbols and noted – ironically – the MD's utterly legible signature. Not entirely aware of himself he asked, "Would you like to help me spend some of this? In a restaurant."

Her eyebrows rose. They were, he noticed, unplucked.

"Just lunch, that's all."

Her face relaxed. "I don't go out. Lunch is sandwiches and the telephone."

"You work too hard."

"So does he," she said nodding backwards. "It goes with the business."

And with the random furniture. "He's lucky to have you."

"Because I do my job? Is that so rare?"

"Probably not. I'm out of touch."

"Being out of touch also goes with the business. None of this is fashionable."

Hatch was silent, surprised. The fascinating upper lip was now a natural element in a face without artifice. Her beige twin-set a senior secretary's uniform in most of the companies Hatch had worked for. A sign of propriety and competence. The only notable deviation was hair in a soft brown cloche rather than a perm.

She sat up. "You are out of touch. Selling isn't your job. If times had been better you might have managed our production. But that's pure airy-fairy. I'm sorry it came to this, for what that's worth."

"It's worth a lot."

"Well, then. It'll be hard, but stay away from sales if you can. Try and be flexible looking for jobs."

"Not my greatest strength, flexibility."

"Bollocks," she said crisply. "Production is flexibility. Doing things differently. Treat a job interview as if - " She gestured impatiently. "as if you had to make that door handle for half the price. Goodness, what do I know?"

"A lot, it seems."

"What I *do* know is you shouldn't spend any of that cheque on a two-hour lunch. It'll keep you going for a couple of months. Tell you what. When you do get a job give me a ring and invite me out to dinner. If you're still inclined."

There was no time to savour this. She had work to do and he got up. "I have a confession. I don't know your surname."

She waggled her index finger. "Flexibility, remember. Lateral thinking. If you can't work that out, well – no dinner."

"I still say he's lucky to have you."

"Get out. You're repeating yourself."

In the sales office the men had left and the two secretaries were bent over word processors, avoiding association with failure. He opened desk drawers. Without his five-year-old company Mondeo which had passed the week in the car park with a failed generator, he would be taking the bus home and didn't fancy an awkward load. The Oxford dictionary dating back to Loughborough could be left to increase his successor's word power. Was the stapler his or theirs?

He took only the bent con-rod. While at Loughborough he been an unpaid mechanic to another undergraduate who raced a Formula Ford. Their differing temperaments ensured the partnership lasted only half a season. At Mallory Park the cautious Hatch had insisted on an oil-change while the driver, unwilling to risk being late on the grid, had ignored him and suffered a partial seizure two laps into the race. Hatch had rebuilt the engine without complaint and dropped out. The damaged con-rod remained as a memento.

Just inside the elaborate portico to the industrial estate was a well-patronised café where Hatch ordered a bacon sandwich and tried to read his newspaper, the cheque a tangible presence in his breast pocket. It would last more than the two months Linda had predicted. It would ease his job search. In some ways being fired had left him shriven.

He pushed away the paper and sipped at his brick-coloured tea, recalling his impetuosity towards Linda half an hour ago, an act of loneliness hiding a more basic need: the thrill of a woman's company with sex as a desirable, but not essential, outcome. He changed his mind: sex, yes, sex.

Sex. Three weeks ago he and Makings had waited for Hester inside a pub. A woman in her forties had entered alone, ordered and ignored a half pint of lager, and had glanced back and forth, detached and seemingly uninterested in what went on. Makings nudged Hatch. "A local lady of the night. Our paths have crossed in the county court."

Hatch's interest was aroused. As a solitary divorcé he was a possible client for this woman. Might it be worthwhile paying for her services? The dead face cut her off from most women he knew. Her hair had been dyed blonde but wasn't this proof of womanhood?

Then an even earlier event came to mind. A Swiss motor manufacturer who supplied Tempest had courted him and his assistant manager at a Swiss night-club where insistent prostitutes had sat on their laps. Language had been the stumbling block, the talk spasmodic and events were moving towards yes or no. At his side the assistant manager said, "Mine's quite pretty. Algerian perhaps. But I could never do it."

"Oh?"

"The AIDS statistics. Far too risky."

"Statistics!" Hatch had laughed.

The young manager looked rueful, ashamed at his lack of adventure. Hatch had disguised his own timidity but his reaction was the same. As in the pub with Makings. Hatch was ultimately too practical to use a whore.

But mightn't Linda be a risk if it ever came to that? The possibility was appalling. And yet…? For once Hatch was in analytical limbo. He raised his mug but knew the tea would now be tepid and set it down again. Time to ring Prudence.

LATE in the afternoon, back from Prudence's disturbing revelation and wanting only to lie on his bed and concentrate, he entered Mister Wee's by the side entrance and took the narrow staircase to the first floor. A door opened and Jimmy stood there sulkily. "Missa Hash."

"A problem with the computer?" Tutoring Jimmy had been taken on casually, a means of ingratiating his landlord. Now it was part of daily life. Inside the lad's room he listened to symptoms, resentfully listed, and slipped into the role of instructor.

"You click on Properties."

A nod.

"And then Statistics."

"Yes."

The child's eyes, wet coal behind cheap circular glasses, stared critically. Why did the Wees have his black hair cut so short? To save money? That was hardly Wee philosophy. More likely short hair was seen as using money - and time - more effectively. Aesthetics wasn't a starter. The lad's hair was mere insulation, radiating from his round cranium like spines on a sea urchin.

"You say menus make things easy. I don't have to think," said Jimmy.

Hatch said gently, "First you must learn why Properties is relevant."

"It's logical, you say."

"Only afterwards, Jimmy."

The child thought, then asked, "Please explain." There was the poignancy. A clever nine-year-old boy, constantly competing, yet adult enough to recognise his limitations. How many adults had that quality? Was Jimmy's cleverness a little inhuman?

It was clear Jimmy would get a scholarship to the grammar school as Hatch had. But that wouldn't mean there'd be less work at home. By then computers would be second nature and some poverty-stricken expert would be dragooned into widening Jimmy's horizons still further. A third language, perhaps. Economics. Hatch didn't envy him this force-feeding. Homework for Hatch had been a tranquil – even enriching – part of his life since his mother's proselytising started later in the evening. In contrast, Jimmy must frequently long for bed. Did children suffer nervous breakdowns?

"Software is always short of space," Hatch continued. "The instructions on the screen are often only single words - labels not descriptions. Sometimes they're almost meaningless. Look at Save As: it really means name and position."

"I couldn't understand that at first."

"Develop an instinct. Click on a tag because you've eliminated other tags. I say this but it's tricky when you're doing something new or something you do rarely. Remember formatting the floppy? Think about format. Outside it has a general meaning; for us it's more specific."

"I was wrong about Properties."

Hatch laughed. "Not so serious. Let's say half-right. Mostly with this box of tricks you're completely right."

"Box of tricks?"

"Silly phrase. A cliché. I didn't want to say computer; perhaps because it was too obvious."

"A tag?"

"If you like. But now there's a bigger problem. These crashes; I think you're short of RAM. We need to speak to your Dad."

"He sleeps in the afternoon. I'll get him," said Jimmy ruthlessly, dropping out of the swivel chair and opening the door of the tiny room.

"It's not that urgent. Let him have his sleep. He's earned it."

"He won't mind."

No doubt he wouldn't. Mr Wee worked interminable hours in his fish chop. Jimmy too would work interminably but at a job carrying more status.

And now Mr Wee, having squeezed in through a door part blocked by the computer table, leant against the wall and looked tiredly and uncomprehendingly at the glowing screen. His hair, normally brilliantined and combed back, was in disarray from the pillow and he had napped in his work-a-day black trousers and white shirt. Father and son spoke in whip-cracking Cantonese.

"I explained to my father the computer crashes. He is angry."

"It's not exactly a fault."

"Computer no go, computer stop. That is fault," said Mr Wee implacably.

"But we're asking it to do a job it wasn't specified for." Too complex an idea; too many short words. As Hatch searched for a simpler yet technological parallel – based perhaps on deep-fat fryers - Jimmy rattled and barked at his father. Certain sounds caused Mr Wee to wince.

Mr Wee made a slow gesture from right to left, his hand held flat, the palm facing downwards. Slicing? Removing skin from a fish? "Computer cost one thousand and seventy pounds." Mr Wee added a bitter coda. "plus Vat." He frowned horribly. "Shop say proper computer. Not a toy. Not a toy. Now computer stops."

"It's working too hard."

"Hah," said Mr Wee, who knew all about working hard.

"We need more memory."

Patiently Hatch explained, basing his sentences mainly on nouns. Mr Wee looked professionally blank when Hatch provided an estimate of the costs, then agreed for Hatch to act as intermediary with a PC specialist.

"I'd forgotten. I can't deliver the computer, I have no car."

"No car?"

Hatch had intended to leave Mr Wee in the dark about losing his job. It had seemed legitimate since the rent would be manageable for a couple of months. Or would have been until he'd spoken to Prudence. "I am unemployed."

Both looked on with abiding horror, a fate more shocking for Chinese than for Britons.

Mr Wee raised his hands as if acknowledging a larger force. "I cannot... Jimmy..." Hatch saw the dilemma. Normally Mister Wee would have shown an unemployed tenant the door to prevent Jimmy being infected. But Hatch had been a model resident and had helped with Mr Wee's strategic plans for his son.

This morning the solution would have been so simple. With deep misgiving Hatch said, "I will pay in advance. A month in advance."

Even this did not remove the stigma. Mr Wee and Jimmy looked anxious, mumbled Cantonese in low voices as if fearing Hatch's comprehension, fell silent again. Then Mr Wee made a very big decision. "Missa Hash, you stay."

Hatch was now alone. His room had never seemed so tawdry, so limited. Ad hoc wiring for the bedside light, misaligned wall-paper, the closeness of the Baby Belling. He sat at the enlarged window-ledge that served as a desk and opened his brief-case. The con-rod, that amusing descant on his professional life, became what it really was, failed metal. Scattered on his bed were papers: photocopies of lab reports, a handwritten recommendation from Prudence's GP, a glossy brochure for a clinic. The cheque still in his breast pocket was no longer a comfort. When Tempest had lost the negligence suit and entered its eternal backwater Hatch had known his own worth and had sought work confidently. Disaster followed. Now it could all happen again.

INTERLUDE

It had been a long afternoon and this was not the time for big decisions. But the under-secretary had promised his master that this meeting – unlike dozens before - would resolve things. Already the soaring cost of comparing the proposed systems had been joked about in The Times' diary. When the elapsed time was leaked, as it surely would, there would be even more pain for the ministry.

In an attempt to appear more decisive the under-secretary lifted the massive assessment document and let it fall on to the table. The fluffy flat sound was not what he had hoped for. "Item five. We have been here before. Heads-up display for the Mark Two Apache. Two proposals. Salisbury's analysis dates back to last November."

Those at the table regarded him warily.

"You all know the details."

Theoretically they did. What they faced was choice.

"I'll take it clockwise. Babbage, this is really your field. Has your opinion changed?"

"Not in the slightest. Our guys put their finger on it in the first appendix. Too close to call."

A collective sigh suggested few dissenters. Doggedly the under-secretary pursued his way round and listened grimly as others attempted to say what Babbage had said, if in different words.

"Well, gentlemen. You're asking me to toss a coin?"

The uncomfortable silence worked on everyone's nerves. In a low voice the most physically distant committee member said, "Company B is very close to the minister's constituency."

No one breathed as they all imagined this detail emerging as a leak. Applicant companies were given code names as a gesture towards blind-tasting fairness but the real names were known to everyone in the room. The member who had spoken raised his voice. "There's a precedent. Remember Heseltine and Westland."

"But those issues were national not local." said the under-secretary who wondered what age most of the committee had been at the time.

Babbage had been looking contemptuously at his peers. "There is one other… political consideration. What would you say the minister's attitude was towards the special relationship? Hands across the water and all that?"

"He loves it. Isn't his son at Harvard? But so what? Both our proposers are British companies. And Hughes makes the Apache; they're American… aren't they?"

"Hughes are American," said Babbage crushingly. "But in the ninth appendix Company A says their display will work with the British gyro-compass."

"Again, so what? There isn't a hope in hell of that being fitted in an Apache."

"Exactly!" said Babbage.

"Exactly what?"

"This system has always been what the Pentagon would call a fur-ball. We could help lubricate our minister's enthusiasm by turning down Company A. Then he can sell Company B in Washington as a pro-American gesture."

"But the likelihood of the gyro-compass link-up is as remote as…"

"Take it or leave it," said Babbage.

4. CLARE

Clear horizons

"FORGET Mrs Kepler, I'm Clare, you're Alan. We're equals now. In fact we always were."

Less than a year out of university he wriggled with little-boy embarrassment. She sighed, edging the Jaguar another ten yards forward as South London traffic contracted like a python's stomach.

"That's not strictly true about being equal," she amended. "You weren't told how these things work. Blame company policy. Sigma embargoed what I could say during the interview."

"You were fair enough, so was Sigma. I knew about MoD procurement and how it works. It was a risk but I fancied this job."

"Fancied *our* job? Did you have other options?"

"I was on a BAe short-list. But I liked Sigma better."

Intent on comforting him, whether he needed it or not, she missed the latter sentence as she juggled the air conditioning. She said, "Don't worry about your CV. Most avionics people understand government contracts. They can be a rough ride. Tell yourself it was good experience. Bigger projects drag on for months without much happening, leaving you twiddling your thumbs. As it was, you got the B Sector module and that taught you something I hope."

"Why was Sigma turned down?"

"I can't truly say. Assessment is supposed to be even-handed: Company A, Company B, that sort of thing. But the committee is in the know. The contract wasn't big enough to attract mainland Europe and only four Brits were contending. At the German armaments funfair I had a drink with an MoD Salisbury technoid. He said we were close. Chances are it was something we couldn't have planned for."

They were in Lewisham now, enjoying London's great cartographic joke, the South Circular. Just passing a set of traffic lights was a useful gain although the big car's aristocratic disdain insulated them from most of the fretting.

"Will you look for a job from London?" asked Clare. "You share a flat don't you?"

"With two others." Alan's head jerked up. "I'll stay in London. I couldn't stand Wilmslow now."

She laughed at the way he fiercely distanced his childhood. "Think of Wilmslow as a fall-back."

"I'd rather stack shelves."

"No reason to do that. Your degree's sellable. You have some cash. And I can afford to be honest with your reference."

He pondered. "You think I was OK?"

"You'd expect me to say so. I picked you out of ten applicants, four I interviewed. Saying you were rubbish would mean I was rubbish. Hand on heart you weren't rubbish. I'm just sorry it ended this way."

"Not your fault."

He sounded defensive on her behalf. She now remembered what she had passed over. "Was there something about our set-up?"

He hesitated.

"It probably doesn't matter," she said.

"It does matter, but it goes back in time." He stretched out, screwing up his face. "Obviously I haven't worked much with women. At York there were only two in the applied stream. Jill and – oh dear, what was her name? – Heloise. She struggled with that name. And both of them were, I have to say it, plain. Poor grades too. Other students sneered." He moved his shoulders angrily. "I was just as bad as the rest. Parrotted what everyone said: that it wasn't a woman's world. Perhaps I believed it."

"I'm surprised."

"I changed my mind because of you. You weren't my first interview. But the others were all men. Condescending twats. 'Where do you see yourself in five years, little chap' sort of shit. But you were different. Quite different."

"How different?"

"You treated me seriously."

"Was that so amazing?"

He turned, looked her up and down. "I suppose not. You are serious, after all. Those dark suits. No make-up. Anyway, you treated me as an adult. Man to man. I mean…"

"I get the idea. But then the job was a man's job. Or a woman's."

"You asked me questions then listened to my answers. I know you listened because you responded to what I'd said. Old hat to you but for me it was almost unbelievable. And you knew the technical stuff. I thought about Jill and Whatnot at York. Imagined how they were doomed to struggle. I suppose you faced all that. And came out on top. I wanted to work for you."

Clare looked out hard through the windscreen although the car was stationary. From that first autumn day at Wadham, as part of an elite enrolment of only eight students, she'd absorbed physics as if it were champagne. Even the first year with all the maths – different maths at that. No real problems during the first job either. But being good at management was not only harder, it was difficult to measure. Especially when it meant squeezing sense out of youths from evolved Polys. What he'd said pleased her.

"Nice of you to say that," she said. "But I had some advantages – material advantages – Jill and Whatnot lacked."

"Your dad's got millions."

"How did you know?"

"First day at Sigma. Spitz, that creep in software, told me."

"In what tone of voice? Envy? No need for secrets now."

"He wanted to slag you off. But couldn't make it stick. You knew more about the attack software than he did. He sort of tailed off, mumbling you had no sense of humour."

Spitz the South African, pallid from years spent in front of a hundred monitors. Humourless? Me? Could that be true? Probably. I don't laugh a lot.

She'd offered him the drive up to London by car for two reasons. He had too much to carry for the train and she imagined he might be in need of succour given he'd just lost his job. His comments were unexpected. She went on, "The irony is we're in the same boat. Both jobless. I'm cushioned if I want to be but…"

"…but it's your line, the one you've chosen. Not getting the contract must piss you off."

"Too right," she said. "It does piss me off. But I'm even more pissed off that it happened to you."

"Bastard government."

"Bastard government."

He asked about her future and she tapped the steering wheel. "Something successful. Not that Sigma was a tragedy. I knew it would be hard and so did they. They paid me a fat salary and promised an even fatter bonus. I didn't get the bonus but I can't grumble at the termination payment. Perhaps I'll go a'whoring at a consultancy."

"Why not start your own?"

Was he on the lookout? She glanced sideways and saw only the innocence that had appealed during the interview. "Hawking oneself around clients is wearisome. And start-up can be a slow death without someone to stay in the office and work twelve hours a day."

His flat was on the fringe of Brixton and she parked on a double yellow line near his front door. He protested.

"It's a Jaguar," she said, amused.

"Pimps drive them round here."

"Then everyone will be mystified about us."

She helped him carry out his loads, enjoying his attempts to dissuade her, seeing it melt before his childish belief in equally divided labour. Poignant freight filled the boxes. He'd stacked university textbooks on his desk imagining they'd bolster his credibility at Sigma not knowing you didn't hark back to your education when you've got a job. With the last box despatched indoors, and under the surprisingly tolerant eyes of a traffic warden, she faced him.

"I'm glad I gave you the job, Alan. Glad to have known you."

Little-boy cringing: no occasion for a peck on the cheek. The age thing, of course; a difference of how many years? Fifteen. Phew. Would a dash of lipstick and a Jaeger sweater have made a difference? Clare thought not. She stuck out an unequivocal right hand. "You deserve to get on. I'm sure you will. You have my address. You know I'll be glad to help."

He failed to engage her eyes and his handshake was limp. She waved over her shoulder and got back into the car. Not once had he called her Clare.

HER mother lay on a recliner, ostensibly acting the Headcorn aristocrat but actually keeping an eye on her new Polish gardener. She wasted no time greeting Clare: "I don't think he understands double digging."

"Hello mother. Surely you only double dig uncultivated land. It can't be necessary here"

"Of course it isn't," said her mother impatiently. "Even you know that. I asked him to dig that bed over there – as a test."

"And he hasn't done it. Perhaps he's clever enough to know it's a nonsense. Perhaps he thinks you know nothing about gardening."

"I've done this garden for thirty years."

"And when did you last double dig?"

Mrs Morgan changed the subject. "Clare, darling, why do you wear such a severe suit? With your thin face, you look undernourished."

Thin and serious! "The perfect outfit for a sacking."

"You weren't sacked, darling. I'm sure there's a more… congenial phrase."

Her mother was right. Alan Harding had been sacked. With Clare the contract had been amicably wound up. "I've brought back the paintings you leant me for the office. I'd love to keep them at home but we haven't the space. I'm terrified Nick will put his grubby hands on them."

"Are they in the car? Just call out for Consuelo. She'll put them away."

"I won't do any such thing. Tell me where and I'll put them away myself."

"You seem a bit snippy, dear. Is it the job? Or something else?"

A 56-year-old retired REME sergeant, taken on for document-chasing, had lost his part-time job this morning; his wife crippled with arthritis. Clare debated bringing this to her mother's attention but didn't want to be told there was a clinic in Godalming where a week's stay would work wonders.

"Mother, do you disapprove of my career?"

"Disapprove? Goodness you are at odds with yourself. No, I'm impressed beyond measure. You've astonished me."

"Like a dog's walking on its hind legs?"

Mrs Morgan giggled. "You always get the quotations right. Most people think it's hinder. That impresses me too. But disapprove? No."

"In your heart of hearts, though, wasn't physics a bit of a comedown? Perilously close to dirty finger-nails?"

"I'm horribly conventional I know. I saw you were clever and expected you to choose some profession where you would succeed, where you'd have the luxury of public recognition. A barrister, perhaps. I knew nothing about physics but I should have taken the hint. Even when you were still at school there were those casual references to Newton's laws of motion and – what was it? - kinetics. Kinetics for goodness sake! But in the end it was your choice. I discussed it with your father. A physicist could well become the Astronomer Royal, he said. Seems you get a knighthood with that. Dame in your case."

"Dame Clare Kepler," Clare said experimentally. They giggled.

"That said, I did have misgivings when you went into industry. I worried your cleverness might not be enough. Those early positions: you always seemed to be persuading people to do things. No reason why you mightn't be good at that but luck obviously played a part too. I didn't want you depending on luck."

It was some years ago. A wearisome technical sales visit to one of the emirates with the Americans one step ahead all the way. Not merely a matter of persuading the impenetrable caliph to look at an over-priced system but trying to rein in the rugby ebullience of the sales director.

"You clever old thing," she said patting her mother on the knee. "I've misjudged you."

"It's a daughter's right. Industry or no you've had your successes. I know you're well paid. Being our daughter allowed you to take risks and I assume you did. But you never come to us cap in hand. Is that what this is?"

Clare mentioned the termination payment. Cosseted as she was Mrs Morgan recognised the cheque's value. Clare said, "It would cover your new gardener for a year."

"A year and a half," said Mrs Morgan with a precision typical of the rich. "So, are you dissatisfied? What work would you prefer?"

"I'm hazy. What was that phrase you used: 'the luxury of public recognition'. Perhaps I need some of that."

They looked out into the garden which hid its acreage in an ingenious series of curves and bowers. "And how is Jerry?" Her mother's voice was bright with obligation.

Clare stood up abruptly. "I'll get those paintings out of the car."

"Time for a salad."

They ate in the conservatory. Clare chatted unnecessarily with Consuelo to tease her mother who had strict views about dealing with servants. But Mrs Morgan was equal to it. "Let's have a glass of wine," she said, directing Consuelo into the pantry.

Sipping, Clare said, "That's burgundy."

"Meursault. You seem surprised."

"I forget how well-off you both are."

"Your father only admits to being comfortable."

"And is he presently reaping further comforts?"

"He's in Zurich. Something to do with the provenance of a Mondrian. He occupies himself most of the time; I don't suppose he'll ever retire. But then the work is hardly nine-to-five."

"And it's entwined with paintings and their value. This must be the only room in the house where there isn't one on the wall."

"Too much direct light. He uses it when he needs to look at detail. There's an easel behind the fern palm." Mrs Morgan pushed away her half-finished glass of Meursault. "That question about our disapproval. I'm intrigued. You rarely ask questions."

"Today's been a day for reflection. A job that didn't come off; could I have done better? I didn't come here directly. There's a youth who's worked on this project, Alan Harding. He had books and things at the office and I drove him to his flat near Brixton. So young. Was I ever that young? I don't often look back, there's not much fun in it. But I wondered how I was at that age."

"You lived in an alien world. We chose the prep school in Surrey and from then on most of the big decisions were inevitable. The scholarship, Wadham. When you were at Oxford your father did ask friends who knew about physics whether a year in America would be a good idea. A Rhodes in reverse. But you were quite firm about not going. We wondered whether you had – shall we say, social reasons - but there was no suggestion of that."

"Social reasons? Oh, you mean a boy-friend. On that side of things Oxford was a bit of a failure. I think I was thought to be somewhat sniffy." She paused. "Yes, that's what it was. Sniffiness. Alan, this youth I drove to Brixton, talked about the way I interviewed him for the job. Said my intensity impressed him. Wadham undergrads looking for popsies were less impressed."

"Intensity? Is that supposed to be a failing?"

"Depends on whether your aim is a good degree or being belle of the ball. No question which way I leant. Wedded to the nucleus. Head down. What a prig."

"Oh no," said Mrs Morgan, briefly raising her soft voice. "You made friends. They stayed here, remember? That Jewish girl, I forget her name, she came here twice. Talked about atonal music. You went to France with her one summer."

"Rachel Boltzman. An authority on Schoenberg. But there was pressure in the family to marry. Dozens of kids. Lives in Leeds." Clare shrugged. "Mother, was I normal?"

"Normal? I'm not sure I can answer that. You're our only daughter. Who should I compare you with?"

"Try, mother. Try."

"Normal... I suppose not but I didn't realise that until you left home. You were assured. I always thought that was why you did well at university, but it was more than that. You rarely needed our advice and we got out of the habit of offering it." Mrs Morgan added neutrally, "Otherwise we might have said more about Jerry. But..."

Clare rolled fat white wine round her mouth. "By then I'd developed my own habits, the habits of success. You can't be blamed. I was thirty-two."

It was, of course, the subject Mrs Morgan most wanted to discuss. But she knew enough to be careful. "You're too adult to catechize. But how about the child?"

Characteristic that she referred to Nick almost in the abstract. "An unsatisfactory holding action at the moment. I make sure he doesn't suffer and the au pair loves him to distraction. Jerry? Absences are the problem."

"Is there a solution?"

"I can't tell. Perhaps you're seeing me trying to face up to things."

Clare would have liked more Meursault but had a half-hour's drive across Kent. The momentum between them had slowed and departure was in the air. But Mrs Morgan had something to say, if tentatively. "I was startled by this matter of disapproval. It meant you knew less about us – about me – than I imagined. It must be my fault. I'm not a demonstrative woman; it's one reason your father married me. During the early years, when he was taking risks, he needed peace here at home. I think I became rather too peaceful."

"Mother… "

"I was astonished by your successes. Pleased I hadn't given birth to another me. I should have said so at the time but didn't. Afterwards, success tended to be the norm. Marking it wasn't necessary. But I must mark it now. I'm proud of you. And I…" The sentence tailed off.

Her mother's eyes shone. Clare could never recall such emotion. Conceivably that final sentence held a confession of love which Mrs Morgan was unable to admit. But it didn't matter, the admission was tangible. They embraced awkwardly. Through lack of practice, Clare imagined.

They walked round the garden arm in arm. A litany of beds reshaped, bushes uprooted and colours mingled restored Mrs Morgan's iron-clad composure. Back at the Jaguar she looked mischievously at Clare. "I'm taking advantage of the new frankness. I meant what I said about dull clothes. It's a man's world but there's no need to dress like a man."

Clare laughed. "Mother, this suit cost… Well, I've actually forgotten what it cost. A lot."

"It's significant you can't remember. You simply went out and bought some clothes. And that's what you're wearing - some clothes. You can't disguise what you are."

"What am I? Defective but passable. A thin face, teeth that aren't right, not much in the way of a bust."

"You're slender and you move well. Highlighting would disguise the grey in your hair. Your teeth; you don't help by not using lipstick. Why not make an appointment with my dentist."

"Mother, I have a dentist of my own."

"All right, none of my business. But why shouldn't what you wear and how you look celebrate what you have achieved. I don't want…"

"Don't want what?"

"I don't want people thinking you *had* to be successful."

It was only after a few miles Clare realised the implications – that success might no longer be an adornment, rather a compensation.

There was, of course, no Range Rover outside the house but then this was only late afternoon. It remained to be seen whether it would arrive before midnight.

Wealth, evident at her mother's, had also paid for this four-hundred-year-old Tudor cottage on the Chiddingstone road. It had the well-preserved antiquity of a museum exhibit and was – always had been – too small. In five years it had doubled in value but Clare had never considered selling for somewhere more modern and more roomy.

Nick, playing in the garden, ran to hug her legs. She felt the dampness of tears against her thigh. The au pair stared.

"He's not normally like this Birgitta."

"You are, er, early. And today was nursery day. He gets on with the other children but he's always keen to leave."

Am I really protecting him? "I'll get him tea," she said, stifling a question about what he normally ate. A protective mother would know.

Nick's tears were as transient as Beethoven's storm. He sat on a cushioned kitchen chair beating a spoon against his melamine Mister Bump plate and shouting a mantra recently learned: "Eat it all up! Eat it all up!"

"Orange juice or milk?" Clare asked.

"Juice, juice."

"Juice, what?"

"Juice, puh-lease."

A boy who had inherited his father's easiness and pale-complexioned English looks. Within weeks of the birth Clare discovered she had no natural instincts for motherhood and in this Mrs Morgan had been little help. But Clare had been lucky. Although fractious at night Nick found objects interesting and his tantrums could be forestalled. Often he looked at toys rather than played with them. Following a hunch Clare bought realistically detailed cars and locomotives instead of the wooden versions said to appeal psychologically to today's young men. Since Clare too responded to detail she was pleased at his preference. Perhaps the gene of science and technology had passed on and her talent for motherhood would emerge later.

Wanting to cover up her absence she half decided to give him his bath, then, tactically, chose not to. This was the day's climax for the heavily maternal Swedish au pair. Clare's favourite moment was receiving Nick, pink and placid in his pyjamas.

Now chuckles and humming crackled sporadically from the hall intercom as Nick glided contentedly into sleep upstairs. Clare sat in her office, a masterpiece of space conservation achieved under the stairs by Sevenoaks' most expensive carpenter. Shallow drawers interacted with a delicately curved façade stained dark to match the aged house's beams. But even the carpenter's ingenuity had not found sufficient area for a desktop and an expensive laptop acted as substitute. Connectivity problems were hindering links to the comparatively new email service and Clare tore off faxes from a machine hidden on a shelf above her head.

The most recent, from the head of the Ministry of Defence laboratory at Salisbury asked her to phone "at her convenience." The unit had assessed Sigma's proposals for the Apache heads-up display and it was from one of its lesser lights Clare had learned just how close the competition was. Now this forlorn request. Knowing she was jobless the MoD no doubt wondered if she was desperate enough to work for them.

Another fax from the Sevenoaks Jaguar dealer suggested she might trade-up when she replaced her sixteen-month-old model. But this wasn't the time to be changing an expensive car. A London book-shop announced that a novel she had seen reviewed in one of the Sundays was now available. Time had passed and she had forgotten why she had pursued this.

The downstairs intercom was now silent and she could afford to mount the creaking stairs to the bedroom, intending to change into something more comfortable. In the full-length mirror she tested her mother's charge of dowd or – worse - the possibility she was becoming mannish. The charcoal-grey suit fitted well and had been altered from a more voluptuous cut. It was obviously expensive but hardly the emblem of a confident woman. It took no risks.

Clare pulled out a pair of tight-fitting trousers in light/dark yellow stripes previously worn in the Bahamas. In vain she flicked through hanging blouses looking for cleavage, knowing this to be her particular cowardice. A sleeveless dark green polo-neck was the only option which clung.

Birgitta met her in the hall. "Many apologies, Mrs Kepler. There is a message I had forgotten. Your husband phoned. A tournament in Berkshire. He will be home for a late dinner."

"Something heavier than we would have chosen."

"I have made meat balls and noodles."

"His favourite Swedish dish. Perhaps his favourite dinner."

Birgitta was in her second year with them and was aware of Jerry's absences, often on pretexts more tenuous than a tournament in Berkshire. Yet today he'd broken with tradition and let them both know about his movements? He was aware that the Sigma contract had ended but surely he wasn't coming home to hold Clare's hand?

Dinner saw Jerry at his best. Face shining healthily from the golf course, he praised Clare's "new outfit" then explained with amused shrugs why he had only taken tenth place in the tournament.. She marvelled at how he could, when it pleased him, disguise his competitiveness with self-deprecation. Despite his firm belief Birgitta was a dull Scandinavian he entertained her with memories of a Bergman film (surely the only one he had ever seen), again claiming to have misunderstood the plot through his own pig-ignorance.

When Clare mentioned seeing her mother he even asked two or three civil questions across that abyss of mutual antipathy. By now Clare knew she was being prepared for a confession or admission which would demand her absolution.

The charade became more self-evident in the bedroom when one or two of his finger-trailing gestures hinted they might make love, a rare event these days. Sexual relations had never really survived Nick's birth, which surprised then depressed Jerry. The subject was never discussed although it weighed on him, especially when he imagined himself unobserved and watched his son apprehensively.

Emerging from the bathroom, wearing only pyjama trousers the better to show off his athlete's upper body, Jerry had almost finished preparing Clare for tonight's final act. "How did the meeting go at Sigma?" A familiar hollow tone.

"Predictably. Lovey-dovey about what I'd done. A larger severance than I expected."

"Any irons in the fire?"

"A fax inviting to me to call the MoD's laboratory in Salisbury."

His eyes sharpened. "But you wouldn't consider that?"

"Only if the balance of my mind were disturbed." He missed the allusion and looked puzzled.

"What do you... fancy?"

"Something different. Less obscure."

"It's your life, of course. I never interfere. But is there likely to be a gap? Will we be on short commons?"

"Would that be a problem?"

"Not really," he said, smiling. "There's some work needed on the Range Rover. But it could wait."

"Does it need doing or not?"

"Body work. It could wait."

"But the car's your billboard. It advertises you."

"True."

"I assume it's serious. And I hope no one else was involved. Get it done."

"You're sure?"

No point in asking for details, they would only humiliate him. Just as she'd never tried to get to the bottom of his late evenings. Golf pros and the women they taught seemed such a cliché. But would it be worse if his absences were devoted to men and drinking?

As Jerry rolled over in bed he muttered something familiar but inaudible. She wasn't in the mood to ask him to repeat it.

5. CLARE

Connubial life

CHUNTERING across the landing was starting to persist but Clare waited it out. Half an hour later it had become a drone, punctuated by half-hearted protests which would soon get louder. At 7.15 she swung her legs out of bed, surprised to find herself alone in the room.

Nick stood eagerly at the end of his cot. Out of habit she led him downstairs but he managed himself competently then rushed ahead into the kitchen. "Daddy!"

Jerry wearing a terry-towel beach robe ate cornflakes and read The Times sports section. He ignored Nick. "I thought you'd forgotten," he said to Clare.

"I think you're right, I have."

"The Captain's Day. I told you last night."

"Am I... did I...?"

"Last year you were in Munich and you said you'd make up for it."

"The Captain's Day?"

Jerry groaned. "The one event where wives are invited."

This was untrue. The Lynn golf club calendar included some appalling dinners which partners were expected to attend. The club was owned by a married couple of great wealth who, two years before, had watched a TV documentary which lampooned a golf club near London run by misogynists and social idiots. This had terrified the Lynn owners. Following an extraordinary general meeting to change the constitution it was now a condition of membership – easily enforced since the club had a long waiting list - that wives be regularly paraded. Dim memories seeped back and Clare recalled Jerry's nervous rage when told last year she would be elsewhere.

"Munich isn't even important," he had protested. "It's a jolly. And you say you don't like jollies."

True, but obligatory for three senior members of the company. She had bowed her head choosing not to remind him of occasions when he'd similarly excused himself for returning in the small hours or staying away for a weekend. And hadn't he been the first to employ "jolly"?

She glanced at Nick, still trying vainly to gain his father's attention. A visit to a petting farm had been on the cards but luckily she had not mentioned it in Nick's hearing. "I forget the rules. Could I take you-know-who?" she asked, nodding at their son.

Jerry's astonishment was unfeigned. Wives were obligatory, children unthinkable. "I was going to give Birgitta the day off," Clare said hurriedly. "I'd better let her know. Perhaps she can take him to the nursery."

Jerry returned to the sports section.

Again Clare riffled through unfamiliar clothes, re-discovering the tweed jacket which otherwise hung unused. Her golf jacket. Outside on the driveway more nuisance when Jerry announced they must take two cars. He would be staying on to present his pro's report to a management meeting.

"Let's have a look at the Range Rover," she said childishly. The offside passenger's door and rear wing were abraded and traces of what looked like Cotswold stone clung to the striations. Clare recalled the clubhouse had raised flowerbeds protected by walls of a similar biscuit colour.

"Don't we have insurance?" she asked.

"Yes, but… there was another repair earlier in the year. We'd lose the no-claims."

"What's the estimate?"

"Er, um, about two grand."

Which probably meant three grand. She walked towards the Jaguar.

Slowly the two cars, as if umbilically linked, moved along crowded roads. Green lettering on the back of the Range Rover proclaimed "Jerry Kepler, golf pro, can simplify your game" a slogan she had thought up for him. But then she had also helped create the reality of Jerry Kepler, golf pro.

Long ago, now. A period that had ended in the mistaken belief – perhaps hope - that Jerry Kepler, not then a golf pro, might help simplify her game.

Crystal glittered in welcome as the guests entered Wadham's huge hall. Above, the celebrated hammer-beam roof enhanced the sense of occasion but it was the glasses – oh, and the napery – she remembered. Trappings of an academic salute.

If the reasons were obvious the event was splendid. So splendid that she had no hesitation in doffing her tailored chalk-stripe for something far more extrovert: an ostentatious silk gown with deeply scalloped neckline, specified and bought for that evening alone, her response to Wadham honouring its brightest and best. Six months previously she'd been appointed UK technical vice-president of one of the world's great software giants, the youngest to hold the job and the first woman. Tonight the college's crystal contained Latour.

She was sanguine enough about the price of all this to envisage the begging bowl. For the moment, however, it was enough to revel in the skilfully arranged ceremony. Spouses were invited and she, unmarried and unattached, was paired across the table with a lone male she took to be unmarried. When she discovered he was a professor of theology she had laughed aloud at their incompatibility, pleased nevertheless by his youthfulness and Mediterranean looks.

What had they talked about? Certainly not their differing worlds. Given their youth, perhaps they had simply shared the night's good fortune. Eventually, though, the grandness of their surroundings shrank and the conversation turned into a tremulous exploration of each other. His eyes were pure Murillo, watching her, deeply meditative, as she spoke. When he kissed her goodnight she knew why he was unaccompanied. His wife, close to giving birth, had said, "You go. Come back and tell me all about it."

In her monkish college cell Clare felt aroused and sickened. Her upbringing was based on a code which resonated with what she saw as science's honesty. She wanted to turn away but had never known the amorality of real passion. It was she who phoned him at his college and she who paid for lunch in a town out on the Fens fifty miles away. When they made love his new daughter was nine days old.

To begin with they hardly spoke. But these were blank not contemplative silences. Much effort went into the logistics of adultery and the grim satisfaction of aligning railway timetables with car journeys to arrive at the designated X. And, if ever she needed reminding of the wrongness of the affair, she could reflect on car-bound contortions in deserted side roads and on rural cart-tracks slipping out of clothes that identified her employment and into those intended to arouse him. Together with that last lubricious detail when she flipped down the sun visor and dashed on lipstick in the mirror.

Afraid of questioning herself she ignored the effects the affair was having on him. His love-making had a frantic quality (Those eyes!) which she complacently imagined to be a version of her own excitement. Only later did she realise his frenzies had as much to do with shutting out his world as a desire for her body.

Uncommunicative, they fell out and separated for nearly a month. But the return, initiated by Clare, was even more charged. They started to talk, but in twin monologues which touched vaguely on the horrors of what they were doing.

"She mustn't find out," he said. "She doesn't deserve it."

"We need a better code when we speak on the phone," Clare said, not looking at him. "Something simpler."

She vowed her work would not suffer. Being single and endowed with youthful energy she stayed long hours to compensate for her absences. The UK president, to whom she reported, was astonished by her application and by her rapid grasp of management, her only potential weakness when given the post. He asked if she cared to represent the company on a government advisory committee, a remarkable suggestion for someone so young. She accepted and worked even longer hours.

Gradually the love-making became less compulsive and less frequent. Occasionally they went for walks, on one occasion a movie. But her need for him did not diminish. With no one else so close she talked to him about her work, discussed staffing problems, described her distant relationship with her mother. The only matter that wasn't discussed was the future.

It had to end. A more relaxed tempo allowed her to see the strain he was under. Fatherhood, a young wife and the ironic nature of his work combined to make him irritable and, latterly, jealous of her position. They discussed full separation in careful terms, as if weighing up the purchase of a new car. For six terrible weeks they remained apart, during which Clare slept badly despite a crushing workload. For the first time she took sleeping pills and woke up uninterested in what she faced at the office.

They resumed the affair and for a week or two enjoyed a tenderness they'd never known. Then, as if tenderness was an unnatural state, he looked at her with dark encircled eyes and for the first time took the initiative. "It's over. It must be."

"It's over."

Terrified of wakeful or drugged nights she resigned her magnificent position and passed a meaningless month on a Greek island believing change would soften things. In London she spent most of her savings launching a consultancy to obliterate her anguish. It failed because she was unable to find a partner willing to share such a suicidal project. The summer dresses bought to entrance him were given to charity. Business suits, ordered originally to disguise her youth, were now worn as a matter of principle, as if their austerity drew a veil over the previous half year. Make-up, particularly lipstick, was swept from her dressing table into a bin liner and then into oblivion.

Short of money and unwilling to beg from her parents she became IT manager of Confexxion, a Croydon sweets and confectionery manufacturer, at a third the salary she had earned before. From this perspective the dinner in Wadham's big hall dwindled into fantasy and she accepted her career trajectory had flattened. But a board decision to invest heavily in automated production encouraged her to lose herself in the company's huge rehabilitation. The benefits of automation became apparent after a single year and the company – institutionally ignorant of her department – ascribed this progress to her. From a seat on the board she was just in time to vote to expand the company's marketing department and later to consider the appointment of an assistant marketing manager.

Jerry Kepler, golf pro, can simplify your game. He'd interviewed well according to Giefel the marketing manager but his
subsequent contributions had, by Jerry's own admission, been
sub-par. It didn't matter. Soon he was to be translated.

To defer meeting Lynn GC officials in their blazers Clare followed Jerry into the pro shop where she wandered around, finger-
ing Pringle sweaters and noting prices with amusement. She sensed
him behind her, keen to show he was one half of a couple, obeying
the club rules.

"Golf's a shocking indulgence," she said pointing to a £20 pair
of socks.

"A mania. Submit to it or go home and watch sport on telly."

"It bit you."

"At age twelve. One reason I was lousy at marketing."

"Give me your arm," she said, "and I'll do my duty."

After an awkward twenty minutes circling the clubhouse lawn
Jerry handed Clare over to "Jack Treens. Club secretary. Very important chap." and sloped away on ill-defined business. Little interested in golf and even less in the club hierarchy, Clare was unsure
how important a club secretary was and fenced for a while until the
exchanges became predictable and risk-free. In fact she had a significant advantage over some of the officials. Whereas many clubs
employed retired Army officers, Lynn preferred the RAF where
Clare's authority was familiar. This at least made introductions more
bearable and suppressed references to the little gel's tasks back
home. Treens himself was an ex-squadron leader, latterly posted to
a navigation training school. This might have been promising had
he not been forced to admit his responsibilities had been "admin
not technical. Not really clever enough for that sort of thing."

He added brightly, "By the way Mrs Kepler I must thank you for
the superb prize you've put up for today's competition. Most generous."

A gesture Clare was unaware of but knew she would eventually
pay for.

"It is suitable, I hope?"

"A Big Bertha driver. I should say so." From her reaction Treens realised Jerry had proposed the prize and quickly changed the subject. "We don't see you on the course, Mrs Kepler."

"Jerry and I had an agreement: I would learn golf if he played tennis with me. I beat him at tennis but turned out unteachable at golf. A pro who couldn't teach his own wife seemed like bad news, so we quietly retired the agreement. Perhaps we were both a little over-sensitive. I understand pros usually ask a colleague to do the teaching in these cases."

Treens' diplomacy wasn't up to this and after an embarrassed laugh he retired to his office. Clare decided she had now been visible long enough, ordered coffee and took it to a table overlooking the first tee. By angling her chair towards the action she hoped to suggest she was fascinated by what she saw and that this would discourage chat. But other women had the same idea and soon there was a shortage of seats. Within minutes she was joined by a heavily made-up woman whose Junoesque contours were emphasised by a close-fitting summer dress where large white discs floated on a brown background. Clare admired, even envied, the way the garment matched the woman's anatomy.

"Alison," said the woman, stretching out her hand. "Would you mind horribly if I had a cigarette? I'm dying for one and yet everyone looks so damned healthy."

"Clare. By all means. But I've never thought of golf clubs as healthy."

Alison blew smoke away noisily. "An aggravating pastime, golf. It encourages what used to be called syncope. I should add I'm not a regular here. My brother's a member and there's some draconian rule that says he must bring his wife. Well Jill's having nothing of it and he's terrified he'll be punished for being woman-less. I'm standing in. A chance to take in the mores for future reference."

"You write?"

"Freelance. Mostly women's magazines. Something says this isn't your preferred territory."

"I'm an obligatory wife. And you're right, I'm here reluctantly. Normally I have a job to go to."

Alison's eyebrows rose. "Electronics," said Clare.

Alison ordered coffee and turned towards the tee. "Another disappointment: golf's practitioners don't radiate much sex appeal. Whoops, I'm forgetting; I could be looking at Mr Clare out there."

"I'll warn you."

But when Jerry did appear, passing on a message to someone overseeing the tee, Clare held back. Alison gestured an elbow. "At least he's younger. But there's something not quite right. He looks disappointed, a bit discouraged.?"

Clare pretended to look. "I think you're right."

It was clear Confexxion's assistant marketing manager had exaggerated his abilities. On the pretext of saving money he had broken with tradition and not used the company's normal PR consultant to arrange a reception for trade magazines. "PRs charge the earth," he had said. "I can do the arrangements in an afternoon."

But he'd forgotten to have the train met and the question and answer session produced not a single initiative from the mulishly offended journalists. A press release rushed out to cover the expected lack of coverage included a handful of grammatical howlers which ensured coverage but not the sort the company wanted. All this was outside Clare's responsibilities – or interest – but she happened to share lunch with Giefel and his aggrieved assessment of Jerry. "He'll have to go," Giefel said.

In the current month Confexxion had fired more people than in any previous year. Increased productivity had caught out those who worked directly with the contracted distribution company and the new bar-codes and other IT systems had been beyond these laggards who were also disinclined to learn. Hand-written orders had sufficed in the old days and – this was the crucial point – they could be decoded by any human being who was half-awake. Data digested by a computer didn't offer this luxury. Two long-established despatchers refused outright to adapt and Clare had been forced to kick them out. This was not well received by the workforce who insisted that new profits were being paid for in human suffering.

Not wanting to open another can of worms she offered to speak to Jerry. "Let's see if there's any good in him," she said to Giefel. "We must avoid another sacking. I know it's your patch and I won't go over your head. But I could approach him from the board if you agree. Perhaps that'll straighten him out."

Thus she met Jerry ten miles from the plant and beyond prying eyes. Until then he'd been a problem not a person. Given her continuing numbness towards men she treated him statistically. His curly brown hair, piercing blue eyes and athletic build were simply CV data rather than agreeable physical components. Two things did surprise her: his deep tan and a Perrier to go with the meal. But there was more.

"I don't want much to eat," he said. "A sandwich. I know I'm here to have my wrist slapped instead of being fired. In which case a long meal would be embarrassing. But I'd like to explain that awful cock-up. I have marketing experience but only in a specialised field which happens to be one of my great interests." He essayed a faint smile. "It wasn't bonbon manufacture."

"No doubt. But forget the sandwich since we've come all this way. And I'll ask the questions." This re-established a pecking order but she also believed there might be something to work with.

His initiative taken away he leant back good-naturedly, ordered an omelette and waited for her.

"You were with this sports goods chain, Goal, for three years?"

"General dogsbody at headquarters. Then list compiler in marketing. Then special events organiser."

"Special events?"

"Golf really. My fascination. Technically it shouldn't have worked. Goal doesn't sell golf equipment. But a golf competition lasts all day and there's time for the sales force to talk socially to the people who matter. It's good value, although it doesn't work if you invite people who don't take golf seriously. That was my talent, finding golf nuts."

"How?"

"I'm a golf nut myself. I play lots of courses, know lots of people. I kept the invitation list fairly short and chose swank clubs. We did four comps a year and got ourselves a reputation. People rang up and asked to be invited."

"Did Goal recognise what you'd done?"

He laughed. "They refused to promote me but they did give me more cash. Sales seemed delighted. But, like all good things... New MD, new policies. Why were we promoting golf when we didn't sell the equipment? They switched to a kids' football league on Hackney Marshes and it ended with a race riot."

"Do you ever lie?" Clare asked suddenly.

He guffawed. "All the time. But not about golf."

"Your Holy Grail?"

"I've never known what a grail was, but yes."

She took it no further and asked questions about his life away from the company. It was quickly obvious there was little more to add. Later she spoke to Giefel. "How about a golf competition...?"

He pondered. "None of our competitors does one."

"Then it could be a good move."

It might well have been. The arrangements fulfilled all Jerry's promise and those invited represented a valuable set of contacts. But the golf was played under the cloud of a hostile takeover and when the Malaysian bidder appeared it was evident the factory would be asset-stripped and the equipment shifted to a place where labour day-rates were conveniently lower. Clare had already received two bonuses in shares and their value appreciated during the takeover uncertainties. These she sold to recoup all her losses on the abortive consultancy. Jerry got four weeks' salary.

Most of the management spent the final raucous Friday in a pub where Clare was kissed, often and wetly, to her intense annoyance. The only person who didn't kiss her was Jerry who shared her displeasure at these assaults.

"Curious isn't it?" he said. "Some men think they have a right."

Clare wiped herself with a handkerchief. "It's an emotional occasion. But they aren't entitled to my lips."

"Saddies, the lot of them. At any other time they wouldn't get near a good-looking woman."

This throwaway compliment didn't entirely surprise her. He'd been grateful for the faith she had shown in him and was careful to behave in a correct – almost precise - manner during their rare official meetings.

"What will you try for?" she asked. "I take it golf's a hard nut to crack? But that's where you should be."

"That's where I was three years ago. Assistant pro at a scrubby club in Essex. I was more than halfway through the PGA course. But I couldn't keep it going; I almost starved."

She sipped her coffee and contemplated him as a manager might. Enthusiasm – about anything at all – was a rare commodity during personal assessments; she knew this from bitter experience. What's more he had converted his passion for golf into an attention to detail needed to organise the competition. Even Giefel, who had never forgiven his earlier gaffes, had been impressed.

"How much would you need?"

"You're not offering to stake me?" he asked.

"Why not? Isn't that sort of thing done?"

"It's a huge gamble."

"Eighteen months ago I took a large gamble and lost. One way and another I've won it all back. Oh, look, there's Desgranges forcing his way over here. No prizes for guessing what he's after."

Desgranges resembled a peeled egg, having gone comically bald. "I have to go, Clare. It's been a pleasure working with you. You stuck it to those dinosaurs who said women can't do the confectionery industry."

"Why George, thank you."

"I'll miss you. But you solved one problem. My wife and I couldn't think of a name for our first-born. Guess what we agreed on." He put his hand forward to shake hers but she leant forward and kissed his cheek.

She shrugged at Jerry's amusement. "OK, I'm inconsistent. Isn't that what I stand accused of: a butterfly not up to Aunt Jemima Humbugs?"

He raised his hands. "I wouldn't know. I'm out of that loop. Gosh, that sounds like a marketing noise."

She waited for him to respond to the point she had raised before Desgranges, then realised he wouldn't. Perhaps he thought she wasn't serious or was playing with him.

"As I was saying, I've got money."

"But why should you? Not that I'm complaining."

"Don't worry. I'm not the foolish older woman trying to buy your body." Though who knew? "Look I could say I'd been lucky, but I'd be lying. I enjoyed university and I enjoy what I do. As my parents like to say, 'I've got on.' But I don't often find that competence in others. Some pretend to enjoy their job but what they really mean is they're terrified of losing it. Point out someone, anyone, in this pub who was a glowing asset to Confexxion."

He gestured an order to the barmaid. "Glowing asset. That lets me out."

"But we'll never know, will we? And that's a shame. However perhaps I can give things a shove in another direction. Sport's trivial but then so are Citrus Sherberts. Unlike sweeties sport is definitely a meritocracy. Do you reckon you could cut it?"

"I haven't the faintest idea. Sport – certainly golf – requires luck. In my heart of hearts I doubt I'd make it out on the circuit. But being a club pro is the next step down and I have that ability. And the hunger. But I couldn't ask you to bet on me."

"Why not?"

"You're not a bank. You're a person."

It wasn't that she was attracted to him; there was no depth there. But there was unexpected humanity and for the first time since her horrors she felt herself responding to a man's company. A part of her once dormant was now awake. His brief compliment – if that was what it was - had no sexual importance; it simply told her she was better equipped to get on with the rest of her life.

"Come up with a figure," she said.

Alison had turned from the first tee and was now examining Clare closely. "You never mentioned your surname."

"Did I have to? You didn't."

Alison said nothing, her scrutiny unbroken. Clare had experience of journalists though not those writing for women's magazines. "Oh for goodness sake. My name's Kepler, my husband's the pro here, you saw him minutes ago and rated him disappointed. For the record I'm moderately well-known, but in a narrow business field that the tabloids don't browse in."

"You under-estimate the tabloids. A successful business woman married to a golf pro – there's half the story straight away. Add in a little sleaze, a piece of paper from your dustbin you neglected to shred. Even an ill-educated guess. Why is he disappointed? No, I'm only kidding." She turned to face Clare directly. "As I said, you appear out of place. The more I see of this club, the more that sounds like a compliment."

"It also sounds like jumping to conclusions."

"Touché. But seriously. You're worth a feature and I'd like to write it?"

"For a woman's magazine?"

"I draw a wider net."

"Why am I worth a feature?"

"Pure instinct. Some people interest me, some don't."

"Have I got secrets worth unearthing?"

"That's a news story. I'm talking about a feature."

"Would I get to read it before it was published?"

"No."

"How would I benefit?"

"You'd get an honest, skilful appraisal. Others would see it too. Who knows about benefits?"

Clare considered her situation. Jobless, vague about the next move. An article might not define her but being interviewed might. "Give me your card. I'll think about it."

Nick was being bathed as she got back. He stood up to be embraced then looked around. "Daddy. Daddy."

"Isn't this new?" she asked Birgitta. "He's never been used to Jerry in the evening. Was he happy leaving the nursery?" Birgitta said yes but offered no comment on the master of the house.

Lunch at the golf club had been heroically stodgy. Clare toyed with a tomato sandwich. Even if she'd been inclined to watch television bright evening sunshine through the tiny Tudor windows would have discouraged her. She killed time for half an hour, daydreaming on the couch.

At eight she telephoned Chantal. "I have a mid-range chablis."

"I take it *le coq sportif* is engaged in putting balls into little holes."

"And I am well aware of our ground rules. Jerry will be late tonight."

"Oh chérie I'd love to but I haven't even eaten. I await my beloved who is bringing home someone he needs to cultivate. I had to change the date since our guest insists on a cassoulet - in this weather, I ask you – and didn't realise it takes time. But we can at least chat until then. How are you? Wasn't there a problem with work?"

"No longer. The work no longer exists. I am free during the day as well as the evenings."

"You sound quite gay about it."

"I have gained a sack full of écus."

Chantal laughed. "Who else in this wretched town – this stretched-out London suburb – could have put it that way? Oh, I wish I could help you with your chablis. Save some for tomorrow or come over here for coffee."

"I'll phone, knowing how you insist on protocol."

"Dear, dear Clare. You are my best friend in Sevenoaks. I love you. But I cannot – will not – love *le coq*. A man should have more in his head than little white balls. Besides, he takes advantages when we embrace. Please forgive me."

"I understand. Truly I do. Even if it does mean we see each other so little. And it's a pleasure to hear your accent. But here's a question. Your Frenchness means you're the only person I can ask. We get on. We like each other. I like your wickedness, your enthusiasm, your lack of inhibition. I have a reason for asking this and it is not vanity - "

"Chérie. You are – How do I say this? Where does the qualifier go? – the least vain woman I know."

"Perhaps I have little to be vain about."

"Foo. You are a scientist. You beat men at men's games. Best of all you are serious but never *ennuyeuse*. You know that word?"

"Boring. But that's a subtle difference only French people understand. In England serious and boring could be the same thing."

Chantal remained silent for several seconds. "I wish we were speaking face to face. I wish to be very clear. Another reason I love you is that you are not French. French women – here in Sevenoaks – they weary me. Fatigue me. They have no restraint."

"And I have… restraint?"

"Yes but that is good. I must explain more. I… Oh, *merde* and even shit. The beloved and his guest are here. We will meet tomorrow. We must meet. Promise?"

"I promise."

Clare took New Scientist out to one of two chairs in the small garden. It was, as Chantal implied, a matter requiring faces as well as voices. An opportunity to backtrack, to delay, to consider. For restraint was as open to misinterpretation as seriousness. Lack of aggression might be lack of confidence. Nonsense, of course. Belief in herself had brought success and esteem. But benefits could arrive via the back door and for misunderstood reasons.

She started reading the magazine and was immediately reminded of Alison. Her thoughts swung backwards and forwards, between the offer of an interview and an account of progress at CERN. For her CERN, or what it represented, was the road untaken. Her professor at Wadham had urged her towards a masters and research, only one step down from recommending her to join the college. Others said research was too often stultified. Who, even among physicists, knew the head of CERN?

"Nothing wrong with measuring competence against a salary," someone said. Her future became clearer over lunch with a headhunter from an oil company. The position he offered was unappealing but she came away with a fair understanding of her worth in industry.

Worth that had prevailed after the Confexxion takeover when she left to embark on a series of short-term contracts where high salaries reflected the risks she was taking. Offering to finance Jerry's entrance into the golf world had meant dipping into what she had saved. Within a few months the costs were covered from her current account.

She was careful to be open about Jerry. Acquaintances and both her parents remained sceptical, even after she and Jerry married. "Did you have marriage in mind?" asked her mother. The short answer was no.

But why had she done it? Well, he didn't complain about the remote and difficult target he had chosen. He was polite and had some social skills. In one rationalisation, adopted and discarded, she saw the project as self-indulgence without any intellectual attachment. Golf was as alien as movie-making or genealogy. More important, she only risked losing money. Recovering from the affair had left her more sensible, more controlled and less vulnerable, or so she believed. Eventually she would meet another man and matters would proceed along Cartesian lines. Jerry was not that man, Jerry was a project. Almost a charity. Looking back now she was able to laugh at these theories but then they had been real enough. Time changed her and her view of herself.

One thing she hadn't foreseen was being required to monitor Jerry's progress. He had insisted. "It's your cash," he said and she knew it would be crass not to show any interest in what she had paid for. Lunches, then, at transport cafes close to golf courses, sandwiches in a layby near an academy where he was staying for a residential course. A Prêt à Manger package in the car park of the gloomy Midlands office where he took his third year examination. Beaming with good health he summarised progress in the compressed arithmetic golfers express themselves and which she followed only dimly. What she enjoyed were his clear-sighted triumphs, the energy he radiated and his ability to put setbacks into a plausible context.

Once, over a disgusting and ignored fry-up, she surprised him by referring to the risks he faced in trying to balance the animal pleasure of long drives against the need to be accurate. "A tug-of-war between fun and money," she said casually, a phrase she'd nevertheless honed.

"I thought you didn't know the sport."

"Just recently it's been difficult to escape. That American competition, on the course with all the azaleas. The constant repetition about having to lay up, if that's the right term."

"Did you... get into it?"

"I didn't watch long enough. But the logic appealed. As did the physics. A crude introduction into aerodynamics but accurate as far as it went."

He stared speechless.

She continued. "I don't understand strategy and the names mean nothing. But I'm pleased about what's happening to you. It is your thing, isn't it?"

"Nothing else matters." She was to remember this several years later.

They became lovers after she had tested her emotions in a half-hearted affair elsewhere. He was a ludicrously handsome professor of English at Bristol who appeared on television a lot. To her amazement he had only just discovered C. P. Snow's essay on the two cultures and seemed determined to fight a rearguard action against science. Not having read Meredith or Beckett left her disadvantaged but dogged. She persisted with him for a further weekend hoping his artfully combed, greying head contained something other than competitive vanity. Driving him back to Bristol from Broadway, which she'd foolishly agreed to before the last arid night together, proved a severe ordeal.

By now Jerry was an assistant pro with prospects at a midranking Home Counties club. They met at the club-house where he had had to lie about her status. "I asked for an hour off and Boris – he's the pro, my boss – said I wasn't to let my girlfriend keep me any longer. I wanted to explain that girl-friend didn't describe you but I gave up. I hoped you'd prefer that to me telling the truth."

Broadway was still vividly remembered and Clare was not in the best of moods. "Gets you off the hook, anyway."

"What do you mean?"

His tone surprised her. "Oh, nothing."

"I'll put this on my tab. Just the drinks, then."

They hadn't met for six weeks and there'd been no time for him to report progress. Yet here he was, escorting her out of the bar with exaggerated formality. Beside her car he attempted to be offhand. "It's just a case of waiting. Boris has got an offer from somewhere near Sunningdale – he won't say where – but he'll take it when the school term ends. I could send you a letter when there's news."

Arranging this meeting had involved some serious diary juggling and Clare's instinct was to protest at cutting things short. Then for the first time, and with unexpected clarity, she recognised Jerry's awkward situation. "I'm sorry. That was bad-tempered. And rather silly."

"Silly?"

"That business about girl-friends."

He fumbled with his hands, an uncharacteristic lapse in his normal decisiveness. "That isn't... silly." His face was troubled.

"Would you prefer I stayed away from these... what are they? Briefings?"

"I prefer you to come."

"There were never any obligations. From the start."

"I know. But I never understood why."

She laughed. "If we're going to discuss this we shouldn't be standing here in the car park. It'll look as if you're breaking up with your girl-friend. Should we resume over lunch? Or would that turn you into a ditherer? I mean, first you get rid of me, then I return?"

He didn't like this. "Let's go back."

"Let's have a proper talk. Why don't you give me a lesson."

"Not in that outfit. It's far too..."

"Formal? I could buy clothes."

"At the prices we charge?" They both laughed. It cost her £200 for items she would never wear again but the childish hint of conspiracy helped. Observing the sale, Boris the pro was only too willing to re-arrange the lessons schedule to accommodate such a willing customer.

Jerry gestured to the buggy and Clare stepped in. "Surely I need more than one piddling club?"

"To get out of a pot bunker; a sand wedge is enough. Our practice area is on the far side and it's not often visited. Amateurs hate pot bunkers but if anyone does turn up we'll gracefully concede and drive off somewhere else."

There was no need for tuition. The serene surroundings were a healing contrast to Broadway and Jerry an uncomplicated alternative to the Bristol professor. They sat in the buggy. "You've done a lot for me," said Jerry. "But there is one point…"

"I know, I know what you're going to ask. My strange act of charity. I've pondered that same question. I used to tell myself it was a folly, but not any more. Not now you're close to getting what you want. It's no longer madness and it's not really an investment - I'm not looking for a return. At the time I didn't look deeply into my motives. Now I'm glad I didn't. I might not have done it and that would have been sad."

He took a golf ball from his pocket, lobbed it into the pot bunker, picked up the sand wedge and jumped down beside the ball. "This is me," he said. "Almost swallowed up by the hole. Look at the steep walls. My target is the green, straight ahead, but I can't see it. This is me. See what I do."

Effortlessly and lightly swung, the club head brushed the sand, the ball rose vertically and dropped on the grass where he had said it would. He turned to face her, well below the buggy yet full of authority. "Many people can't do that. But there are many things I can't do. I know I'm a sportsman and not much else. During that last week at Confexxion I wanted to ask you out: dinner, or whatever. But there was too much confusion. I delayed until the pub booze-up and waited for the right moment. Out of the blue we were talking about me being financed and the opportunity had flown. Afterwards I was glad. What would we have talked about?"

"I can't speak to you down there," said Clare.

Sitting next to her again he started tossing and catching the golf ball. "Would you have come?"

"Perhaps." She shook her head. "Probably."

"What would we have talked about?"

"What everyone talks about. Themselves."

"I'm not sure I have another self."

"You're begging for sympathy. Golf absorbs you - you could have told me why. And if that was too damned philosophical we might have discussed what doesn't absorb you. You could have tossed up an abstraction – like that goddamn ball – and simply started talking. Disillusionment. Beauty. I don't know what. Stop being childish."

He slid the ball into his pocket. "Are you surprised?"

"I'd have thought I wasn't your type but not for the reasons you suspect. Not because you think me clever. I suspect you see me as distant, managerial. And then..." About to refer to her looks she stopped short. She didn't want to imply he was drawn to big-busted women with lots of self-evident hair.

"And then...?" Had he guessed?

"Something I've changed my mind about." She waved a hand defensively. "Let's have dinner and find out?"

"OK if I call you in a week's time?"

"So I can say I'm washing my hair if I want to turn you down?"

"Say 'Hair' That will be enough."

As they rode circuitously round the fairway edges she felt he'd got the better of her. More surprising, she didn't mind. They had dinner a week later and she discovered something new - he could be trusted with her feelings. She asked about life beyond becoming a pro. He thought about this for some time, to the point of seeming half-witted. Finally he said: "Stability." Astonished by this she looked for evidence of posturing but saw only honesty. They kissed goodbye like people who'd been neighbours for a decade. The next time dinner was in London and he stayed the night.

Now with New Scientist on her knee and the stillness of the house weighing on her pleasurably she re-examined the foolishness she'd been accused of. All she remembered was her own detachment. It had not been a meeting of like minds but why should a physicist seek out another physicist? Why not the pair of them in two separate daytime worlds entering a third shared world at home? Businessmen did it with stay-at-home wives and professional couples worked in fields as different as law and politics. If it was a theory there was empirical data out there to support it. But the flaw, visible through hindsight, presumed they would retain those earlier versions of themselves. Neither could have foreseen that his forcefulness and obsession would die away when he gained the stability he craved and discovered he wasn't as good as he thought he was. That comparison had continued to harden forcing him to recognise – in terror – his average achievements. To his credit he adapted and the routine of being a golf pro became a protection. But the thrill of the chase was lost. And when Nick was born unexpectedly through a failure in Clare's method of contraception the retreat into routine grew. Nick was irrelevant because there was nothing Jerry could point to with pride as a father. The absent evenings were followed by weekends at distant, footling competitions. Jerry needed a barrier against his wife's confidence and successes.

Clare, who might well have sympathised had she been asked, was never asked. She fiddled with New Scientist as she might have fiddled with an outmoded theory.

Later she wrote a reminder on the kitchen calendar to call Chantal. Purely for social reasons since Chantal's quickness had answered the question Clare had in mind. This was typical of Chantal and was one of the reasons Clare had been drawn to her. Not that the Keplers' social circle in Sevenoaks was particularly broad. Both worked uncongenial hours and Jerry, despite his gladhanding at Lynn, could be a social liability. There were couples - in effect wives – who were keen to share his company and others, for almost the same reasons, who were not. Distrustful husbands together with those bored by golf kept invitations to a minimum.

Chantal had been very explicit. Having met both Clare and Jerry at a particularly bibulous party and entertained them both with her exhilarating gossip, she then contrived to have coffee alone with Clare some days later. "At last," she had said, "someone who doesn't talk about gardens, their children or their cars. Or the way they drive their cars from here to there. I hope we can be friends but perhaps we cannot."

Clare had an inkling. "You'd prefer we were alone? As we are now?"

"You understand. Ah, that is a relief. Sometimes it is difficult… " Chantal lapsed into a brief burst of French from which Clare detected *le coq sportif.* And a protocol was born.

As it happened meetings were comparatively rare. Chantal, living with her "beloved", had an international career as a management consultant which meant weeks away from Sevenoaks. But any rendezvous that could be retrieved from crowded calendars was always scandalously enjoyable. Jerry took these defections without complaint assuming that Chantal feared his sexual magnetism. Clare was less sanguine, suspected an ironic interpretation of the French phrase and made a point of not asking for an elaboration. From time to time she wondered whether she ought to have shown more uxorial support but this went out of the window when Chantal, perverse as ever, took a liking to Nick.

6. HATCH

Connubial retrospective

THE MORNING sun shrivelled Hatch's eyes. For three hours he'd been cloistered in a car parts store, trapped within cramped shelving that lacked natural light, searching out customer orders. A part-time job to bring in cash, hard-earned on the worst shift of the day between seven and ten.

The shop manager stopped him. "You picked it up quickly."

Suspecting sarcasm Hatch mumbled.

"I mean it," said the manager genially. "Most people take weeks."

"It isn't easy."

"I'm forced to fire people regularly. I'd go electronic but a bar-code swipe would cost two-hundred-kay. Hang on here. I'll get you a better shift as soon as I can."

A new career!

Prudence's flat, off the Ashby-de-la-Zouch road, required three buses but he set out on foot to savour air and light. The parts store had been a logical step. Such systems were an essential feature within Tempest and he knew how they worked. But he'd used them as a manager: ticking off shopfloor requests, approving space layouts, authorising audits. He had never picked orders, never fingered through mini-bins for items with ten- or twelve-figure codes, never known the childish relief of tracking down a large and recognisable starter motor compared with scrabbling for yet another tiny spring. Whether he had the temperament or not he knew he couldn't be choosy. For unexplained reasons he'd been turned down for counter jobs at a kitchen equipment shop and at an off-licence.

His route took him away from Tamworth's centre through one of the unrenovated streets where brick frontages in gothic revival style had a Lego-like charm; where the cheapjack plastic shopfront displays were dominated by differing widths of window and their bulky surrounds.

Tempest's office block in Bloxwich had been gothic style and a PR consultant, brought in to advise on modern gloss, wondered whether it "encouraged positive twentieth-century thoughts". Tempest was divided. The older managers, terrified of being thought fogies, wanted to demolish the block. Others, including Hatch, favoured refurbishing. The argument came to an end when it was discovered the building was listed. Later a brochure was proposed to celebrate the company's twenty-fifth anniversary. Since no one else seemed interested, Hatch volunteered to explore the building's history and contribute a few paragraphs.

It left him with an interest in late nineteenth-century architecture and a residue of professional doubt. Previously he had always argued that industrial buildings should conform to the processes they housed; that distinction was now clouded.

At a local library, offering more cheerful gothic, he picked up a leaflet of forthcoming Birmingham Symphony Hall events and sat down to read. He needed to prepare himself. For several weeks Hester and, occasionally, Tom had practised charity by stealth, inviting him to concerts and recitals. Attending these events was not wholly enjoyable. He didn't like the role of pauper nor did he approve of their attempts to widen his musical tastes. Like most engineers he favoured instrumental Bach and had in his time regurgitated tedious argument to justify this. Over the years this view had solidified and he now avoided Elgar, let alone Prokofiev. Didn't mind being thought unimaginative. Since it would be churlish to turn down the Makings' generosity his tactic was counter-attack. He ringed a performance of Monteverdi Vespers. It wasn't keyboard or stringed Bach but, more important, it wasn't Birtwhistle.

Having dawdled he now hurried to the station and caught a bus to the suburbs. It was becoming more difficult not to think about what lay ahead. He reminded himself he was seeing Prudence not to argue but to test his own responsibilities.

The final bus, which followed a continuous rural circle, took him past farms with meanly defined fields, typical of the Midlands. After the divorce Prudence had insisted she wanted room to move but Hatch saw this area as a very urban form of countryside. Also, to come all this way and then live in a flat, however luxurious, seemed self-defeating.

Prudence had a private hallway and a solid teaklike door. He pressed the doorbell, breathing shallowly.

She gestured him in and he stood aside so she could lead the way to her living room. A hall lamp with a Tiffany shade threw checkerboard flickers on her head. The deep carpet pile absorbed the tips of her stiletto heels.

Hatch was directed to a leather sofa: bulging upholstery, in an inhumanly clean shade of beige, that had surely never been sat on. "Can I get you some tea? I have that valerian flavour."

The conversation would be civilised. Except that Hatch had gone off valerian soon after they parted. "A little later if that's all right."

She sat on a matching easy chair, elevated by its over-stuffed curves. They said nothing as they became re-accustomed. When a draughtsman at Tempest told him Prudence resembled the American actress, Anne Francis, the comparison was too obscure to mean anything. But when someone else repeated it Hatch followed it up. The resemblance was irresistible, down to the beauty spot, displaced in Prudence's case to the top of her left cheek. He had watched cassettes of Bad Day at Black Rock and Forbidden Planet as if they were porn, furtively alone with these counterfeit images. The resemblance had never been discussed and he wondered now if Prudence had known about it. Years had passed, lines on her face had slackened but the slightly sulky mouth and loose blonde hair still recalled the films.

"You're wondering, aren't you?" she said.

"I usually do."

"We were different then."

He shook his head. "I can't see it. Anyway, the Featherstones agreed about the lease. They'll move out in two months' time. It'll cost us four months' rent."

"I said they'd behave well. They're our friends, Andrew."

"Perhaps. But this is only the start. We need a bridging loan until the house is sold. And I should warn you, the house has hardly appreciated. We paid too much in the first place."

"I liked the house."

Oh, he knew that. "We took out a big mortgage."

"There was so much to put right. We needed the en suite. In this day and age it's barbaric doing without. You agreed. I remember."

"When I was a senior manager at Tempest."

She winced, not wanting to hear this. "You don't resent finding this money, do you? I could ask Doctor Lindsay again, find out whether there's somewhere in Britain. Somewhere cheaper."

Hatch spread his hands. "I can't support you with my income just now. I hardly have any income. We're lucky I blackmailed Weldworth into a bigger pay-off. That will cover initial expenses in Switzerland. But the house will only bring in so much."

"You never showered me with alimony," she said wanly.

"A salesman's pay didn't allow it…"

"A salesman! Something you were never cut out for."

This selective view of his working life would once have enraged him. Now there seemed no point. He turned on the couch looking sightlessly onto the bland landscaping outside.

"Well, Weldworth was a silly job," she insisted.

"Don't," he said.

Her blonde eyebrows, thick and unplucked, rose in mild indignation.

"It was your decision, Pru."

"I don't know what you're talking about." But she did.

How long had they been divorced? He'd lost his job through no fault of his but had looked elsewhere full of confidence. Justifiably. A good offer from Hotpoint had required a little patience and alimony would have flowed. But for some reason she'd been terrified. Get a job, any job, she'd said.

I deserve it, she'd said when he protested. Should he have held out? No point in speculating. He hadn't. And the pain and humiliation of what followed would never go away. "What was it you wanted from me in the first place?" he asked to change the subject.

"A home. Someone reliable."

Hatch laughed. "You could have had that and more without me. The Egyptian, el Saouid, was crazy about you. He'd have promoted you into a princess. Why not him?"

She turned away.

"OK, you were too good for him. But there were others. That peer who owned the boutique hotel in the West End. No miscegenation problems there. Why not him? More important, why me?"

No answer.

The anger faded. "Switzerland must happen. I can't walk away from ten years. But selling the house takes all our assets. I'll bite on the bullet but I have to say there aren't any great jobs in the offing. It may be a long wait."

He stared into her violet eyes. "Look, I need a favour and it's going to seem strange. I know I'll end up as a fool. Over the years I've shut my mind to what went wrong. Finding out didn't seem important. But now I need to know the real reason you married me. Not the reason I imagined." He paused. "Two weeks ago I asked a woman out to lunch. She refused and it's just as well. I doubt she'd have enjoyed my company. Was I always like that?"

"I'll make some tea," she said and rose from the chair. He followed her into the kitchen where he watched her filling a kettle. Turning, she stepped back, startled to find him there. "That's not like you."

"What isn't?"

"In the kitchen. It was never your place. Not where you did things."

"Times have changed." He thought of the Baby Belling and the room above Mr Wee's fish-shop. "Did I never wash up? Peel a potato?"

"Not man's work." Her lack of acrimony surprised him.

On the coffee table, by the pot of tea, was a plate of biscuits. At the supermarket he never considered biscuits. Why? Too many damn questions.

"Are you working at all?" he asked. "Or am I prying?"

She shook her head. "Three mornings a week at the solicitor I mentioned. It isn't the money – the pay is Dickensian. It's a routine."

He opened his mouth as if to speak but she guessed what he was going to say. "The answer to that is no. I discourage it. Perhaps that's why I'm going to church again."

A major difference between them although not a source of argument. Prudence hadn't required his company at Holy Trinity and he'd always been grateful. He assumed it had been a middle-class necessity. Like doylies and antimacassars. Certainly it had never led to any of the discomforts of his mother's religious obsessions.

"So," she said briskly, bringing her knees together and smoothing the skirt over her thighs. "The whys and wherefores – and after all this time!"

"This wasn't a subject we ever discussed. At the end you simply said you'd had enough and I took you at your word. Perhaps you expected me to protest, I don't know. Perhaps you were undecided and hoped I'd react positively. A terrible thought that's only just occurred to me. If that was the case I'm sorry. You meant more to me than just a blind agreement to separate. But I never felt I had the right to argue against the break-up."

"It's true I expected more of a struggle. I thought you simply lacked interest. Now I know. With you it was the honourable thing, wasn't it?"

"The practical thing. I couldn't bring myself to harass you."

She laughed. "Weird, really. You had my feelings at heart. But it didn't seem like that at the time. In any case that wasn't the issue."

Hatch waited.

"I'm not sure I want to do this," she said. "It will hurt you. You understood about the house and I'm grateful. Can't you let it be?"

"I'm facing a rocky future. I may not come out of this professionally intact. We're talking about one of my failings. A big failing. I need to know. But what I believed then still holds. I won't harass you."

"Even so, you're squeezing me."

"And perhaps I don't care if I harass you," he said, smiling grimly.

"God, we sound like a Terence Rattigan play."

"Not my field."

"On the contrary. You could be one of his characters. The honourable victim."

"A victim?"

"Very much so. Wanting to know why you're asking the wrong question. People get married for all sorts of reasons. Some of them even romantic. Most reasons don't last and others take their place. After all, why did you marry me?"

"You're stunning to look at and intelligent. Also I had a conviction – no doubt mistaken - I was right for you. I thought you wanted a settled life. Yeah, it doesn't sound good, does it? Perhaps it qualifies as being practical."

"Did those reasons – your reasons - endure?"

"More or less."

Prudence sighed. "OK, let's start at the beginning. It's a banal tale, very obvious. Both of us were victims." She raised a hand. "Don't be so stubborn. I'm a victim too and this isn't special pleading. We're victims because of who we are. Being an engineer made you vulnerable, my face made me vulnerable."

Now she stared down at the neglected tea tray. As she poured out the two cups the herby smell rose towards him. It was easily the best feature, the taste was disappointingly sharp, could have been an aperient. But he would drink it as his part of this rather tense encounter.

She handed him a cup, saying, "What was I talking about? Ah yes, my two-edged gift from God."

For some reason the words appalled him, but then he heard a faintly familiar bell tolling.

"I was born pretty and at fourteen I was beautiful. I can say this unselfconsciously because it was generally agreed. As a result I became unpleasantly over-confident. Also I could link cause and effect. I didn't suffer as an adolescent I learnt things and set aside the lessons."

She stared into his face. "When you were brushing up your A-levels I was being asked out by the school's main hunk, famous for his Caterham Seven."

"I'm impressed by that detail."

"Saying he had a car wouldn't have typed him well enough. He had a fantasy car. Most Seven owners are in their fifties and they've bought a childhood icon. My classmates babbled about the car but didn't know what it signified. I investigated, found he came from a wealthy family, that his parents indulged him, that he was an amateur when it came to girls."

"An amateur?"

"A Caterham Seven is a motorised pair of trousers. Getting into it with the roof up is almost impossible. So it's nearly always hood down. It used to be called a tart trap but it lost its appeal in the lightest shower. The Seven was a pawn in my game. I should add the lad had other plus points: handsome, enough money for a decent restaurant. A worthwhile scalp in fact. When he asked me out – as I knew he would - I said, fine, but we'll travel by taxi. The little lamb."

"Thank God we didn't go to the same school."

"You've forgotten that I too was a victim. I grew up quickly. I used to say to the few girl-friends who could stand me that men came in two varieties: those awed by pretty women and those who wanted to subdue them. With the second lot it was a matter of discovering their Achilles heel, their Caterham Seven weakness. Rather deliberately I became engaged to one of the awe-struck ones just to see if the awe died away with familiarity. It didn't. And by then I was twenty-seven."

"Then I turned up. And that didn't solve the problem either."

"I thought it might."

Hatch said, "I knew you'd had an active social life - I knew several of the hangers-on. But all this mechanistic stuff is new. It's astonishing we found each other. I was way out of my depth at the time."

"The Ideal Home Exhibition. Why were you there?"

"Tempest was exhibiting. The usual – washing machines and dryers. However we'd suffered one of those managerial brainwaves. Senior staff to spend a couple of days on the stand, mingling with the customers. I found it hard going. As I recall you were one of several women working for the organiser – wearing yellow and white stripes. You asked me if you could help. Didn't expect me to say yes but, I thought, why not?"

"Ah yes. A bad case of shop assistant's dilemma. When does the vendor break into the customer's browsing? And how is it done?"

"I was impressed. 'Make a virtue out of jargon,' you said. You asked about my job and came up with a perfect tactic. I remember it to this day. Sidle up and ask if the browser knows the drum is triple polished. 'Or some such jaw-dropping factoid,' you added. Factoid was new to me."

"And then we…?"

"I was starving. You took me to the VIP restaurant and used your pass. You stayed for lunch and I couldn't work out why."

She laughed. "Nothing flattering. I needed to sit down – a chronic complaint at exhibitions.

"Even so I was privileged."

"We chatted. I couldn't categorise you. You weren't bursting with testosterone nor transfixed by my breasts. You were relaxed, rather innocent. And you were – are – good looking. Interesting, perhaps. Why? You seem astonished!"

"You've never said that before."

Both reflected on whether this mattered. Hatch said, "I was hopelessly unobservant. It was only after lunch I realised how you appeared. In that yellow outfit you were just another functionary. But perhaps we don't see the faces of women who are helpful. I got the hint from men at other tables; they couldn't take their eyes off you. Or me, for that matter. I remember thinking, 'She's a blonde!' as if that was the explanation. Obviously I'd joined the awe-struck group."

"Far from it. You were easy with me. That was unusual."

"You invited me to the exhibitors' party."

"To avoid somebody there."

"You were good company, even flattering."

She sighed. "I even made it easy for you to get in touch."

"You sound regretful."

"Aren't you?"

He said, "I was slow picking things up. Who knows what marriage is supposed to be? At the time it was simply a struggle. When difficulties cropped up I assumed the failings were mine."

"Are you sure you want to go on with this?"

"You mean the problems *were* my fault?"

"I suppose I do. But I'm bringing them to the surface, and I'm not sure it's necessary."

Hatch leant back on the sofa and saw another Tiffany lamp-shade. A decoration his former wife had chosen. An attentive husband would have known her taste ran to Tiffany lampshades, yet here it was, alien and unexpected. Had they disagreed about furniture, the way rooms were arranged, about paint colours? Nothing came to mind. But had he simply forgotten or had such differences never arisen?

Her expression was distant yet pained. He said, "You don't want to do this?"

"I avoided telling you when we divorced. It seemed unnecessary and cruel. That's still the case but as you say, you're entitled."

"Could we have some lunch somewhere?" He needed to break the spell of this feminine room, although he hadn't enough to pay for two meals. Prudence said, "Don't waste your money. I'll put something together. It won't be terribly interesting but we aren't celebrating."

They sat at the kitchen table over toasted cheese sandwiches and more valerian tea. Another preternaturally clean room. She said, "You were wrong about el Saouid. He wanted me all right but he had plans. I was to be dressed by St Laurent and dragged round the earth's surface to sit in on property deals. His theory was I would distract those he did business with. I turned him down and he started a sort of auction, upping the ante again and again to find out where I would crack. We would stay at the Plaza in New York. Not good enough? The Gritti Palace, then. We would charter a jet. No? Buy one. All I could think of was the Egyptian bazaar writ large.

"But it wasn't el Saouid who forced my hand. It was somebody much younger, an act of pure vanity. The son of a Russian oligarch who had no business talent and nothing to occupy himself. He was very quiet but underneath lurked a dreadful drama queen. I refused to meet his father in Moscow because I'm not at my best when it's cold. But previously he'd boasted about me to his family and getting me there was vital. He threatened suicide and I said 'There, there.'. So he went away and tried. But he was no better at suicide than business. Aspirins! They left him with kidney damage and while he recovered I moved out.

"I lived for six months with my mother in Banbury, a perfect place to review my love life. I realised not a single man I'd slept with would have been bearable as a spouse. I was fed up of tending to myself when times got fraught. I wanted to try out peace and quiet."

"Peace and quiet," said Hatch. "Welcome to the walking dead."

"There was more to it than that. I wanted a man who'd defined a place in the world and found it. Enormous success wasn't a factor but I needed a man who could think and who had recognisable values. Because I am who I am he had to be presentable; I didn't fancy explaining a geek to the social world I might be entering."

"Well, there's a compliment or two."

She was raising the tea-cup to her lips with both hands. "Does this sound like me?"

"Not really. But then you're explaining yourself - something you rarely did when we were married."

"Hole in one. But ask yourself: did I compile this list before we met or is it the result of ticking off what I saw in you? Hmmm. I'm turning out to be pretty calculating, aren't I?"

He said, "I knew I was under scrutiny but that seemed natural. I guessed you'd been a high flyer and accepting me would bring you back to earth. I tried to show you a version of me I hoped was truthful. But I assume I misled you."

She lowered the cup with a decisive clatter. "Within six months I knew it was a mistake. I married you on a theory and the theory was incomplete. The other nine years were devoted to changing you – clearly impossible – and making hellfire sure I didn't conceive."

Hatch was silent, remembering Hester's unbidden question about children.

"You were born with instincts that not only made engineering attractive, they made it inevitable. And being a good engineer made things worse for us. You too had a theory although yours was better thought-out than mine. You decided to be decent, to ensure there were no money arguments, to consult me about decisions, and – wherever possible – go with what I wanted. You accepted (via osmosis because we never discussed it) there would be no children. How you guessed I'll never know. Leisure activities were mine not yours. You neither encouraged me to take a job nor prevented me from doing so. The perfect basis for a marriage, the prescription for a happy wife."

She poured out more tea.

"Only the most perverse woman would have complained. And there was more. From the start, when the rules could have been bent a little, you made love twice a week, admittedly on different days. When I took you in my mouth you suggested – God knows how – that you enjoyed it but it wasn't a requirement. Decency at that level can, my dear Andrew, drive away passion."

Silence again.

"Let's take a smaller matter. We started going to the theatre. It was new to you and you enjoyed yourself. But you needed to understand this new world. The drives home were a continuing stream of analysis and conclusions. As if you were getting ready to sit an exam. I realised this was how you took your pleasure but often you neglected to say whether you'd enjoyed the play or not."

She gazed at him questioningly.

"Lumping it together distorts things. I make you sound like a pedant and you're not. Often you made me laugh. You bought me thoughtful presents. You were supportive when my bad temper got the better of me at parties and dinners. But it was no good. I was always waiting for the other shoe to drop. I imagined I could predict your responses but you're far too intelligent for that. What I was sure of was that you *would* respond. You *had* to. It's part of your balanced world."

She took another sip of tea and shuddered. "I'm not sure how long I'd have gone on. And after a while I could see there was no fun in it for you either, just duty. You may think I was grateful when Hester recognised our joylessness and decided to drive in a wedge. But watching you was painful. I've no idea whether you took what was on offer from her and I wouldn't have blamed you. All I can say it didn't help much if you did. You say you still see her and her newlywed Tom. It's none of my business but I doubt she's let go of you entirely."

Prudence spread her hands. "Does any of this help? I was a smart little girl; smart enough to know your virtues would come at a price. How much did I want – or need – to be married? Just now the idea leaves me cold. One thing I am glad about is I was able to crawl away alone to church. Just as well. These days I let my mind go blank during the services."

Hatch pushed his unfinished tea to one side. "I want to walk a few steps. Here in the room. I thought I'd warn you."

He prowled hoping the physical exercise would settle his mind. Spotted two newish novels on a corner table but neither the titles nor the authors meant anything to him. And now the prowling made him feel awkward and self-conscious. After less than a minute he sat down.

As he started to speak she urgently forestalled him. "I should have mentioned this before: you are due a terrible apology. When you lost the Tempest job I panicked. For reasons I cannot justify I imagined you were dropping me when you asked me to be patient; that sordid arguments about alimony were just over the horizon. I felt I had to be decisive. I may have ruined your life. I'm - "

But he cut her off. "Don't apologise. We shared the unpleasantness. As I said, the Swiss clinic is the important thing. I'm not sure I could say anything more that's coherent."

The phone rang. Faint but shockingly intrusive. He stood up quickly, glanced around at the small room but saw no options. "I'll go outside."

"There's no need. The phone's in the bedroom."

He could hear her indistinct speech and hummed foolishly to blot it out.

She was quickly back. "Just a friend. Nothing really. But it gave me chance to think. There is one more thing, isn't there?"

"What's that?"

"You've just asked me tear you apart. Isn't it your turn now?"

"I don't understand."

He thought he knew but he didn't.

She asked, "How did you know I didn't want a child?"

"I'm not sure I can… "

"Sauce for the goose, Andrew!"

"Are you sure…?"

"The goose!"

He felt small and weak. As if he had floated up towards the ceiling and now gazed down on a humunculus that was Andrew Hatch, a being neither interesting nor capable of emotion. He said, "I misread you. Got the right answer for the wrong reason. A rather horrible reason. I became unofficial guardian of your body. Imagined you cared too much about yourself to fit in children."

Prudence laughed. "I suppose I deserved that."

"Hardly. You were never a flaunter. Never self-regarding – not with me, anyway. If I'd seen you more clearly I'd have realised that."

"But does it matter? I didn't want a child because I knew sooner or later we'd break up. How very considerate of me. But if I'd been slightly more considerate perhaps I ought to have warned you about the break."

"Put it out of your mind. Please."

They stared at each other.

There would be a long wait at the bus-stop but he was not tempted to take out the whodunnit or piece together what he'd just heard. "I let my mind go blank during services," Prudence had said and he strove for that type of emptiness.

JIMMY was due to learn about spreadsheets. His marks at school would be entered into the cells and a graph of his performance derived. But within ten minutes Mr Wee had rushed in. "Damnfool Albert not come. Big queue." He addressed Hatch. "You come." It sounded peremptory but commercial stress always affected Mr Wee's English.

For three hours Hatch shovelled chips on to sheets of paper. His sole instruction was a gruff whisper ("Too much."). The customers, glum faced, monosyllabic, quickly let him know about his failings ("Ah baht sawlt?"). During a lull he peeled more potatoes and turned them into chips, standing back from the cramped conditions and taking brief pride in operating the machines. When it was over Mr Wee offered to fry him a final piece of cod. He had never been a fish-and-chips enthusiast, now even less so. But he reckoned refusing the offer would be more painful than acceptance and took a hot package up to his room.

The evening's work had sidetracked Prudence's judgements. Now he would have to start acknowledging them. As he plucked a chip and put it in his mouth he realised he had failed to scatter his supper with salt from the large aluminium shaker downstairs. He

had his own salt but the effort of getting up from his bed was beyond him.

7. HATCH

Right about turn

"I WONDER, might I borrow part of your paper?"

His hands, liver spotted and arthritic, clenched the sheets. "You must wait your turn."

"Only the advertisements. A quick check. No more than a minute."

"I want this paper." The old man had a toothbrush moustache. To his left a walking stick hung from the edge of the table; close by an old corduroy cap.

"It's all right. I'll wait til you're finished." It wasn't as if Hatch had a full diary.

The man's face remained suspicious but his hands relaxed. Hatch realised he was being set in context. Other readers, their silver heads bent over the tabloids, were of an age with the Telegraph reader. Hatch was the odd man out.

"The adverts, you say." Fingers like ringed sausages sorted the pages and detached that section of the newspaper.

"I appreciate that. Thank you."

Newspaper classifieds were a daily chore which reminded Hatch he needed also to consider unemployment benefit. He had often reached this point and had held back, despite his acute poverty. It was just possible his father was to blame. A severe single-parent after his wife had condemned him to Hell and departed, George Hatch was a Midlands traditionalist. Umbrellas must never be opened indoors, mirrors were covered to propitiate the death of a neighbour or a relation and drinking during a meal was either unhealthy or bad manners. Hatch no longer observed such superstitions but the prospect of discussing employment with a civil servant left him irrationally uneasy. Some inner sense suggested it would be a step that carried its own momentum, officially linking him to the underprivileged. At job interviews the distinction between "Looking for work" and "Unemployed" was probably important.

Assuming there were job interviews. It took no time at all to trawl the pages he'd borrowed. The very category, Engineering, had been debased and now included fruit machine repairs and fitting car exhaust systems.

There was, however, grim satisfaction in saving money. At first he had bought the Telegraph every day but slender pickings led him to the central library reading room. Now, lacking other diversions, he was tempted to take Whitaker's from the shelves and daydream the morning. But this too was close to stigma.

Carefully he reassembled the pages and handed them back. No longer startled the Telegraph reader was more alert, more in tune with things. He nodded at the returned pages. "Work?"

Hatch nodded back. The man was on the verge of saying more but decided not to. A humane gesture. Unemployment was not a casual topic.

LONDON. How long had it been? Probably a conference at a featureless hollow hotel in Bayswater. At Euston he was repeatedly reminded he was a foreigner: swaying back from purposeful natives, distracted by the bright red flow of buses beyond the station concourse, trying but failing to follow loudspeaker announcements heavy with Caribbean accent.

A short walk east, towards Kings Cross and then south. To his left were the gothic temptations of the St Pancras façade but this was not the time to stop and admire. This was London and London didn't care. Menacing streets to cross, lights to watch, angry traffic.

Kings Cross had once been just a station. Now it was said to be depraved, a flesh market. He saw few signs of accosting whores but would there be customers at this time of the morning?

Hatch paused to consider crossing a huge spread of tarmac, a playground for bellicose taxis. Defeated, he walked a further hundred yards towards Islington.

After turning south he found conditions less noisy, vehicles more restrained. In residential streets, once middle class, the houses were coated with light brown dirt cast up as mud by traffic and allowed to dry. A shabby place to work but at least an opportunity to do so even if it was an odd variant on Hatch's previous employment.

Shabby inside, too, with furniture pushed against the walls of a former living room. "I have an appointment with Basil Greetham. He's the editor - "

"It's Mr Hatch, isn't it? Sign this receipt. Proof you've used the rail ticket we sent you. That's brill. Take a seat – oh, let me move that stuff first."

Greetham's office had cells of space grudgingly excavated between columns of paper and Hatch was gestured to a paper-free chair. "Tea? Coffee?" Hatch saw a mug on Greetham's desk but boggled at the logistics of being served. He shook his head.

"You read the mags I mailed? You know our competition because I see you're a PES member. They call theirs PES Monthly; we call ours Real Production. That says it all. We're a proper magazine, theirs is a freebie to justify the membership fees. We kick their arse on ad revenue, we run stuff they wouldn't dare to. And – damnit – we're read."

Greetham was tubby, bald and shone with energy. "Notice I don't sound like an engineer? That's because I started in newspapers. How did I learn about milling machines? I'll tell you some day. It's you we need to talk about. OK? We're an editorial team of three. My deputy is joining the FT and my assistant editor will step up. Three journalists."

He picked up his mug, frowned at its lightness and shouted, "Stella, more tea. Sure you won't have one? It's Andrew, isn't it? I'm Baz."

"Coffee. No milk, no sugar."

"Black coffee with nothing. Did you hear that, Stella?"

"For shit's sake, Baz, they heard it in Streatham."

Greetham grinned. "I command absolute authority. What was I saying…? Three journos. If it's too technical we find the answer somehow although mostly we know it all. That's what we've always done. But Dave – he's the one going to the FT – thinks this isn't the best set-up to handle new stuff." He looked at Hatch who realised this was a question.

"New stuff: just-in-time, cell manufacture, laser cutting, CAD."

"Had experience of any of that?"

It wasn't the sort of interview where one lied or blurred the issues. "Some, but I've been in welding sales for a while. Not by choice, as I explained. I saw advanced cell manufacturing in France several weeks ago."

"Got any contacts there?"

"The owner."

"Would he talk?"

"Almost certainly."

"If you get this job that's your first story. You see the way we're going. We hire an engineer and convert him into a writer. Not the easiest thing in the world but it can be done. Brought any work?"

"Three sorts. Two or three articles written for your competitor but I doubt they'll ring any bells. Even I could see their standards weren't high. Pathetically grateful and they didn't change a word."

Greetham flicked through the tear-sheets. "I'd have junked two of these straight away. Familiar blather. The third might have hacked it but at one page, not three."

Hatch said, "I've done learned journal papers. Good info but written to a formula. You don't publish that kind of stuff."

"We do but it's disguised, completely rewritten. Guess what's the first thing we change."

"Kick out the experimental stuff."

"Not bad," said Greetham approvingly. "That's the second thing. What we do first is move the conclusions from the end to the start. Know why?"

"Because the conclusions are what matter."

"You'd be surprised how many mossbacks resent that. And the third category?"

"Papers I've given at conferences. They'd be closest to what you want."

"Correct. Any idea why?"

Hatch pondered. "Simpler writing?"

"Even more important."

"Not the foggiest."

"Conference papers come with visual stuff. We don't just publish words."

"Stupid of me."

"Don't knock yourself."

The mugs were delivered and Hatch balanced his on a tiny open triangle at the corner of Greetham's desk.

"At the moment you're unemployed."

"I fear so."

"Yeah, you and a million others. We've never advertised for an engineer before and it's a buyer's market. I could strangle that silly bitch."

It took a moment before Hatch realised the bitch was the prime minister.

"So far we've talked about the easy bit. Info arrives in an unsatisfactory state and we re-shape it. You'll be OK at that. Just to make sure I'll give you a so-called learned paper and you can cut it to six hundred words at home. If we use it I'll pay you... peanuts. The harder side is writing an original piece. Asking questions, turning the answers into an idea, asking more questions. My job is to find out if you can do that. Help me; tell me why you'll be a shit-hot writer."

Startled, Hatch thought briefly of Prudence. "This is pretty personal but what the hell. A sense of dignity won't get me a job here. I'm divorced and recently my ex told me why that happened. She introduced me to the theatre which I enjoyed. But it seems I blew it. I spent the drive home analysing and concluding. Boring for her. But a writer needs to do that."

"No shit?" said Greetham. "My ex would have explained my heave-ho in coarser terms. OK, you need to be analytical. But journalism is more. As I said, it's asking questions. More, it's *wanting* to ask questions. You see something or somebody and you say: why? As I'm doing now." He leant back in his dangerously creaking chair. "Guy I knew joined the Middlesex Press Group. Oxford, modern languages. Prepared to do the grind, the long hours, the lousy pay. Got sent out on a house fire and came back worried. 'What do I do? I couldn't think of anything more to ask. With more time I could have made a list. But I didn't have the time.' I thought it wasn't time you lacked, mate, it was instinct. I gave him three months but he was out in as many weeks. Works in PR at three times the salary. He has the hair for it; long, light brown, keeps falling over his eyes. Point is, can you ask questions? Or will you run out of steam?"

Hatch sipped horrible coffee. "I could ask you plenty."

"Great! Go ahead. Ah, but just a minute. We have to make it realistic. The real bind is writing down the answers. And sometimes the questions. No use seeing the word 'No.' in your notebook and wondering what that was all about. Want to try?"

Hatch reached for Greetham's notebook and ball-point then asked, "There's not much money in it, not much status, what keeps you going?"

Greetham beamed. "Same as Faulkner said when he got the Nobel. Creating something new, something that never existed before, something instructive and – most of all – something someone will want to read."

"Is it anarchic?"

"The methods are, they're mostly self-taught. But the piece mustn't be. It must be well ordered."

Hatch said, "Take a milling machine. Even if it were the first one ever made you couldn't describe it in words alone. That would be too tedious, too hard to follow. How do you get round that?"

"Don't forget our informed readership. There's stuff you can miss out. Just what, well that's not easy. But graphics comes in here. If there's a pic you won't need to say the equipment stands on a single-piece base and that the operator's controls are here and there."

"So, you ask what's new, what's improved?"

"Exactly."

"Suppose you think the guy's lying?"

By now Greetham had been drawn into his role. "You tell me. Why the suspicion?"

"Experience. Reading up beforehand."

"You suspect he's lying. What's the next step?"

Hatch too was getting carried away. "Shit, I'm not sure. I'm… No, tell you what. You lie back at him. Something like: I saw Joe Bloggs's new machine at Hanover and they had nothing like that performance. Are you sure you can meet those figures?"

Greetham clapped his hands and gestured for Hatch to continue.

"Here's a nightmare. You're half an hour into the interview and you realise you've misunderstood the answers. Do you confess or hope you can get things back on track without being noticed?"

Greetham looked at Hatch. "How the hell did you come up with that?"

"Because it's happened. I've spoken to equipment suppliers, building sub-contractors, even consultants. Stuff can be complicated – simultaneous functions, either/or options, or just misinformation. Do you come clean or preserve your professional face?"

"Obviously you know the answer."

"Come clean, every time."

"And risk looking like an idiot?"

"Admitting something like that relaxes the guy you're talking to. Makes him feel superior. He's no longer just a words machine. At worst he'll be easier to understand, at best he may tell you more than he should."

Greetham raised his hands. "OK, no more fake interview. You've proved your point. You were good. So good I'll have a handy new tool when I'm tackling some of your competitors for this job. Let's get back to the real world. What can I tell you?"

"How is Real Production doing, financially?"

"I won't show you our trading statement," said Greetham laughing. "But I'll be as honest as I can."

"You're a free magazine."

"To qualified readers, yes."

"You depend on selling advertisements. But times are hard."

"And political attitudes are against manufacturing. So times are even harder. You're asking the sixty-four dollar question: how am I protecting the magazine? Any ideas yourself?"

"Diversify, I suppose. But I haven't a clue how magazines do that."

"If you had I'd be worried about my position. The clever answer is don't wait until things are difficult before looking for answers. That's why I'm paid a bonus. Some years ago, when we had the cash, I came up with an international conference where we pay big names a fee and expenses to speak about costing in production engineering. It's a narrow topic but it's never out of fashion. We couldn't start it up now because the risks are too great. But, because the quality is recognised, we have an international attendance and most people book year-on-year."

Greetham looked reminiscent. "PES Monthly copied us, did it on the cheap, never made a profit and this year will make a very big loss. There are other things. Our annual directory of equipment and services has a lot of value added. Helps increase the pot. That should answer your question. I guarantee we'll be in existence in a year's time and the year after. Beyond that we are in the hands of that brass-headed gorgon."

"Does an assistant editor find his own stuff or does he do what he's told?"

"There are regular parts of the magazine he's responsible for but they are mainly re-writing and elaboration. My dream is a staff member who thinks up features, finds out who to speak to, does the interviews and drops 1500 – 2000 words on my desk, ahead of the deadline. But it is a dream. Usually we have discussions about subjects, thrash them out and then go, go, go."

"I guess I've run out of steam," Hatch admitted.

Greetham glanced at Hatch's CV. "I can't be bothered to dredge through all this again. What's your background?"

"Working class. Father a Black Country lathe operator. Scholarship boy. Production was the only job I ever wanted."

Greetham was uncharacteristically silent. "Won't writing about it be a bit of a come-down?"

Job interviews required you to lie. But there were limits. "I suppose you're right. But this is a parallel world. The experience can be converted, I think. I'd rather write about manufacturing than install fitted kitchens."

"Let's hope it doesn't come to that." Greetham flicked his bottom lip. "I suppose that's all I need."

Hatch stood up. "Good. Thanks for seeing me. I'll be on my way." Greetham said, "I never asked you any of those shit questions human resources are always so hot on."

"About my motivation? I like making complicated things and being in charge. I like finding ways of making things cheaper and better. I like bringing people on. The usual… shit."

Hatch hadn't eaten. That plus the intense scrutiny had left him slightly faint. But he knew exactly how much money he would spend at the supermarket late that afternoon. He made his way to Euston along streets now less aggressive. Unoccupied seats were rare at the station but his came with a discarded copy of that morning's Telegraph. Perhaps it was an omen but if so it was a hollow one. He could send his CV to a headhunter looking for a mining engineer in the Congo or apply directly for a vague managerial position with something that sounded like a Middle East bank, the ad laid out in a rectangle without margins and using a unique and obsolete typeface common to such announcements.

Instead, belatedly, he turned to the news pages looking for coverage about the brass-headed gorgon and her inexplicable policies towards companies that made things. The Telegraph seemed in favour; talked about her courage

On the Birmingham train he dozed and woke up suddenly to an unexpected view. From the back of the carriage the unhindered perspective was that of a tapering tube flying at low altitude, the windows on both sides unscrolling scenery at great speed. A spectacular sensation, a sellable sensation yet he'd never previously noticed it. Because the carriage lacked internal walls the long clean lines were enhanced but why hadn't the railways bothered to draw attention to this effect, typical of the twentieth century's addiction to rapid transport? And there were also production implications. The speeding effect depended on a design with an uncluttered interior where strength was not compromised. Was this an article? He made notes as he recalled Greetham's eagerness.

The bus from Birmingham station confirmed the uniqueness of the train. Handrails prevented a clear view end-to-end and the bumpy ride, together with grindingly slow corners, meant there was no continuous or consistent unreeling of views through the windows. Would Prudence have responded? Probably not, she behaved uneasily on public transport.

Hatch made his way towards a discount supermarket surrounded by military fencing and intended mainly for car users. Pedestrians, baulking at a lengthy detour, had bent rails apart and now squeezed through more directly. Hatch saw no reason to be middle-class and followed a hardened track between dispirited rhododendrons. Inside - as ever - the sense of illusion. Cans and packets which appeared to carry internationally familiar names, labels and colours but proved to be middle-european substitutes. None of which mattered to Hatch in his relentless search for low prices.

Two tins of baked beans – from Rumania – would supply three, possibly four, evening meals when combined with toast. A foil tray which would surely have contained Irish stew at a larger emporium was marked goulasch and might have fed him over two days had he owned a refrigerator. Slovenian orange juice as a specific against scurvy (Hatch now worried about malnutrition) would be drunk tepid.

The walk back to Leyfield took forty minutes, made more tedious by the potatoes he had added to his shopping bag. But he was inured to walking; in any case, time was expendable. Passing a filling station he noted the litre price of petrol, worked out the cost of a gallon and decided walking saved him the money spent on half a week's meals. Always assuming he had the option of a car.

The light on his answer machine was blinking. Phone and machine were expensive but essential. Replies from job applications were rare enough and he could not afford to be unreachable. The caller was Hester at her crispest, reminding him he would be picked up at six and, although Monteverdi wasn't on offer, the programme had been restricted to the late eighteenth and early nineteenth centuries. "So we'll see you at six," she said again, softly, more possessively

That proprietorial tone evoked Prudence a few days ago, sipping tea, shuddering, describing the end of her marriage to Hatch. Observing for the first time, and with surprising clarity, how Hester had recognised their situation and had reached out to him. "I doubt she's let go of you entirely," Prudence had said.

That was understandable. Without Prudence those had been dark days for Hatch and Hester's amiability and sympathy had meant a lot. But what had she expected in return? Obviously more than Hatch was prepared to give. Hatch had seen it as friendship but friendship and gratitude were thin gruel for Hester.

After a few months of dispensing sympathy Hester had grown out of sorts, became impatient, behaved irrationally. Abruptly she started to cultivate Tom, Hatch's friend and long-time bachelor. They married quite quickly. Hatch had disappointed her and knew it but was secretly relieved. This was not however the end of the matter. Tom continued to invite Hatch to dinner and to musical events. Hester now became enigmatic as if using her marriage as a stalking horse, as if reminding Hatch of his earlier failings. Or for something else entirely. Hatch knew, for instance, who would sit beside whom at Symphony Hall tonight.

By concentrating he was able to toast two slices of stale bread on the Belling without burning them. The loaf had to last another two days and he inspected it carefully for mould before wrapping it up. Heating the beans demanded constant stirring, causing him to yearn for the mindless utility of the microwave rented out with the fully equipped house and now in the hands of the Featherstones. Tomato sauce seeped into the unbuttered toast. He deliberately slowed things down by using a knife and fork but the meal took only four minutes to eat and left him a further hour to kill

The television had also stayed in the rented house so he had joined the library. This was still newish territory and presently he was picking out books with authors' names that were dimly familiar. After a week he realised this limited him to classics, most bringing no immediate rewards. He had not actively disliked English literature at school but preferred some guidance as to a book's value. Now he faced an unlucky dip. The present novel was by Conrad who, he was astonished to discover, was born a Pole and had gone on to write in English. Why then, with an infinite range of styles to choose from, had he opted for gristly prose and a crablike approach? Because the dust jacket was unadorned he knew nothing about the contents and had had to read the summary, something forbidden at school. It told him to expect the sea yet, after fifteen pages, the sea was still distant. He put the book down and tried to write a description of the effect he had noticed in the railway carriage. Fifteen minutes slipped by and he was unable to come up with a satisfactory initial sentence. So much for his confident interview. However he was sure Greetham would have some plausible explanation for this.

They were on the motorway in Tom's car. "Still a Volvo, I see," said Hatch. "The compromise car."

"What compromise?" asked Hester sitting in the front passenger seat. "Would I qualify for a Volvo?"

Tom said, "I thought you liked the Renault. The commercials suggest it's a vehicle for infidelity. No, my love, the Volvo isn't for you. It's the solicitor's in-between car, transport for anyone who charges fees. Drive a Roller and the client says to himself it was paid for out of his sweat and blood. Drive a Lada and the client worries about his adviser's competence. Not too lavish, not too cheapskate, that's the Volvo?"

"Andrew used to drive an aged sports car. The Austin-Healey. What would that say about a solicitor?"

Tom said, "Very subtle but, in the end, a non-doer. Andrew's Healey proved to the world he had the technical nous to keep it going. Also, that he didn't care about pitted chrome and sagging seats. A solicitor with such a car would be an object of suspicion. But here's the subtlety: he might get away with it if the car was in showroom condition. Implying he paid someone to keep it nice and shiny."

"Would a solicitor admit to reading Conrad," asked Hatch.

"Not to a client. Who wants a literary solicitor? Is that who you're struggling with?"

"Not any more."

"Would you say Conrad's an engineer's author, Hes?" asked Tom.

Hester turned to the back of the car, her eyelids slightly lowered. "He's not explicit enough. Doesn't get on with the story."

"Then recommend someone," said Hatch. "The names I pick are hard going."

"Somerset Maugham."

"Steady on, Hes," said Tom. "Andrew's lips don't move when he reads. You could aim a bit higher."

Only Tom's reaction told Hatch he was being teased.

When Hester didn't reply, Tom filled in the gap. "Classics can be up to date. Why not Anne Tyler?"

"Could Andrew stomach the domesticity?"

Still being teased.

Hatch said, "Domesticity? I'd make it welcome in my bare room."

They had ice cream at the interval. "Were you overwhelmed by the Brahms?" Hester asked.

"Very lush. It's not a Brandenburg."

"I can't argue with that."

Hatch felt it was time he showed he could take the initiative. Without thinking ahead he started to describe the effects he had noticed in the railway carriage but never got past the first few words. "An Intercity train? Going where?" The question snapped out.

Hatch recognised his mistake and downplayed the magazine interview with its sense of exhilaration. But it wasn't enough.

Even Tom was surprised. "You'd consider working in London?"

"Or the Orkneys, or Timbuktu," Hatch said, levity that missed by a mile. "It's hard to find the job I prefer in the Midlands."

"But there's no immediate hurry," said Hester sharply. "You got a decent severance cheque. You could wait it out."

Were they entitled to know about Prudence and where the cheque had gone? The prospect of plausibly lying his way out hung like a weight. "I have other problems," he said slowly, only to be interrupted by the bell for the second half of the concert.

On the way back to Tamworth he did explain his finances but from the back of the car. Thus there was no immediate reaction. The Makings were too skilled socially to start resolving a husband and wife problem over their shoulders. Neither would they suggest Prudence was taking advantage, that he was weak-willed, that he was risking professional oblivion. They would touch on these matters at meetings even now being planned. Hester would be the more impassioned but Tom too would lay down another more jocular gauntlet. Their attitudes were apparent as both of them got out of the car outside Mr Wee's, Tom to shake his hand solemnly, Hester to provide a forgivably intense kiss. London, uncaring London, was now a backdrop.

8. CLARE

Bared soul

"HILDEGARD, don't apologise. You recommended a perfectly legitimate job. I enjoyed the afternoon; a chance to flex my muscles."

XXX

"*You* thought he was young! My dear, he was embryonic. The give-away were his jeans; he hadn't enough rump to fill them. I wondered what the merchant bank thought, but perhaps he wore a suit when going cap in hand. After all, he went to Oundle. Can't knock that, can we? A £7m line of credit. There were times I felt like his grandmother, never mind his mum. Don't spend it all at once, dear."

XXX

"A perfect gentleman. The right level of deference to my gender, my experience and my age. And a relaxed authority, as if we were on his yacht. He understands management as well as the hard stuff. The little devil had read my CV from cover to cover. Picked out the step down when I went to Confexxion. Then came up with another beauty: 'I could ask if you've had trouble squaring the job with looking after your son. But I don't think I'll bother.' See how clever that is? Asking the question but in a way he could deny afterwards."

XXX

"That's not sharp practice. I'll use it myself the next time I interview a married mother. God, if we played by the HR rules we'd never find out anything."

XXX

"One slightly iffy matter after he'd asked me how I'd structure the company. I said Bristol, came up with a square-footage figure, drew him a management chart, rough-costed the IT and found him taking notes. Perfectly entitled to, of course, but I went vague after that."

XXX

"By all means send your other clients. He's funded for three years and telecoms is solid. It's a good routing system and I couldn't see any obvious development problems. My reservation – as I said – is it's a start-up. Long hours, young people who know their stuff but nothing about the outside world, arguments about car-park spaces and regular panic attacks. If everything goes to plan he'll be rolling in it in about ten years. Me too but I'd be ten years older and possibly a little tired."

XXX

"A good question. He knew I could do the work. And that I could handle his techies. But perhaps he was counting the years on his fingers. My years. Give him credit, nothing he said touched on that. On balance I think he'd have made an offer, and at the right salary. But it wouldn't have taken me forward. Besides which - "

XXX

"I'll put on my best face for that one even though I can't say I love banks. By all means, keep me informed."

XXX

"In a fortnight's time, then. Oh, one other thing. At one of these ghastly golf-club dos I met a journalist, Alison Fenner. You might check her out. She tends to write for women's magazines but not exclusively. We got on well and she's taken a shine. Or perhaps it's what I represent. She wants to do an article and I got the impression it wouldn't end up in Woman's Own. Good idea?"

XXX

"Later this afternoon? Call me back and I'll get in touch with her. I didn't know she was that well-known. Good. Nice to talk to you again, Hildegard. Cheers."

CLARE made coffee in the new Krups Jerry had bought a couple of weeks ago, the fourth percolator in two years. Others had been discarded still operative but condemned because of "design faults". Percolators were a small but declared battlefront and he was disproportionately angry when she refused to become interested.

"You're the specialist. Can't you feel it jam when you slide the pot in? It's that spring-valve under the reservoir. Surely it's not beyond the wit of man to design a smoother action."

She experimented, noticed the effect but was inclined to pass on. He insisted, "It's bad design, isn't it?"

"I suppose so," she said, searching through the spice cupboard.

"Doesn't it irritate you?"

"Certainly it will now."

"You never noticed it?"

"I don't expect much from domestic equipment. Ever since I took the back off my father's television set and saw components mounted on wood."

"But more people will buy that coffee pot than the stuff you work on. More chance of something going wrong; a lawsuit."

He went on like this for some time. His fervour was unusual as was the way he confronted her, standing forward slightly, arms apart from his body. That night, as she lay beside him, listening to the light snore she assumed was common to all athletes, she played through the percolator scene. Was he trying to say he belonged to the real and useful world and that her abilities were only theoretical? If so he must have his way. Pretending to be ignorant about something so simple irritated her but she was prepared to let him prowl this new vantage point. The Krups had cost three times as much as previous percolators and seemed to be flaw-free. But to him defects were possibly more important than carefree coffee-making.

Post fluttered into the hallway and she took her cup of coffee, picked up the letters and moved to the lounge where custom furniture, smaller than standard, gave an illusion of space in the low-ceilinged room.

A hand-written address roused interest; hand-written contents even more so. A stalker? The letter was from Alan Harding her former colleague at Sigma who clearly needed a typewriter to make a splash on the job market. But what was this? A job offer already? Aha, the MoD testing facility at Salisbury

Clare laughed aloud. I must tell him, she thought. It will boost him to know he's come second even though it won't be for the same job. I can tell him how to pull strings in the MoD. How to play off senior officers in appropriations. Lunch, somewhere in the centre. Somewhere expensive.

Abruptly she sat up. How many weeks had it been? She tried to reconstruct his face and all she could come up with was a sketch. More adult, decisive, sexually confident than the real thing. No resemblance to that foetally-curled lad who had sat beside her in the car. But then she'd never been enthusiastic about youth as such. Why was she deluding herself with maternal thoughts? Perhaps they weren't maternal.

Her last bout of love-making – if that's what it was – had occurred in the spring. Jerry had won a minor competition at Lynn, had stayed for the presentation dinner, had swallowed beer on top of the introductory champagne and had phoned her, apologetically, asking her to pick him up. She would have agreed anyway but the apology, delivered in that frank, shrugging manner that recalled his days at Confexxion, put her in a forgiving mood. At the clubhouse he caught her eye, boyishly mimed his drunkenness and kissed her when she reached the bar. Kissed her in front of a semi-circle of men who whooped staidly.

Since she was also required to chauffeur two other crapulous club members there was no significant talk in the car but the way Jerry disposed his legs, turned himself towards her and sighed rather breathily proved his earlier friendliness was still alive. In their bedroom, as he slid hands over her hips, she remembered when such caresses caused her to react rather than ask questions. Nevertheless she moved into the approved position and made encouraging signals.

Drink or some other restraint prevented him from entering her. Even when she encouraged him with her mouth – not her greatest bedroom skill – it was clear he was incapable. More remarkable was his anger as he rolled away. Making love had been important for him. Perhaps sometime soon but without the beer.

But it had never happened, the failure weighed too heavily. Clare knew she lacked the emotional stamina to bring him to that moment again and the impulse lapsed.

Why shouldn't she consider a lunch with someone half her own age? Deliberately she thrust aside matters of organisation, evasion, money. Plus uncertainty.

The letter slipped to the floor and in reaching down she noticed a PS: "I'd appreciate your advice. Perhaps we could have lunch together. My treat." So at least age wasn't a problem.

A subject to discuss with Chantal. Not directly or as a request for advice. But in an abstract way, the sort of talk Chantal loved - deconstructing the fantasy of the older woman, pouring scorn on *Le Blé en Herbe*, launching little darts about *le coq* and checking whether Clare was able to keep a straight face. But Chantal was in Atlanta, no doubt doing her best to disguise her feelings about American society while submitting ever larger invoices.

Clare stood up, walked into the kitchen and did a tour of inspection. Finding nothing that required her attention she walked quickly round the garden, searching out tasks she'd promised to do. None were apparent although she knew, infuriatingly, they existed. Vaguely, she even knew their nature – that they would be quickly achieved, and how and what the benefits would be. As she moved from location to location she sensed their nearness, even though the tasks remained undefined. Then the phone rang.

"Hildegard here. Your Alison Fenner is well liked. She writes for the Sunday colour supplements and I think that's what she has in mind. She'd be worth your co-operation because her features are reasonably long: several thousand words. Space to spread yourself and to lay some impartial CV before the bank."

"Assuming it's favourable."

"Take your point. Nothing comes for nothing. If the newspapers like her it won't be for writing puffs. But you've handled the press before. And you say she likes you."

Clare laughed. "What journalists like is not always likeable. But that's the price for impartiality."

"Did she hint at any line?"

"Being married to Jerry ups my status. But unless she's good at lying it's what I've done that matters."

"I think you may ask about the tone of the article."

"I'll do that."

Hildegard said, "Get in touch with her as soon as you're able. These things often take time – both the interview and the delay before publication. But if it hasn't appeared beforehand you could mention it during the bank interview – casually, of course."

Clare phoned, got the answerphone and approved of its professionalism: "Alison Fenner speaking. Leave your details and I'll get back in a couple of hours." The return call interrupted Clare in the middle of an experiment.

She explained: "My son's four and still too young for Beatrix Potter."

"She has her dark side," said Alison. "Graham Greene pointed that out."

"Graham Greene? The Catholic author? He read Mrs Tiggywinkle? I'd better save the books until Nick's in his teens."

"Oh bollocks. Kids like a bit of sturm and drang. Try him in six months. But what do I know? So, you're OK?"

"You come trailing banners. My job-hunting is handled by a fancy management company and my next interview is something of a biggie. Your piece might help; even just the mention of it. But my advisor says I'm to ask you what line you will take. Does that offend Fourth Estate ethics?"

"Successful woman in a profession dominated by men. At least that's the background. But the hard stuff – the physics - must go up front; I don't want it drowned out by a sub-feminist text. I want to be clear about what drew you to this work. It's a piece where detail drives the story."

"And where will it appear?"

"If all goes well, The Guardian magazine."

"The Guardian!"

Alison laughed. "Have I trodden on your Tory toes? You didn't seem like a blue rinser at the golf club."

"I'm not a Tory and I'm not the other lot. I've voted in both directions. I'm not worried about The Guardian but wouldn't they prefer a politicised woman."

"I'm betting you'll turn out to be politicised. Just not party-politicised. I'm glad you've decided. We could get this published quite quickly. Are you readily available?"

"Just one no-no. Next Tuesday I can't be reached. I'm trying to get Nick into Sevenoaks' best primary school and that means doing pretty-please with them. I've been asked to talk to the children about physics."

"See if I can sit in. With a photographer. It's the sort of event I'd go large on."

"A photographer?"

"It's a magazine, Clare. There'll be pictures, lots of them."

"Oh."

Jerry arrived soon after five. Recently he'd adopted a mechanical joviality but today he was deflated. "Any mail?" he asked offhandedly.

"Just your magazine."

He slumped into one of the miniaturised easy chairs and looked vacantly at the fireplace.

"You're early. No lessons?"

"A couple of teenage girls. I passed them on to Alex. I thought I could teach golf on auto-pilot but these snooty ones with rich fathers…"

"You look down in the dumps. Do you want a proper dinner or chili?"

A flicker of interest. Jerry preferred meals he could eat with a spoon and didn't care about the dictates of the weather. "Nothing like a bowl of chili," he said dully.

It wasn't Clare's favourite evening meal: images of the beans piling up inside, solid and indigestible, later releasing their anti-social vapours. Beans spoke more of animals than of humans. But chili was easily prepared and as she sat down at the dining table his enthusiasm was a minor reward.

"The telecoms job. You turned it down?" He didn't sound terribly interested.

"The usual juvenile whizz-kid. I'm sure he'll do well. But he's starting from scratch and I'm a little too dignified for all that hassle."

"Dignified?"

"Elderly, if you like."

He looked up. "At forty-one?"

"I'd be spending half my time building up the company and creating its inner workings. It's not stuff that interests me. I prefer running a project, processing ideas, finding people's limits. Hildegard says there's another job in the offing, one I'm better fitted for. It concerns… whoops, I'm supposed to keep my mouth shut about it. Let's start again. One financial institution is acquiring another and there will be IT incompatibilities. But it's more than just technical. There are wider responsibilities which haven't been explained yet."

"Wider responsibilities?"

"I'm guessing. It may be something like the NHS's IT system, but in reverse. That's seen as government work so they don't use a techie spokesman. Hence long delays and costs that go up and up. But a financial institution would need to calm down the shareholders and the markets."

"You'd be a whipping boy."

"Only if I cocked it up. I'd have one advantage. Nobody would know more about the system. That would help in press conferences."

He frowned. "It's not something you've done before."

"That's what tickles my fancy." Clare reached over and took his empty bowl. "Mother raised this subject two or three weeks ago. She thought 'public recognition' might tempt me. Well, it's too late to start up as a civil rights lawyer but perhaps this is a side door. Fruit?" The invitation was hardly necessary. Athletic pernicketiness had long ago made fruit the only possible dessert.

Ostentatiously he began peeling an apple. "You mention civil rights lawyer as if it was like flipping a switch," he said peevishly.

"Oh no. It would take oodles of cash and lots of time."

"I don't mean that. Could you, now, learn a completely different profession?"

"Well our prime minister, whom you love so much, has degrees in chemistry and in law. I'm at least as clever as her."

"You could do law?" he insisted.

She noticed his tone of voice. "I wouldn't be a complete novice. Managers need to know law. I've taken courses."

"You're confident you could down tools and emerge as a solicitor or a barrister or whatever in a three, four years' time?"

His tone of voice was rising. This had nothing to do with the law. "You seem surprised. In fact you seem..." It wasn't profitable to complete the sentence.

"Envious?" he asked, sneering.

"I don't know what."

"Let's stick with envious. Are you really surprised? Can't you see your stupid jock of a husband is occasionally pissed off in your shadow."

"Jock! But you have the male dream. The job you've always wanted."

"Oh sure, sure. But how *old* is a jock? What age does he stop being a jock?"

She had seen this coming once he'd recognised he couldn't win tournaments, especially four-rounders.

She said, "You're still young enough. I've met pros who are older."

"They're not golfers, they're businessmen – in a small way."

"So I didn't do you any favours?"

Because he had no answer he got up abruptly and went out. She took the few items of their sparse meal into the kitchen and washed up. Then found him in the lounge with the television turned to some unlikely programme – amateur variety acts from Birmingham – a just bearable alternative to staring out of the window.

"Have you any ideas?" she said.

He shrugged awkwardly.

"I take it you were asking for my help."

He reached forward and angrily switched off the television as if he hadn't been responsible for switching it on.

"Don't you ever consider our marriage?" he asked. "The oddity of it?"

"That we have different jobs? Is that so odd?"

"We have different jobs because we're different people."

"Don't different types of people marry?"

He writhed against the cushions. "I have no idea. At Lynn married couples play golf together. I watch them. They seem to fit. But we're separate."

"We don't work normal hours." She didn't mention Nick. To Jerry his son was a remote side issue.

"But are we together because we want to be? Holidays, for instance. We go somewhere hot and expensive. Swim. Lie on the beach. Drink ridiculously priced wine. Wouldn't we be better off doing something quite different? Alone?"

They were now on the fringe of something larger and she was shying away. But Jerry was in full flight.

"I've asked you before. Was it a good idea to marry a jock?"

"I didn't see you as a jock. You weren't one. Damnit – I don't like the word; it sounds so horribly sexual. You're an enthusiast, you work hard, take risks. The fact you became a sportsman wasn't an issue. Hardly anyone has a goal in life, you did."

They sat in silence. She resumed, "It's ironic. I'm not an enthu-siast. I took physics because it attracted me. But that was all; I suppose I could have taken other degrees. After that there was no job I felt I had to have. To some extent I've wandered. And I've never had feminist instincts. I admired the way you took on the world."

"You slept with me." he said almost sulkily.

"You were – are – physically a catch. Honest. Lively. And – it shocks me to say it but I must – grateful for what I was doing."

"Gratitude doesn't go very far in bed."

"No it doesn't. Perhaps I got it wrong."

This time the silence was longer.

"When were you first disappointed?" he asked.

"I'm not disappointed. I try to be adult about marriage. The only guarantee is that things will change. For me changes must be ridden out. I never thought I had much in common with my mother but perhaps I was wrong. I think she was convinced during the early years my father was unfaithful. He was away an awful lot. But she didn't complain. She endured it; this was what she had bought into. And she was right. Once the careless raptures were over – if they ever happened - he re-discovered her. They are an affectionate couple."

He got up and went to the drinks table. "I notice there's a word you don't use. About them or us. Not that I'm one to talk."

"It's a word I've always distrusted. Always found it extreme. I've worked with Americans and they use it far too much. They're always saying they love their wives and often it's a prelude to hanky panky. I try to be honest but the state of love is too hard to define. I chose you. I want to be with you. I'm willing to see out the difficulties."

She stopped briefly, terrified at the accumulation in these claims.

She went on, "Do I love you? Does what I've said suggest love? Perhaps not. Could I live without you? Yes, possibly. But I'd be diminished."

She realised he was staring at her and had jettisoned his complaints and anxieties – at least for the moment. His face reminded her sharply of the last moments at Confexxion, in the pub, when her offer to help had prevented him from inviting her out. Was that love? And what were her exact feelings then? An exhilaration, a willingness to be swept along?

He put down the bottle of scotch. "It's not a word I use." He sat down in his chair with some reluctance as if wanting to stand, to prolong what he'd just heard. "If I'm honest it doesn't fit my feelings. There was always awe."

"Awe?"

"You knew your own mind. When you slept with me I thought: well, that's all right then. Only your opinion mattered. You said you trusted me but it was the other way round. I trusted you to make decisions for both of us."

This at least she recognised. Did this mean the marriage was not a shared responsibility but hers alone?

He reached for her hand. "We could go... upstairs. I'm not sure... Last time..."

"Let's do that," she said, attempting to be brisk.

They lay entwined in a bed deliberately large enough for them to sleep comfortably apart. Again he needed help but this time her obligations were clearer. This time her mouth was more decisive, as if she were taking an examination in technique. As they coupled she knew it wasn't for love - whatever that was - probably not even for sex. Confirmation? Her love-making took on new vigour and eventually he sighed with what sounded like relief. Soon the bedroom rustled to his athlete's snore and Clare, lacking her climax, was left to wonder if anything had been clarified or eased.

9. CLARE

Awakened innocence

ALISON surveyed the contents of the wardrobe. "Well equipped for funerals or foreclosing mortgages. Not much else."

"Come on! There are holiday clothes as well."

"Good heavens, you're right. Provided you're satisfied with Bournemouth or – ah, yes – Edinburgh."

"Stop teasing."

"I'm hardly the expert. I wasn't married long enough to have children and I haven't noticed how mothers dress when they pick up kids from school. My impression is they wear clothes on the far side of casual. There's nothing here to offend. It's a professional visit so you could justify one of these oh-so-charming greys. Provided the kids don't imagine you're a school inspector."

Clare flicked the hangars left and right. She said, "That summer dress of yours is perfect. Why have I never bought anything like that?"

"Because you're a boss, not a worker."

Still dubious, Alison approved a light grey skirt and a loose-sleeved white blouse with modest unbuttoning at the neck. Then there were the shoes. Alison said, "These are all for men with very small feet. Don't you have any heels?"

"I went to Henley, once. Are those sandals any good?"

"Sandals are supposed to be fun. These are just shoes in drag."

They took their coffee outside so that Alison could smoke. From a bench seat under a tiny arbour they watched Nick thrust his hands upwards, attempting to throw his ball, then grin wryly at his own clumsiness. Clare said, "My lack of clothes sense - even my mother chides me. I have no talent for casual wear but I didn't think it mattered. I've always gone in for authority."

"You don't need authoritative clothes. You've got the real thing. You could boss your way around in Laura Ashley." Alison let smoke drift up into the still air. "I changed my mind about what I wore. For ages journalists have turned up in rags, wanting to be separate from the establishment. But I kept on noticing the distaste it caused. It seemed pointless antagonising people over such a small matter. I started spending more on conventional clobber and found interviews flowed better."

Alison took out her pocket recorder. "Tell me about Nick."

"I will but now you've raised it I need to clear my mind on clothes. Perhaps they're more important than I've allowed for. At school I had no opinion; I wore what my mother bought. In any case, the school uniform simplified things. One thing I did notice, though. On an exchange trip to Auxerre I knew - dimly - my things were not like everyone else's. They were casual, of course, summer dresses and the like. But different. It took me some time to pin it down."

"Bet I can guess," said Alison, smiling almost wolfishly. "Bet they were more expensive."

"You've spoiled my story. But you're perfectly right. The French girls noticed, straight away."

"Making you unpopular, I'd say."

"Linguistically I was shown no mercy. My mother continued to buy my clothes when I went to Wadham but by then I'd become more savvy. I was at university to show off my brain, not my family wealth. So I bought jeans and tee-shirts out of my allowance."

"Leaving your Kensington stuff in the closet. Gawd, you've lived a pampered life Mrs Kepler."

"I know, I know. But you don't begrudge me taking on protective colouring, do you? Actually, being a student suited me. With no dress sense and no views about colour matching, jeans were perfect."

"Still would be," said Alison. "You've got the right bum and the right legs."

Clare coloured slightly. "Well, thanks for that. Anyway the crunch came with my third job. American executive suite, every formality. Tailored business suits were inescapable. In any case, I wasn't that all-fired keen to look too young. Sartorially you could say I'd come home. My tailor chose the colours – from a very small range – and when I put on a suit it felt right. I was a manager so why not look like a manager?"

"Except there's another part to your life. The part where you're not managing."

"And that's where I still have problems. Holidays, dinner parties. The fact is I'm given to rationalising. Why, I ask myself, can't I play in the clothes I wear for work? Oh yes, inertia and incompetence are my problems but my argument – however feeble – is that austereness is nothing to be ashamed of."

Alison looked as if she disagreed, as if she wanted to ask further searching questions. Ran her eyes down from Clare's close-cut hair to her ankles, as a man might, thinking he was unobserved. Then her face relaxed. "I'm not sure if I'm going to use any of this. But what I do need is information about your son. Let's cut back to Nick."

"He was unexpected but happily I'd moved up the ladder. I'd worked for fifteen years, I was well established and well paid. I could afford an au pair. Best of all there was no sense of resentment. I knew he wasn't going to rob me of my profession."

"Is that the worst thing?"

Clare looked startled. "I suppose it is. But I hope you aren't going to get hypothetical about it. Having me choose between my work and my child. Or my husband."

"Were there no dark days? No doubts?"

"Of course there were doubts. But to understand them you need to know my world. The first years were technical, small-scale problems often part of a larger project. If I'd had doubts then I'd have worried. It would have meant I was under-educated. No problems as it happened. I opted for industry rather than research and spent a couple of years developing bio-medical systems."

"Weird. I don't associate that with physics."

"I'd done student work at the Clarendon on lasers. The company I joined designed equipment for measuring physiological stuff like heart rhythms."

"Yet you didn't stay in that line of work," said Alison.

"A tide in the affairs of man. During that time most of us found development work had more to do with using computers than, shall we say, visible engineering. And computer skills transfer to other branches of industry. I made a rather ironical move – from medicine to armaments. A very large step, in fact: a tank gun-sight with three sub-systems under one stratagem. I headed a sub-system team and had one of those lamp-bulb moments journalists like writing about. A useful idea about how the project fitted together. After some argy-bargy I ended up managing the contract."

"And that's when the dark days started."

"You are clever," said Clare, laughing.

"I've done this before."

"Obviously. By then I wasn't looking for answers, but getting others to look for them. Management, in fact. And I had the bad luck to find myself among a group of misogynists who weren't terribly good at their jobs. Who did everything they could to bring me down."

"But you kicked ass."

"Definitely I kicked ass," said Clare.

"Tell me how."

"Well, it's still OSA so I have to be careful. At first I tinkered around and got nowhere, they were one step ahead. They could always point to the way their jobs were defined. Very vague definitions. I cried myself to sleep for a week or two, I must confess. What's more there was no way I could take the problem upstairs. I'd be seen as weak-kneed woman"

"And so?"

Clare said, "I took the problem upstairs! But not as a disciplinary matter. I asked for permission to run each team for a fortnight with a view to improving efficiency. On top of acting as project manager. A huge task – so huge my boss couldn't see any obvious benefits in it for me. Of course the scum thought they knew what I was up to. They made sure things worked smoothly as I passed through. But my real aim was to use what I learned to cut costs by re-writing the job definitions. My boss loved all this and quickly approved my re-writes. The scum thought this very ingenious but I still wasn't finished. I reversed the situation. I forced one team to meet the new requirements knowing they were incapable. I took chapter and verse on the leader, lead him into my boss and to everyone's surprise I had him fired."

"Sounds like a passage out of The Prince."

"I've never read it though I've been meaning to. The exercise taught me two useful lessons. Firing early is always easier than firing late. And firing not only impresses those below but also those above."

Alison said, "Do you remember my original question?"

"You asked about Nick. To some extent I've told you. Soon after he was born I realised I wasn't an instinctive mother. It took me ages to understand his tactical crying, for instance. To get his own way. When I mentioned this to other mothers – though not mine, alas, she was just as baffled – they saw me as slow. So I now tend to look after him by rote, if you like. And we get on well. But to make up for being a poor mother it's important I have jobs that maintain my self-confidence and are sufficiently senior to let me get to him if he needs me."

Alison looked at her watch and pressed a button on the recorder. "Time to prepare for your audience."

As they drove to the school, Alison gestured at the burred walnut on the dashboard, "Nice wheels."

"An accessory to go with all those grey suits. I bought my first Jaguar when I found big cars are easier to drive than small cars. I kept on buying them because of the effect they had on male colleagues."

"We don't seem to have touched on what you do in your spare time."

"I don't suppose reading New Scientist counts. I'm a member of a tennis club but I don't have a real friend there and I find it hard to get games. When I got the scholarship to Wadham my father – who's as rich as Croesus – said I could pick anything I wanted as a treat. I asked for tennis lessons from a member of the British Davis Cup team. This was twenty years ago and you won't have heard of her. No great shakes internationally but more than good enough for me. The problem is none of the women in my club want to play me. After I beat a couple of men the list got even shorter. So I have to pay the pro."

"Holidays?"

"Anywhere hot and unimaginative. The Carribbean by choice. I used to feel guilty about lolling on the beach, ignoring architecture and all the other cultural bits and pieces. But by the time I'd done the reservations, packed our bags and got on to the plane damn management had caught up. I felt tired and I didn't need picturesque scenery."

"Tell me stuff you're lousy at."

"Languages. I've tried but I have a tin ear. I don't enjoy most social events, probably because I'm no good at breaking ice. I could say I have no small talk but that always sounds like boasting. Politics baffles me because none of what's said ever sounds credible. Scary sports scare me; I don't even like watching speed. I have no sense of history."

"Fears?" asked Alison

"Isn't that rather psycho-analytical?"

"It's a journalist's question. Leaves you damned if you do or damned if you don't."

"Try me again later this afternoon," Clare advised.

"Does all culture bore you?"

"My father knows paintings: he values them, tracks them down, authenticates them, buys and sells them, loves them. It's something that tempts me but I've never had time to study. And – given my background – I don't respond to non-representational stuff. I'd like to acquire one real masterpiece, stick it on my wall and glance at it as I walked by. For ten years."

"Theatre?"

"I prefer film, but you'd expect me to say that, wouldn't you? Film is controlled; I don't worry that someone's going to trip over or forget their lines. That way I can concentrate on the content. The Swedish director – Bergman – I like his pared-down world."

At the school Alison conferred with the photographer while Clare took Nick from the car-seat. She explained to Mrs Thorold, the head-teacher, "He's going to act as my stagehand."

The school-children, sitting on the floor of the main hall, regarded her gravely, their interest rising as she laid her unexplained props on a table. Even more so when a chair was found and Nick sat down, close to the props.

Mrs Thorold slipped easily from talking to Clare into a dry unspringy voice many adults adopt when speaking to children. "All of you are still too young to be thinking about what you'll do for a living but perhaps some of you have ideas. Anyone? Yes?"

"Start a rock band, miss."

"Do you play an instrument, Darren?"

"No, miss."

"Perhaps that might be the first step. Anyone else?"

"Do the weather."

"You mean for television, Chloe? Why does that interest you?"

"Everyone talks about the weather, miss."

"Indeed they do. Tarquin?"

"I want to be a crocodile, miss."

This produced a wave of tentative laughter. "That doesn't surprise me in the slightest, Tarquin." The head continued. "Well, three of you are thinking ahead, though in one case not entirely seriously. The reason I asked is because our speaker today, Mrs Kepler, tells me she was fairly sure – even at your age – that she wanted to be a physicist. Does anyone know what a physicist is?"

There was no response and several children deliberately lowered their gaze to avoid being asked. "Well Mrs Kepler you may need to start right at the beginning."

Clare leant over and whispered, "May I have them call me by my Christian name?"

Mrs Thorold recognised this as a tactic and bowed her head approvingly. "But don't be disappointed if they revert to type and call you 'Miss'. You're looking at an awful lot of conditioning out there."

Clare waited until the head had taken a seat at the side of the hall. "Hello everyone, I'm Clare. I know I'm terribly old but I have Mrs Thorold's permission for you to call me Clare. I won't mind if you forget and call me 'Miss'. And, since I have a husband, you may even call me Mrs Kepler.

"I not only have a husband, I have a son. Here he is, this is Nick. He's going to help me with my talk.

"Now Mrs Thorold said when I was at school I wanted to be a physicist. But I didn't actually use that word 'physicist' because I didn't know what it meant. What I was sure of, though, was I wanted to understand the world around me, the world I could see. Take this table. It's made of some sort of plastic, it has a wooden frame and the legs are this shiny metal called stainless steel. Three materials – plastic, wood, stainless steel – which we can easily see are different. But why and how are they different? Physics can tell us the answers."

At which point the first flash of the photographer's camera occurred. Although forewarned the children, in unison, sighed with a sound approaching wonder. It reminded Clare her performance was not confined to this afternoon or to this assembly hall.

"Physics can tell us much more. Funnily enough it can tell us why this plastic, this wood and this metal are in one sense the same. They don't look the same, do they? But if you looked through a very powerful magnifying glass you'd see they were made of the same things. Does anyone know what those things are?"

A boy who sat languidly and whose hair was cut in an adult rather than a child's style partially raised his hand as if it weighed more than a hand should. "Atoms, miss."

"Excellent. What is your name?"

"Leonard." A name that went with his ensemble. An adult name.

"Well Leonard, you answered very quickly. Perhaps you can tell us what you are made of?"

"The same – atoms."

"Leonard is quite right. He's made of atoms just as all the rest of you are. And I am and Nick is and …even Mrs Thorold." This brought a subdued giggle.

"Just think of that. All of us made from the same tiny things, just like the table. Perhaps you can understand why I wanted to find out as much as I could about all this. Now I did say the visible world – the world we can see – but what makes atoms even more fascinating is that we can't truly see them. We have to find out about them in other ways. We can squirt them about and notice the effects they make. We can do sums about atoms which tell us how they behave. We can do other sums which tell us how much they weigh. We can't see them but we can be sure they really exist."

"That's why we made the atom bomb."

Inevitably, Leonard. "Quite right. Leonard have you thought of becoming a physicist?"

Leonard shook his head. "Going to become a doctor, like my dad."

"You'll make a good doctor, I'm sure. Now, I'd love to be able to do some experiments that prove atoms exist. Unfortunately I'd need complicated and rather large equipment. So let's turn to something else that fascinates physicists. Unfortunately it too is invisible – truly invisible – but it's much easier to show its effects. And Nick is going to help me, aren't you Nick?"

Nick looked dubious.

"Everyone knows what's in Nick's hand." Heads nodded vigorously. "And Nick is going to do something very simple with that apple. And you're all going to say: there's nothing to that. But let's see. Hold your hand out, Nick. That's right. Grip the apple tight. Turn your hand. Now, let the apple drop."

In a flicker of photoflashes, the apple made a satisfactory thud on the wooden floor.

"Thank you Nick. Go and sit on your chair for the moment. Could someone tell me what you just saw. Yes, the girl in the blue blouse."

"Nick dropped the apple, miss."

"And…?"

The child looked baffled. "It just dropped."

"Yes, it dropped didn't it. On to the floor. But tell me: it didn't drop up did it? It dropped down."

The child shrugged. Clare said, "Yes I know it seems a bit silly. Apples drop down. Everybody knows that. Well, once upon a time a very clever man is said to have seen been lying in his orchard and he saw an apple drop. But instead of saying to himself: everybody knows apples drop, he asked a question. Can anyone guess what the question was?"

No answer, no raised hand.

"You're all forgiven for not knowing because it's a very big question. He asked himself: Why? And you're all forgiven too for not knowing why because the answer is even bigger than the question. This very clever man – perhaps one of the cleverest men that ever lived – went away and thought about it and came up with the answer. He said that a force between the very heavy Earth where we all live drew the much lighter apple towards Earth. And he called this force gravity. And for me, as a physicist, gravity is very important."

"Because gravity doesn't just draw apples to earth." Clare pointed to a red-haired boy in the front row. "Can you tell me your name, please?"

"Phillip, miss."

"Well, Phillip, I'd like you to stand up. Now, on the spot, jump. There, you all saw Phillip jump. But what happened afterwards?"

"He did what the apple did." Yet again, Leonard.

"Thank you Leonard. He dropped back on to the floor. And if I tossed my pen up into the air what would happen afterwards? Yes, it would drop to the floor. So, does everything that you throw up or let drop fall to the floor? I see everybody agreeing. Perhaps it's time for Nick to do another experiment."

Having seen others perform to general approval Nick was quickly off his chair. Clare took his hand and slipped it into a loop of ribbon attached to a balloon. "In a few seconds I'll ask Nick to let go of this balloon. Will it fall like the apple?"

A wariness descended, followed by self-congratulatory murmuring when the balloon rushed upwards. And Clare was finally free from apprehensions about the photographer and engaged only with the fresh minds in front. Free too from the pedagogic tone of voice she'd instinctively adopted, free to be enthusiastic rather than merely simulate enthusiasm. The paradoxes of the magnet and the paper aeroplane were demonstrated and explained and soon Mrs Thorold was at her side and she found herself bowing to the tinny cheers that children make only when their attention has been held.

Alison, leaning against the car, smoking by necessity, watched Clare strapping Nick into his seat. "You were enjoying yourself."

"I can't bear inertia," said Clare.

"Who's guilty of it?"

"Sorry," said Clare, laughing at her own outburst. "Eng-lit types who think only George Eliot holds the spark of life."

"Good quote."

By agreement Jerry was home for a foursome dinner which included Alison and Birgitta. Afterwards, also by agreement, Clare drove over to her parents' while Alison interviewed Jerry. "Is this normal?" she asked. Alison shrugged. "Is anyone normal?"

This time her father was at home and they both came out of the substantial wooden porch to greet her as she stepped from the car. Yet again she was struck by her mother's awkward formality com-

pared with the naturalness of her father's embrace. The trio passed
into the house arm in arm.

"Do you trust Jerry?" asked her father genially. He turned to his
wife. "If I were being interviewed about you, Melanie, would you
prefer to be out of the house?"

"My dear, no one disputes your talent for discretion. It's the
foundation of your fortune."

Mr Morgan frowned. "I wish you wouldn't use words like that.
We're simply - "

" - comfortably off," said Clare and her mother in unison. Mr
Morgan smiled complacently.

"Dad, never in a thousand years would you hint at your assets.
But what constitutes being rich?"

"Rich? It's not a word I'd use about anyone."

"Because it's unnecessary. You only mix with rich people. Surely
you'd admit that Mr Lazlo, the one who lives in Eaton Square, is
more than comfortably off.?"

"Ah, but he inherited a great deal from his father. At one time
the family owned a large part of Coblenz."

"Dad, Dad. Neither of us cares where it came from. We're only
concerned that it's there, like a huge inflated life-belt, surrounding
and protecting. It's the means to buy a Klee on impulse."

Her father reached up to straighten his tie; Clare couldn't remember ever seeing him without one, even on holiday. "I know you
and your mother are teasing me. But I like to differentiate between
inherited wealth and earned wealth. I had a few thousand when I
married your mother. What we're surrounded with now is the result
of fairly hard work and the support your mother gave me when
things were nip-and-tuck."

Gracefully put. How much did those infidelities – imagined or
real – mean now? To either of them?

Clare said, "I was teasing. I don't give a toss what it all adds up
to. I've always admired the fact you earned it doing what you liked.
What you were good at. And that was your greatest gift to me. It
meant I could do what I liked."

Slightly embarrassed Mr Morgan looked down at the creases in his broadcloth trousers. The chosen cut resulted in wider legs than were currently the fashion. Often his deliberately unfashionable clothes enhanced his authority especially when set against the habits of his natural coteries – groups of wealthy continental businessmen. "I'm sure Melanie would agree we're twice blessed. We were able to provide the assurances and you never needed to take advantage of them."

The silence that followed was broken gently by Mrs Morgan. "Speaking of which Oliver…"

Mr Morgan fluttered a dismissive hand. "A trust fund for Nicholas. I should have done it much earlier. I'm sure he'll be clever enough but one can never be sure of scholarships. Schools are such a burden these days."

Her father was the only family member to call him Nicholas. Clare wondered whether this gift had to do with his parents' deteriorating view of her marriage. A trust would no doubt be inviolate. "That's very generous of you, Dad."

Again the dismissive hand. "And what's happening on the job front?"

Clare told them about the likely interview and linked it to an awakened interest – triggered by her mother's phrase – in public recognition. Mr Morgan, who had conducted the whole of his business life outside the spotlight of publicity, shuddered slightly. "As John Paul Jones said, you want to go in harm's way."

"It's a type of progression. If I get the chance to run a large company I'd need to address different forces outside the company – the press, bankers, shareholders - on many different issues. This job would give me a start."

Her father nodded. "A long way from physics."

"Sometimes the distance is even further. I've known managers with degrees in medieval history, in PPE, even medicine."

"You're far braver than I could ever be," said her father. "But would you enjoy it?"

"Enjoyment comes from doing something well. That I've yet to find out."

Her mother interrupted them briskly. "Leave your father to The Connoisseur for the moment. I've got some ideas for the garden I'd like to chat about before it gets dark."

The ideas proved to be merely an excuse. Out of earshot and encouraged by Clare's recent willingness to talk about Jerry, Mrs Morgan asked for domestic news.

"We have discussed things," Clare said, not hinting at how those thing had ended, inconclusively, in bed. "He's dissatisfied with his job and he is trying to work out dissatisfaction on me. What I took to be apathy is not that; there's even some affection. What worries me is his attitude towards Nick. It's as if he had no son."

"So… what will you do?"

Clare looked directly at her mother's face framed in neat waves of white hair. "For the moment I'll endure."

Clearly Mr Morgan knew why they had gone out and looked up expectantly as they re-entered the room. Realising quickly there was nothing new he stood up and took Clare's hand, "There's a narrow line between wanting to help and nagging. Neither of us wants you to suffer from our neglect."

"It hasn't reached that stage. I can't compensate for golf's hollow centre. He must work it out for himself."

"Bring the child to see us," said her mother. The child that lacked a name.

At home Jerry was watching the late news on television, a glass of whisky by his side. "She only left half an hour ago. It was hard work. I've said things that surprised me."

Clare picked up the glass and took a sip. "I suspect I have, too. But that's the whole point. An impartial view."

"Would you like to know what I said?"

"No. Not because I'm not interested. You should be allowed to say what you think. For both our sakes."

He'd been apprehensive, obviously. Relieved, he was turning over the implications of "both our sakes". His mouth opened with a question then closed. She found him regarding her with that attentive slightly puzzled look that dated back to his rehabilitation at Confexxion; she too was transported to that uncertain, slightly daring time. She leant down and kissed him but found no renaissance in his lips.

10. HATCH

Touched in parts

PRUDENCE had borrowed a car, no doubt from some admirer, and Hatch drove her to Birmingham airport. This break from public transport and from trudging felt like a holiday.

As they queued at the check-in, Prudence said, "I'm grateful, of course. But there's something demeaning about your doing this."

"I don't resent it, honestly. Not that I'm any kind of hero. Turn it the other way round and I'd feel a shit if I wasn't doing it."

She looked surprised. "That's an uncommon word for you."

"I make pocket money at a parts retailer and it describes what I think of the work."

"No progress?" asked Prudence.

"A possibility with a trade magazine but it's in London and not well paid. Yesterday I met someone I knew at Loughborough. He's been at Marconi ever since. Or he was until a fortnight ago. Now he's bewildered by the outside world. Astonished he isn't already re-employed. Quite put out that I couldn't recommend half a dozen openings."

They had coffee at a gaudy franchise devoted to Mexican food. Scenes from their marriage re-played as he sat down and noticed the covert glances Prudence attracted. The dark smudges beneath her eyes, more prominent now, only added to her appeal.

"Is Hester more evident?"

"She's appalled I might consider London. So was Tom. When I get back I'm expecting two quite separate messages on the answer machine. But I can't be picky. In the past Hester has hinted she may be able to swing a job."

"My advice – if it carries any weight – would be to stay clear. But that might be a luxury in these troubled times."

Hatch looked amused. "You think she'd gobble me up?"

"She's not the problem, you are. You're too guileless. Though just how you'd divide yourself between Hester and Tom I shudder to think." She looked out over the shoddy foreground, causing a couple of male faces to bob up at nearby tables. "Speaking of which we've never really discussed what I'm doing, where I'm going. Spending our money. I put the facts to you and you agreed."

"Usually I'm blamed for being over-analytical," he said wryly. "The decision made itself."

"With some misgivings, surely?"

"We see each other differently; we proved that when I visited you. I'm not allowed misgivings. I disappointed you and it was awful being told why. But deep down I wasn't surprised. Even when we got married I always I thought you were entitled to leave me. But did that mean I expected you to? I don't know."

"Oh shit."

"You see how useful that word is. I was in despair when you forced me to take that sales job but I couldn't hate you. Even though it was a high price for a decade spent in your radiance."

Prudence looked at him tensely. "And now? If I weren't so vain there'd be no need for Switzerland."

"No Pru, that's not vanity. You've never been vain. You never preen. But even if Switzerland were pure self-regard why would anyone expect you to act any differently? There's more at stake than having your head shaved."

She stared, unnerved by his sympathy. "A man I know whose life I may wreck got quite shirty. He couldn't understand. 'You don't mind being seen in a headscarf by the Swiss; why would Brits be any different'?"

"Go ahead and wreck his life. I would. He sounds like - "

" – a real shit." And they both laughed.

Quickly she was serious again. "You wouldn't want me back again, would you? Before you answer let me say I have no intention of returning. Under any circumstances."

"No I wouldn't. I haven't the confidence I had ten years ago."

He accompanied her to the departure gate. "Do you want me to telephone?"

"Do you want to?"

"Yes. You are a sort of investment. But the calls will be short."

"Then call."

He knew she wouldn't look back as she went through the gate. He, on the other hand, watched. Not from any romantic impulse but as he might have reacted to a possession now seen in a second-hand shop. The golden head upright, like that of a martyr. But that was a nonsense.

It was pure luxury simply to be driving a car and he was briefly tempted to turn the journey back into a scenic detour. But geography was against him. With Birmingham to his left all worthwhile countryside lay to the right and would have required an unjustifiable dog's-leg eastwards. Within half an hour he was parking outside Prudence's block of flats trying unobtrusively to hide the key beneath the floor mat. The windows of her bedroom looked out emptily on the car, an apt image of her life's mysteries since they divorced. That some man would lend her a car was surprising yet simultaneously inevitable. Nothing she'd said suggested a present-day hinterland, other than the admission that she might be wrecking someone's life. Perhaps the car belonged to that someone.

Reverting to buses was particularly tedious but he arrived home late enough to call in at the fish shop and ask if he were needed. He'd now done several stints behind the counter. Payment had not been discussed and there'd been no change in his rent. But Hatch knew Mr Wee's conscientious view of cash.

"Ah, Missa Hatch. You come eight o'clock? OK?"

By now he was acclimatised to the work, even welcomed it since it absorbed time and discouraged reflection. Upstairs the machine flashed three messages. The first, recorded minutes after he left to pick up Prudence, was from Hester, insisting he ring her immediately at home. Tom on the other hand wanted Hatch to ring him at work. The third call was from Lodestone Engineering in Stourport, not the type of company to require a production engineer as such, but who nevertheless asked for a meeting. Quickly he dialled the number, got an answerphone and left a message saying he'd call back the following day.

That left Hester and Tom. Hester's tangible urgency might well have disappeared if Tom were now at home. So Hatch rang Tom first to find he was with a client. This allowed him, somewhat nervously, to ring Hester. She insisted they meet that evening.

"Difficult. Mr Wee wants me at eight."

"Mr Wee! The man in the fish-shop?"

"The owner."

"Is it important?"

"I'm assuming he's going to pay me."

This silenced Hester's impatience. Hatch and money were subjects both Makings approached with great delicacy so there was no more to be said. Perhaps apprehensive about Tom's imminent arrival, Hester agreed to call the following day. Half an hour later Tom phoned back and this time the subject was money although there was much manoeuvring before he got to the point. Having um'd his way through Hatch's much edited account of the drive to and from Birmingham Airport he became portentous:

"Now look here, Andrew. These problems you're having with, er, cash."

"Yes."

"These problems… are they severe?"

"I've cut down on the claret," said Hatch to encourage a lighter tone. It was as if he hadn't spoken.

"Truly severe?"

"I'm surviving. I do early-morning work at a car parts shop. I lend a hand with Mr Wee."

"Mr who?"

"My landlord."

"You work in the fish-and-shop?" asked Tom, astonished.

"I'm not intending to make a career out of it."

"A fish-and-chip shop," said Tom distractedly. "Have you heard from the magazine in London?"

"The editor said it would be a week or two."

"And you'd actually consider London."

"I may have to, Tom."

"Look, there's probably some detail chasing with us. Would that help?"

"I'm grateful but it sounds like busywork."

"Then what about - " Hatch could almost hear the mechanisms straining against a lifetime's caution. " – what about... a loan?"

"It's good of you Tom, but by my reduced standards I'm not that desperate. What's more I try to keep cash in step with spending. I have no idea when I'd be able to repay you."

"If you do get desperate you'll let me know? Promise?"

"Promise."

Tom's sigh of relief showed this was the hoped-for reply and that he'd discharged his duties. Had the offer really come from Hester? Hatch pulled the suitcase from under his bed and sought clothing that already carried the stench of cooking oil.

WORKING at the parts store was becoming increasingly more depressing. Hatch was particularly irritated by the manager's hints that the two of them were "us" while other less competent assistants were "them". Also he suspected he was being deceived, that the matiness was a front to delay giving Hatch a more congenial shift.

It was his job to unlock the store for the seven o'clock opening. Within the racks Hatch smelt the bitter yet oily atmosphere cooked up by early morning sun on the corrugated-iron roof. At the reception counter he swung up the wire netting shutter then unbolted the customer's door. Two sleep-deadened youths in garage overalls shuffled through, making their needs known in the oral shorthand Hatch had had difficulty understanding a few weeks ago. Cash changed hands. Both worked for back-street car-repairers lacking the financial clout to carry spares or operate an account with a manufacturer's supplier.

To Hatch's surprise the third customer was a woman, mid-twenties, lipsticked, a swirling summer dress – very much a rarity. Her face seemed overwhelmed by this concentration of masculine grubbiness. She said, "I do hope you can help me. I'm completely out of my depth."

"In effect we're a shop – but without the display window."

"It all looks so secretive."

"True," said Hatch. "That's because here the customer is the expert. There's no impulse buying. No packets of chewing gum round the cash register."

She giggled pleasingly. "That much I realised. Think of me as the expert customer's runner, gofer. I do the books at Monckton Motors but we're a mechanic short. The boss was able to spare me rather than someone who does the real work. He's given me a biggish list. I thought it might help if I typed it out instead of worrying you with my terrible handwriting."

Hatch looked at the sheets of paper, then at her. "The perfect customer," he said ambiguously

"Well, thank you."

"Are you going to wait? It'll take a few minutes to pick this lot. If you like, I'll put the coffee on and you can serve yourself. That way you'll know it's fresh."

"That's very kind." She turned uncertainly, looking for somewhere to sit.

"For goodness sake don't let that breathtaking dress touch the couch. The last thousand customers were just the teeniest bit oil-stained. I've got just the thing." He reached back into one of the racks. "A plastic cover for a car seat."

Hatch tucked the cover round the beaten leather surfaces. "As to reading matter, the very finest. A year-old issue of Car, an ava-lanche of Automotive Supplier and some aged Sunday supplements. If you're tempted I'll get you some disposable gloves."

She watched as he went to work on the percolator. "All this service," she laughed, "I wish my order was bigger. Gosh, you're opening a new packet of coffee, just for me. Doesn't it smell delicious? I think I'll forego your very specialised library, I do have my Guardian."

"A Guardian reader, too. The day's starting well."

Keen to get back to the counter Hatch nevertheless sought to move slowly, purposefully, hinting at his expertise. Within the bowels of the store he moved up and down among the parts bins picking items into a plastic laundry basket. Briefly he hummed a theme from the Bach double violin concerto but stopped after a couple of bars. No need to appear so obvious.

When he returned to the counter she looked up, cup in hand, but he shook his head. "Finish your coffee. I need to set up the invoice. We're not blessed with speedy automation here."

As he keyed in part numbers he sensed her watching him. "I'm rather ashamed," she said.

"Why's that?"

"I was dreading this. I thought it would be lads together, nudge-nudge, wink-wink. But it's not like that at all. I can only think you're out of place."

"The squalor's a bit deceptive and the work's more demanding than it looks. Many of the parts differ in only a tiny way. If I get them wrong I irritate customers profoundly. I'd hate to do that to someone who's brought in light so early in the day."

She refolded her newspaper. "No rewards for getting it right, I assume? Only complaints when it goes pear-shaped."

Her sympathy broke into his keyboarding and he stared at her dress, trying to commit the pattern to memory. She added, "It's rather the same with book-keeping. But I take it this wasn't your lifelong ambition."

The subtlest of compliments. He recalled her newspaper and its traditions. "Just another Thatcher victim. I used to make things."

For a while she said nothing. Then: "My older brother too."

When he printed out the invoice she took a thick company cheque-book from her handbag. I'll find out what her name is, he told himself. But she signed the cheque pp A. S. Robertson and it wasn't her surname, dull in all conscience, he was after.

All that was left was to carry the substantial collection of packages out to her car. She opened the door. "That was… very civilised."

"A pleasure. A real pleasure."

Back in reception he picked up her cup and noted the faint traces of lipstick. He regretted the store was empty, that there were no customers to occupy him.

Released at ten o'clock he bought – The Guardian, what else? Having called Lodestone Engineering to make the appointment he sat on a bench in the pedestrian precinct and flicked through the paper guessing at what she'd read, unwilling to let the memory go.

Hester had said she would phone him at the bed-sitter. Because he was unemployed she, like others, assumed he would be permanently available. But he couldn't bear to sit on his bed and wait for the phone. He wanted to be elsewhere, unharassed, able to dwell on the fading details of the unknown customer and the phenomenon of women.

At the library, after an unprofitable glance at the Telegraph, he looked at technology reference titles and picked Metallurgy Basics. At Loughborough metallurgy had been hard work, a science on its own. As he went through the book he noted its editorial structure for the first time. Unyielding metals - chromium, copper, magnesium, nickel and titanium – evolved into progressively more exotic alloys which, themselves, turned into qualities (hardness, corrosion resistance, toughness). Finally the book listed the tasks such materials would fulfil. An orderly logical world in stark contrast to that of job-seeking, where the CV was quickly put to one side and personality – What could be vaguer? - warred with experience and knowledge.

The prime minister regarded manufacture as ponderous, old-fashioned and unprofitable. When it came to technology she favoured a covert world based on electronic transfer of information. Hatch, conditioned by the Midlands, regarded these visible and invisible worlds as typical of the conflicts in companies he'd worked for. Accountants promoted to financial directors saw profits as a natural result of their supervision. Whereas those who made the finished product were chided for the costs of bought-in goods, for overtime payments to meet contract deadlines and – a particular favourite – for the "wastefulness" of "non-contributory" functions such as packaging and delivery.

The details of Hatch's fresh morning customer were fading and he could no longer recall the dress pattern he had worked hard to memorise. She said she "did the books" at a company which Hatch knew specialised in repairing out-of-warranty Volkswagens. Hatch hoped she was not a bookkeeper training to be an accountant.

He closed the metallurgy book firmly. Reading was pure sentimentality. The government and city money-spinners sneered at the under-financed workshops in the Midlands as sentimental and mired in the past. It wasn't sufficient these days to make something, it had to be glamorous, obvious. And newsworthy.

Outside he bought a Cornish pasty and re-read The Guardian for information that confirmed his prejudices. He was hardly cheered by a trio of paragraphs on increasing unemployment and a hyper-thyroid Midlands MP who feared a "deskilled generation" in his constituency. When Hatch got up from the bench and started for home he realised he wasn't walking but ambling. Ambling was a side-effect of unemployment; journeys on foot were passages in time as well as of distance.

THEY faced each other over a table at a department-store restaurant in Sutton Coldfield, a novel environment for Hatch and, it seemed, for men as a whole. Some older patrons wore felt hats. Country Casuals and Jacqmar were on sale beyond the restaurant's dividing wall and this added to the claustrophobia.

"The magazine hasn't let you know?" asked Hester.

"Not yet. I do have an interview with Lodestone Engineering in Stourbridge. A bit of a mystery. I knew them from Weldworth. A fabrication shop doing one-offs and batch work. Larger than most but I can't see how I'd fit in."

"How many employees?"

"At a guess, less than fifty. I saw the ad in the Birmingham Mail. Pretty vague. The usual rubbish about 'taking part in our exciting future'. Seemed worth a punt. As you know I'm less choosy than I was."

Hester drummed her fingers, nails varnished a strident red. Too strident? Stealing a second glance he was detected.

"Surprised?" she asked.

"I wasn't sure your hair was dark enough to go with that colour."

"And is it?"

"Oh, yes."

"Nail varnish in general? The mark of a tart?"

"Absolutely!"

A risky reply but the right one. She had adorned herself for the occasion, was out to make an impact. "How about the eye shadow?"

Which he hadn't noticed. "Very dramatic."

Hester gestured. "Something I need to know. How long can you support yourself?"

"This fish-shop work will cut my rent but I don't know by how much. Car parts should cover my living expenses, the phone, some of the electricity."

"Have you nothing else? I can't understand. Weren't Weldworth quite generous? Has Prudence got it all?"

In the past he hadn't gossiped much about Prudence but Hester was offering to help him. Hatch looked round the genteel restaurant. Felt hats were turning: Hester's sharp voice was attracting attention since everybody else whispered. The audience – most of whom had ordered cakes – were not shoppers but elderly women in best-dressed limbo. Back in the fifties they'd have used the Kardo-mah.

"You're going to say I'm easily pushed around."

"Am I? Are you?"

"Maybe. But the alternative's unpleasant." He gathered himself. "Prudence was diagnosed with a brain tumour. She saw a specialist and he was optimistic, said it was probably benign. As a result she dropped down the NHS totem pole and had to go private for immediate surgery. I can't argue with that but we've only one asset - the house. As you know we bought just before we separated. A big step up. The price was highish and the market has fallen since."

Hester said nothing, dwelling no doubt on her own home comforts. Tom actively bought and sold residences almost as a hobby. As a solicitor he discovered bargains. The Makings presently occupied a five-bedroom house worth half a million pounds, mortgaged for a mere hundred thousand.

"So there's not too much equity," said Hatch. "But there's another factor. Prudence doesn't care to have the surgery or – more truthfully – to spend her convalescence in Britain. She's quite frank, says it's pure vanity. I can't disagree."

Hester said, "She's going foreign and it will cost a bomb. Can't be America because I doubt you could afford it. Europe, somewhere fashionable."

"The specialist said Switzerland. As I told you and Tom I gave her the Weldworth cheque for immediate expenses. A bridging loan will cover the rest until the sale goes through."

Hester was fenced in morally. Any criticism would discount Hatch's generosity.

"Have I been pushed around?"

"Of course not," she said. "That was good of you. But did you have to give her the *whole* of the severance?"

"I didn't want to…be petty. A brain tumour, for Christ's sake."

"Water under the bridge. So, here's the question; are you likely to starve or be kicked out during the next few weeks?"

"The short answer is no."

Hester rubbed her hands briskly. "Good. Here's what I'm trying to arrange. I have friends from university who went into television. They formed a production company and did several programmes for ITV. Since then they've grown. They need a technical adviser. Not televisually technical, technical as you'd understand it. You'll have to trust my judgement but I'm sure you're capable. They say the work is interesting and I'm sure it pays better than Weldworth. Would you consider it?"

"Of course."

"It's not traditional manufacturing but it will mirror what you've done. The atmosphere will be different but the work…"

"I've adapted in the past. As part of my job."

Hester said, "The thing is to hang on. They assure me new investment will be in place shortly. From what I've told them they like the sound of you."

"Of course I'll hang on."

Her shoulders sagged with relief. "God, this place is where elderly ladies come to die. Let's have a drink, a real drink."

In the nearby pub Hester's first gin and tonic went down quickly and she ordered another. "Unemployment's such a waste," she said.

"That gets my vote."

She raised her glass, "Here's to happier times." And her hand slid over his.

11. HATCH

Selling his wares

THE FOOTBALL ground was owned by the local authority and lacked facilities other than goalposts. It occupied valuable land, awkwardly trapped between rows of houses. Hatch paced it out. At just under a hundred metres long and forty-seven metres wide it could have accommodated an official game provided the spectators – perilously close to the action – were limited to two hundred. Incidental matters for Hatch abhorred all team games. What the land did offer was a measured circuit round which he could jog, provided he picked his moment. By nine-thirty most dogs that needed to had defecated (in the centre of the pitch - a pleasing discovery) and it was too early in the day for holidaying school children. Five and half laps represented a mile, his initial target.

He would jog a mile and then take stock. The exercise had less to do with health and more with escaping from the bed-sitter where he felt the walls were closing in. There'd been the matter of clothing, partially solved by cutting the legs off jeans used for painting during his house-owning days. Feet were another matter. He had nothing resembling the whitish footwear he belatedly recognised as trainers and which he hadn't the cash to buy. So he put on his oldest lace-up brogues and bumped off on earth hardened by several weeks of sun.

Those same shoes turned out to be a calling card. The first lap passed off easily and in solitary self-confidence he increased his speed. After three laps the remainder seemed beyond him and he was being harried, twenty yards distant, by another jogger. Spurred on he completed the mile and stood to one side, concentrating on concealing an acute lack of puff.

The other jogger did one more lap then stopped five metres away for much the same reason. Their faces met in complicity; the other pointed at Hatch's brogues. "Very athletic," he said breathily.

"I'm a style failure."

"Your first jog? Are you filling in time?"

Hatch looked more closely. Noted the man's unfashionably short hair, still parted, a tee-shirt contoured for someone much younger, shorts for the swimming pool not the track. Remembered the time of day. "Strange what unemployment can force us to do."

"Did you have a grippy spring for building up wrist muscles as you made phone calls?" asked the man as his breath eased.

"Just a bent con-rod. Andrew Hatch, production engineer, no present means of support."

"Tony Gallagher." They shook hands. "Ergonomist. Time and motion. Now it's all time and no motion. On my side of the marriage, anyway. My wife's a teacher, thank God."

"Mine's in Switzerland."

Gallagher pointed. "There's a greasy spoon that way. The council dustmen use it. A cup of tea gives you a seat on a bench."

"I didn't think I'd need cash, jogging."

"Doing another mile tomorrow? Buy me tea then."

Gallagher had designed work stations for television assembly lines and had been out of work for two months. "After a while you ask yourself what you'd settle for."

"I'm trying a detour. An industrial magazine. Doesn't pay much. But it's one way of staying up-to-date."

Gallagher sipped tea from a plastic cup yellowed by caffeine. "I thought about lecturing evening classes but it's a one-way trip into the outback. When I took up ergonomics it interested me, now it seems like a whim. Too specialised, the personnel spooks say. But hell I'm an engineer. I've learned once, I can learn again." The way he put down the cup and pushed it away suggested he wouldn't pick it up again.

He went on, "My dad ran a foundry. My brother became an insurance broker and my dad sneered, 'What kind of a job is that?' Dad knew nothing about ergonomics but he approved of what I was doing. Now I'm dumped and my brother drives a Merc. Dad has nothing to say."

"Back at Loughborough," said Hatch, "the future wasn't jobs, it was work that needed doing. And there'd always be work because the world needs useful products. That's still true. The stuff just isn't being manufactured in the Black Country."

"A poncy lot at my school. Everyone wanted to 'escape' from the Black Country. Not a good school for physics or chemistry. Milton bored me rigid. By then I'd spent time in the foundry and done work experience in light engineering. At school they had this debating society and they came up with: 'Literature is the preferred civilising influence.' Nobody wanted to speak against it. God, the English master was so patronising. 'Gallagher, your father is in, er, industry. How about you putting the literary types in their place'."

Hatch's eyebrows rose. Gallagher continued: "My point was literature's inadequate. There's nothing in Milton about lathes and yet the school was surrounded by machine shops. No poncy poet ever took on manufacturing and I couldn't see why. Watch a drill bit go through machined steel - the power's fascinating? Swarf on the workshop floor? – the hell with autumn leaves. Beauty isn't just the fucking Lake District. I was never going to pick up many votes but that shitehawk English master chaired the debate and got them giggling with talk of Gallagher's purple passages. In the come-back at the end I said I hoped they all went home on a bus put together by a poet. But I lost my rag and added in foul language. Had to speak to the head afterwards. Couldn't wait to get away from that school."

A well-remembered trauma. Hatch said, "I'm slightly ashamed. My school separated out the streams and I never got Milton shoved down my throat. Loughborough wasn't exactly a haven for the liberal arts either."

Gallagher was still pawing at accumulated unfairness. "Perhaps I'm paranoid but wordiness is increasing. Do you ever listen to what's said in a job interview? The words? The so-called concepts? The shit about facilitating, deliverable projects and team players. It irritated me in management meetings but it's far worse when you're on the outside trying to find out what's going on. I thought they spoke that way to show off, to prove they knew the lingo. But if you chase it down it's a cover-up for nothing at all."

He twisted angrily. "I was interviewed by an instrument company in Wolverhampton and it was plain they didn't like me, I wasn't going to get the job. But the department head kept blethering so's my feelings weren't hurt. I'd have sat it out and been polite if he hadn't mentioned an analyser which was going to 'leverage the market'. I had no idea what he meant so I asked him to explain but it still didn't make sense. He floundered for a whole minute. Did he mean, 'Sell more,' I asked? 'In a nutshell, yes,' he replied. And so we went our separate ways."

Gallagher looked around the shabby café like a caged animal.

"Christ, let' s get out of here. Fancy another mile?"

Hatch didn't but couldn't walk away from another member of the clan. After one lap of the football field, at a far too ambitious pace, Gallagher was clearly intent on driving away his frustration. This was achieved. The remaining laps were leaden.

"See you tomorrow. My turn to buy the tea," said a heavily sweating Hatch.

Gallagher had a distant look. The next day Hatch waited in vain for ten minutes, jogged his mile and even peered through the unwashed windows of the café but there was no Gallagher. Faced with the interview at Stourbridge he walked away regretfully. Gallagher had been uncomfortable but had cast light on another aspect of being without work. Perhaps it was important to be angry about things, to avoid acting the gentleman.

And then there was Gallagher's profession. During Hatch's time at Tempest ergonomics was practised in university labs and workshops. If anyone assembling a dryer at Tempest suffered crick in the back it would have been Hatch's job to find a higher stool or to cut away part of the bench. Now specialised engineering had emerged to address such problems. Hatch had never worked alongside an ergonomist but he knew there were more of them about. Being out of work was an unlearning process.

In the library Hatch checked bus time-tables knowing a rail ticket to Stourbridge would cripple him. Arranging the interview he had allowed for buses and now found he would need to leave his bed at dawn.

Travelling from Birmingham out west he was curious to know what he would find at Lodestone. Fabricators normally had no use for production engineers but when he arrived there were clues that the company had outgrown this restriction. Instead of a jumble of rusting box pallets out front there were flowerbeds and a little landscaping. A free-standing company sign had been professionally conceived and engraved on an impressive slate slab. The building had been extended in brick to the rear and the extension had plenty of skylights. The receptionist doubled as a typist and switchboard operator but receptionists were a rarity in an industry where customers are traditionally received by the proprietor in a beige warehouse coat with large pockets.

In fact he was met by Roger Fairbairns who wore a tailored shirt with cufflinks and a Liberty tie. "Mr Hatch. I own Lodestone and you'll notice I didn't switch off an oxy torch so I could shake hands. That should tell you I'm not wasting your time." He followed Fairbairns into his preciously designed office decorated with prints from pre-war Autocar.

"Any ideas why I'm interviewing you?" asked Fairbairns.

"The obvious one. Instead of waiting for orders you're going to make up products and sell them across the counter."

"What kind of products?"

"Probably small items in low volumes."

"How small?" asked Fairbairns intently

"Up to a metre but not bulky. Probably nestable. It depends on how much of your new extension is productive. You could have off-site storage but I credit you with better planning. The big question is how you split fabrication from the product line. Tooling won't be interchangeable so you'll be tight for space." Hatch added. "But fabricators are always tight for space. If it happens you can always turn down work."

"Fabricators never turn down work." said Fairbairns robustly. "You're pessimistic about dual-function machine tools?"

Hatch noticed the asperity. "You can design for adaptable equipment - accept the compromise. I take it you know your own peaks and troughs, what you can live with. Multi-purpose kit will give you sensible cash flow during start-up and the first couple of years. By then you'll know whether it's a good or bad idea."

"Aren't you being cautious?"

"Me? Cautious? You've told me nothing yet. I suspect it's the biggest single decision this company has ever made. You're a successful fabricator, I can tell. But switching to continuous production means marketing and sales and your new manager must be hand in glove with both, especially at the beginning. Another thing: the new man could save you thousands by looking out good secondhand machinery. But you know all this and I'm teaching you to suck eggs. As I say, you've told me nothing."

"You're quite aggressive, too."

"First I'm cautious, now I'm aggressive. Balancing the two – that's good for a start-up."

"I take your point," said Fairbairns keen to shift the balance of power. "But you know what they say about job interviews: if the man on my side of the desk is uneasy the feeling will grow with time."

"Only in personality checks; mainly for sales staff. I'm not marking your card but you need someone who knows production and won't keep quiet if things go astray. If you don't like my manner kick me out or just ask questions."

"Here's one: how do I come over to you?"

"One thing I like. Adding a production line is ballsy and I prefer working for bosses who make decisions. It's astonishing how many can't."

Fairbairns laughed. "Let's have some coffee."

It was good coffee, served in bone china cups. Fairbairns said, "I can't tell you about the products for the moment. But how about this? Lodestone was my father's company and I started on the shopfloor. I've taken time out to learn marketing. So far that's worked because fabrication is an odd nut. I can't see justifying a marketing man for the new products and I'm thinking of doing it myself. Does that sound OK?"

Hatch pondered. "I hope you take this the right way. Has your marketing been somewhat under-employed recently?"

"Possibly," said Fairbairns curtly.

"Then planning will depend on the pattern of fabrication work."

"Hmmm. What sort of salary would you expect?"

"Lowish but with a simple bonus scheme, based on productivity – not like the bankers where it's just extra salary. Also, if you delay making the appointment full-time have me in as an adviser on a per-day rate. Especially if there's plant to acquire."

"Tell me a couple of details that aren't on your CV."

"I suspect you're not interested in leisure activities."

"Try me."

"Baroque music. DIY home improvement, although that's taken a bit of a knock in a bed-sitter. In my time I've been mechanic for a couple of car racers – both extreme amateurs. Books? Mainly biographies, the more academic the better."

"You're just an engineering stick-in-the-mud," said Fairbairns, his geniality returning.

"Guilty as charged. One other thing was hard to describe briefly so it isn't on the CV. A lot of effort at Tempest went into cost engineering. To cut out repetition I wrote some primitive software to give me a first-pass analysis of new component costs. Unsophisticated, based purely on machine time. It wasn't foolproof but it avoided blind alleys."

"Clever stuff. I haven't used a computer as much as I should. Just invoicing, quotes, accountancy and letters. I looked at CAD but we're not big enough."

"That could change when you add the product line. Stock control problems will be an indicator."

Fairbairns leant back in his chair, hands supporting the back of his head. Hatch recognised the ploy: simulating friendliness, even vulnerability. "OK, you've got some idea of what I'm aiming at. What's your reaction?"

"Give me a clue about the products."

"No can do." But he wanted to. "Oh, what the hell. Garden tools. The market is sewn up by a couple of nationals. There's so little choice. From one garden centre to another you're faced with the same range. No problem for the DIY chains but there's a slew of smaller outfits who'd prefer something different."

"Will your range be different?"

"Young lad in from a design college on work experience; wonderful stuff. He's under contract now."

"Garden tools. Simple enough. Not too much capital investment. A concentrated market in the Midlands. Two salesmen to begin with. What about the thing everyone forgets? A publicity budget?"

"I've had experience of that on the fabrication side. It's a weird proposition. If I can do that I can do products…"

"The right kind of flyers can sell both sides of your business." Hatch sat up. "Are you going to be successful? I have no idea. There's always a good chunk of luck needed. As you well know. But it could be a winner. I'd enjoy working with you…"

During the twenty-minute walk to the bus station Hatch glowed with energy. It had been a good interview and for the best of reasons – he'd been back in the real world. Aggression, even the risk of alienation, an opportunity to parade himself. This minor triumph deserved the company of a woman. Sex, perhaps, but first an opportunity to talk. Ideally a virtuous woman capable of listening and understanding, wanting to listen and understand. Linda at Weldworth? The mythical woman who had bought car parts? His throat contracted at the thought.

His need was partially resolved by the Makings. Perhaps to save him from the fish-shop they'd invited him to dinner. And to ensure the talk didn't dwell on employment a couple had been brought in to widen the range. Both guests were demonstrably employed - he a thoracic surgeon, she an actuary.

"Why did I think all actuaries were men? Andrew Hatch, by the way."

"Jean Galsworthy. Because it was true until the seventies."

"What's to say - actuarially - about production engineers?"

"Mostly grief, I'm afraid. A shrinking profession. Many PEs have problems adapting to other parts of industry."

"Because we're pig-headed?" Her rimless glasses were impressive, worn as weapons, sharpening her and shortening her reflexes.

"You tell me," she said, laughing. "There is one obvious factor. Line production has tended to become line assembly with manufactured items outsourced. It's a simpler discipline and those in charge don't learn as much. If you're a mech-eng you'd be over-qualified to run one of these so-called production lines."

Hatch said, "I was re-reading a book on metallurgy, one of the harder parts of mech-eng for me. Nowadays it's probably unnecessary."

"It's not all gloom. Things can look bad when a large manufacturing plant closes and it happens a lot since many are foreign subsidiaries. Shift the pain from the home front to the colonies. The skills fragment for a time but come together again in smaller units. If a production engineer is going to come back he's has to be a real multi-tasker. Not frozen in history."

They were under scrutiny from Hester and Hatch gestured. "Jean knows more about my line of business than I do."

But Jean was above easy flattery. "Another misunderstanding. People think actuaries only work for insurance companies. But industry is full of probabilities. My last contract was with a company making curry meals."

"Really!" said Hester, her exaggerated interest perilously close to no interest at all. "And did you reveal the curry meal market to them?"

"Easily." An argument seemed a distinct possibility and Hatch was relieved to see dinner announced by Tom wearing a Fortnum and Mason apron. Hatch took his seat determined not to mention engineering but needn't have worried. The Galsworthys were equally strong minded and determined to dominate each other. The others round the table tended to be sidelined.

As an unpartnered divorcé, Hatch often scrutinised couples for signs that they might be breaking up. Here it was hard to see what held husband and wife together but he now knew marriages had more than one aspect. It was quite likely the Galsworthys would take to their car in high good humour at having controlled the dinner. He wished Prudence were here. She had a talent for spotting behaviour that passed by Hatch completely, as if each had attended a different event. Prudence often refused to believe Hatch had missed signs of mutual hatred or lurking infidelity among guests, unable to credit he could be so unobservant.

Tonight Hatch might have daydreamed indefinitely had silence not broken out. In full flow about the NHS's failure to support its true stars, Greg Galsworthy, thoracic surgeon, tailed away. "Hogging the conversation as usual. Sorry about that. An occupational failing. Please, someone, fill in the gap."

"Well there's that old war horse about the doctors," said Hatch. "They grumble about guests buttonholing them and putting questions better suited to the surgery. Good luck to them, I say. When people ask me what I do for a living – and most don't these days – I tell them and that's an end to the chat. I'd welcome lay interest."

Characteristically Greg's wife answered on his behalf. "I always thought doctors misread the Hippocratic oath. They resent being at the public's beck and call. Not that I've noticed surgeons holding back at parties."

"Jean is too kind," said her husband with practised insincerity. "What about solicitors?"

"We run doctors a close second," said Tom. "But there's an added frisson. Received wisdom says we charge extortionately for work more humane people would do for free. So there's always a sense of flirtation. Those asking questions are on the look-out for the moment when I become silent through pure greed."

"In both cases we're talking self-interest," said Hatch. "But why does no one care about the way manufacturing works? Once magazines carried cutaways of rolling mills and canning plants. Explaining technology. In Victorian times engineers were heroes. But these days, nothing."

Greg Galsworthy's mouth opened but not quickly enough to forestall his wife. "Once things were mechanical and comparatively easy to understand. Now electrical or electronic controls are hard to illustrate and harder to penetrate. I took my car in because it misfired. The bill was, of course, enormous and I asked what had been done. Immediately we were into talk of 'chips' and my mind blurred."

"Tom holds Andrew in awe on technical matters," said Hester. "And for just that reason. The explanations are so beautifully obscure."

Hatch protested, "Neither surgery nor law are really accessible."

"Both have been dramatised in books, films and on TV," said Greg shortly. "The lay public don't understand but they think they do."

At which point Tom asked everyone to judge the Pontet Canet and the talk drifted. Because the Galsworthys would, not surprisingly, be driving off in the opposite direction to Leyfield Hatch remained mute about transportation. Tom acknowledged he'd had more to drink and volunteered Hester as chauffeur. Uncertain on dark rural roads she hardly spoke but when they arrived she drew him to her and kissed him on the lips. Earlier he'd yearned for a woman's company but not this. Morality fought the taste of lipstick and the rich undertow of perfume.

12. HATCH

Corvette interview

"I ASKED for Carolson but they said 'There ees no such name'."

"Reception has my passport to stop me running off without paying the supplementary charges. I'd forgotten to change the name and it was simpler answering to Hatch." Prudence sounded tired.

"What's the news?"

"Do you actually care?"

"Why else would I spend my time gathering up coins to make this very expensive phone call?"

"Sorry. I'm told there are after-effects. Lack of judgement is one. I wondered how it might show up and now I know. To answer your question, the tumour was benign but I'm not exactly home and dry. They're evasive about the details."

"Shit."

Prudence laughed weakly. "Don't worry. When I'm stronger I'll start harassing them."

"How do you feel, generally?"

"Distant. But tell me about you."

"You were right about Hester. She's fixed up a meeting with a TV production company. I know, it sounds weird but it is logical. I won't explain now, there may no point. No need to tire you."

"Will there be a price to pay?"

"Hester seems to think so. Her goodbye embraces are becoming more intense."

"And you? Will you be the grand chevalier?"

"Do you really want to talk about this?"

"It takes my mind off these bandages, the belief I'm lying in a hospital bed in Wallsend. Perhaps you're right. Holding the phone to my ear is a burden. No, that sounds crass. I'm glad you called. Call me after you've seen the TV people. I'll be better value."

"I'll do that. I'm sorry things are so…"

"…shitty?" Again the weak laugh.

Hatch had fed the slot throughout the call. Now he totted up change in the pocket he reserved for food and "others". Meals were his most flexible expense and their cost could usually be adjusted to cover the unexpected. Breakfast no longer happened; he could nourish himself in the middle of the day or in the evening, but not both. He preferred the latter even though it meant he had to occupy himself at midday to break up the afternoon's emptiness.

Today he planned to visit the recently opened Tamworth Power Station Museum. Not a mainstream attraction, even for him, but preferable to judging Crucifixion paintings in an art gallery. From his bed-sitter the 1½-mile walk would absorb time although there were disadvantages: a hole in his shoe was widening. Perhaps the "restored under-type semi-portable steam engines – the only two of their kind to be found in the world" would compensate.

In the event he was denied thrice over. When he arrived, more interested in sitting down than in the exhibits, he found the building was open Wednesday to Saturday. Today was Tuesday. Had it been open it would have closed in twenty minutes at 1 pm. In any case there was a £2 admission fee. The only positive discovery was a low wall on which he could sit and read Albert Speer's autobiography until an intermittent breeze flicked the pages once too often.

Nothing distracted him that evening. Jimmy was with an uncle, being trained for his long-planned entry into the business world. And Mr Wee was apparently satisfied with the counter assistance in the fish shop. Despite a growling stomach Hatch postponed preparation of his packet soup and tried yet again to find entertainment on his radio, a filling station freebie during the days when he drove a car. Since Radio 3's composer of the week was Alban Berg he turned to Radio 4 to find an alarming programme about saturated fats. However static made listening unbearable. He resumed Speer wondering how many of his engineering acquaintances would have responded as Speer did and grabbed the treasure trove Hitler made available.

The packet soup was a mistake. Remaindered down to a few pennies it belonged to an earlier, cruder era when adding water created a clotting agent rather than a foodstuff. Despite energetic stirring beds of unabsorbed powder formed like algae on a neglected garden pond and each had to be spooned out before Hatch dared sample a mouthful. During the spooning a blob of algae fell on to his shirt where it dried into a chancre. Wiping did nothing and the pea base left a green stain. This at least occupied part of the evening – crouched over the small hand basin, rubbing in Fairy soap, then precariously hanging the damp shirt on a loop of string outside the lavatory window.

The book kept on slipping away. Why, he asked himself, had he never noticed how slowly time passed? What were evenings like, shared with Prudence? What cured the fidgets? Neither he nor Prudence liked television. There had been DIY but it was hardly an obsession. Casting his mind back he wondered whether some of the DIY work had been unnecessary, simply killing time. Fairbairns had called him stick-in-the-mud, accused him of lacking intellectual resources. There was music but not on light summer evenings; CDs were for winter nights. The obvious solution was a woman except that he lacked the money, even at the most modest, non-carnal level. He also doubted his appeal, his ability to gain sympathy from women in general.

After all his early track record was variable. During his late teens women found him physically attractive but rarely agreed to a second date. He had a habit of driving conversation into stale and unprofitable byways, leaving the woman mute. Once, as a sixth former, he persuaded an exceptionally pretty girl to come to the cinema. What's more she came enthusiastically. Knowing she specialised in French he had booked tickets for an arts cinema showing of *Un Condamné à mort s'est échappé*. Fine. But when the prisoner cut his way through the door with a sharpened spoon handle Hatch objected on metallurgical grounds and continued to rehearse this on the bus home, unaware he was burying Bresson's delicate complexities under pettifogging detail. Hatch got the message when he was denied a final kiss – virtually a given in those days - and told sharply this outing was both the first and the last.

At university he worked at making his studies more enticing to others but then, more often than not, those interests were shared by Loughborough's somewhat distant female undergraduates. The trick was to be laconic, throwaway and confident, especially the latter. He could do that. He wanted to do that. But here, in what Mr Wee called an "efficiency" (Mr Wee had spent time in the USA), there were no women to practice on.

The phone woke him at seven-thirty in the morning. "It's Zach Ericsson. We're seeing each other later today."

It took Hatch time to connect the name with Gamester, the TV production company. "Yes, ten-thirty. Your offices in Edgbaston."

"Yesterday's plan. How flexible are you?"

"Totally."

"Could you get yourself to the Hilton Park service station on the M6 by eight-thirty? Taxi, obviously. If you're short keep him there and I'll pay. I need to get to Wilmslow by ten for a money matter. A must for the company. I'd postpone our meeting except I can't see fitting it in during the next fortnight. Thought I'd do the interview in the car as I drive; kill two birds with one stone."

"I'll get there. I take it you'd prefer me in trousers."

Ericsson roared with laughter. "Put 'em on in the taxi. You'll recognise me. Beard. Tee-shirt. Big vulgar car. A typical TV scenario."

Hatch had two twenty-pound notes, both allocated. That was it until the parts retailer paid him. It seemed risky but he suspected Ericsson would appreciate his enterprise if he paid the taxi himself, smoothing out transfer between vehicles. He dialled a local taxi company – an almost forgotten experience – and was relieved by a quote of thirty-three pounds. As he shaved he considered Ericsson's tee-shirt. Would he expect Hatch to be casually clothed? Probably not. Ericsson's view of engineers was likely to be as stereotyped as Hatch's view of TV executives.

"I didn't recognise the car so I can't tell if it's vulgar," he said as Ericsson gunned the engine down the sliproad on to the motorway.

"Chevrolet Corvette - the only sports car the Americans make. Longer than a Bentley yet it's only a two-seater. What it proves is I was a telly babe. A Corvette figured in a sixties series, Route 66. I promised myself I'd have one. Horribly impractical but I'm stuck with it now. Part of the image."

"I've heard of the model. Huge engine but quite primitive. Overhead valves if I recall."

"You could be right since I've no idea what overhead valves are. Guzzles petrol, if that's anything. Refresh my mind about your background."

Ericsson responded "Uh-huh." to most of the details. Only the mention of Tempest produced a reaction. "Washing machines. No shit!" Perhaps the brand name caught his attention.

"So – production engineer. What does that mean? Sounds dull-ish. Did it test your imagination?"

"All the time. Keeping production running is easy. The hard part is making things cheaper, standing a design on its head. The door lock on one model had nine separate pieces. I got it down to six and saved fifteen percent of the manufacturing costs. Thinking in 3D."

Ericsson liked the phrase. "Thinking in 3D," he said. Repeated it.

"I've been a racing mechanic. Cutting down weight without compromising car body strength."

"Compromising" pleased Ericsson too. For several minutes he squirted the Corvette up the outside lane, intimidating vehicles and forcing them to swing back into the centre lane - as if he were clearing his mind. Then he too took the centre lane. "We're designing a new show and I need to be secretive. Can you keep your mouth shut when you're out and about?"

"No problem. I lead a circumscribed life."

"Circumcised?"

"Circumscribed. Limited. Don't get about much. Tiny social circle."

"So it's not your dick," said Ericsson. "OK, here's the scene. Provisional name Superwoman but we're changing it because of copyright issues. Women compete on intelligence, strength, technical skills, social abilities, articulacy and... some other things. Back in the Bronze Age there was a similar show but it was a washout. The contestants just sat down and punched keyboards."

"I remember. The women wore plastic jump suits, as if they'd come by space ship. Beehive hairdos and lots of make-up."

"Why do you think it failed?" asked Ericsson.

"No spectacle. They could have been working supermarket check-outs."

"Supermarket check-outs! Yeah, I like that." By which, Hatch assumed, he liked the phrase. "You shoulda been around at the brain storming. Hester didn't say you were a words guy. So what's the answer."

"Something visual."

"Any ideas?"

Hatch thought for a moment. "You said technical skills. Making something? Assembling something?"

"That's half of it. The other half is a puzzle for the viewers."

Hatch saw how he might fit in. "How about a puzzle based on mechanics. Imagine a lop-sided see-saw: one end of the plank much longer than the other. At the short end, near the pivot, there's a heavy weight. The contestant has to place a light weight in the right place at the other end to make it balance."

A screeching occurred below the car as Ericsson braked from 95 mph to enter a slip road up to another service station. More screeching as he parked the car, engine still running, in a space intended for HGVs. "Draw me that out. There's paper in the glove compartment."

Hatch did so. Said, "Welcome to the Law of Levers. The pivot is called the fulcrum. The length of the plank makes up for the lighter weight. Not that viewers need know any of this. They'll know the contestant's got it right when the lever – or plank – is horizontal."

"Hey, neat. The Law of Levers. Anything else?"

Hatch paused, but only to underline what he had to say. "How about a set of gearwheels? All in different sizes. The task is to arrange them in the correct sequence. Viewers know it's correct because the competitor rotates the gear at one end – it could have a handle on it like a starting crank – and the gear at the other end turns just enough for a pointer to move from two o'clock to two thirty."

"You've lost me. But I get the general idea."

"No one counts the teeth or measures the wheel diameters. All they see is a clock face which scores the points."

"And you've got other ideas?" asked Ericsson.

"Of course. Dozens if you like. All visual."

"Based on bits and pieces generally available?"

"Some made up specially for better visuals. Take the set of gears: it makes sense for the clock pointer to move from two o'clock to half-past rather than some odd figure. But that wouldn't cost much. One other thing - the tasks would be designed to make sense for the audience."

Ericsson was chewing on a cocktail stick which had appeared from nowhere. "The gears, they'd be scaled up of course. Done in plastic?"

"Sure. Easier to colour. Er, shouldn't you be back on the motorway?"

Back in the outside lane Ericsson drove at over 100 mph but not, Hatch suspected, because of the money business in Manchester. Rather he'd been touched by the unexpected

"You were mech-eng at uni so none of this is new. I did PPE. There's a snobbism, isn't there? The art-farts think mech-eng is for people who lack imagination. But without trying you've turned ideas into television, something the densest viewer can see and understand. That's TV's job. When we get it wrong we end up with pictures of bearded men, dirt on their faces, lit by flames, pretending to be barbaric. That's when words haven't been turned into real images."

He chewed on the cocktail stick. "Is there more?"

Hatch was uneasy about the Corvette. "It might take five minutes' thought and a drawing board to work things out. Don't forget, the puzzles needn't be mechanical. Chemistry is even more fun. Even more spectacular."

"Chemistry! Yeah!"

"Er, you're doing 110."

In Manchester Hatch stayed in the car and used pen and paper to outline these new – ostensibly trivial – projects. He designed a load-bearing structure out of balsa, filled a defined volume from different containers, lifted via a combination of pulleys – all laboratory demonstrations made more entertaining by enlarging and decorating the equipment. With a dozen ideas sketched out Hatch leant back and feeling like Little Weed dozed off.

Noisily, ebulliently Ericsson swung open the door. "You got what you wanted?" asked Hatch, yawning.

"A shower of spondulicks. Ever heard that word?"

"Well, yes." Ericsson's deflation was palpable and Hatch hurriedly added, "After all I'm older than you."

Ericsson glanced at the paper on Hatch's lap. "More wizardry?"

"Competitors must calculate the answers not guess at them, that needs stressing. We're testing intelligence not luck. Superwomen must know the Law of Levers even if the viewers don't. Or, if you like, a boffin could explain the test beforehand in simple words."

"A boffin? You?"

"Good God, no. I'm not wearing make-up for anyone."

But Ericsson examined Hatch's face as if it were a map that led somewhere.

Back on the M6 he held the car to a considerate 85. "The boffin's good. Suppose we dressed you in a white coat and gave you some glasses…"

"With a slide rule sticking out of my pocket?" Hatch said. "Boffins are nothing if not old fashioned."

"Let's think about it. Look, I can't offer you the job until I've discussed things with the others but your suggestions are what we want. They must become Gamester's intellectual property. How do I do that?"

This was exhilarating. "I could number and sign the drawings and have you pay me cash for a day's consultancy. My receipt cedes ownership."

"Cash?"

"Haven't you got any?" asked Hatch, remembering the taxi.

"Well, sure. But not enough for that."

"What sort of…" His voice faded as the world of entertainment opened up. At first Ericsson had appeared naive and Hatch's suggestions infantile, unrelated to his working life. Now Mr Wee's bed-sitter, Prudence and Switzerland, the emptiness of his stomach were becoming fabulous pre-qualifications. "Write in a figure for the consultancy fee. Give me some cash, deduct it 'On account' on the receipt."

"That would cover it. For twenty-four or forty-eight hours at least, until Gamester's bean counter can look at it. Trouble is I'm not carrying much cash. Never do. Just a couple of hundred or so."

"Half would be ample."

Ericsson glanced across and laughed. "I'd forgotten the shitting taxi. Obviously, you're down to your last sou." He glanced at his watch. "Plenty of time. I've got a better idea. Let's go to Edgbaston."

Leaving Gamester's glass-enshrouded office and stepping into the rear of a pre-paid limousine, his back pocket wodged with £20 notes, Hatch was bemused and apprehensive. Between the front seats were decanters in a velvet lined tantalus and a working television which he quickly switched off. Ineluctably he heard Baudinière speaking proudly, perhaps gleefully, about cell manufacture in his Breton factory. Speaking from another world. Of another world.

THE computer session, ostensibly about databases, was long gone. Jimmy's voracious mind quickly grasped the principles and converted the data into a grid based on pocket money from his father and Mr Tan, his uncle. Tan was an accountant who paid Jimmy for sorting through clients' invoices. Hatch thought it more likely Jimmy was being taught book-keeping as part of his father's master plan. Jimmy confessed financial matters were beneath him

"They're not a career," said Hatch. "Just one of the skills if you run your own business."

"A fish shop?"

"Well, yes. Your father keeps books. But he probably hopes you'll take up something else."

"Money. He says I must learn about money. I'm not sure. Is money interesting?"

"Very interesting," said Hatch diplomatically. "And very exciting. Listen to the prime minister. But what would you like to do?"

Jimmy moved uneasily and looked at his shoes. "I am too young. My father says."

"Too young for what?"

More shuffling then Jimmy stared down into Hatch's soul. "A dancer."

"A dancer!"

"At school we saw Firebird. You know Firebird? It was perfect. That is what I want. In my heart. " His eyes shone with tears.

Hatch envisaged - with something close to horror - the disappointment and misery that would pile up in Jimmy's life. A life based on division. Wrestling with economics in sixth form, something similar at university, but always the secret yearning. Did Mr Wee know? Suspect? And now Hatch's dismay shifted from Jimmy to his father. Dancing! It would betray the family. Worse, it would prove Mr Wee didn't know his son, that those hard-worked expectations were built on sand. Not that the future would change, of course. Jimmy would go on to do economics or whatever else had been laid down. But now his father would know his heart wasn't in it. Or was Chinese stoicism inborn, would Jimmy be shown the error of his ways? And accept them?

"You have not discussed this?"

"I dare not."

And then, quickly, Jimmy's worries disappeared; another fascination had emerged. A secret thrill which fascinated both him and his father. "You still do not work?"

"Untrue. I worked today," said Hatch and took £20 notes from his back pocket.

Jimmy was disappointed. "And tomorrow?"

"Perhaps."

Ah, the unreliable occidental. "Do you know Firebird?" Jimmy asked casually, as if the answer didn't matter.

"It's written by Stravinsky," said Hatch. "He was Russian."

Jimmy was apparently satisfied.

Hatch left by the side door to avoid being asked to work at the fish shop counter. At the Harvester, just opened for dinner, he ordered a large steak and a carafe of anonymous red wine, paid in cash and demanded plenty of change. A kiosk at the restaurant meant he could avoid the two urine-tainted phone boxes in the street.

Prudence sighed and said, "It doesn't sound like you. I've no doubt you're capable. But – entertainment! Am I being horribly uncomplimentary?"

"It's a mystery to me too. And there's no guarantee I'll get the job."

"Will you take it?"

"There's another possibility. A fabricator who's switching to product manufacture. More my sort of thing."

"And no indebtedness."

Hatch said nothing.

"I'm glad there are options. You need work, it's your true source of oxygen."

"Sounds as if you're improving."

She laughed. "One of my vital signs."

"Is it… bearable?"

"Your call helps."

"No more real news from the doctors?"

"Professional mumbo-jumbo."

"I'll call tomorrow. A pocketful of twenties is reassuring. I had a steak for dinner."

"You never cared for steak. Said it was unimaginative. The American default for a luxury meal."

He hadn't eaten steak for decades. "Perhaps I'll see what's on at the cinema."

"Now that would be totally against the grain."

13. CLARE

Bank charges

NORMALLY erect and stoic, Birgitta entered the kitchen crouching slightly as Clare sipped an early-morning coffee. Whispered words about unbearable tooth pain. Clare welcomed the opportunity to be decisive, phoned her dentist (University of Otago 1984), and forced him into an out-of-hours appointment which left her smug and pulsing with adrenaline. Having delivered the numbed au pair to the equally numbed New Zealander she drove home again to pick up Nick for nursery. Rather than tackle the complexities of transferring the child's seat to the Jaguar she took Birgitta's Fiesta and passed an awkward ten minutes at odds with the manual gearbox.

The nursery was close to Knole Park and announced its presence ostentatiously. Road signs hectored motorists not to put "society's future" at risk, a welter of flags fluttered their multi-cultural messages and the playground was equipped with durable, obviously expensive equipment. Nursery visits were never a favourite experience and Clare loathed the forced community of mothers. Several actively resented that she could afford an au pair; others with part-time jobs in and around Sevenoaks asked intrusive questions about her employment. Nick, freed from the car seat and unaffected by Birgitta's absence, walked quickly towards the children milling around the entrance. Clare had hoped to be away like a wraith but the carer who received Nick's lunchbox was new and asked her to identify herself, alerting nearby mothers.

"Is Birgitta not well, Mrs Kepler?" asked one, standing tactically between Clare and the exit.

"Just a dental appointment."

"I hear Nick is fitting in very well."

Keen to depart Clare nevertheless stopped and turned. No mother, however impatient, could walk away from a compliment to her child. "He wasn't clinging to me when we arrived this morning. Never a backward look"

"Everyone's impressed with Birgitta. What agency did she come from one? We tried a couple and weren't impressed. You were lucky to get a Scandinavian."

Birgitta's father was a divisional director with Electrolux. They had met at a defence contractors' conference in Berlin and Clare found him keen to separate Birgitta from the drug scene in Stockholm. But this inquisitive mother surely knew that. "I avoided the agencies. I got to know Birgitta's family through a business contact."

"Through work! I believe you do something terribly specialised."

Clare had suffered these attempts at intimacy before. This one seemed only seconds away from an invitation to coffee. Brightly she replied, "Not at all specialised. To tell the truth I'm out of work at the moment. A charge on the state, you might say."

Questioning had its limits. "I'm so sorry to hear that."

No doubt they were all watching as she unlocked the Fiesta, agreeing among themselves about a loss of status, confirming that the news of her unemployment was true. News that might start a few hares, not least among the nursery owners fearing for their extortionate fees. Clare didn't mind about this. Not being an instinctive mother left her uncomfortable among those who believed they were. As well as hideously bored.

Birgitta was sitting outside the surgery in the sun, operated on yet cheerful. Clare was glad to hand over the Fiesta and its manual gearbox. She asked, "Do mothers at the nursery insist on chatting?"

Birgitta laughed. "They try. But then they discover my English is really quite bad."

Clare laughed back. "You're so well organised and I've been terribly remiss. I don't think I've ever asked whether you enjoy yourself here. It must be terribly dull."

"Observing the English? That's not dull."

The great attraction was Nick as Clare knew.

THE grand house had a porte cochère wide enough to take the Jaguar. Which was just as well because the alternative approach would have been to drive over the adjoining lawn. When Clare stopped under a ceiling of biscuit-coloured stone the passenger door was opened by a youth in a striped waistcoat. "Good afternoon, Mrs Kepler. If you'd like to leave the keys in the ignition I'll park the car and have luggage brought to your room."

In the cavernous reception area a slightly older youth, in a similar waistcoat which Clare saw was decorated with the bank's logo, came forward smiling. "Welcome to A Bras Hall, Mrs Kepler. I'll show you to your room."

They entered a lift artfully hidden from eighteenth-century splendours and rose soundlessly. "I'm Jeremy. Number five on the phone system if you need anything. The background information and your agenda are in the room. There's plenty of time before your first appointment if you fancy a stroll in the grounds. To the northwest there are a couple of Henry Moores."

Room hardly described the suite she'd been given but by now Clare's scepticism was unchecked. The laptop computer, the bottle of Cristal and the selection of never-to-be-read hardback best-sellers were intended to say she was here at the behest of big money. Picking up Swarowski binoculars to examine the distant reclining figures she reminded herself that money's comings and goings needed electronic systems. Eventually the interview would resort to mundane talk of data storage, processing speeds, levels of security, back-up and customisation and at that point the lavishness of her bed would cease to be to the bank's advantage.

As it happened the most remarkable item was Adam, a functionary from human resources who had mysteriously managed to avoid

the taint of his profession. Casual, witty, self-mocking and sometimes profane, he explained the programme.

"We start out by intimidating you. And none too subtly. You
wouldn't have been the first to wonder whether you'd scratch your
car getting it through that ridiculous horse-and-carriage job at the
front door. After which a waistcoat probably suggested you might
care to inspect the Henry Moores. Fine if you've had an education,
not so if you haven't. Henry Moore? Didn't he play for Darlington.
And did you notice the Cristal? Who in their right mind would dare
drink champagne when they're down here on a job interview?"

"I might if I thought I'd ploughed it."

"You see!" said Adam. "Education! Nobody at my comprehen-
sive ever ploughed an exam. OK. Starting in half an hour you talk
to a couple of guys – always guys I'm afraid – about your career so
far. Not a railway timetable account. Say what you're proud of, your
management triumphs. Blow your own trumpet.

"Dinner follows. Not really an interview more a social event.
Discuss your interests with some of our senior managers. The side
of you that isn't covered in a CV. Proof you're a human being.

"Tomorrow's different," he added. "It is the nature of the job.
In a phrase – the bank's spokesman about the bank's IT. You'll
study a couple of scenarios and then answer press questions. You'll
be tested but not to destruction. We need to know how you handle
technical information which might show us in a bad light. By which
I don't mean lying or even covering up. Rather, telling the truth in a
way the media won't – preferably can't - misunderstand. A good tip:
imagine you own the bank. Anything I can tell you?"

Clare poured out Evian. "It sounds like a short shortlist. Given
you're assembling the great and the good"

"Well spotted. It's a very short shortlist."

"I'm a woman. Is that significant?"

"You want me to cut my bloody throat? I repeat, it's a short
shortlist."

Clare opened her brief case. "I wasn't sure about this. Last Saturday I appeared in a longish article in The Guardian. Not exactly

CV material but it is an impartial view of who I am and what I've done. Needless to say it's entirely independent and it includes one or two warts. Is it of interest?"

Adam took the colour magazine and glanced quickly through the story. "How did it come about?"

Clare explained and he looked surprised. "She volunteered? Well she can't have taken you for a simpleton. Attracting a journalist's interest – for the right reasons, of course - is definitely a black art. I'll have copies made and pass it along. Only one thing better than blowing your own trumpet and that's having someone do it for you. Anything else?"

"Just a thought? Is the bank changing its image?"

He looked at her differently, more professionally. "Why do you ask that?"

"Are you head of human resources?"

"Too young?"

"Not only that. It's obvious the bank takes this appointment pretty seriously. That's what I'd expect and that's why you're here. Yet you're quite different from any HR manager I've ever met."

He laughed ruefully. "You'll be delighted to learn I'm not at liberty to comment on that. But if you bring it up at some appropriate point I won't dissuade you." Now he became brisker. "I'll get the photocopies dispatched. If you'd like to wait here, read a magazine, I'll be back soon and take you through."

Instead she took stock of the lounge. Luxurious of course and he'd been right: luxury intended to intimidate. Yet the conversation would in the end play to her strengths rather than theirs.

The two male interrogators were not bank employees and had been hired to ask questions and sift answers. Both were besuited and serious. "Our names are not important, Mrs Kepler. You won't meet us again. You won't object if we record our exchanges. If your application is unsuccessful you are entitled to have the recording destroyed."

The Guardian article was treated as if it might be an elaborate fabrication. The origins of her meeting with Alison took almost ten minutes to discuss causing Clare herself to wonder about the plausibility of meeting Alison by accident. Did such encounters really happen? Were they by their nature suspicious?

Finally the two suits turned to the article itself. "Is it fair? Is it accurate?"

Clare suppressed a sigh. "Fair? It's the reporter's opinion, how she saw me. I was surprised she found me slightly pedantic but I can't argue. There's always that risk when you deal with technical matters for a lay audience. Explaining systems has been part of my professional life and if I come across as pedantic I'm disappointed. At least she understood me. If I had to choose between being exact or being populist I'd go for the former."

"She doesn't provide an example of this... failing."

"She includes a phrase about a module in the Sigma heads-up display. It's not a description rather a label. If she'd asked for detail I'd have held back. The information is classified. That was at the back of my mind and perhaps I sounded stiff."

"It could be a factor here... with the bank."

Clare said, "I take your point. It's the first time I've been accused of being official and you'll notice there's no hint when she describes how I spoke to the school-children about physics."

"She talks about your confidence. Neither of us is sure whether she's suggesting you're over-confident."

"I agree. She's ambiguous. I 'dismissively' reeled off a summary of the student work I did at the Clarendon. As if I were pooh-poohing what she imagined to be advanced particle research. As if I were keen to prove I was very clever. In fact the particle work was low grade and I didn't think it worth her attention."

"What about accuracy?"

"As far as the physics is concerned, there are slip-ups. But I sympathise there. I've written for consumer publications and been limited as to how much I could say. The trick is to use a sort of shorthand which is comprehensible to non-physicists yet doesn't make me wince when I read it back. Her shorthand isn't as fine-tuned as mine. But she's pretty accurate about the business side, although she does make me sound a little too prescient. I was quite lucky the balance sheet improved a year after I arrived at Confexxion."

"Confexxion? Tell us about that."

"Nothing I've done anywhere else did so much good. But I started almost from ground zero. The company was backward about information flow and when you replace hand-keyed destinations with bar-codes you can fairly expect higher throughput and fewer errors. On the other hand it was a big change for the despatchers; there should have been interim technology before I arrived. As it was the despatchers resented what I'd done and some refused to use it. There was conflict and some job losses."

"But the board were, shall we say, grateful?"

Clare said, "It's a shame the company was acquired. The directors were ready to move into the twenty-first century; to take a long term view."

There followed close analysis of the Confexxion changes after which she gave them a sanitised account of removing the dry wood during the gunsight contract. In her heart of hearts she still saw this as a feminist triumph but her deliberately dry words turned it into a series of logical management steps and a hoped-for response.

"You were quite young?"

She looked demure.

They wanted to know why Sigma's tender had failed. Clare speculated carefully without appearing to complain.

"In the end I can't explain it. But I did hear from an impeccable MoD source that the two tenders were very close; the implication being there was technically nothing between them. I know enough from sitting on government advisory committees that in such cases procurement often feels free to look for political reasons which can help the minister make up his mind. I'm not for a minute suggesting it happened but the prospect of additional employment in an area can be a consideration."

"You're philosophical about the failure?"

"I know our system did everything they asked for. If it hadn't the decision – which was long delayed – would have been made much earlier. For what it's worth the MoD approached me within forty-eight hours to see whether I cared to join their facility." She shook her head. "Not my cup of tea, really."

"Too institutional?"

Clare saw that trap a mile off. "I prefer the ideas side. Even though Sigma didn't get the contract I know we came up with a good system. I'm proud of that."

She reconsidered a recent dilemma, then made up her mind. "There was one other positive outcome. I appointed someone out of university to the Sigma contract and gave him real responsibility. When I turned down the MoD they approached him. Not for the same job. But it was clear they recognised the quality of our work."

At the dinner everyone made strenuous efforts to prove this was an interview that wasn't an interview. The head of investment gave a spirited and articulate defence of Benny Hill as the key to British humour.

"But would he have had a place in the bank?" Clare asked.

"Proof of lateral thinking. Running his videos in a sealed-off room like the Japanese are said to have. Frustrated employees beating seven bells out of an inflatable model of the chief executive. Benny would be ideal preparation for our planning meetings."

They discussed winding down after a hard day. Clare noticed no one mentioned stopping off at a bar. And despite noisy comments about the Richebourg that came with the rack of lamb various tactics were used to avoid taking a third glass.

Being under scrutiny Clare knew she had to initiate as well as respond. And to take risks. She asked whether banks generated loyalty among their employees, whether they expected to do so. This turned the tables. To some extent the managers were also on trial and found it necessary to match her, risk for risk, and to avoid predictable PR boilerplate. One of them offered a dubious proof of loyalty on the grounds that banks did little mutual head-hunting.

Clare wryly pretended to ask for advice about lack of competition at her tennis club. Adam, the unconventional human resources manager, suggested she tested herself in tournaments.

"They usually last a full weekend. Tendering involves tight deadlines and I do work odd hours."

"And you're a mother," said someone else, making the point for her.

"A mother who already makes good use of the au pair."

"So you play the pro and you're careful not to beat him," said Adam, laughing.

Tempted to add, "Especially since he's a man." she held back.

Perhaps because most of the managers were of an age to have teenage children they asked, wearisomely, about school holidays. Should these be a source of improvement or relaxation?

"My son is only four so I've yet to decide," said Clare. "But based on my own holidays too often it's a case of parents showing off. No kid would ever opt for, say, a transatlantic exchange. My father, who is otherwise a sweetie, wasn't above trying it on. When I said I favoured Italy he suggested I stayed with a fine-arts friend of his in Florence. I'm sure he wanted to drop hints about it at some future business meeting. But I wanted to lie on the beach."

"And you ended up on the beach?"

"As I said, he's a sweetie most of the time."

And so it went on culminating in the offer of digestifs, turned down almost in unison. The strain lay not in avoiding errors or devising impressive ideas, but in maintaining the fiction that this was a social event and that she and they were supposed to be enjoying themselves. Finally it was over and she retreated to her room to take her second bath of the evening. Lying in a comforting soup of one of the many free unguents she turned, as she knew she would, to Alan Harding.

They met for lunch at a temple of haute cuisine in Belgravia which somebody much older than him must have recommended. It was a mistake but merely the first in a chain. Because she'd encouraged and reassured him he decided her interest was more than professional. This was quickly apparent and Clare was astounded she could ever have looked forward to the meal. To have briefly regarded him as adult was pure delusion. The shyness was still there but mixed in with a desperate and disorganised sense of the chase.

He had stood up at the table, saying "Hello Clare," kissing her with great awkwardness on the left ear. His fragile confidence evaporated immediately and he sat down as if his legs had given way. The change was so complete she felt she had to comfort him or at least pretend she hadn't known what was in his mind.

Complimenting him about the MoD job she gabbled. The sommelier stood unregarded as she transferred helpful names and telephone numbers from her address book to the back of an envelope. Only after the frozen look had faded from his face did she sit back.

But this was only the prelude. As he had misread her before, so he misread her again. In sparing his feelings she was thought to be affectionate and he became predatory, watching her keenly, tacking double-entendres to the ends of her sentences.

"Procurement, like everything else at the ministry, is impossibly hierarchical," she said. "But there's no need to start at the bottom."

"As the actress said to the bishop." He may even have winked.

It wasn't the offensiveness so much as being out of date, as if he'd read it up in a phrasebook.

It was depressing watching him re-assert himself. He leant over the table, causing her to sit up and draw away but this too was an error. During a break in conversation he suggested they go for a stroll in St James Park, loading "stroll" with clumsy meaning.

From then on it was a matter of endurance. Her short, discouraging answers eventually blunted his hopes and he became sulky. She paid for the meal, horrified that he'd intended to spend such a sum. Outside she made a commonplace excuse about hurrying away but he wasn't quite finished.

"I got it wrong?" he said, truculently.

Subtlety had had its day. "Yes, I think you got it wrong."

"You aren't looking for someone young."

"Nor middle-aged nor elderly. " And walked away.

Now, in a cooling bath, she realised why teachers who interfere with the taught are said to have broken a trust. To ease her conscience she had mentioned him to his advantage during the afternoon interview. That done she knew there was no one in whom she could have confided her embarrassments during that lunch. No one. Not even Chantal. She would have laughed: *aucun probleme!*

Breakfast was followed by another briefing from Adam. Again he stressed the importance of the two role-playing exercises. As if to raise apprehension.

"Your technical abilities yesterday were more or less a given. These two tests will prove whether you can handle the job. Whether you can think on your feet. You've done role playing I take it?"

"Oh yes. But I'm assuming these exercises will be properly designed. Not the usual childishness."

"Properly designed?" he said, surprised.

"Not a scenario which holds the candidate to only one reaction. A deliberately loose set-up is much better and really does test reaction times."

Yesterday he had joked about the bank's attitudes. Not today. Had he a personal stake in the tests? She went on: "The tight scenario is really just a memory test: restriction A leaves only option B. A bit like a pinball machine. With the loose one you're forced to look several steps ahead. If the setters are playing by the rules there may be several legitimate conclusions."

Now his face was a mask. "I see you've gone into this thoroughly. Which would you prefer?"

"The loose one. Riskier but success means something."

But she had not told him everything. Having read her 500-word briefing she had seen fruitful holes. Holes which could be exploited. She would be required to explain why an eight-figure sum had been transferred to the wrong account, simultaneously causing a string of incorrect entries on the records back-up. Other disasters had then happened downstream, offering the press a field day on the bank's poor IT security. Since Clare had no prior knowledge of banking systems the setter had used jargon and inter-system complexity to confuse her. All pointless since the daily newspapers and TV reporters would be equally ignorant of such arcane information and the proper response would hinge on simpler matters.

Three young men played the role of the putative journalists. Clipboards showed they were working in concert and that they would lay traps by cross-referencing Clare's answers. Each was jacketless to give meagre evidence of authenticity, trickery that would have been more plausible if they'd dispensed with their braces.

The initial questions were plodding and covered the brief's inarguable facts. Clare answered half a dozen of them curtly then took events into her own hands. "Perhaps we could hurry up things. The bank admits that the transfer failed and that this appears to have caused a chain reaction. At the moment there's a prima facie case for saying this was not accidental but fraudulent. The key technical issue is that the local records back-up failed. Now I don't need to tell you gentlemen - " Her tone teetered on the sarcastic. " – that no bank would ever install a back-up which was likely to fail accidentally. Banks depend heavily on accurate record-keeping and this particular link is potentially the most vulnerable. Because of this security here is raised to what computer specialists describe as a 'redundant' level. But, since systems can still fail and it's vital to prevent erroneous data feeding on, the design would of course be failsafe. This didn't happen."

The three journalists had ceased to be interrogators and now gazed at Clare, lips slightly parted. She went on, "I invite you to draw your own conclusions. The most likely reason for a non-failsafe failure is human intervention. By a person directly familiar with the system or informed by someone who is. Because of this strong likelihood we have done what any responsible financial institution would do and called in the Fraud Squad. You'll appreciate this is as much as I can say on the matter though the minute we have positive news I'll be pleased to pass it on. Any questions?"

The final sentence was rhetorical. The journalists cleared their throats and looked around for guidance while the two adjudicators talked to each other in low urgent voices. Adam, who sat close to the adjudicators, had resumed the mask he had worn earlier that morning.

They broke, ostensibly for coffee. Clare walked out through open French windows on to a terrace and tried to imagine the dénouement as she gazed out over the artificially trim landscape: a banker's landscape. Finally an adjudicator found her and told her that her interview was "complete" and that she might now leave. She would be informed in due course.

Having packed her bag and taken the lift to the huge entrance hall she found that neither Jeremy nor her car keys were immediately available and was left waiting in a part of the building where time, it seemed, stood still.

It was still mid-morning and she was home before lunch. Since the interviews had been negotiated by her management agency she rang Hildegard and gave her a complete account which Hildegard recorded and agreed to transcribe. "You'll get the transcription tomorrow morning. What's your reaction?"

"The first day's interview was thorough and competent. They made good use of Alison's article and I've no complaints. The dinner was a diffuse affair, but justifiable, I suppose. Since they stressed the job has an important public side they were entitled to see how I behaved socially. The role playing just hadn't been thought through. I could have trotted along but there was a risk they were setting a trap and I would have looked like a technical nitwit. I don't think it was a trap, judging by the reactions of their impossibly young human resources guy. I behaved exactly as I would have done if I'd just come back from holiday and someone had thrust a hot potato at me with ten minutes' preparation. It may be argued I should have behaved more smoothly. I was told that I was on a very short shortlist and have no way of knowing whether the others had already been interviewed or not."

"I suppose we'll have to wait for their reaction."

This came two days later. Clare had not met "the bank's high standards" and would not be offered the post. It was the first time she had been rejected for a position she had applied for.

Hildegard was angrier than Clare. "You're entitled to a fuller explanation. Would you like me to do some probing?"

Clare was inclined to let things drop. But perhaps it was better to be completely informed, however salutary. "Why not? Go ahead."

That evening she and Jerry had dinner at a pub they'd used throughout their married life. Years ago it had offered simple but good cooking, now it had aspirations – just this side of intolerable - towards a gastropub. They ordered an old favourite, liver and bacon built up into a mini-architectural dome, and she brought Jerry up to date. "That's a first," he said.

Jerry continued, "On the other hand cock-up is more likely than conspiracy. They were all men, weren't they? Perhaps they put their heads together and decided you knew too much. A rare case of leaving the pisser outside."

"What pisser?"

"LBJ. If someone's pissing into your tent it's better to ask him inside. Political savvy."

She was surprised, even touched. Comforted too by the familiarity of the scrubbed non-matching tables and the good quality, if expensively labelled, paintings. "Do you think I had this coming?"

"How do you mean?"

"I've had an easy life. Nobody's ever smacked me in the face."

"You've earned your easy life."

She laughed. "You thought differently a couple of weeks ago. All that talk about the ageing golf pro."

He frowned. "I was just jealous. Hell, I'm entitled to be jealous. Besides you were right. For a man with my brain I have the perfect job."

"Including teaching daddy's little darling to use a nine iron?"

Jerry looked puzzled. "Which one was…? Oh yes, Daphne. Drives a two-seater Merc. Wrists like jelly. You know, golf pros are supposed to be true money-grubbers. Boris was typical. Half what I earn comes from lessons and theoretically I'll teach anyone. But if after the first ten seconds there's no point, it gets distasteful."

"Yet she persists?" asked Clare.

"Having lessons gives her status, the only status she's got. She's spoilt rotten and she's failed at everything. So she chats her silly head off, saying 'Jerry tells me this.' or worse, 'Jerry says I'm improving.' God knows, I need the money but teaching her is like going on the streets."

Clare touched his hand. "You seller of dreams. But there are other, better days?"

"Days when there's just golf. Even now nothing beats a well struck drive, down the fairway, knowing it's an iron to the green. The buzz was always there; it's still there. But how about you?"

She giggled. "I've just been slapped. Perhaps I'll be a better person." Without referring to him she ordered kummel digestifs and he approved of their past associations.

HILDEGARD called before nine, her voice urgent, perhaps fearful. "Can we talk. Not over the phone. Can you come up to town? No, I'll come down. That's not right. I'm sorry, I don't know what I'm saying."

"Hildy, calm down. It's bad, is it?"

"It's bad."

"Then I'll come up. Sandwiches in the park."

"To hell with that. I'll book the Caprice."

"Sandwiches in the park, Hildy! Restaurants are rotten for bad news. Everybody stares."

Sitting on a bench she watched Hildegard from two hundred yards away. Long legs and long ash-blonde hair reminiscent of Hildegard Neff. Once, she'd asked whether there was an intentional link with the German film-star but, inevitably, her Hildegard was too young to know. Clare stood up as Hildegard approached and they linked arms and moved round the lake. Eventually they sat on the grass, creating a cordon sanitaire.

"Two shrimp salads, two splits of New Zealand sauvignon blanc and two disgusting plastic wine glasses," said Clare opening an M&S bag.

But Hildegard, normally brisk, managerial and confiding, looked strained. Clare became less brisk. "Come on Hildy. I'm a grown up."

"It's so barbaric." After agreeing at least to poke at her salad, she started to speak. "I knew I wouldn't get anywhere with anyone senior. Especially since this sickening Adam seems to be implicated. So I worked on one of the juniors, fibbing my heart out. A serious effect on your career, that sort of thing. Promised her secrecy."

She laughed harshly, "Surprised myself. Proved I can be a complete bastard."

Clare waited.

"She phoned me from a call box during lunch break. She's too junior to have any direct connections but she picked up what mattered. There have of course been ructions. Adam was closeted twice with his supreme boss and now keeps his door closed. That's significant; previously he claimed to be an open-door manager. What a wanker.

"According to my snout there seemed to be no link between the role playing and your not getting the job. So she took an enormous risk. Waited until Adam was out of his room and glanced at the file. And it's true, there is no connection – or, shall we say, no official connection."

She stopped and looked away. Clare continued to wait.

Hildegard took a piece of paper from her purse. "Here it is verbatim. 'Although we emphasised the public nature of the post Clare Kepler paid no attention to her appearance throughout the two days of the interview. Her clothing was drab and unimaginative. She wore no make-up and her short-cropped hair was obviously cut for convenience. We have no argument with her age even if this were legally permissible. After all, it would have been simplicity itself not to shortlist her. Her technical competence is everything we required. But it was beyond our remit to guide her on physical presentation. Interestingly she asked the HR manager about changes in the bank's image. He neither confirmed nor denied this for obvious reasons. Mrs Kepler failed to make the further inference that a change in our image might well require a change in hers. This is a delicate matter and it is important that we re-emphasise, if we have to, that the appointment of Miss Flanagan was based on both her technical abilities and her skills as a communicator.'."

Hildegard stopped reading and lifted her head. "It's a cover-up, isn't it? Why else would he talk about your business suit as drab and unimaginative? He cocked up the role playing and he's got out of it this way."

"So if Miss Flanagan played her role before I did she swallowed the defective brief?"

"It seems so. But what matters is this memo. We have concrete grounds for discrimination. We could - ".

"Oh Hildy, we will do nothing."

14. CLARE

Redressing the future

AS A journalist, are you corruptible?"

"You're asking the Humbert Wolfe question, aren't you?"

"Never heard of him!"

> *"You cannot hope to bribe or twist*
> *(Thank God!) the British journalist.*
> *But, seeing what the man will do*
> *Unbribed, there's no occasion to."*

Clare laughed. "I'm turning that on its head. It's bribery I have in mind. Lunch at The Savoy for five minutes' advice."

"Do I choose the claret? I take it the job fell through?"

"And I fell with it. One thing I must insist: everything will be off-record. I warn you, you'll be tempted. But no notes. You can pick claret as far back as 1968 if that will soften the blow."

"Sounds like a deal."

At the Savoy Alison read the memorandum. "You were right about going off-record. I could make a mint."

"Does that mean you want more compensation? On top of the claret?"

"Good grief, Clare, I'm not that greedy. Your secret's safe." Alison looked out at the dining room with its widely separated circular tables. "This is the place for just such a discussion. A haunt of male privilege. There's nobody here with their mistresses. Or their wives for that matter. How was the article?"

"Honest. A reasonable account. My interviewers used it to ask questions. That part went well."

"So it's the other bit we're discussing?"

"More or less. Let's order and make this a proper lunch. Here's the wine list."

After the briefest scrutiny Alison pointed to a comparatively modest Chateauneuf. "My palate isn't sophisticated. I like Rhone wines. A pricey Bordeaux would probably be wasted. Besides, after that horrible memo I prefer to show solidarity, not take advantage. What I said still holds. I liked you then, I like you now."

"I can't say how much I appreciate that."

The conversation and most of the wine were postponed until they reached the cheese. Clare leant back. "You mentioned something off the cuff – other journalists dressing scruffily as an act of independence. But you took the other option. A decent appearance makes interviewees more comfortable. I should have taken that to heart."

"It's no big deal. Try any boutique."

"It's not just the clothes. I lack the ability to assess myself. Until now I've been lucky. Grooming wasn't important. With some employers it would have even raised suspicions. But things have changed. Appearance counts when you're in the public gaze. Certainly if you're a woman. And, much as it irritates me, I have to consider my age."

"Hell, Clare, you're hardly - "

Clare raised her hand. "You're not here to dispense comfort. Look as hard at me as you looked at yourself. I have no idea how old you are and that's the point. I see a lively intelligent professional whose age isn't a factor. The first time we met you wore a strongly patterned dress. I remember thinking I'd never wear that in a hundred years. For you the dress worked. It matched how you saw yourself. Tell me how you see me."

Alison sipped her wine. "You're asking a lot."

Clare sighed. "I suppose I am. I have a friend in Sevenoaks, a Frenchwoman. It just so happens she's out of the country but I'm not sure she would be the right person for advice. Very heavy make-up. Clothes that are savagely fashionable. An attacking spirit.

I'm British. Correction, I'm English. I need to emerge with my nationality intact." She stared. "Are you worried I can't stand the truth? That I'm not used to being vulnerable? Let me lay the groundwork."

Without sparing any detail she told Alison about Alan Harding, about the embarrassment and the sense of responsibility. About her inability to strike the right note. "It's odd, really. In one sense I might have felt flattered. A youth like that. But it should never have happened. Ultimately I was desolate I couldn't discuss it with anyone. Yet here I am."

Alison listened intently. "I wasn't serious. I'll do what I can. But I have my own vulnerabilities. Like cigarettes."

They walked along the Embankment and Alison told her what needed to be done. It was easier than sitting face to face. On Westminster Bridge they did face each other. "These are just my ideas, Clare. I could be wrong."

"I don't think so. You've confirmed what I couldn't face up to. What you say has a ring of truth. My dear, I'm very grateful."

"I called you pedantic. I didn't get that right."

Clare said, "You were probably right at the time. Now there are changes to be made so why shouldn't I change that as well. We will meet again, won't we?"

"My treat. A ploughman's at the Lamb and Flag?"

"Where's that?"

"I'll let you know."

DOCTOR Panchauri was either Indian or Pakistani. His sibilants were still noticeable but the sing-song cadence had been absorbed by the need to speak comfortingly and often evasively about his patients' ability to smile.

"A slight forward misalignment of the two incisors. Easily corrected. I am surprised this was not done when you were a schoolgirl."

"I had different priorities."

"What greater priority is there than a wonderful smile?"

"I wanted to become a physicist."

"Ah." Sales patter took second place to an advanced profession. "Which of course you did."

Clare opened her eyes. "Why are you so sure?"

"My dear Mrs Kepler, I am a cosmetic orthodontist. I am concerned with appearances. For ten years you concentrated on your work. I suspect you were successful. Now you are taking a step back, reviewing yourself. You are looking for the extras. A good car, perhaps. A charming expression. I can at least give you the latter."

She smiled at "ten years".

Doctor Panchauri continued. "You ask yourself whether a woman of your intelligence should take trouble with your looks. Your intelligence makes you a confident physicist. Your smile will make you a confident – and even more desirable – woman."

"Will it be worth braces?"

"Mrs Kepler! This is the twentieth century! No more unsightly cables. No more obvious metalwork. I will give you a system which is almost invisible. You can even take it out for short periods."

"And how long must I wear it?" Clare asked.

"Ah, if it's speed you're after there is a system with a single thin wire – hardly noticeable. In your case, say six weeks."

"Uncomfortable?"

Sometimes even Doctor Panchauri's euphemisms ran out. "You will need… to get used to it."

These were the initial assessments; fitting would be in ten days. When she was about to leave he used both hands to take hers. "It will change you, I promise."

Turning from Wimpole Street into Wigmore Street she noticed a boutique and stopped at the window, something she would never have done a few weeks ago. Two silken dresses: one far too celebratory, perhaps suitable for Ascot, the other for a beanpole eighteen-year-old. The impulse that had taken her to the orthodontist caused her to push open the boutique door and left her standing in the centre of the shop, mute, without a plan.

"May I help you?" Was that a subjunctive? At least she hadn't been called madame.

"I'm rather at a loss. I tend to have clothes made for the office. Dark colours, conservatively cut. I'm looking for something lighter, more casual."

"For the office?" The assistant was probably Clare's age but tricked out for effect. The colour on her cheeks moved through several gradations, the eye shadow was satanic.

"I suppose so."

"I'm not sure…. At the moment we're outdoor-themed."

Was that it, then? Had this uncharacteristic effort been wasted? "None of your clothing is meant to be worn indoors?" Intending to express surprise Clare knew she had sounded sarcastic.

But the assistant laughed smoothly. "I'll take that as a challenge. Let me see, I'd say you are a ten?"

"Closer to a twelve, I fear."

"And your colouring. Mild tawny, perhaps? Hair mid-brown but it looks lighter because it's cut short." No mention that grey might be the reason. "Blues I think are out. You might get away with a suede effect. Probably green but it would have to be one of the matts, moving towards sage. So let's stay with those two."

Clare ceded all authority. She emerged forty minutes later carrying two carrier bags in a deep gloss material which shouted extreme expenditure. In one a two-piece lightweight suit in Elgin green, its pseudo-Armani looseness secured ("but not too tightly, I beg of you, Mrs Kepler") by a sash-like belt in the same colour. In the other a cream sleeveless dress on which two brown bamboo prints spiralled round the left hip and diagonally across the breasts. Both purchases angered her. She had still learned nothing about clothes.

She knew inevitably what the next step must be yet wandered another ten minutes, trying to delay the decision. Finally and fatalistically, she entered a pub just off Baker Street, ordered a gin and tonic and dialled her mother.

"I am taking your advice. Changing my appearance. I went to an orthodontist but now I've fallen at the second hurdle – buying casual clothes. I put myself in the hands of a Wigmore Street virago and spent seven hundred pounds. But I'm no more the wiser. Are you capable of educating me?"

"Good heavens, Clare. You sound out of breath."

"Just a case of supreme irritation. Surely what I'm doing isn't complicated yet I have no instincts for it. How did you teach yourself?"

Her mother spoke softly. "I fear I'll irritate you further. It is a simple thing. Find someone you can trust and let them make suggestions."

"Did you know I was a mild tawny?"

"No dear, I didn't. But it doesn't matter. That's someone else's concern."

"So your answer has been to visit that place in Tenterden? Could they do the same for me?"

"They could. And you could turn their suggestions down if you wished."

"Am I competent to do that?"

"This isn't kinetics, dear. Nothing's defined. You're either comfortable with clothes or you're not. It's that simple."

"I'm feeling impatient. My car's parked at Hyde Park. Why don't I drive down to Headcorn and take you to Tenterden?"

"By all means. But calm down. For many women this burden you talk about is their greatest pleasure. Something tells me it may fall short of that for you."

Beth, her mother's couturier was less forcefully groomed than her competitor in Wigmore Street. Perhaps in her fifties she specialised in soft-spoken authority and, best of all, she had a strategy.

She said, "Not everyone has an instinct for fashion. The problem clients are those who don't realise this. Let's be practical. Put on the clothes you bought and we'll discuss them."

Because Clare felt adrift in the loose-fitting suit she used the sash to eliminate the folds. When she emerged from the changing room Beth immediately loosened the belt. "The jacket's meant to hang provocatively. It suits you because you're slender. Look in the mirror. The looseness has a hint of swagger."

"Should I be looking to swagger?"

"The clothes do it for you. They say you're not afraid to. They're the clothes of a confident woman. With a well-educated swagger."

Clare looked at her mother who said, "I see what Beth is getting at. And you can't argue with 'well-educated' can you? What do you see, Clare?"

"Much embarrassment for a start. I should have solved all this in my teens."

"Well, I did try to help. But you went bohemian at Oxford and then insisted on looking businesslike, on being taken seriously. Aren't some of your suits from a men's tailor?"

Clare looked at her free-flowing reflection. "It seemed the way to go. Beating men at their own game. And I still want to be taken seriously. But not earnestly."

"While still taking advantage of your looks."

"Assuming that's a possibility."

Beth intervened. "I have the feeling this is an old argument. First, does the suit feel comfortable?"

"It's unnervingly lightweight but yes, there's no restraint."

"Look carefully. I may sound over-cautious but do you feel undermined in any way? It's a cliché that women dress to look younger but some hate to be accused of disguising their age. Whatever age that is. Can you see yourself at a business meeting in that suit?"

Phrases from the bank's memo flitted through Clare's mind. "I can. Though there'd be other changes too. Make-up; longer hair with more styling."

Beth and Mrs Morgan sighed in unison. The remainder of the visit involved cloth swatches, sketches by Beth, flicking through magazines and writing down orders until Clare could stand no more. "Enough. I need one more word of advice. Wigmore Street said I have a mild tawny complexion. Mother thinks that's too technical to bother about. Is it a pointer to the make-up I should use? Does it mean anything at all?"

"I haven't the foggiest idea," said Beth, laughing. "Generally speaking your make-up and lipstick should veer away from bright red towards brownish red. Not brown, brownish red."

"Finally, hair. It needs to be longer if it's to be styled. And the grey must go. To be replaced by what?"

"Try henna until you're satisfied."

"Isn't henna the colour of tea?"

Beth said, "The one I use comes in fifteen shades."

In the car Mrs Morgan said timidly, "I'm pleased about this change of heart. I'm fairly sure it wasn't your dear old mother's recommendation."

"You were the verb sap. if you like. But since then I've had an unpleasant experience which I'd prefer not to discuss. It will only hurt you and it doesn't matter now. It taught me not to be stubborn, something I should have learnt a long time ago. Stubbornness is a terrible fault for a scientist."

"If someone was unpleasant to you I'd rather not hear about it. I suppose that makes me a coward."

"It says you're a mother."

GARTON had sent her brochures, organisation charts, three years of accounts and she'd done her own research. Even so she was surprised when she saw the size of the company plant. Modern electronics manufacturing tended to be space hungry, spread out on one storey – like this one – to ensure free-flowing logistics. The aluminium cladding, the wide yet shallow windows, the lack of clutter and the ostentatiously designed administration block were typical. Her Jaguar was now in a visitor's slot close to a management car park populated exclusively with BMWs. High-tech wheels for a high-tech company.

She'd arrived twenty minutes early, time enough to attend to her newly furbished looks. The first act was to remove the device which aligned her teeth. Unobtrusive, made of transparent plastic, it was socially unexceptional but it changed her voice slightly. Getting used to it had been difficult but without it she now felt incomplete.

Her compact mirror showed careful grooming still intact. Eyebrows plucked into high arches paralleled the outline of her face and the beige tones of her powder and lipstick were now quite familiar. No eye-shadow today.

There remained her hair, easily the most radical change and the least expected. Having experimented with henna and formed a preference for Persian Copper she bit the bullet when picking up Nick and asked assorted mothers to recommend Sevenoaks' best salon. The consensus was for Hair Lines ("shockingly expensive").

Hair Lines was out of the centre on Pembroke Road and surrounded by its own car park. This was significant. Few customers arrived by public transport. Clare had imagined something opulent and comforting and found neither. The atmosphere was closer to a pop concert: over-amplified guitars and young women, girls rather, strangely dressed and strangely decorated.

Her recommended stylist, Kylie, had black hair in broken-glass spikes and was pierced with studs, one apparently penetrating the skull above her left eye. Clare said, "You come well regarded but perhaps I'm a little aged. Can you do anything for me?"

Kylie screamed with laughter revealing a ball of chewing gum nestling on her tongue. "Don't fancy my spikes, eh? I can style anyone. What did you have in mind?"

Clare explained the henna experiments, meanwhile appreciating Kylie's attentiveness and the way she ran speculative fingers through Clare's hair. She concluded: "It seemed a suitable colour. Perhaps you could take it from there."

Kylie said nothing and continued to feel out the contours. Finally she said, "I could do better than that."

"Would it be… extreme?"

"Nah, not that. See, you think you've got a thin face, don't you? It's really oval. Quite pretty once it's freed up. But I need to streak a mix of colours - " She raised a hand to forestall Clare's quick alarm. "Nothing strong, just subtle highlights. Then I want a sideways line to take away the dull old balance. Tell you what: if you don't like it pay me a pony and no tip. But you'll like it."

Trying to remember whether a pony was twenty-five or fifty pounds Clare was persuaded by Kylie's confidence, her topological analysis and the way she conveyed – mainly by hand movements – what she intended to do.

And here it was, a transformation that Clare had covertly inspected many times during the past few days. Multicoloured highlights, running from root to tip, varying subtly from light brown to dark gold, like trapped sedimentary layers in an exposed cliff. A sauce where cream and chili oil had been added and gently stirred, just once. Colours that simulated movement.

But what really mattered was a lock of hair taken diagonally across her forehead towards her right ear, disturbing "the dull old balance", proving her face was an ellipse not a cylinder. A line that transformed a merely adult face into an interesting secret.

Habit said it wasn't her. Reflection told her she was no judge. She got out of the Jaguar, facing the sleek yet heartless entrance to Garton's headquarters. Modernism for modernism's sake. A good place to try out the new carapace.

He too affected a carapace. Wearing jeans, trainers and a loose white shirt with billowing sleeves he shook her hand warmly, directing her to the end of a long couch as he took the other. "Mike Gardner. I don't defend my sloppiness to banks or even customers but I'll make an exception for you. I founded Garton twenty-one years ago. Last year we turned over eighty million and made a profit of nine percent. I don't have to be formal any longer. Being interviewed doesn't allow you the same option, hence the history. I could say you wear your rue with a difference but it's probably politically incorrect. Accept this left-handed apology."

"There are Silicon Valley precedents."

"Out there it's youthful and daring. Here they think you're off your rocker. OK. You know something about Garton. We're a contract manufacturer of electronic systems. The job is technical director. It's a new post which takes away some of my responsibilities and allows you as much entrepreneurial elbow-room as you want. I'd like to talk as little as possible from now on."

Clare put her briefcase on the floor. It would be better not to open it. "I expected it to be all new to me but parts are familiar. I've specialised in tendering projects and I can see the similarities. Tightly defined work, tight deadlines and I presume tight budgets. Those are things I'm good at. However the differences are just as important. With tendering marketing is presumed, here marketing is open-ended. One priority would be to work closely with marketing, perhaps take on some of their function. Or create them. I've done that before. The reason I mention this straight away is because I've often found poor liaison between the technical and marketing departments. Worse still stand-offishness. A famous British ailment."

"I can always get good engineers. But good marketing people…"

"I have a memo I could leave with you. The solution's hardly rocket science, in fact it wasn't truly a solution. I proposed a joint committee between the two with alternating chairmen. What it proved was marketing didn't understand the business we were in."

"What then?"

"Sounds so clever but I couldn't think of anything else. I split off active marketing and ran it myself. The rest just withered away."

"If you get the job circulate that from day one."

He glanced at her CV. "You've done military coms. That's one of our smaller sections. Process control instrumentation is bigger; got any ideas there?"

"Big strides at Confexxion but only because their information flow was terribly backward. I'd hate to face re-opening that can of worms here. But then that may not be in Garton's hands, it may depend on how advanced your client companies are. I can help smooth things out if technical changes stir up labour relations."

Gardner was as good as his word and his contributions were limited to questions. Gentle forays to check if Clare understood the other product lines – subjects she'd read up if they were outside her direct experience. The long couch combined with his easy approach turned the exchanges into something of a conversation. Eventually he switched to domestic matters.

"Is Basingstoke a long haul from Sevenoaks? Would you need to move?"

"I arrive early so it's no great problem. I doubt we'd move to begin with." She explained Jerry's needs and he listened with interest. "Something says you're not a golfing family," he said, gesturing vaguely at her faux Armani.

"I play tennis but it's not a sport we share."

"And your son? He's four, I believe."

"A Swedish au pair stands in. It's worked well for a couple of years."

He leant back. "Am I entitled to know how you pass time in Sevenoaks? Be quite blunt if I'm not"

"It's a question I find embarrassing. Do I really have leisure interests? I read a few novels but more often than not I'm dissatisfied. Similarly with most films and nearly all TV. I think being educated as a physicist encourages a rigid mindset. I'm irritated by things that don't work out. I want definitions and don't get them. I look for facts and get motives, ponderings and guilt."

He laughed at this. "I'm ashamed I ever read War and Peace. Tell me your impressions of Garton."

The entrepreneurial side made things different. As did managing separate technical disciplines. If the military coms side was small she'd hope to enlarge it through her own experiences. The variety of the contracts suggested a modern adaptable company; she liked that. No doubt a quick tour would confirm things.

"My fault. We should have done that first. Too much gassing. Let's do it now."

The tour showed heavy investment in automated handling of workpieces, a printed circuit assembly line that went on for ever and might have been transported in a box from Japan. She noted a high percentage of women working neatly and quickly. In mentioning these points she noticed he was slightly distracted, shrugging off credit for his advanced factory.

Back in his office he apologised and asked her to re-state her impressions following the tour. He was silent as she spoke, still seemed relaxed but not as before. She felt he was watching her, almost covertly. When she finished she crossed her legs selfconsciously and discovered that both he and she were looking at her light-brown court shoes with their unaccustomed one-and-a-half-inch heels.

Gardner seemed on the verge of speaking, then changed his mind. Instead he glanced at her CV. "No problems about your referees, I take it? I've learned to ask that question. One salesman I nearly appointed was only a step away from a county court judgment"

She reassured him and he got to his feet. As he escorted her from his office and through the main entrance she felt his hand lightly guiding her but, very properly, touching only the small of her back. As they reached the car park he pointed at the Jaguar, "You're a techno-patriot I see."

"And you're a lover of complexity."

He was caught short, then laughed. "It's true. Germans rarely go for simple solutions. I started out in engineering design and it's a cliché weakness."

She offered her hand and he took it rather slowly. "I'll be in touch soon."

In the car she slipped the alignment system back into her mouth and appreciated the security it re-created. Long ago she had stopped deconstructing interviews. Excepting the bank all had been successful but two had come as a surprise after she'd been subjected to early truculence and indifference. The change in Gardner's attitude seemed odd and possibly marked a shift in sexual awareness. Nothing carnal, perish the thought. Perhaps initially she'd simply appeared as a man in odd clothing. Then, in a Damascene moment, he'd looked in on himself and asked some internal questions.. Hence the light hand on her back. Or perhaps he had been testing her against future rough and tumble when he overruled one of her decisions, solicited her support or guessed at her views. Clare had known even enlightened managers confess – usually in their cups –

to a secret fear about women employees, notably the gush of tears after a difference of opinion.

He phoned mid-afternoon the following day to offer her the job. "I called three of your referees and it was sweetness and light. As I expected. I've asked for written assessments but they're just a formality. There'll be a letter in the post tonight if you accept."

"I accept."

"Would you like to know why I want you?"

"Can I guess?"

"Go ahead."

"I'm qualified, I've got relevant experience, I interviewed well. But the clincher is I'm a woman."

He laughed delightedly and she credited him for that. He said, "Was I that obvious? You're quite right, of course. Based on your CV and your proposals you'd have got the job anyway. But during the tour I looked back on how I've run the company. I've never discriminated against women but I've ignored them for all the important jobs. You made me think about the opportunities that may have slipped through my fingers. To use a word that doesn't come naturally you were cool. It's not a quality I associate with men. I talked to my wife last night and asked her whether Garton could use some cool these days. She said it had lacked cool for the last twenty-one years."

"Thanks for that. My best to your wife."

"I'll pass on the message. Two other points. Your suggestion about marketing is a logical step and I'll add it to your remit. Not immediately, perhaps, but as soon as you can. Does that sound sensible?"

"Provided you're happy. I'll be working by instinct rather than training."

"I've had it the other way round and it didn't please me at all. The other point is salary. I seem to recall some weasel word like 'competitive' or 'attractive' in the job spec. We need to talk that over. I sense you'd prefer a performance bonus rather than a fixed figure. I'll be happy with that. Come in and see me soon and we'll discuss it. Bring in a single-page summary of your first six months."

"May I mention this to my executive search agent? You may want to keep the appointment under wraps for a day or two but I have a particular reason for letting her know. I promise she'll be like the grave."

"That's fine. See you soon… Clare."

"I'm looking forward to it, Mike."

HILDEGARD'S voice broke. "I'm so glad. So glad."

"Oh Hildy, the bank wasn't your fault. You couldn't have known. But I'll bet Miss Flanagan is already finding out."

"Speaking of whom, there's a couple of tit-bits I'll pass on when we speak next."

"Make that soon, Hildy. Come and stay the night. Bring your boy-friend – he can talk golf with Jerry."

"Clare, I'm so glad."

15. HATCH

Do it!

THE NEW trainers were lighter on Hatch's feet and he unreeled a mile round the field without effort, even completed two more laps. Afterwards, breathing heavily but not desperately, he saw Gallagher enter through a gate on the far side to embark on his own circuits. Jogging past Gallagher raised a hand that asked Hatch to wait for him.

As they walked away from the field Hatch said, "I owe you for the tea. It's been a week or two now."

Gallagher seemed marginally fitter. "On a whim I took a course. Computers. Actually, computers for idiots. Waste of time. Average age about sixty-two. The first lesson devoted to booting up. I watched the tutor to see if I could pick up tips. I'm now inclined towards teaching at the technical college."

No one had cleaned the table surfaces in the greasy spoon and the tea was the same faded mahogany. Gallagher described an abortive job interview and Hatch wondered whether to mention Lodestone. Gallagher's willingness to move laterally made him a potential competitor.

Instead, he asked, "What's your attitude towards signing on?"

"Medieval superstition. And I'm not alone. All the out-of-work engineers I've met see it as the beginning of the end."

"I thought I was only one. So much for scientific practicality."

"There are jobs that need doing round my house but I leave the toolbox where it is. I'm scared a neighbour will spot me and I'll end up the local handyman on thirty quid a week."

Hatch said, "From time to time I have to be outdoors. No big deal, really. I live in a scruffy bedsit in Leyfield. Indoors on a summer's day I can convince myself the world has left me behind."

Again Gallagher hadn't touched his tea. "Working-class chap I knew started on the shopfloor as a press-brake operator. After ten years he became foreman. Did night-school and the rest and got promoted to manufacturing manager. That was ten months ago. A month later the company lost a sub-frame contract for transits - forty percent of their business. Terrible cash flow; went into administration. Three weeks ago he hanged himself. If he'd stayed on the press-brake he'd have got another job. Could even have found work as foreman. No chance as a manufacturing manager. He knew his stuff but couldn't handle an interview. Moral: don't promote beyond your accent."

As they parted he and Gallagher wished each other good luck and shook hands awkwardly. Gallagher said he didn't envisage much more jogging.

Entering the bed-sitter Hatch found three letters slid under his door. A luscious if ambiguous discovery but he delayed opening them in the room he had grown to hate. Instead he stripped off his shirt, mopped himself with a cold facecloth, dressed and walked round to the library. There he prolonged the discipline by gathering the day's newspapers and checking the classified ad sections. Even stretching his abilities to the limit there wasn't a single relevant job. Things were worse than they'd been four weeks ago. The three letters now took on more significance. Quickly he opened the envelopes, skimmed the words to get the worst over, then re-read them more attentively.

Calmly he got up, entered a nearby newsagent and bought a copy of the Telegraph with a twenty-pound note. In an adjacent sweetshop he paid for a bag of Maltesers with the ten-pound note he had just received in change. Loaded with a pocket-weight of coins he walked to the bus station where the telephone boxes had shelf-like seats.

"Oh, it's you. But then who else would it be?"

No suggestion of another life. Did no one else telephone? "How are you?"

"Somewhat gloomy. I'll be out of here in a week but they want me back in about two months."

"Oh, hell. Are they… encouraging?"

"They're optimistic, which is a change. I didn't like their fibbing, pretending their English wasn't good enough. Any news at your end?"

"Quite a bit. I wanted your advice but only if you're up to it."

"You don't ask for that very often. Go ahead, if you've got the money. Anything to take my mind off all this whiteness."

"I'm OK for money. I had three job offers today which sounds terrific. But they're all flawed. The first you already know about: technical editor with an engineering trade magazine in London. I like the boss and it could be fun. But it pays twenty-two kay and half my net would go on accommodation. The job's secure for a couple of years."

"You'd be stepping a long way down.. What's next?"

"Something new. A metal fabricator up here in Stourbridge. Normally there wouldn't be anything in it but they're adding manufacture. No guarantee that their new products will succeed, of course, but I interviewed well and he knows I'm capable. Unfortunately he's shifted the goal-posts. I think the prospect scares him and he's cutting the investment. Including the thirty-kay he first offered. It wasn't especially generous and now it's down to twenty-seven. As I say it's risky. I have the impression he'll fail because he's secretly lost his bottle. I guess he wants a plan where he can pull out with least damage."

"I see what you mean. So, number three?"

"This is the TV job Hester had a hand in." He summarised the complexities and oddities, trying to reduce the work into what viewers would see and understand. "It's fascinating and creative. Done properly it'll be a completely new television show. The pay's good at thirty-six kay but there's a snag: it's a one-year contract."

"But if the show's a success…?"

"Indeed."

"Do it!"

"Take the risk? Me? Aren't you forgetting my history, the faults that irritated you so much?"

"It's because of them I'm saying yes. Take the worst case: you're looking for a job next year. But it won't be the same you. You'll still have your background plus something else: a new way of thinking. Do it!"

"There's that other risk, you know."

"That's up to you. I can't pin on your nappie and protect you from Hester. And if it isn't her it'll be some other harpy wanting to trade on your sense of duty. I'm sure television is full of harpies. But it sounds like fun. You could use a bit of that."

Hatch thought. "But what about you? These next two months?"

"I spoke to the surgeon. A hotel would become unbearable but perhaps I'd do better elsewhere. There's a guide I've seen: *Ferien auf dem Bauernhof.* Swiss farms taking in lodgers are at altitude. Gorgeous views, tranquillity."

"Sounds healthy. Take lots of books." He rang off and took out his address book.

LE GRENIER was French-style, the sort of place Tom might choose. A plethora of waiters with razor-trimmed sideburns and white ankle-length aprons. His table for two was crowded out with glassware, cutlery, crockery. Someone had already asked if he wanted *"quelquechose à boire"* but he'd said no for tactical reasons. The ordering would be done together. It was just after eight and only one other table was occupied. He would have preferred some noise at the outset when the relationship – tenuous enough in all conscience – would be re-established. How casually he'd gone about organising this evening; how far from casual he now felt.

Seeing her come through the swing doors startled him. A handsome self-assured woman: Who is she? He'd no idea. When she acknowledged him he breathed out through an open mouth.

She said, "Isn't that an orchid?" It stood alone on his table in a slender, vulnerable vase which he noticed for the first time.

"In three seconds a waiter is going to ask - in French – whether you want something to drink. I thought I'd warn you."

"Suggest something. Stop me making a fool of myself."

"Gin and tonic? Dry sherry? White wine?"

"That's three things; too big a choice."

By now the waiter was hovering. "Would mademoiselle wish…?"

Hatch cut him off. "Two dry white wines, please."

With the ordering out of the way Hatch got things going by describing the new job. She was attentive but then he'd a real story to tell. Each time she sipped her chardonnay her upper lip slid over the rim of the glass.

"A new world," she said.

Do it! Prudence had said. "But I'm still just an engineer?"

"It's not an illness."

"A social disease, then? No, that's something quite different."

"Stop it! I've only worked for engineering companies and I do it by choice. The stereotypes are wrong. Engineers do take risks. I started as a teenager at Hadley's, the structural specialists. I remember taking notes about a support frame for a railway bridge abutment that was starting to crack. I loved it. First the rough calculations then the refinements to save money. Of course they weren't really risks. But cutting twelve mil RSJs down to nine mil seemed so daring."

Her knowledge surprised him. "You know my job, you know me. I know nothing about you. Except that you're conscientious."

"Not much of a reference. I could be a serial poisoner."

He said, "Being fired made me reckless. I wanted what I thought I saw. A couple of hours' chat. Not unreasonable. All the same it was sheer bravado. I'm glad you're here."

She looked away from him, unfocused, slightly distant. "I was reckless in accepting."

"Shall I order wine? No, that's a question. We'll have an expensive Rhone."

The sommelier overheard them and slid in quickly. He complimented Hatch on the Gigondas. Hatch resumed, "We're here to chat. How about…oh I don't know… music? Interrupt whenever you like."

"A short odds guess. You're a Bach fan."

"I've already noticed – you're quick."

"This is the downside of engineering companies. Once an aerodynamicist, a biochemist or a metallurgist did the steady thing: mentioned how he'd re-discovered the wheel in Bach's symmetry and so-called maths. Quoted some differential calculus to prove it. Since then you and your brothers have parrotted all that stuff without thought. Me, I like Lutoslawski and Cage but last night I listened to the Goldberg all the way through. It reminded me of you. I'm not saying you don't like Bach but you should re-think why."

"Forget the formats, the key relationships, the repetitions?"

"Do you have the complete Goldberg?"

"Just excerpts by Glenn Gould."

"Get the whole thing, listen to all eighty minutes. It's more like opera. You'll throw away symmetry and remember the range."

What had he expected? An evening of strained reminiscences about Weldworth? "Tell me some facts, please. Nothing confessional. Some slivers of background. Otherwise you're just a force."

She looked vaguely at her *salade tiède*. "I'd rather not."

"Well, that's music. Engineering would be coals to Newcastle. But I do know unemployment. And it's a matter of space. When I was working, the bed-sitter wasn't a curse. I'd come home knackered and it supplied a bed to lie on. Out of work and it turns into a slowly closing vice. I go for walks but outside can be just as bad. Too much space, space I don't belong to. I can't stop looking at my watch. To pass time painlessly I need to do something. So I come full circle. I'm not doing anything because I'm unemployed."

"I knew you'd be rotten at doing nothing. And rotten too at busy work. Occupying your hands isn't enough, you need the luxury of solving problems."

He nodded. "Work is a sort of luxury when it's not there. My mind's empty."

"And if you can't stand an empty mind you'll never make a salesman," she said. Perhaps she'd meant it as a joke. He'd forgotten that phase of his career and was reminded of what they had discussed in her office.

He poured her some more wine. "Since I can't ask you if you like it I'm forced to order you to drink it." He tried to behave casually as she brought the glass close to her mouth.

She said, "There's no fool-proof way of describing the matured stuff – like this. One man I knew said, 'Think of an unfinished wooden chair from Pine Market and one from Heals, properly smoothed, waxed, four times the price.' All the rough edges gone, no distractions."

Hatch wondered about the man. He said, "The space problem is bad but the talk problem is worse. Nobody speaks my language. If I say 'reaming' no one picks it up. Of course I'm from a specialised world and not having anyone to talk to is partly my own fault. I'm a one-trick pony. A liability at cocktail parties (not that I've been to many of those) and a sort of deaf-mute when talking to newsagents or librarians."

As she listened she pressed the bowl of the wine glass against her cheek which Hatch found intimate and, yet, a barrier. There was no way into that intimacy for him. She said, "You need another rethink. If all you talked about was cast aluminium I wouldn't be here."

"I'm OK where things are well-defined but I lack imagination."

She shook her head and the casually brushed hair swung from side to side. "Anyone who lacked imagination would never admit that. They wouldn't recognise the condition."

Hatch stared.

"Everyone at Weldworth knows I lack a husband so I get propositioned. For reasons I won't go into no one stands a chance. Even if I were inclined the arrangements would be too difficult. Yet here I am, at dinner. Why? You could say I'm an expert at propositions, the way they are put and why. I find men at their worst when crossing the bridge that leads to a women. They lie obviously and badly. Worse, they're insulting. When I'm approached it's simply to check out my availability. At the point of contact I have no other existence: I am either a yes or a no."

She sipped and hummed with pleasure.

"Perhaps you came for the wine," said Hatch.

"I've been known to take over a wine list. I'm strong on value but even then the price can be high. This would have been above my ceiling."

"You trusted me?"

"You've ordered wine before. This wasn't the second cheapest."

"But all that stuff at the beginning? Being spoilt for choice."

"It works with those who are used to booze and those that aren't."

Hatch finally felt the pleasant fatigue of relaxation. "Finish what you were saying."

The glass again rested against her cheek. "I'm trying to remember if anyone else has asked me out for a chat. Probably but, if so, it would have been a form of words. With you I knew it was the truth. Men are more interesting when there's no need to disentangle the code."

"Were you reassured I wouldn't be a threat?"

"I'm not afraid of men who want to sleep with me. I simply have good reasons for avoiding them."

Hatch shook his head. "I wanted somebody to talk to, true. But it had to be an attractive woman."

"That's OK. It makes me more than a bimbo."

The main course arrived breaking into their exchanges. But when they were alone again she was ready to resume. "I'm not out to take confession or offer my own. You aren't without charm. And you buck received wisdom. There's a myth that men need to be slightly wicked – even wholly wicked – to qualify as desirable. If anything the theory confirms the dumbness of women. These setbacks made you doubt yourself. Isn't that right?"

Hatch recalled the disintegrating relationship with Lemazaire, the envy he'd felt for Baudinière, the growing belief that selling was not the route to rehabilitation. Plus the squalor of the bed-sitter and the financial restrictions Prudence had imposed. Had he known despair?

"Getting fired was necessary," he said. For the first time he allowed himself to look directly at her, taking as long as he liked. The light brown, near-shoulder-length hair had been simply washed and brushed – there was no art to it. Her face had a slight permanent tirednesss, an asset which suggested sexual languor. The surrounds to her eyes drooped a fraction. And there was the unique upper lip. How old was she? Possibly younger than she looked since she'd worked unremittingly. It was a face to provoke argument. No woman taking the details one by one would ever agree about her overall sexuality. Yet men, reticent about being drawn to a woman who met none of the usual male criteria for beauty, would come sneaking. As Hatch himself was now sneaking.

"I'd forgotten what a woman's company can mean. Did I ever know? You said getting here took some effort. All I can add is my gratitude."

"Did I arrive here as a woman?" she asked. "I admitted you had charm so that must be the case. I'd have liked to be genderless." She paused. "Although that wouldn't have satisfied you. Most of my life is routine and routine makes me forget what I am. It's easier that way. I haven't exactly given in but I do hoard my resources."

"Oh, come on. What do you see in the mirror?"

"The decline."

He said, "But am I not a better judge than you?"

"A better judge? Not in a thousand years. Your objectivity is in abeyance tonight. If I asked you – which I won't – every line would be fortitude, every wrinkle character, lack of make-up a badge of the feminist intellectual. Physiology and laziness are simpler, more likely explanations."

"You're wasted at Weldworth."

She looked as if she were measuring what he'd said. "Just one women of many. But I'm not here to talk about me. Have you tested your faith against the future? Once, you helped make things that were then sold. But television is different. Much of it is show, fashion and public acceptance. Being dogged may not be enough."

He said, "But isn't television The Boy's Wonder Book of Railways brought up to date with a handful of extras? Showing how things work and turning that into magic lantern slides? Plus understanding the audience and catching their attention. Mind you, I'm the one to talk. When we divorced the television stayed in our old house and I never replaced it. I should buy one tomorrow and watch everything, the junk as well as the good stuff."

"A bit late."

"Perhaps. But I was thrown in at the deep end. My interview was in a car between Manchester and back. My interviewer was a creature of television, a techno-innocent who responded with frightening speed to what I said. His very enthusiasm encouraged me. I may know enough to leave doggedness behind."

"But hang on to the rest."

About to pour out more wine he paused. "You see me as vulnerable?"

"Misplaced sensitivity."

"Good grief, it must be true. My ex-wife warned me only a day or so ago."

She laughed briefly and for the first time. "No doubt other women will want to guide you. Your ex-wife even. It can't be a matter of self-interest then."

Hester, a cool presence close at hand, reasserted herself. "There is someone else. She may want to control me simply for the sake of it."

"That's not unknown. Do you want to talk about it?"

Her directness was shocking but he grabbed the opportunity. "I don't read an awful lot but a Kingsley Amis novel stuck in my mind. One male character said it was an article of faith never to mention his dealings with one woman when talking to another. It seemed wise at the time. Being here with you turns that into nonsense."

If he'd expected appreciation he was disappointed. Once started, though, he told the story with relish: the early flirtations, Hester's abrupt decision to marry Tom, her unwillingness to leave well alone, the insistence that he should stay in the Midlands, the machinations about the job.

"She's been married, how long?"

"Two or three years. Perhaps more."

"And her husband…?"

"The soul of honour."

"Another honourable man. Your ex-wife believes you may give in to a sense of duty. But neither of you need worry. You can do rational thought and you're not impulsive. I doubt you would have told me – would have wanted to tell me – if you believed it might happen. You wouldn't have opened up this embarrassing confession if you really thought she'd get her way."

Hatch was slightly stunned.

Linda continued. "I don't think she herself is too serious. She enjoys tormenting you but she doesn't sound like a woman who would flee her husband. She sounds a mite too comfortable."

The adjective alone silenced Hatch.

Coffee was taken in a lounge on a small couch with both turned towards each other. Now he could inspect her clothing: an anonymous black skirt, a white blouse with only vertical pleats for decoration, no jewellery and only the faintest application of lipstick. Almost like a restaurant waitress sitting down to rest her feet.

Searching for something new to say Hatch was interrupted. "You should read more. I know engineers regard it as a badge of office not to open novels but you're moving into a more literary world. Unless you want to be elbowed about by arty types. And there will be arty types."

"I can always bring up the Moh scale."

She said, "No you can't. Any more than speaking Japanese. You'll be ignored. Read some author who will tax your brain, who'll make you sweat. Patrick White, for instance."

"Biographies won't do?"

"No proof of a flexible mind."

When they finished the coffee she looked at her watch. He wanted more but knew enough not to plead. "I'll get them to call us a taxi."

She looked at him sternly and he rephrased. "A taxi for you. But you must let me pay."

Outside he waited until she'd stepped into the cab to show he wouldn't hold her with too much talk. "You must know I would like to see you again. I won't bombard you, I promise. I accept your lack of freedom. I won't ask why."

She sighed. "We'll see. Call me at work at lunchtime. But wait a few weeks."

As the taxi drove away she had neither thanked him nor commented on the evening. But not through rudeness. Perhaps banality wearied her. He would have liked to think covetously of her but that clearly wasn't right. It seemed he might never see her again and that was agony. But if it had to be he accepted it. As he waited for his own taxi he thought of other women who had affected his life but found it difficult to concentrate. He walked backward and forward, jingling his keys and looking up at the summer sky.

16. HATCH

Into the tube

GAMESTER'S basement was stacked with cardboard boxes and orphan piles of paper. "I'm told this is our store," said Ericsson. "It's the first time I've been down here and I'm appalled. Television is transient; there's no need for storage. If this junk were removed would there be enough space?"

Hatch glanced round. "Easily."

Ericsson shouted up the stairwell, "Celia."

After a whirlwind introduction to the company Celia was the only person Hatch could put a face to. Perhaps because she wore a tee-shirt with an obscene slogan. Elsewhere she would have been Ericsson's personal assistant. Here she was an assistant deputy director or some such. But then Hatch himself had been given a similar triple-barrel title and was still unsure about the exact order of the words.

Celia remained at the doorway suspending herself by her elbows from the jamb. How insolent she looks, Hatch thought admiringly.

"Ceel, what is this stuff?" asked Ericsson.

"All sorts. The models we used in Great Fire of London, for instance."

"Jesus Christ," said Ericsson as if she'd talked of the Ice Age.

"Then there's - "

Ericsson interrupted with spectacular rudeness. "Don't give me a history lesson. Have we used any of this a second time?"

Celia wasn't put out. "Never. But it all cost money and it stays here until someone capable of making a decision has it moved." It was clear who the laggard decision-maker was.

"This afternoon," said Ericsson, "and I mean this afternoon, have it shifted to a self-storage unit. You can manage that can't you?"

"Except for one tiny thing," said Celia with a smile. "How long should it be stored for? When it's out of your sight and you're asked to sign the renewal order for the store you know what you'll do: you'll have it junked. No sense in having a long contract in the first place."

If Ericsson's intention was to out-stare Celia, her mockery insisted he would lose. He sighed. "Shit, I was right first time round. In this industry we plough the past under. Junk it."

But Celia wasn't finished. "You're such a knee-jerker. Why not a charity?"

"A charity?"

"I pick up the phone, call Oxfam, say 'As used on TV' and they'll take it away themselves. For free."

"Ceel, I kiss your arse. Metaphorically, that is."

Hatch said, "So that's what an assistant deputy director does. These weird jobs, they're not just to swell out the credit titles."

"Hey Zach, isn't Mister Hatch supposed to be a dumb engineer?" She allowed Hatch a concessionary grin. "You're right, an ADD is a poodle poop-scooper. If there's anything you need sing out now. You won't see much more of our chief blowhard this week. Unless you phone the Manoir au Quat' Saisons."

"Steady on, Ceel. That sort of info undermines staff morale."

Hatch said, "Give me some of these boxes, a Stanley knife, some gaffer tape and a self-assembly workbench from Ikea."

Ericsson and Celia spoke in unison, "Boxes?"

"I'll recycle them. We could work from drawings but crude cardboard models are better. Give me a couple of days for three projects. With your feedback I'll have designs you can test in front of the cameras. Of course I could go straight to finished work but that will cost you. And we've got to be careful. From what I've seen of Gamester I suspect you change your mind a lot before you're satisfied. More expense."

"A couple of days?" said Celia. "Can you work that fast? Aren't you used to metal?"

"If I thought you could understand drawings I'd work faster still. But that needs practice. Later on, perhaps. For now let's keep it simple."

Celia exchanged glances with Ericsson who laughed. "You always said I was shit at appointing people. Now, say you're sorry."

"I'll say sorry to Andy. I thought he'd be a dead weight, a perfectionist we'd have to dynamite into action. Looks like he's doing the dynamiting. What was that about Ikea?"

"Their bench is ideal. It's cheap and big and I can assemble it in an hour. But they don't deliver. We need to pick it up and I don't have a car. And the Corvette hasn't enough space."

"Forget old man Zach," said Celia. "Never let it be said I'm a wart on the arse of progress. We'll go in the Land Rover."

Ericsson said, "But he needs to be measured for Gamester's three-piece suit, taught the company song, given the - "

" – key to the executive washroom. At least he knows how to lick our backsides. Speed, Andy, it's the way to our heart."

Outside the tower block the car park was generously proportioned and defined with shining white lines. Celia's Land Rover was an old model, bare aluminium showing through the paint, the aerodynamics of a chicken hutch. Out on the M6 they shouted over the engine roar. "Are we what you expected?" Celia asked.

"I couldn't risk being seen an old fart."

"We've had specialists. Advisers, experts on this and that. The difficulty is getting them to shut up. We need essence not background. You're different. We're improvisers and we could set up these rigs ourselves. But it'll be quicker and more certain with you. More time for improvements, for making things viewer-friendly."

"I've been thinking about that," Hatch said. "I have some detail suggestions. Do people at Gamester actually read instructions or is it all done orally?"

"Here's how it goes. Headings on one sheet of paper, simple sketches and ten minutes round the table with Zach or whoever he delegates. You keep notes. Chances are we'll never look at them except where there's an argument about costs."

Although elderly the Land Rover was exceeding 70 mph. Celia noticed his glance. "You're right, we're speed mad. There's never enough time. Which reminds me: I haven't seen your CV and don't know your domestics. Is working late a problem?"

"It won't be when I've got some wheels. Otherwise I'm a solitary."

"Gay?"

"Not yet anyway. But give me time in the giddy world of entertainment."

"Backstage entertainment, not so damn giddy. Most of us are solitaries."

Deceived by her scruffy clothing and her ill-chosen horn-rimmed glasses he hadn't previously noticed her engaging face. Or her well-defined hips. Younger than he was, but by how much?

"Who do I speak to? Gamester has no recognisable management and these titles don't mean anything."

"Nine times out of ten I'll know. Otherwise I'll point you in the right direction."

"One thing occurs. Who pays for the bench?"

"My plastic. That's right! You're skint. I'll get you an advance if you want."

"That would be truly Christian."

"Oh, that's me."

After manhandling the large pack from Ikea into the Land Rover they resumed their seats but Celia made no move to start the engine. She was sweating quite heavily now and gazed at him like a confident raptor. Hatch knew he was going to be kissed and wondered why. Perhaps this would mark the end of a well-ordered world and the beginning of another that was speed mad. He concentrated on not being surprised even when her loose glasses slid awkwardly between their faces.

"Did you like that, Andy Hatch?"

He removed the glasses. "I'll like this more."

The kissing was mere reconnaissance. Soon they were back on the motorway and Celia resumed telling him about the oddities of TV production. He had wanted to ask about the slogan on her tee-shirt but was glad he hadn't. What had seemed a mild obscenity turned out to be word-play on blow-job.

With a salary advance to support his long dormant credit card he called in at a motorcycle dealer the following Saturday. He inclined towards a nearly new 125 cc scooter but suspected Gamester might see that as old-fart evidence. Instead he put a deposit on a five-year-old green 1000 cc Kawasaki with a mere seven-thousand miles on the clock. This despite its terrible riding position - knees tightly bent, feet well off the ground. Discomfort had probably encouraged the previous owner to sell and Hatch knew he would eventually need a car. Before that the Kwacker would allow frightening bursts of acceleration and a high level of risk.

The ride back to the bed-sitter was restricted by traffic and narrow streets. When he arrived he had nowhere to park the beast. He asked Mr Wee if he could use the backyard.

"You got job?"

"I started today. Edgbaston." Hatch was reluctant to talk about leaving the bed-sit. Mr Wee had been generous in setting fish-shop earnings against his rent and now regarded him as the perfect tenant. The relationship with Jimmy was a further benefit.

Mr Wee looked at Hatch and said nothing. Normally his imperfect English gave him the courage to override social embarrassment. But not now. Like Hatch he avoided talking about the future.

Hatch rang the Makings and got Hester. "Are you both free for dinner tonight? My treat. Celebrate my return to the middle-classes."

"You sound bright."

"Only a one-year contract. Good salary. Looks like fun." As he spoke he recalled Celia's sweaty cheek against his. And the reversed droit du seigneur.

"Fun!" said Hester. "That's rare these days."

"If you could book a table for about eight. I'll be over at seven-thirty."

"You don't need picking up?"

"I've got myself some wheels. Only two, but there's an engine between them."

"Two wheels?"

The bike was much discussed over dinner and time passed before Hatch realised why. It was a step away from the Makings' comfortable environment, incompatible with the suburban permutation of cars. It meant Hatch would, for the most part, now travel alone, without Hester as his chauffeur. Had he realised this?

"A bit juvenile, don't you think?" said Tom, normally tolerant of Hatch's oddities.

"I've joined a juvenile part of society. I need to fit in. What's more I've got to give them credit for employing me. When Ericsson did the interview I was still a solid citizen. Despite that he decided I was what he wanted. I find him and them infectious; I'm caught up in it all."

"Caught up in what?"

"Ideas instead of fifteen-page proposals. Talk not measurement. I came up with something half clever and Ericsson applauded: 'Hester never said you were a words guy.' How about that for a transformation?"

They observed him gravely across the restaurant table as if he were their son caught smoking marijuana at university. "Have you thought this through in terms of a career path?" said Hester.

"Career path? That's the one measured in decades. Rungs on the ladder. Steady progress. I wonder if anyone at Gamester has a career path?"

"You've changed," said Hester disapprovingly.

Hatch poured out sancerre. "I've had to. Head of production for Tempest should have been for life. But that liability suit was the finish. Being forced to get a job quickly put me in sales where I got fired – and deserved to be. The only suitable job offer was poorly paid and doomed to failure under a boss scared to go all the way."

Hester frowned at Hatch's dismissal of his past life. "I approached Mr Ericsson for something to tide you over. A one-year contract won't help you progress. You need to be patient."

"For how long? Manufacturing jobs are disappearing. Whatever I found would be at a lower level. Gamester may seem a joke but it's teaching me something new."

Hester waved her hand. "It's just playing at work."

"When bosses ask if I'm adaptable – if I can do lateral thought – I offer them cost engineering. But I'm fibbing. Cost engineering is simply part of production. Gamester tests my imagination. What's more it proves I have some. Ericsson doesn't know manufacturing but he's quick, very quick. When I explained my ideas he responded. He knew they'd be good television."

Disturbed by Hester's negativity, Tom tried to change the subject. "Tell us about these ideas, then." Without thinking Hatch dived in and summarised the gear train project. Then realised it was hopeless. The physical relationships were beyond them and as he doggedly embarked on the simple arithmetic their faces went blank. It was the first time he'd noticed this gulf between what he was and what they were. Since neither wanted to admit ignorance the conversation moved elsewhere.

Hatch listened half-heartedly to Tom on white Loire but his mind was elsewhere, reflecting on Ericsson. His admiration had taken a knock when Celia bated Ericsson but he knew now the banter had been good-natured. Ericsson could teach him things.

They had arrived at the restaurant in Tom's car and Hatch had to be transported back to the Kawasaki. He refused cognac but accepted coffee which Tom went out to make. Hester smoothed folds of skirt over her thighs.

"I'm pleased the interview went down well," she said insincerely.

"I'm very grateful."

"Perhaps we should meet."

Once this would have worried him. But something had changed and perhaps Celia had accidentally helped him to a different view of himself. "Yes, why not?"

And it was Hester who looked surprised.

"I'll be moving from the bed-sitter soon but I'll pass on the new telephone number," he said matter-of-factly.

The good-night kiss was glancing, perfunctory.

HATCH was not surprised to have Gamester to himself at eight in the morning. Downstairs in his atelier he prepared for work, marvelling that this rough and ready stuff would bring in a salary, amused by the Makings' incomprehension. He started fashioning the gear-train in cardboard but in a simplified form without the tedium of cutting dozens of teeth.

Celia sauntered in close to ten. "Is that your green bike in the car park?"

"It is."

"You're determined to go native."

"I pondered not shaving."

"Big mistake. You're our wonk. We need you to look reassuring, capable, a member of the real world." She fingered one of the wheels he'd made. "How long's this going to take?"

"Another hour. I'll have the other prototypes by tomorrow afternoon."

"Concentrate on this one. Tart it up with felt-tips to make it more real. Then explain it to an audience later this morning. Would that put you on the spot?"

"I take it the idea's to get feedback?"

"Everything we do is tested against low-browed Mr Ordinary. Since he doesn't work for us we need to think like him. Tell yourself it can never be too simple."

Hatch drew teeth round the rim of the cardboard discs and spinners in the middle; labelled the discs with information; added other vague decorations. This wasn't his field.

At three he faced half a dozen Gamester employees, all younger than him, all shabbily dressed, all incapable of sitting upright. "This is a techno-test based on understanding gears. The contestant sets up a sequence of gears - a gear-train - on this frame. If she's done the arithmetic and got it right she turns this wheel here at the bottom full circle and gets the necessary result on the sixth gear at the top.

"I know 'result' sounds vague but I've been learning how to dumb down. At first I had the bottom and top wheels as clock faces. That way two o'clock became, say, four o'clock. But it wasn't dumb enough. Now I favour the correct result being flagged on a panel that says 'Bingo'. Or whatever.

"Here's what the viewer sees. The contestant does her sums, puts the gear-wheels in the right order, twiddles the bottom gear and increases her score. The arithmetic is simple and it's based on the number of teeth per wheel. Plus one other factor. Can anyone guess?"

No one spoke. Hatch said, "I take it you all did eng-lit. I can demo it, though cardboard isn't the perfect medium." Hatch slotted two wheels on to the frame so their rims touched. "I turn the bottom wheel clockwise and, lo, this drives the second wheel. But the second wheel turns – wait for it - anti-clockwise! That complicates the arithmetic a little and the contestant must allow for it."

A long-haired woman in a kaftan said, "That point should be made clear for viewers. It's got a low-grade woo-factor."

"I'm glad you told me," said Hatch, grinning. "A woo-factor. Something terribly complicated that can only be understood by scientists?"

"More or less."

"Mr... er, Zach said a boffin figure might explain the test. If so your point could be included."

A youth with shoulder-length hair asked, "How long does it take to set up the gear train? Could somebody who's really clever do it in less than a minute?"

"Good point. That's up to the producer. But remember: the techno-test is just one of five contests in a given programme and there'll be four women competing. I could come up with a longer version if necessary. OK? Now I'll mount all the gear wheels in the right order and you can tell me how the camera should cover this."

Celia stood at the back throughout. After the reactions and suggestions had been considered she joined Hatch. "A good suggestion about the size of the frame. It's a key issue."

"The minute I started I realised these components aren't big enough. Viewers need to see the wheels being attached." Hatch frowned. "But I'm disappointed. In the end it was so dull."

"Wait until it's part of the TV programme. When there's some tension, when it's all in colour and not cardboard and there's a good-looking woman figuring things out. When getting the gear train in place affects the results. That's our side of things."

"I need to do some desk work. Scale up the drawing, check the price of sheet plastic and find out the cost of gear-cutting. You need some cost estimates, I assume?"

"That and a timetable. Use my desk and phone. There's some film I need to see in the studio."

As he scaled up the drawing other ideas occurred. Turning the demo frame into a tripod. Creating a simple rack to hold the wheels. He made phone calls and wrote out the estimates in his legible hand. Applying what he'd learned he immersed himself in dramatising the see-saw project he'd first suggested to Ericsson. Absorbing work.

When he looked up Celia leant over the desk. "It's half-past two. Have you eaten?"

"It's not mandatory, is it?"

"Reduced blood sugar. Slows your brain."

"This isn't work."

"I'll remind you of that sometime. Two hours before we go into the studio and you face a remake 'for technical reasons'. Then you'll need your blood sugar."

"I'll get a Mars Bar?"

"A Mars Bar? You'll start coming out in spots. I thought you were the practical sort. Or are you only good at nuts and bolts?"

It sounded like banter and that's how he was treating it. But the tone was bossy. "Don't tell me I have to find a pub. There'll be nothing left."

"There's a vending machine upstairs. But don't for God's sake depend on that. Most of us use an Italian round the corner."

The following lunchtime he allowed Celia to propel him into Mia Tesoro where he ordered a bowl of minestrone. "I did without breakfast and lunch when I was out of work. Now my stomach's shrunk. I couldn't possibly manage your fettucine. But I'll finish with an expresso, I promise." He looked at the surrounding tables. "Where are all the others?"

"I fibbed. Most are at The Red Lion. And not for the cottage pie."

"You're saving me from myself?"

For the first time she hesitated. "A bit stupid of me. Fact is, Gamester's got talent but lacks discipline. The work gets done but only when a deadline threatens. Too much of it is instinctive. Zach told me who you were, how you adapted during the interview. You're clever enough to go beyond making models and handing out advice. Provided you don't join the boozy high-wire set."

"I'm flattered."

Celia forked up fettucine. "I came here with a degree in sociology. Sociology! Can you imagine? I felt damned lucky not to be sitting behind four-inch thick glass at a Job Centre. I worked hard and Zach recognised that. Now I sort of run things in his absence. I say 'run things' but there's a snag. I'd like to look further than next Friday evening. Get rid of one or two idiots, send a couple more on training courses. Can you see what I'm getting at?"

"If Gamester's ying, I'm yang. I've got too many straight lines, I'm too predictable. Those straight lines are one reason my wife divorced me. She's recuperating in Switzerland and I phoned her because I needed impartial advice. She said take this job. I probably would have, anyway, but her advice helped."

Celia laughed. "An ex in a million. I'm glad you're here."

Their eyes engaged and Hatch wondered what complexities were building up. Celia said, "I'm not sure about your love of straight lines. You weren't outraged in the Land Rover."

"Different world," Hatch shrugged. "A rite of passage. A new scalp in a land where genders are more flexible."

"Christ, you make me sound like Medea. But then perhaps I am."

"I didn't mind."

"Didn't mind? Mr Puss-in-Boots."

"I thought I did very well. Being necked doesn't happen on the washing machine line."

"Think you can stand the pace?"

"Easily."

The week flowed into the next and Hatch did finished drawings for three more projects, phoned for quotes and provided interim budgets. As a new boy he sat in on response exercises for other parts of Superwoman where contestants' general knowledge, mental dexterity and physical abilities were tested. Never having watched competition TV he was astonished by the discussion, the need to examine and resolve aspects of political correctness. Suppose a fat woman had to climb a ladder – How would that be handled? Would it be better avoided? And should the filming compensate for ugly contestants? Throughout, Celia was fairly close at hand, interested in his reactions, teasing him about his ignorance of TV. He was pleased to resist her jibes and wanted to know more about her. But she regularly opened their conversations and he wasn't sure he had the right to ask.

Over the weekend he put down a deposit on a one-bedroom flat in much more salubrious Bonehill. Rather than give notice to Mr Wee he sought out Jimmy who listened with a blank face and shrugged at the news. His slack posture suggested he had been betrayed.

"I'm not moving far away. I could visit."

Another shrug.

If anything Mr Wee's face was even blanker. "When you go?"

"Two weeks' time, if that's convenient."

"You go now. You want?"

Hatch explained he needed to buy furniture. Perhaps the offer to visit Jimmy would soften the blow? Suddenly he lacked the energy. "In two weeks' time, then."

The following Tuesday Celia insisted on lunch at the Italian.

"All settled in?" she asked.

This was banal. "You could say so."

"Domestically?

"I'm moving the weekend after next. If I don't die of claustrophobia."

"How's your social life?"

"Moribund."

"Good. Ride me home tonight on your big green bike. I'll give you dinner."

"No can do. You need a crash helmet."

"I took the precaution."

He resisted asking how. Or why.

When they met in the car park he was glad she had also found an anorak even though it was a warm summer's evening. She ran her hand over the Kawasaki's rear end. "The pillion's for someone with no-bum at all And have you seen those foot-rests? It'll be like tucking my toes into my trouser pockets."

"We're talking speed not comfort. Imagine you're a foetus."

"Or the beast with two backs."

Hatch buttoned up his waterproof jacket. "I take it you've ridden pillion. You won't sit up when I turn into a corner?"

"An on-and-off boyfriend had a bike, hence the helmet. And yes, there are no women's rights on the rear seat. You're the boss."

The bike was more powerful than any he'd ridden and continued to exhilarate him. But as he took the handlebars with Celia behind him he knew this would be different. Her body sleekly engaged his, her knees underpinned his thighs and her hands rested provocatively on his hips. He was now more than just a bike rider, part of a coupled couple perhaps. He rode briskly but within himself; she was the perfect passenger, an immobile sack of cement. Held up by a red light he heard her say, "You ride well."

On an empty dual carriageway he touched three figures but she remained relaxed. Only the pressure of her body and the passage of air marked their speed. Adam stirred.

Celia's tiny starter-home semi was in a modern development masquerading as a Midlands village halfway to Redditch. She hopped off the bike athletically and removed her helmet, keen to show her face. "That was great. I'd almost forgotten… Park the bike round the back and come inside."

Hatch took off his jacket, left it on a kitchen chair and followed her into the living room. There she took his hands and pulled him down onto a two-seater couch where their knees touched. Briefly she disengaged a hand and pushed the black rimmed glasses up her nose. "I've never brought someone home like this. Blatantly, like. We can do it straight away, if you like. Or we can delay things – a meal, a walk to the pub. Or you can say you don't want to and I'll bear that as best as I can…"

The glasses slid back down. "Why am I talking like this? It must be how I see you. Old-fashioned, gentlemanly, given to seeing women as ladies, timid about demanding sex. Oh yes; one practical matter but not quite a deal-breaker. I left the Land Rover at Game-ster. You can stay the night or make a long dog's-leg to pick me up tomorrow."

Pushing the glasses back up again she laughed. "Perhaps I'm nervous. You've seen them on the tip of my nose before. What else? It's not Mills and Boon, not love at first sight. Sex at first sight then. But if it doesn't happen, it doesn't happen."

Her face was triangular. Slightly girlish, younger than her years. Certainly the heavy glasses were confusing since they added an alien harshness. Dark blonde hair fell round her face like an inverted tulip cup. Her eyes were grave. "Is this all too quick for you?"

He shrugged. "It's the irony. I'm like most men, I have these in-ner monologues. I look at a women and ask: would I want to sleep with her? It's quite automatic, quite secret. Age, looks, figure, attitude, it doesn't matter. Perhaps women do it too. As I say it's secret, mostly nothing happens and all of us get on with our lives. Down in the store room you sparred with Zach and I was fascinated, saw you were unique. Answered yes to that inner question. You kissed me in the Land Rover and I wondered why. Why me? Now things have moved on: you're talking about it openly. I still haven't caught up. Why me?"

He squeezed her fingers and said, "I'm a child of my time; what I do know is I don't want to fuck you. I hate the word. Dogs fuck. If pressed I'd probably say 'sleep with you' which is silly because sleeping's what it isn't. There is a better phrase in the Bible: to lie with. And that's what I'd like. However there is a 'but' and it probably sounds feeble to you but not to me. I can't bear the risk of hurting you."

She opened her mouth but he hadn't finished. "Stupid, isn't it? You've got more power to hurt me. And you might well. Even so, I don't want to hurt you."

"Why might you?"

"I'm involved with women. My ex-wife recently had surgery and I feel some obligations; the thread isn't entirely broken. From my side, at least. Another woman has wrung my heart. She came into my life just once and I think she's gone out of it for good." He laughed nervously. "Finally… there's the wife of a friend, an unwanted complication."

He shifted uncomfortably on the couch. "I sound like Bluebeard or Don Giovanni. Being out-of-work has softened my backbone. Perhaps I've become vulnerable. Who knows whether any of these sad involvements are significant? I like you and – I'm a sucker for this – I admire you. Perhaps you're tough enough. Perhaps I can't hurt you. I hope so."

"Come here, Bluebeard," she said. "Sit next to Celia, number four in your harem. Did Bluebeard have a harem?" She kissed him. "When a man and a woman do sex either can end up hurt. It's the dark side. A risk we take."

He held her face and kissed her hard. "If this is an affair it started gloomily. You know why? We didn't take lunch seriously, we're under-nourished. Scramble some eggs – no, I'll do it for you, and the toast. Get out the jam and the Nescafé. And then we'll -"

" – put an end to talk."

During the snack he spread egg on a toast finger and held it for her to bite. Saw her small white teeth. Afterwards, as she had teased Ericsson, so she teased him. Double-talk about load-bearing structures, nuts and bolts, screwdrivers. For the first time Hatch saw sex as a game. Neither silence nor solemnity were part of it.

Hatch said, "I know nothing about you."

"All you need to know is this… and that."

"Yes, but I need more. It's a vital part of sleeping – of lying - with you. Otherwise it risks being fucking."

"History isn't my strong point. I'll tell you, I promise. Not now."

"I've just remembered: 'Making love in the afternoon, With Cecilia up in my bed room'. Paul Simon didn't say the f-word."

"Too right. The word's too short. Let's make this… last."

For a time he played the older, steadier man, conscious of technique, meeting norms practised in films, read about in books. But the sight of an ear concealed beneath strands of hair, moisture on her lower lip, the sound of breath in her mouth - all put paid to detachment. He too breathed through his mouth, tried to hold back for her sake, recognised it was impossible, sighed. "It's been too long."

They walked to the pub, ostensibly to wind down but said little. Slumped in their seats, vacant, as if overtaken by an unpleasant surprise. What had sex told him about her? That she was not an innocent, that she'd been keen to explore him. And now? When he took her arm he felt her cling on.

"It wasn't what you wanted?" she asked.

"Tell me about yourself. Not your secrets. Who you are."

Mundane details. Middle-class parents whom she'd obscurely disappointed; conventional wildness at Essex, a poor degree. Jobs that led nowhere. Only in talking about her marriage were the admissions slower, more blurred. Hatch was surprised given the off-hand references to her "ex".

"That's enough. I don't need to know. Obviously it hurts." He grinned exaggeratedly. "Favourite films. Holidays. Anything."

They were back in the house, again on the sofa. She said, "It was the way it ended. After two years, struggling financially like most young couples. I thought I'd done what was expected. Very quietly he told me he was leaving. He ticked off the reasons; got up to eight if I remember. All those failings and I honestly didn't recognise a single one. I lacked a sense of responsibility, was shallow. I had no reason to think he was lying and I accepted it all. He could have been talking about a neighbour for all the sense it made."

Hatch recalled Prudence reluctantly outlining the husband she'd left. Decency and thoughtfulness turned into grounds for divorce; sympathy that had aggravated things. Finally, a man any woman would have rejected. "You could have just described the way my wife left me."

When they kissed her brisk dominance had gone. As they made love there was even a return of innocence, a reconstruction. The sex was prolonged and, unless she was fearfully skilled at protecting his feelings, her climax was both real and mixed with something like relief.

As he fell asleep he now knew he could hurt her.

BASED on Hatch's figures, Gamester's accountant provided a budget for his year's work. It was more generous than he expected and Celia explained this was company practice. A twenty-five per cent contingency was normally added to cover the eternal bugbear - emergency costs close to the deadline.

"Suppose I finalise the work and I'm under budget. Could I spend some of the balance?"

There was affection between them. "How final is finalise?"

"If I'm comfortable would you be happy?"

"I guess that's why we employ you. Dependability plus imagination. A solid combination. What had you in mind?"

"An electronic stopwatch which shows how the competitor's doing against the clock. Makes things more visual and adds buzz for the viewers. Here's some sketches to give you an idea. I'll get quotes. We may get a discount or even a freebie if the supplier's name is prominent."

"How commercial you are, my dear."

17. CLARE

Speaking professionally

THE PLASTIC brace was slacker now which meant it was doing its job. But she'd have liked proof in the mirror and this was hard to assess. Beyond that there were the social aspects of leaving it in or taking it out. That very morning she'd had to tick off a marketing assistant for missing a deadline in analysing some raw data. Brace in or out? Where lay the greater authority? She'd tried a novel compromise; brace in, comment uttered through compressed lips. It hadn't worked. She sounded angrier than she felt. Also she'd over-specified her visitor's chair and the girl, though terrified, looked too comfortable leaning back against the soft leather upholstery.

Her secretary buzzed. "Do you have time for Mrs Gardner?"

"Mrs Gardner?"

"Mike's wife."

For whom it would be brace out.

"Hello Clare. It's Barbara, by the way. I brought in mail for Mike and I've wanted to meet you for weeks. I won't waste your time. I'll be away in five minutes."

"Don't rush, please. Give me chance to show how well organised I am."

"No proof needed."

"Coffee? I buy Colombian and have my own system. It's much better than Mike's."

Barbara said, "Now there's a surprise."

Filling the percolator she glanced back at her boss's wife. The pale green linen suit was clearly tailored, the shoes bought in London not Basingstoke and the hair styled by someone as skilled and as expensive as Kylie.

They sat on Clare's rarely used chesterfield. Barbara said, "I'll spare your blushes for the moment about what I've heard. How's life at Garton?"

"Well, I can't spare *your* blushes. Mike's perfect. He wrote my job description and it's no more than five hundred words. So the work and the responsibility are what I make of them. When I took over marketing he rearranged things within a week, even moved their offices nearer mine. On the other hand he's no pushover. I suggested a new layout for management minutes and he agreed immediately. But when I told him I could cut two work stations from the PLC assembly line he told me I couldn't and told me why. That was a relief."

"He knows his company."

"Oh, he's the boss."

Barbara inclined her coiffed head. "His decisions usually turn out well as you've seen. And he has the knack of foresight. He recognised where point-of-sale was going long before the manufacturers did. Urged two of them into a merger and took over their lines. We had seventeen percent growth that year."

"He's earned the right to do without a tie," said Clare

"The tie was a conscious decision. He tells me he saw grounds for another as he interviewed you. Women are rare in this business, even rarer at your level. It wasn't just a matter of appointing a competent woman to a senior – technical – position. It said something about the company, showed Garton as confident. He's sorry he never thought of it before."

"There are CEOs who never would."

Barbara said, "Indeed. What Mike doesn't know is I'm here on my own. I want to take things further but I need to talk to you first. I used to be in executive PR and you have qualities which could be actively exploited."

"You'd better explain."

"You may find what I'm going to say embarrassing. Certainly Mike did. But remember this is what I'm good at. During your first few weeks here he ran on about your triumphs and I asked, 'What does Clare look like?' Pretty direct, eh? You needn't feel offended. He bollixed his answer so badly I had to find out myself. As I suspected we could all profit from your abilities... and the way you look."

Barbara held out her cup and Clare, confused, re-filled it.

Barbara continued. "Don't be shocked, please. I'm not talking strapless bathing costumes. It's far more casual and subtle. The first step will be to make you Garton's spokesperson. You're worried, I can see, but you needn't be. This is how it works. To begin with I'll pick conferences where you'll give industry papers or appear in forums. Nothing new or frightening in that?"

Clare shook her head.

"I'll target events that get press coverage. Your material will be written vividly, even controversially. Again, don't worry. If you aren't comfortable with it we'll change it. After that I'll be relying on the laziness of British journalists. It's a double whammy. Memorable stuff from a good-looking woman. Journalists love that combination."

Barbara sipped her coffee. "That's all you have to do, Clare. Success breeds success. Eventually TV newsmen will ask you to comment on the rise in copper prices, the techno-brain drain, and whether A-levels are getting easier. The final stage is delicious. You'll be able to say you're too busy and can't see them. Making you even more desirable. How do you feel about my scheme?"

"How does this benefit Garton?"

"By expanding on Mike's initial reaction. By emphasising how clever we were to swim against the tide and give you this job."

In the growing silence Barbara spoke less coercively. "If you don't like it we'll drop it immediately. You're far too valuable as you are. I know that already. The question is: do you fancy a public persona?"

Clare put her coffee down untasted. "I took this job because I knew I could handle the work, liked the company, liked Mike. As I said, my job is quickly described which means it's wide-ranging. If releasing me to the media helps I can't really say no. It doesn't scare me although there are risks. Let's go ahead." She laughed. "But there's a huge irony in my recent history. I have to decide if I should explain that."

"Dwell on it first."

As expected, just before she was due to leave that evening Mike knocked on her door. "I understand you slapped a marketing junior on the wrist," he said, taking the delinquent assistant's comfortable chair and hitching an ankle over his thigh.

"No big deal. Just a little tardiness. Has she complained?"

He laughed. "She wouldn't dare. But the story has got around."

"How do I come out of the story?"

"With awe. But I must say there's a sideline: have I been complacent in the past? I hate companies that bully and I want Garton to be contented. But have I bought contentment through lack of discipline? I don't care what her fault was or how you dealt with it. But the general reaction suggests in-house disciplining is fairly rare. We can't be so perfect, can we?"

Clare reflected. "Garton *is* contented. Too contented? I don't have a view. Talking about disciplining there's the small matter of my gender. Women can't afford to be weak nor must they overpunish. I'm probably tougher than a man would be. Marketing is my lesser responsibility and I can't let it take up too much time. I need to be able to ask for something then switch off until it's done. That's what this morning was all about."

"Any advice?"

"Discipline shouldn't be your concern. If it is then it spools back to a bad appointment. I'm hardly likely to say that's one of your faults?"

"Am I too impulsive then?" asked Mike.

Clare shook her head. "Only to people who can't keep up with you. I agree with Barbara. Garton proves you have a talent for looking ahead. Which is what I want from any boss."

"How about not being in control? How else could my wife slip in under my radar and subvert senior staff?"

"How about sneaky delegation? Having your wife raise a subject you didn't care to?"

Mike said, "Touché, even if it's untrue. Seriously, are you happy about Barbara?"

"I am. Did she mention the irony."

"You're considering revealing all. Sounds interesting."

"I think you should know. It explains why I accepted Barbara's idea."

As she described the bank interview he lolled on the chair, became grim then unhooked his supported ankle and leaned forward. "Incompetent bastards."

"I'm glad they showed their hand. Hindsight says it wasn't the job for me."

"But what's this about your appearance…?"

"Ah, I took the hint. You're seeing Clare Kepler Mk II. The remake."

"Am I the other side of the bank's coin? Influenced by appearance?"

"They were looking for a figurehead, you for a techie. I assume you wouldn't have employed an airhead."

Mike got up. "I'm having second thoughts. Barbara mentioned 'exploit'. Isn't that what the bank had in mind?"

"Exploitation has another, more innocent, meaning. In any case before I'm exploited I need to show I can do my main job. Also it's not all one way. Spokespeople can fall on their face and I haven't any real experience. On top of that there's a limit to how much we can control the outside world."

"Perhaps the risk is too great," he said, shaking his head.

"Come on, Mike. What's the worst that can happen. I make a booboo, there's some temporary embarrassment and I learn to operate within my means."

He stared at her then stuck his hands in his trouser pockets and laughed ruefully. "I've just remembered something. You are cool, aren't you?."

"Am I really? I had a comfortable upbringing: able to take risks, able to run home to Dad if anything went wrong. As to getting slapped down there are not many people – men or women – who reach forty without being hurt. The bank was a first. A Sevenoaks hair stylist, my mother's couturier and greater sense of realism got me over that."

"You're willing to do this risky thing?"

"I want to do it," said Clare firmly.

"Well, there's an end to the agonising. Another thing. You've met Barbara and she says you both get on. How about coming over for the weekend? With your family."

Her reaction must have been unmistakable. "Later then," he said quickly. "I've interfered too much."

Although her position qualified her for a large BMW she continued to drive the Jaguar. Perhaps for moments like this when its quietness eased her along the motorways after a long day's work. Ahead lay domesticity and quiet moments with Nick.

Jerry wouldn't be home for dinner nor would he have phoned in a reason. Once these absences had been irregular, now they were the rule and dated back to Clare's transformation. Seeing her fresh from Kylie that evening had caused his shoulders to sag, as if her dowdiness had been acceptable and now the game was up. His sense of defeat was especially noticeable at their rare social appearances - a fundraising cocktail party for the library and yet another inexplicable golf club dinner. Previously he'd treated Clare to a form of belittling that passed for spouse chat in that part of middle-class England. Now he remained hangdog by her side.

The disenchantment had grown. When Clare joined Garton Jerry forced her to predict her salary with possible bonuses and it was

was as if the last of his family duties had been blown away in a financial welter. Their main contact was reduced to the few moments in the early morning when his careless return to bed left her tugging the blankets back over her bare hips. Because their quaint but impractical house had only three bedrooms the only other option would have been for him to use the couch. Clare, however, saw this as forcing the issue and remained silent.

Birgitta now had a boyfriend and often took the evening off. To ensure she wasn't constrained Clare employed Sharon to prepare the evening meal and sometimes to babysit Nick for brief periods. Sharon, a single mother who had once run a local pharmacy, was however keen to get back to her own two daughters and there was little opportunity for conversation. As the evenings became progressively more silent Clare had to resist the temptation to keep Nick up beyond his normal bedtime.

Thus the exhilaration of working for an enlightened company dissipated on the drive home. Once, hardly believing what she was doing, she stopped at the Clackett Lane service station and wandered distractedly round the newsagent's, glancing at magazines that were of no interest, at pop CDs remote as planets. Aware of the solitariness that lay ahead.

Birgitta noticed Jerry's absences but avoided mentioning them even when Clare would have liked an opportunity to rant. Instead Birgitta urged visits to the theatre and cinema but these had never been Clare's preferences, certainly not on her own.

"There is that journalist friend. Who wrote the article."

"I'd feel I was using her. Worse she'd guess I was." When they'd last met they'd talked enthusiastically about further meetings. But Clare didn't want to play the disadvantaged wife.

Now she left the M25 and swung into the tight Sevenoaks exit travelling far too quickly, causing the tyres to protest. Speed had risen during her moody thoughts at the wheel. On narrower roads she drove cautiously.

As she bathed Nick that evening he said abruptly: "Sha'n give me Twix cos I was good." which had Clare counting the words on her fingers. Was it his longest sentence so far? She couldn't be sure. A mother would know. Should know.

A week ago she'd shared a carafe of terrible red with Chantal at an over-priced wine bar crammed into The Shambles. The atmosphere between them was semi-valedictory since Chantal was due to start a three-month contract in Hong Kong.

"My best friend, my best most interesting friend, you have become beautiful. And yet you always were beautiful. Just hiding. Now out in the open, attacking. And yet completely English," said Chantal. "I fear I express myself badly."

"Not a normal failing."

"You want something else, something better. Obviously."

"Not really. I simply - "

"Not really!" cried Chantal. "You wretched Englishwoman. How you understate."

"I needed to be different."

"For dull professional reasons. But changes will happen. And you will change other people."

"Oh my French cartoon. How I'll miss you."

Alone apart from the sleeping child Clare found to her minor despair she'd read all her copies of New Scientist. Too many reflective evenings. She turned reluctantly to her unopened Reviews of Modern Physics, a subscription which should have been cancelled a decade ago. At random she read "Electromagnetic traps for charged and neutral particles" for less than five minutes then tossed it aside. The text was difficult enough let alone the narrative logic. Physics had been the basis – the springboard – of her professional life but that time now felt more like adolescence. It hadn't helped her to address a marketing assistant who had ignored usage patterns in the south-east. Nor would it help her re-assess the PLC assembly line. Physics was a pension fund which doled out smaller and smaller payments, more of a reminiscence than a management aid. Yet it was still a reassurance which kept her on the right side of a fence dividing them and us. A snobbism? A defensible snobbism.

BARBARA Gardner now visited regularly to discuss Clare's public role. This time she brought the industrial magazine, Real Production. Clare's chesterfield was getting used more and more.

"Read this," said Barbara. "We get much better coverage when we bring up Garton's manufacturing activities rather than staying with electronics all the time. And let's have no more ye-of-little-faith protests. Slipping your photograph into the press pack paid off."

Clare hadn't seen the point of speaking to production engineers about electronic point-of-sale systems but the results were spectacular. Seven other speakers had addressed the one-day conference yet her paper took up a third of the magazine's coverage. An authoritarian head and shoulders had been spread over two columns.

"The key was the title we chose," Clare admitted. "Engineers believe EPOS is too costly for anything less than a supermarket. Aiming at small storage operations brought in bags of questions. The editor of this magazine wants details of a fully costed installation."

"We don't want you wasting your time with small potatoes. I'll get our freelance PR to write it. Controlled-circulation mags are always keen to print good nuts and bolts stuff. But now we're shooting higher."

"You've hit another bull, haven't you?"

Barbara laughed. "My dear Clare if it wasn't for you I'd be organising coffee mornings for Age Concern. Instead I'm turning you into a star. No, that's not right. You are a star. I'm adding a little twinkle."

"So where will I be twinkling?"

"The perfect forum. Organised by The Financial Times so we'll get a wider audience. And a nice broad subject you were born to tackle: women in high-tech industry. We'll have some new photographs taken."

That afternoon Clare returned to the PLC assembly line. Mike had insisted the layout could not be improved but she couldn't leave it alone. Working with the line supervisor and the operators she had created a mock-up component feed which had tested well. Close up with those it would affect she was careful to explain that removing a station would mean redeployment not redundancy.

"The line becomes ten metres shorter and we save lots of lovely space," she said.

Wearing a white lab coat was a bad decision since it inflated her status and made it difficult to get sensible answers about whether the new station would be too cramped. Everyone knew what she was looking for and tended to be over-optimistic, trying to please rather than inform. She was making a quick dimensioned sketch so she could play around with the positioning on a drawing when the supervisor tapped her shoulder and pointed to the tannoy. "You're wanted: outside call."

The interruption broke her train of thought and she spoke brusquely on the supervisor's phone. Only to hear her secretary transferring Birgitta.

"Mrs Kepler. I am sorry to worry you. Perhaps I should not have phoned. It is difficult."

Clare thought immediately of Nick. "Let me call you from my own office."

Hurrying along corridors that were long and unsympathetic, Nick's name drumming in her ear, she took fleeting comfort from Birgitta's "difficult". An accident wouldn't be difficult. Was pain difficult? Injury? At her desk she breathed deeply, her finger-tips slipping on the phone buttons.

Hearing Birgitta's voice she butted in. "Is it Nick? Nick?"

"Nick?" Birgitta sounded puzzled. "No, not Nick. He is at nursery."

"Then - ?"

"It is Mr Kepler."

Changing direction required prodigious effort. "Is Jerry all right?"

Birgitta continued to sound puzzled. "He is all right, I suppose… He came here an hour ago. Said I should not phone you."

"Just a minor matter?"

"Not a minor matter. He has gone. He insisted I should not call you. 'Let her find out when she comes home.' He said that. But I have called you."

"Gone?"

"Taken his clothes. But I must not phone you. I have phoned you. Is that correct?"

Birgitta's concern with nicety was comical yet her voice was agonised.

Clare said, "You did the right thing. Has he left a message?"

"Perhaps in the bedroom. But I didn't enter the bedroom."

The sense of etiquette. "It doesn't matter. You sound disturbed, Birgitta. I'm sorry about that. Should I come home and pick up Nick?"

Neither of them was on the same wavelength. The question outraged Birgitta. "Of course I can pick up Nick. I am not disturbed. It is you, Mrs Kepler. An unhappy time."

When she had put down the phone Clare tried to decide whether there was any point in returning home early. As it was her secretary opened the door. "I'm sorry. I overheard and got involved. Take the afternoon off."

"Thanks. It would be better if I did some explaining first."

"Of course. Silly of me."

She hated calling Mike without warning. It broke her terms of employment; managers should manage. But was the phone subtle enough? She too found herself struggling with etiquette.

"Is he free for two minutes, no more, I promise?" she asked Mike's secretary.

Mike's great indulgence was sailing. His office, home to models of all the yachts he had owned, resembled a room at the Greenwich Museum. He stood up, tanned and robust, among these fragile ornaments. "Take a seat. This is a first. It must be serious."

"Perhaps you can decide." Quickly she summarised the vagaries of her marriage, ending with, "I can't see how going home would help. But would staying here type me as a heartless, career-driven bitch?"

"And Barbara's up in London. Why don't you try me with something easier? Let's see, there may be a note on the kitchen table but I don't see that helping. Given the way he spoke to the au pair, it seems unlikely. How about taking your son out of nursery and going to your parents'?"

"I'm not sure I'm up to a wordless session of 'I told you so'. Not that they'd be so cruel but it would be ever-present."

Mike spread his hands. "I'm slightly useless. I feel my advice would be second-best to whatever conclusions you reach. It's why I employ you." He grinned. "And why it tickles me to hear you couldn't leave the PLC line alone. I should be angry, of course, I am the boss. But what a hypocrite I'd be. I'm straying from the point. How is this going to affect you?"

"As far as Garton is concerned, very little. I've always accepted I'd adapt to any changes Nick caused. That's why we have a cleaner, an au pair and now a woman who prepares our evening meal. After all Jerry was never an attentive father even though Nick thinks a lot of him. If this is permanent, he's too young to require an explanation, thank God."

"Are there close friends nearby?"

"No. Nor any a long way off. Our jobs have prevented that. And although Jerry's golf demands social skills I get along without them."

"I find that hard to believe."

"I fear you see the best of me at work. I was always too serious during the early years. Now I'm stuck with it."

"Rubbish. But this isn't addressing the problem. Take the afternoon off anyway. Phone me at home if you need more time. What do you think of Barbara's latest bit of stage management with the FT?"

"Her deviousness astonishes me. It's only taken a few goes and I'm already in the spotlight."

"She enjoys it. It makes more sense working for Garton than killing time with a charity. What's important is she likes you. I don't want to take advantage of your problems but you might now reconsider a weekend with us."

At home there were emptied drawers, a wardrobe that now held only his unwanted clothes and the strange absence of several video cassettes. Clare tried to recall the missing titles but couldn't. The digital clock from his side of the bedroom was another absentee and a vacant peg showed where his coffee mug had hung. The expensive Krups percolator had left with its master though this could have been predicted. He'd obviously planned his departure; why else would he have sorted through the cassettes?

She was inclined to let him make the next move but decided this was irresponsible. At the pro-shop she was told it was his day off. Was there a contact telephone number? It remained the one she was calling from.

Unwilling to linger in the house she overturned a lifetime's prejudice and took Nick to MacDonalds where he stared open-eyed at others of his age eating chips with their fingers and was overwhelmed – touchingly so – by a box that came with the meal and contained a disassembled plastic toy. As Clare put the pieces together he watched while she, in her turn, felt her stoicism drain away. For the first time she recognised Nick's tendency to be charmed by events and places which didn't appeal to her.

Unfortunately this was not one of Birgitta's nights out and she warily set the table while Clare heated the prepared ragout. Birgitta was embarrassed by the memory of her disjointed phone call and responded in monosyllables. Some bridge mending was in order.

"You're right, Gitta. Mr Kepler has left, certainly for some time and perhaps for good. I'm sorry you were involved. If he comes to the house or phones, tell him to send me a note. You shouldn't have to act a referee."

Birgitta shook her head gloomily and Clare wondered how long she would stay in this now lopsided domestic unit.

18. CLARE/HATCH

Intersection

NEITHER Clare nor Jerry wanted to meet each other in the immediate future but domestic trivia ensured it happened. Access to a joint savings account had to be revised. Some clothes, majestically left behind, were now found to be necessary. A roof-rack for the Range Rover was retrieved from the garden shed. Keys returned. And Clare had Jerry's new telephone number.

As a result she now knew he was living in some splendour with one of his clients. Whether it was Daphne, the pupil who had derived status – if not golfing skills – from her lessons wasn't clear but it seemed likely. Jerry didn't elaborate but this was understandable given the contempt he'd expressed for that particular daddy's pet. Clare was curious about her age.

"She must be quite young," she said over the phone.

Jerry allowed an indeterminate grunt. Confirmation by default, then. Presumably he had solved his problems as a lover. A woman in her twenties could hardly be expected to sympathise with such a crucial shortcoming.

"Anything else?" she asked, hoping for, but not expecting, a glancing allusion to his son. None came.

Emotionally Clare was in control. Jerry's departure had been on the cards too long for her to feel newly hurt. Yet she could not escape feeling broken in some way. Even defeated. This was most apparent later in the month when she took Nick to spend a weekend with Mike and Barbara and found herself installing him in the bedroom of one of the Gardners' sons, presently at university. Rock posters, suspended model aeroplanes, a copy of Swallows and Amazons and a pile of tee-shirts were proof of a normal upbringing. Nick's progress now seemed disrupted, in danger.

Downstairs she discovered herself to be a social solitary and it came as a shock. At both evening meals there was a lack of balance which other guests could not disguise. Everyone tried hard but she quickly recognised she was a conversational obligation, a single mother like the woman who prepared her evening meals.

Birgitta's trauma became a memory and her mothering of Nick resumed, perhaps intensified - an important benefit. Clare was finding that after even a normal-length working day, the drive back left her little time for motherhood. To compensate she left early if uneasily on Wednesdays. Another new tyranny included finding time for regular salon visits.

Because the Financial Times forum represented "a rich opportunity" Barbara proposed bringing in a professional writer.

Clare baulked. "I've always written my own material."

"But mainly for specialist audiences. If you take the right tone this could be picked up nationally."

"The right tone?"

"The exact level of controversy. Not shrill - even-handed, justifiable."

They stared at each other but Barbara knew her trade. "I won't have you misrepresented. Tell the writer what you want to say and he'll shape it for the media. You'll still be you."

But with a rather more polished voice. The writer made quick notes and asked a dozen questions. It was her answers which formed the bulk of the paper. And, Clare discovered to her secret shame, the end-product was easier to read than her own efforts.

Tweaked by Kylie and wearing the palest of grey suits over a striped blue and white blouse she moved to the lectern and opened with a light-bulb joke which wasn't even new but which she improved by treating the second line as a throwaway. Guidance for this was there in her notes in square brackets. She enjoyed the pleasing ripple of laughter.

She admitted few women had worthwhile senior jobs in "the technologies" – a locution invented by the writer. "But I have." Others had told her she'd passed through something called a glass ceiling. "I'm asked how I did it and people seem to expect an answer that's mystical or carnal."

Pause, said the instruction. Again laughter rippled. "The answer is neither. With a sociology degree I could be still banging my head on all that glass. Instead, it helped that I'd done physics. Or maybe I was just lucky."

Look out at the audience now. She did so, grateful to Kylie. "And that's where it all starts. Not enough women take degrees in physics, in chemical engineering and all the other so-called hard subjects. And not enough people ask why. And even fewer educational analysts – most of whom seem to be men (Pause.) – provide any answers.

"So it's up to me to explain. Except that I'm not sure I can. But I can explain about skiing. I tried skiing in my teens and one thing was clear. There were those that had seen it on TV and liked what they saw – liked the grace, liked occupying that landscape. And there were those who booked a winter holiday on the slopes because their friends had. The skiers who went parallel first all came from the first group. They'd responded to ski-ing's aesthetics. The others simply took the classes because that was what one did.

Again she looked out - following a written instruction to find and address an individual from the crowd. Most wore suits, including the women, since the forum was aimed at middle to senior management. But one man had shed his tweed jacket and even rolled up the sleeves of his green plaid shirt. An easy target. "You can see where this is leading. A majority of kids – male and female - pass through school with little enthusiasm and no idea of where education might lead. As the terms go by the choices harden as their performance is totted up and their teachers and/or their parents look for the short odds bet. Surprise, surprise, this turns out, more often than not, to be English, history or one of the other easier options

(A pause to check whether the audience sympathised with this attitude.) and you can guess the rest."

The bare-armed man appeared to nod. "So the universities fill up with students who fitted in well with the biased matrix formed round secondary education. Referring back to our skiers, degree hunters tend to be those who accepted being taught and, willy-nilly, seemed suited to it. The ones who had a clear, keen view of the future? Well, there weren't many of those.

"So the situation is worse than we thought. Enthusiasm for a given career path is uncommon to begin with. It is eventually manufactured by a system which favours the line of least resistance. And since these generalities also favour boys over girls, the outcome is more or less inevitable.

"None of this is news. Nor is it surprising that there is little desire among girls for hard science. Parenthetically, I'll use physics as a science shortcut from now on. But if instead I chose, say, chemical engineering things would be even worse. (Pause.) I think we all know why young girls are not seduced by physics – the science, perhaps even the word, doesn't exist for them. They can be forgiven because the history of physics has been hard on their gender. No female Einsteins, no female Bohrs. Once we've ticked off Marie Curie and – in the case of the very well-informed - Rosalind Franklin –"

Look at your target listener, said the bracketed instruction. Clare addressed Bare Arms. "Just checking. But of course you all knew about her, didn't you?" A confirming ripple.

"Since we're so rare I better get down to cases. And I'm afraid you'll have to make do with the case I'm most familiar with - mine."

Becoming more conversational she summarised her own progress beginning with her first exposure, aged six, to technology (When her father had ordered the x-ray authentication of a Reynolds), the pig-headed way she had resisted teachers who attempted to push her into medieval history or – failing that – archaeology, on choosing between commerce and research ("Can anyone name the

head of Cern?") and finally the difficult step-up into industrial management ("Difficult because it seems counter-intuitive.").

"There were real problems in my first managerial job which
concerned an MoD contract, still the subject of the Official Secrets
Act. The work was broken down into sub-groups one of which I
headed. Competition was very strong. I must say other groups discriminated against me but then they discriminated against each other. I have thought long and hard about whether I – as a woman -
was seen as a soft target. The trouble is I was also a novice so I
suppose it was a bit of both."

This time she not only looked directly at Bare Arms but smiled
modestly. "Fresh-faced and keen I worked hard and was promoted
to project manager. But if I'd played by the rules after that I'd still
be there. The others enjoyed the commercial equivalent of academic
tenure; this took the form of job descriptions which protected
them. My solution, which I doubt would be available these days,
was to assume responsibility for the administrative and analytical
work which no one else wanted to do. From this I proposed cost
savings based on changing the job descriptions. As a result the
problems departed as – I'm glad to say – did several of my recalci-
trant colleagues." Clare could tell the audience approved of this.

Disguise the change of subject by turning to a new sheet and
flicking through what remains, she was told. In compiling the notes
she had wondered whether she should touch on her most recent
experience of discrimination. But the writer had been quite firm on
this. "You're under no obligation to tell the whole truth. However
you arrange that information there is no way you can avoid doing
yourself a disservice. You're not required to bare your soul."

Clare resumed. "There is of course no better asset than understanding your brief; if possible, rather better than your line manager.
But I'm sure you all recognise that as one of the great truisms, the
equivalent of favouring good hygiene and democracy. What is far
harder to define is picking the right moment to use this knowledge.
Here I must confess I had a secret weapon not generally available.
Wealthy and indulgent parents! I apologise for being so wretchedly

Sloane. But I learned an important lesson that is generally applicable. I was able to take risks that were more or less risk-free. And most of them came off. After a while I realised that speculative proposals from subordinates are accepted more often than not. Does that sound like a very big claim?"

Bare Arms wasn't lolling in his seat but sitting up, looking straight at her.

"Put yourself in the senior manager's position. What do you want from your juniors? Management by rote or flashes of imagination? Or are all those pep talks about motivation just so much hot air? Personally I welcome those flashes and so did my senior managers back in the dark ages.

"Am I telling you anything you don't know? Probably not. But here's something you may not know. Given the subject of this forum and given my position at Garton you could be forgiven if you anticipated a list of all the dreadful gender barriers I overcame to get where I am. In some respects quite the opposite. In twenty years I've done a lot of defence work and it's my conclusion that women get a better crack of the whip in the weapons business than elsewhere. So-called brass-hats listen politely, ask good questions and defer to women managers. Why? I haven't the foggiest idea. If I had I'd bottle it."

Despite this, said Clare, women had to struggle in certain peripheral industries. She named them. What was the answer? "Visit schools and spread the gospel. Deny your daughters sociology. Seek out women at conferences like this and ask them about their careers rather than about their drink preferences. Re-examine job interviews and see if fear played a part. Risk positive discrimination where job applicants are virtually equal. Don't expect all colleagues to be crazy about soccer."

The applause at the end of her talk followed a murmur of approval.

At the lunch break speakers and chairman sat together at the same table. "Doesn't this defeat the point of having an audience?" asked a woman who worked for one of the drug companies. The organiser shook his head. "Trust us. If you mingled with the punters now they'd ask you all their best questions and there would be slim pickings at the open session this afternoon."

As they began to drift back into the auditorium a man who looked faintly familiar smiled at her, tentatively. "Just a quick word."

It took a second before she realised it was Bare Arms. Except that he looked more formal wearing his tweed jacket. He said, "You speak well. And regularly. I saw a report in Real Production."

"Thank you. They were quite generous."

"You deserved it. I'm a production engineer and if I'd known you were speaking I'd have been there. How would you feel about Garton getting a wider audience?"

"How wide?"

"Television."

It sounded pre-arranged. Surely Barbara wasn't that skilful. "Really."

"My name is Andrew Hatch. I am nominally a production engineer but my career has taken a strange turning and I work for a TV production company. There is no time now but I'd like to discuss co-operation on a TV programme we're creating. If you'd like me to call here's my card to get me through your switchboard."

"A strange turning?"

"Oh, yes. I'll need to explain that too. Should I call?"

"Well I'm not against strange turnings."

HATCH stayed for part of the open forum but sneaked away after deciding that there were only two types of questioners: men who wished to boast about their deep understanding of feminism and how this had paid off in the appointments they had made, and women who described the scope and glamour of their present position then slipped into a vengeful mode about the victories they'd won.

Under the scornful scrutiny of the hotel's cloakroom staff Hatch pulled on his waterproof suit and walked out through the foyer, thighs rasping audibly, to the scrap of car park the Kawasaki had been assigned. His helmet shut out the susurrus of London traffic and he followed signs to The North – that alien land – roaring effortlessly up Archway Road. On the M40, still remarkably free from traffic, he repeatedly broke the speed limit by large margins alternating this with periods in which he hid behind goods vehicles. The concentration required to control the powerful bike absorbed both distance and time and he was back at Gamester by late afternoon.

"You remember I asked whether there was more cash available for my techies?"

"Here it comes," said Celia.

"Well there's a good chance I can get what I want without it."

"Ah, walking on water!"

Hatch explained where he'd been and who he'd seen. "Garton could probably provide the display systems to guide viewers. Probably for free or a small amount of publicity. But I've got another idea. The woman technical director I heard could well be our boffin. Makes sense having a woman boffin."

"Good looking?"

"Well… er, yes. The point is do I have Gamester's permission to open negotiations?"

"This is one for Zach."

Ericsson asked the same question. Hatch said, "We're not talking about Miss World here. She's in her forties but well turned out. Not a Rank starlet but authoritative."

"So your plan is to visit the company and check out these – what are they? – displays? Fine, that's your side of the business. But anyone who goes – or might go – in front of the camera is my business. I'd better come with you. It's not that I don't trust you but anything like this has mega-chances for embarrassment. If she passes muster I'll give you a nod and you can explain what's needed. Without my nod you stay quiet."

"Christ, it sounds like a bloody cattle market."

"That describes it exactly. What we don't want is to say, 'Come and be a TV star.' and then, five minutes later, 'Sorry, we don't like your face.'"

Hatch shuddered.

OVER the past fortnight he'd spent his evenings furnishing and decorating his new flat with no time for Celia. Now she walked past his desk and raised her eyebrows.

"How late can I arrive?" he asked.

Celia shrugged, meaning anytime. It was a gamble but Hatch was in a gambling mood. The first part of the evening would be spent with Hester.

Hester's rendezvous was at a Solihull art gallery open evening, part of an ironclad alibi. "Proof absolutely positive if you bought a painting into the bargain," said Hatch.

But Hester wasn't amused. "I'm here with a single man and haven't told my husband. The meeting's perfectly innocent but I'd rather Tom didn't know." They wandered around the rooms for half an hour pretending to inspect bloodless landscapes of The Peak District. Only then did they cross the street to a wine bar and order a bottle of syrah.

Weeks had elapsed since Hatch had bought the Makings dinner and disappointed them with his motorbike and his delight in Gamester. He was surprised but not alarmed when Hester phoned him to insist they meet. The table between them had been awkwardly fashioned from a wooden beer barrel.

As he looked at her he recognised the changes. Back in the dark days, soon after Prudence left, Hester's open face had a certainty and a strength he had welcomed. Even now he still appreciated her rounded, firmly held contours. But the immediacy had gone and decent, seemingly naïve Tom was present in spirit. What remained was whatever he owed Hester.

She spread her hands out on the barrel top. "Thank you for coming."

"Gawd, Hes, that's a bit formal."

"Yes it is, isn't it? But then we're here for my benefit. You could say I'm indulging myself even though it doesn't feel like it. There's this alibi for one thing. I've never betrayed Tom and I never will. Having a real reason to be here is one way of making sure he isn't hurt. Except it isn't a real reason and that casts a shadow."

Hatch wanted to agree but said nothing. Hester noticed. "Already we're at cross-purposes. You think the way I've occasionally embraced you betrayed Tom. Those lingering goodbye moments with my husband looking on approvingly. But they weren't treachery. He urged us both to be less formal." She flashed him a mirthless smile. "We'll get around to that in good time. First things first. Did you come here willingly?"

"Of course."

He asked, "Expecting what?"

"Reminiscence. Minor revelations. My knuckles rapped for being too serious about an unserious job. Statistics about older men and motorcycles."

"How about disinterested chat?"

Hatch shook his head. "Could our chat ever be disinterested? Pre-Tom we thought a lot about each other. All that may be dead but the reasons still exist. In me at least."

"Really!"

"You sound surprised."

"Ever since I married Tom you've been so uneasy in my company. And I'm not talking forbidden fruits. It's as if I worried you."

"For fuck's sake," He chose the word deliberately. "You got married, we bid each other goodbye, afterwards you lurked, wanting to control me. Or that's what it looked like."

Hester no longer smiled. "So that's what it looked like?"

"And you got Tom to think the same way. Got him to manage my miserable social life. So you could hide behind him, it seemed."

"Why did I do this?"

"There's the puzzle. You used to be a great comfort. Instinctive, doing the right things. And then…"

"And then…?"

"I started to irritate you."

"Irritate?" Hester straightened up, crying the word aloud. In doing so her knee hit the bulging side of the barrel causing her to wince, to reach down and massage her pain.

"Don't forget Prudence taught me to recognise irritation. I understand I got up her nose so I assumed I eventually got up yours. The usual stuff: because I was dull, predictable, uninformed about the big things in life, a social liability. Who was I to dispute all that? I suspected both of you were right. Irritation was the real me."

"Whereas it wasn't that at all."

"You don't deny you changed?"

She said, "I won't deny that. But not because of your nature. I liked that steadiness. You never irritated me. There was a much more obvious reason."

Until now this had been his received wisdom. He'd never considered he might be wrong.

Hester's eyes softened as she continued to rub her knee. "God, there's no dignity in this place. Who dreamed up this wretched furniture? But honestly… couldn't you work it out? It was pretty simple."

"I saw… antagonism."

"You saw despair."

"Why?"

"Oh Andrew, Andrew. Moments ago you said I comforted you. Did the right things. And so I did. In the black dog days post-Prudence. But those days didn't last and you recovered. You didn't need comforting. I don't know what you did want but it wasn't anything I had. And it happened horribly quickly. Over one weekend."

"When? When?" This time Hatch moved incautiously and banged his knee even harder. Under different circumstances it might have been funny but Hester was far from laughing.

She said, "I'm not sure I want to re-live it. Oh, what the hell. This is why we're here, I suppose. A bloody suicide mission. I only hope to God you still remember those early weekends."

"The stately homes? Of course. Quite new for me, a revelation. You knew so much and I knew so little. You were marvellous…"

"Oh, I was marvellous all right. I had the whole of your attention. And that's a great thing to have. It's one of your talents that you accept being taught. But then it fell apart. Don't you remember?"

He thought back, trawling for clues. "It must have been that last visit. Shropshire, near Bridgnorth. Budmaston Hall. But what went wrong there? We had a wonderful day. Free as birds, guilt-free."

"You had a wonderful day out, my dear. Mine was rather less wonderful."

The "My dear." was not lost on him. But no obvious breakdown came to mind.

Hester shrugged. "I thought you might remember for me. Save me the agony. Gosh, I enjoyed those house tours, one of my brightest ideas. Having you passive and appreciative. Until Budmaston, that is."

He continued to look baffled.

"It didn't take long to recognise your resurrection. Quite simple, really; you started to talk on your own behalf. You remembered what I'd told you, you pointed out the style of architecture, the way the house was built, the system for managing the servants. Our roles were reversed. I became the student, listening to you."

"Wasn't that something to be proud of?"

Hester said, "In itself, yes. But it was a symptom of something else. You'd lost your sorrows. You were a functioning, thinking person again. You didn't need to be cherished. It was only then I realised comfort was all you'd ever needed."

They were silent. Their wine glasses long since emptied. "How could you be so sure?" Hatch asked.

Hester ignored the question, focusing instead on some distant memory. "We stopped doing stately homes. Just meals out, the cinema, walks. I tried being sympathetic again, working out what you wanted and you turned things round. Come on, Hester, never mind me, what do *you* want? There was no way back in. Then I truly screwed myself. I pretended nothing had changed. That I was still relevant. But you pushed me away - for the best of reasons, of course. You looked to do me favours. A tiny voice inside me kept saying no, no, adapt. But it didn't work." She spread her hands. "Lo and behold I got irritated."

This time the silence lasted much longer. Hoarsely, Hatch said, "How bloody horrible for you."

She raised a hand to her mouth muffling what she said. "I can't bear it. That you should say that. That there's still some feeling."

"Feeling? Why not? Am I supposed to be completely inert?"

She came close to tears but tears wouldn't have been Hester. She pointed to the bottle. "Pour some more wine. We need to wet our whistles. Stupid words."

That small break allowed them to retrench, to speak in more normal voices.

Hester sipped her wine. "This lurking. Not a pleasant word but it will do. I did the decent thing. Gave you up. Attached myself to Tom. Married him. But I could never quite give up the ministering angel. I lurked. I overdid the interest. I made sure I had Tom's support. And there you have it."

"And what's life like now?"

"I'm not ready to go broad-brush on that." Quietly she asked, "Do I seem slightly less menacing?"

"Do you still want me to come round?"

"Oh, yes. If you stopped it would be too exhausting to explain why to Tom. And when I'm properly relaxed it's a pleasure to see you. On the other hand if you arrived as part of a couple I might react differently."

He wanted to reassure her on this but knew he had nothing to say.

"Goodness, how old-fashioned this place is," she said briskly. "Not just the terrible tables. Candles in chianti bottles. The dark wood. Just like the seventies."

She was trying to make things easier but he was still exploring what he'd done to her. "Have we finished what we came to Solihull for?"

"You came. That was all I wanted."

"Has it helped?"

"Not particularly. But I don't suppose it was pleasant for you either."

"Not pleasant. But now I know why. I can cope better with the three of us."

He walked her to her car. With the key in her hand she turned to face him and he was reminded of a dozen other happier occasions. He said, "This business of kissing."

"Ah yes. Not much fun for you. My fault, I didn't try to make it any easier."

On a street where teenagers walked carelessly, swinging their arms, barking half sentences, he kissed her properly on the mouth, lips apart, her body against his. She offered no detectable movement, probably as a matter of pride. "I don't think you'd better do that again," she said tightly.

"No. But I had to do it. Wanted to."

Hester drove her Clio away quickly, noisily, as he walked back to the Kawasaki. Hatch too rode dangerously as if speed might blot out the ambiguity of that kiss. He sensed the depth of her pain, sorrowed for her. Now it was at an end. Once he'd been drawn there but that hadn't survived Tom and now she was a minor chronic ailment. Quite different from the brilliant and wounding memories he had of Linda who had arrived out of mythology and returned to some inaccessible pantheon. Regularly he dwelt on Linda's knowingness, her power and her distance. A week ago he had phoned her and had found her voice remote. More time, please. Why, he had no idea. Certainly she was beyond persuasion and beyond questions, while Hester had been only too ready to explain. Abruptly he pulled up at a red traffic light. It had been there, two hundred yards ahead of him, yet he hadn't reacted to its redness.

Celia had prepared a meal conventionally laid out on a plate: chops, roast potatoes, green beans. The arrangement dissatisfied him, it didn't fit her racketiness, the things that made her memorable. Afterwards the talk went nowhere and he saw she was simply waiting until they went to bed. He remembered his concern about hurting her and realised she had guessed he had seen another women earlier that evening. Halfway through some vigorous love-making, intended to drive away her doubts, he knew his intensity might well draw attention to them.

19. HATCH/CLARE

Strange turning

ERICSSON had come and gone. His role had been to speak to Clare and Barbara about Gamester, to outline their range of programmes and to provide more detail about a competition now provisionally called T-Woman. He warned them about confidentiality and then handed over to Hatch for "the nut and bolts". Hatch described three technical tests and showed how an electronic display – illustrating the contestants' options and their progress – would add visual impact while providing Garton with useful if indirect publicity.

They needed to decide how data could be induced to drive the display. Hatch and Clare became immersed in the options and as each was discussed Ericsson leant back, assessing Clare's telegenics under lidded eyes. Conscious of what Ericsson was up to, Hatch writhed uncomfortably, silently urging her towards articulacy and wit. He was hugely relieved when Ericsson visibly relaxed, laid his arm on the table and imperceptibly moved his head.

Hatch had a hurried private exchange before Ericsson left. "She'll do well," Ericsson said, adding outrageously, "You shouldn't have played her down,"

"Played her down?"

"Just kidding. You get to tell her the glad news. In a qualified way, of course. Mention it'll depend on a screen test."

When Hatch returned to the conference room Barbara was about to leave. "I assume the rest will be even more technical. You don't need me."

"There is one other thing," Hatch said. For the first time he mentioned the expert commentator, pointed out that the contest was for women and that Clare would fit in naturally if she wanted to. To get the point across he hinted at the size of audience the show would attract. "There will a screen test but I doubt that'll pose a problem."

The two women looked at each other then laughed in unison. "Sorry about that," said Barbara. "This is almost too good to be true. As you know I handle publicity for Garton and I've tended to push Clare as a PR asset. Even so I stopped short of television. Your offer is great news. That is, if Clare's prepared to accept."

"Let's not be too eager," said Clare. "Don't forget the screen test. What sort of qualities does this boffin require?"

"Qualities? Those you showed this afternoon and at the FT forum."

"Which are?"

"Ease in front of an audience. The ability to explain technology in simple terms. Natural authority. And…"

"Yes?"

"… a pleasing personality."

There was a brief silence. Hatch continued smoothly, "Don't forget I've seen you in action before today."

Clare asked, "Aren't you really looking for glamour?"

"Glamour that can think and chew gum," said Hatch, laughing.

Barbara had looked on, amused. "I take it a caption on the screen will give Clare's position?"

"Something like that. I can't say exactly but we'll want to take advantage of her background as much as you will."

Barbara said, "So, what do you think, Clare? It's a marvellous opportunity and I'm certain you'll do it well."

"How can I refuse?"

"And Garton can handle the equipment side?" asked Hatch

"Oh there's a range of options," said Clare. "I'll discuss them with the floor manager."

Barbara stood up. "Good. I need to go now. I'll leave you both to discuss the details."

Clare gave a long sigh and reached for one of the bottles of fizzy water at the centre of the conference table. "I may be the first Garton manager who's ever opened one of these. It may even be a wax model." The bottle uttered a hiss. "Ah, thank goodness. I've talked too much. Help yourself, Mr Hatch."

Hatch took a bottle. "Wax models; I know what you mean. All those gatherings about nuclear proliferation, war on want, EU member state agreements, the next Olympics. Delegates hemmed in by barriers of bottles that are never touched. Perhaps they're diplomatic symbols – full means a strong currency. Would you mind horribly if I drank from the bottle?"

Clare laughed. "I'd take it as a compliment. Suddenly I feel so middle-class using this tumbler. So, Andrew Hatch, the man who took the strange turning?"

She remembered.

"And yet you'd hardly know, would you?" Hatch replied. "Here we are talking about LED displays, data capture and gear trains. Echoes of my past life except everything is ridiculously simplified. What's strange is telly. Have you had experience of telly people?"

"Not yet. But that'll change if Barbara has her way. Not that I'm complaining. I share Mike's view – Mike's the boss, Barbara's husband – about women in industry. I'm the first woman manager at Garton and they're making a song and dance about it. I can hardly say no."

"You could be facing a strange turning yourself?"

"Mixing with telly people. Tell me about them."

Up to then the conversation had been neutral. Now a handsome, authoritative woman wanted his opinion on the company he worked for. He paused.

Clare noticed his hesitation. "Look," she said, "the floor manager's back this afternoon. An hour with him and we'll probably have an outline design for you. Before then we could have lunch. Quite frankly I'd like to pick your brains. I've taken on marketing responsibility for Garton as you must have guessed. I should know more about television than I do."

It was a legitimate bit of arm twisting. By now Hatch was confident Garton's hardware would come free and Clare was entitled to her quid pro quo. "I'm more than willing but I'm a novice myself."

"That makes you even more useful. Your card said BSc Eng and I'm assuming you worked in manufacturing."

"Production manager with Tempest."

"Tempest. Ah yes, washing machines. So Gamester was a culture shock?"

Hatch warmed to Clare's knowledge of industry. "What they're really good at is a quick grasp of the essentials. Let's put it this way, at university you read...?"

"Physics."

"Very fashionable. Imagine you've just introduced Garton to the atom. It's completely new to them. But they like the jargon. You explain the wider implications and they listen carefully. When you're finished someone says 'We could show it like this.' Proof they've understood everything well enough to do neat, accurate visuals of a difficult subject."

Clare's eyebrows rose sceptically.

Hatch laughed. "You're a physics snob! And I was once an engineering snob. I had to remind myself Gamester isn't there to machine engine blocks. Their job would be to tell the world how engines are made – in pictures and in eight seconds. It's a way of thinking and it's a rare skill. You and I learned our trades grinding away at maths and data. Gamester comes in by the back door."

"And there's a future in it for you?"

"Perhaps, perhaps not. I'm on a one-year contract. If I want that extended I'll have to move quickly. But I think I understand the set-up."

"Was it a big step down?"

"At first, yes." Hatch shrugged. "I loved manufacturing and loved my job. I had the right temperament for detail, for planning. Had it to excess according to several women I've known, including my former wife. Detail, they all said, made me a real old dullard. But Tempest shrank almost to nothing and I had to look elsewhere. I tried sales and it wasn't me. I almost went back into production, but at a lower level. Then this came along. A chance to show I'm an adaptable old dullard."

"Has it worked?"

"Let's put it this way. I was a lousy salesman. Deep down selling meant giving up too much of what I'd learned, what I valued. With Gamester I'm back to what I learned, but at secondary school - the basics. Yet the basics remain important. They're what took me into engineering in the first place. So now I use basics differently and – this is something I wouldn't knock – I reach a wider audience." Hatch thought for a moment. "I never imagined I'd hear myself saying this. But it's fun."

"And what do the women think now?" Clare jerked back. "No. Forget that. A question too far."

They were drawing closer, nevertheless. At the forum lectern she'd been a successful speaker, brilliantly lit for the video cameras. Earlier this morning she'd been the other half of a negotiating dialogue, flirting – as he had been – with compromise. Now she had shown she was capable of mistakes.

So she was clever, confident and human. Noticing it for the first time, she looked well too. Prudence was the yardstick for beauty and Clare did not belong to that exclusive tribe. But her long face – forceful and aristocratic – was easily remembered. As an article of faith Hatch prided himself in knowing nothing about clothing but Clare's embroidered white blouse with buttoned cuffs and full sleeves cleverly drew attention to the person rather than the garment. She appeared restrained but not severe, both qualities which fitted his way of thinking. And then there was her hair: finely graduated layers of colour deliberately angled and posing the question: What's so marvellous about symmetry?

"You're entitled to ask," he said. "I raised the subject of women in the first place."

"I was intruding."

"Do you really want an answer?"

"Oh, yes. But not out of idle curiosity. I'd say the women got it wrong; their view of engineering, and engineers, was knee-jerk. In your heart of hearts I'd say you thought so too. But you passed on their message which shows a desire to be fair. As a woman who works in engineering I'm interested to know whether your women friends were equally fair."

Neatly done, even if she was fibbing. "All I can say is my former wife advised me to join Gamester because it sounded interesting. But then she left me because she'd had enough of the standard model. Another friend, who helped set up the interview, is put out by my new enthusiasm. She seems to prefer unreconstructed Hatch."

"Snap. I took a big sideways step in my professional life and it didn't come off. It's still quite a raw memory. We seem to have got off track though. Tell me more about Gamester's ways and means."

Hatch swigged at his water, felt a burp rise up his throat and managed to suppress it. "Some of it is communal. About a dozen projects are on the go, some purely guesswork. When it's necessary to test a project against an audience a herd of employees is invited in and asked to comment. It works. Made me wonder if it could work in manufacturing. I know this is partly why managers write progress reports but they're so stilted, so formal. And they don't get read."

"Careful. You could go entirely native."

They both laughed. Hatch said, "In the foyer here I saw your list of client companies. That's quite a range. Would there be any percentage in one division commenting on another? Or would it be tanks on lawns? Protected interests?"

"I'd need to think about that via our floor managers - the heads of the different divisions. They're surprisingly various."

"Covering so many activities is a core asset I suppose. Is there any gain in bringing them together?"

Clare imagined discussions between the divisions and asked Hatch whether Gamester's spectators were allowed to be honest. There was interest there and the time slipped by.

"Time for lunch," said Clare.

"Outside?"

"Oh, I think so."

"If I supply the wheels you'll need a crash helmet."

"You really have gone native." They went in her Jaguar.

At the pub their discussion resumed. "You talked about a lateral step you almost took," said Hatch.

"Painful and embarrassing. It's safe to say you're seeing a different me these days. Funnily enough I'm taking that lateral step here at Garton. There's an assumption I can link up with the outside world but that remains to be seen. This boffin role could be a pointer."

Hatch forked up unaccustomed salad. "I assumed that when I recommended you to Gamester. You seemed confident enough."

"Oh I can communicate. But can I do it well?"

"It starts with how you're seen."

"And how am I seen?"

Hatch gratefully put down his fork. Salads were for those who paraded their food and now he could push the plate away. Here was an opportunity to engage her.

And she him. What she saw was stiffly projecting brown hair that would always be boyish, despite grey borders in his sideburns. Prominent, irreverent ears. Coloured cheeks and a pointed chin which had something in common with an old-fashioned child's top. The eyes were green and half-way towards surprise. Muscles in his forearms extended down into his square-tipped fingers – fingers that were a badge of his profession. His tweed jacket just failed to go with his dark green moleskin trousers, suggesting a modest wardrobe where colours were misunderstood or unimportant and garments were interchangeable.

It was a face she wouldn't forget. Those ears, in particular. Might they be described as muscular?

Hatch repeated the question slowly: "How are you seen? I'm hesitating and here's why. Would I dare ask myself that question?."

"Because you're a fellow? A chap?"

"Good God, no. Because I prefer to stay a mystery to myself."

"You're lucky you can be dismissive. And I was right. It's because you are a chap."

He thought for a moment. "Women can't afford to do that, can they? If I comment on your appearance all I'm saying is whether you fit into a man-made background. What's more, and with the best will in the world, anything useful I say is going to sound like flattery. I'm ashamed any of this should be a career factor."

Clare said, "It's even worse. Perhaps I'll tell you why, some time. What do production managers do?"

"Everyone thinks we just keep the wheels moving. We do but saving costs was probably my biggest contribution."

"So why didn't you start out in design?"

"Too airy-fairy. I'm strictly form-follows-function. I hate chrome strips and multiple curves that are hard to press. I'm told it's all obvious in the way I look and talk. Mr Predictable. But you did physics at – let me guess – Oxbridge? Yet here you are in charge of a slew of production lines. What happened?"

"Wadham pushed me towards a PhD but I preferred industry. I wanted real rewards for being clever: cash and position. A couple of papers in Nature weren't enough. I fancied competing with men."

"And beating them, I suspect."

She said, "That was just part of the score."

"It worked out? Obviously."

"Garton is a marvellous company. I have freedom and support. And esteem."

"But…?"

Clare said, "There's been a price. You too, it seems?"

"Spend too much time at the office and you lose touch elsewhere. When the marriage broke up I'd no idea why. I thought I was a good guy. What's more I only discovered my bad side a month or so ago. It was like finding I'd been disabled but never suspecting. What are your plans?"

"I want to stay where I am for the foreseeable. I'm being invited to write my own ticket here. And you?"

"Gamester's a release. I'm capable of more than I imagined. But I've got to keep learning and use what I've learned pretty damn quickly."

Back at Garton Hatch, Clare and the floor manager discussed three options for capturing the data and settled on barcodes. "They work with the projects you've mentioned," said the manager. "But they may restrict your imagination later."

"It's simply a matter of bearing it in mind."

"Mrs Kepler is visiting Gamester…?"

"In a week's time."

"I'll have some exterior sketches made."

Clare walked him to the car park and watched with mild amusement as he put on his waterproofs. "No worries about managerial dignity, then?"

"Proof I'm not an old fart."

"I think that's now a given."

"Well, thanks. And you'll make a superior boffin."

"A strange turning."

In her office there was a message to inspect the PLC assembly line she had tinkered with. "One station gone, twenty square metres saved," said the floor manager.

Clare touched the station operator on the shoulder. "You're taking components from two sources now," she said. "Are you comfortable? Is the work more complicated?"

"I made mistakes," said the girl. "But there's a rhythm and then it's easy-peasy. I'm not half as cramped."

Clare turned to the floor manager. "Kevin, I should never have got so involved. I should have sent you a memo and let you get on with it."

He grinned, "Ah, but could I have solved it so neatly?"

"Spare me the applause. It was bad management and I've been lucky. For one thing I should have found a use for the saved space before I touched the mock-up. In fact I'll be as good as my word and drop that one in your lap. But take your time."

"You're being hard on yourself. But I look forward to absorbing the space. How far can I go."

"Two suggestions: blue sky, minimum cost."

"Blue sky? Oh, I get you."

Clare looked out over the chattering conveyors. Through one of the building's rare windows she could see the metal-clad stockade round the fledgling military systems division. It touched off a fugitive memory. "Kevin, are you familiar with the other divisions? It's not a trick question..."

"Familiar?"

"In the technical sense. Shared technology, that sort of thing."

Despite her reassurance he looked guarded. "I know we share some systems. After all we're linked to the same IT."

"But there's no official exchange of manufacturing information between the divisions. Suppose floor managers met, say, once a fortnight to discuss detail problems and solutions. Would there be any value in that?"

He spoke slowly. "I'm not sure I'd want to stand up and confess to problems."

"How about letting everyone know about your solutions? This line modification, for instance."

"But that's yours."

"Kevin, it's yours. I won't breathe a word."

"Well…"

"See me in a couple of days."

BORED with the M4, Hatch went north via Old Sodbury and Nailsworth. The road suited his exuberance and he was able to pick curves, drop a gear and lay the bike over, sometimes switching back smoothly on to the opposite angle for a succeeding curve. Mrs Kepler's qualities and triumphant trajectory pleased him. He was proud he'd spotted her potential and relieved that Ericsson had concurred. There were burgers in his fridge but self-catering didn't suit his mood. A hot curry and a couple of bottles of Kingfisher were more the mark. Then he noticed the speedometer and throttled back.

20. HATCH

Crack propagation

CELIA hooked her foot round the leg of an adjacent chair and dragged it over to Hatch's desk. She pushed back what he had written. "Too long. Too many words."

Hatch stared. "You said forty seconds. That's OK for a hundred words. I timed it; I read it out aloud."

"I should have video-ed you. Shown you gabbling. This isn't for radio – the audience has eyes as well as ears. Give Mrs K some show-and-tell and slow her down."

"Show-and-tell?"

"Let her point to things, move her hands to suggest rotation, hold up three fingers for gear three."

"Shit," said Hatch deflated.

"Humiliation is the best teacher. And there's another thing. Sentences needn't be complete – subject, verb, object. Think about her as you write. You say she's clever - make her sound clever."

"Have I still got a job?"

"This isn't your line but it pays to know what we do. If it's any comfort we all made the same mistake. Say script and everyone thinks words. You'll be amazed how few words you need."

"Fewer words. I suppose it's more fun that way."

"Don't go overboard. Don't have her signing for the deaf. And you'd better get on with it. She's due here the day after tomorrow. You need to fax it mid-afternoon."

Hatch picked up his ball-point but Celia wasn't disposed to move. "What's this?" she asked.

"That? It's a con-rod."

"Con as in deceive? Flim-flam?"

"Con as in connecting rod. Connects the crankshaft to the piston. In an engine."

"But it's bent. That can't be right."

"Well spotted. If you over-rev, valves get out of synch with the piston. They touch at great speed. The con-rod bends, a valve flies into pieces, fragments do horrible things to the inside of the cylinder and it all costs a fortune to repair."

"This is a memento?"

Hatch shrugged. "Even engineers can be sentimental. Off and on I've done racing engines and this is a reminder. Racing drivers think in tenths, mechanics in days spent spannering." He indicated the piston. "This belonged to an engine with old oil in the sump. I hadn't time to put in new. I told the driver to keep the revs down. He got excited, as drivers do, left his braking late, changed down with the engine screaming and bingo – a cloud of smoke."

"Memento of a failure?"

"It celebrates the wisdom of engineers."

Celia laughed. "Did you ever race?"

"Not as such. I've tested cars on the track. But I'm far too cautious."

"Oh, I don't know. You don't hold back with the Kwacker."

He liked her using the slang word. "That bike's the last few hours of my childhood."

She stood up and propelled the chair back to its desk. "Let's see the script in - " She glanced at her watch. " – in thirty-two minutes."

The words melted away as he scribbled. Celia had urged him to imagine Clare delivering the summary and he saw her mouth opening and closing, her hands moving as the ideas presented themselves. He counted what he had written: fifty-seven words, six the longest group. After re-reading he took out four more.

As Celia bent over the new draft he noticed two smooth ridges in the back of her neck. Why hadn't he seen them before?

"It'll do," she said. "Use a yellow highlight for the instructions, that way you separate out the spoken text. Ask her to memorise it for Thursday." She looked up and he realised why she had lingered. He said, "You've bought rimless glasses. I didn't notice. Your fault. You were too busy bollocking me."

"Very unprofessional. Next time keep your wits about you during a bollocking. What's the verdict?"

"Huge improvement. The horn-rims looked like an act. And they didn't fit. Now you're an expert. And hard with it."

"Hard?" Her face habitually shone, as if she were about to start perspiring.

Hatch said, "You're a good bollocker. Oh, I'd almost forgotten. Once I've faxed this off I'd like to dash off to the airport. My ex needs a lift home."

"You won't be taking the poor girl home on the bike?"

"Give me credit. I'll rent a car and leave the bike there. Pick it up again when I've delivered her."

"How is she?" Convinced that Prudence was no threat, Celia affected concern.

"Reflective. Pleased about my liking this job. Different. Not so surprising given what she's gone through."

THE SHORT blonde curls were a surprise. Throughout their marriage Prudence had retained a smooth, autocratic bob. Now she looked younger but no less serene. Men on tip-toe outside the international arrivals gate followed her stately progress.

"What's this you're wearing?" she asked.

"My motorbike jacket. But I've got a car for you."

"Do you have a bike? You never told me."

"Not your kind of detail."

"On the contrary." She pulled at his sleeve. "Stop a minute. Let me a look at you. You look upbeat. Have you found a lover?"

It wasn't the word he would have used. "You could say so."

"Good. I'm glad."

As they eased out of the car hire park he glanced at her. It had been nine weeks; her face was less tense. "I am different," she said. "If you're interested."

"We'll call in at a supermarket to stock up. I could do you something when we get back."

Prudence was overfaced by the Sainsbury shelves. "For two months I've lived in a farm at nearly four thousand feet. We were almost self-sufficient. None of this packaging, this glitter."

"Muesli, then?"

"Oh no. Porridge. *Haferschleim*. With morning milk from the cow."

Hatch pushed the trolley to the vegetable section where she was more at home. At the check-out he loaded a monstrous amount of cheese and pasta into bags. When they reached the flat she unpacked her cases while he put away the groceries. Then he cooked falafels adding just butter and parmesan. What little she ate she did so enthusiastically. Afterwards there was real coffee.

She held the cup in the palms of two hands. "I didn't tell you when you phoned. I was pessimistic. Death was always a possibility and, to tell the truth, I'd have preferred it. Having that… growing there, poisoned me. I worried I'd wake up as someone I wouldn't recognise."

"You hid your feelings."

She looked round at her uninhabited living room. "There are limits to offloading one's fears. Especially after that horrible talk we had."

"But I forced you."

"I could have lied. Under those circumstances most do."

He said, "I look at myself differently, joke about my stodginess. Find new ways of not acting my age."

"Buying a bike."

"More radical than that."

She looked at him as she had at the airport. "Is she younger?"

"How did you guess?"

"You've been on my mind. Along with many other things. But you in particular." She placed the cup back on the saucer. "At first the farm was a bad idea. It was remote; the tiny village was a three-kilometre walk and the farmer's wife didn't like me languishing in-doors during the day. I took a book but there was nowhere I could sit comfortably in the village. The next day I walked to a bar in a larger village but after two hours I felt resented. Switzerland isn't terribly hospitable."

"Banks and drug companies."

"I was reduced to sitting in the church. Not one of those gilded lilies of the catholic baroque. A stern Calvinist interior which suited me. I read my book but mostly just sat and thought."

"It helped, obviously?"

"I doubt I have a talent for real meditation. In any case, after four days the pastor approached me. He was friendly and I thought he deserved a censored account about what I was doing. But he already knew. In the way of these rural communities I'd been seen in church by someone who knew where I was staying. This was relayed to the pastor who called the farmer's wife. She knew I was convalescent and imagined my vigils were unhealthy. The pastor simply asked if I needed to talk."

Hatch wanted more coffee but left the pot where it was.

"Seeing him as a foreigner – albeit with pretty serviceable Eng-lish – meant I could be frank. I said I'd been scared, especially of ending up... altered. I expected him to tell me to have faith, but he automatically assumed I was an unbeliever. He reassured me with-out mentioning God. I felt I was a character in a clever catholic novel where the priest says exactly the opposite of what you ex-pect." She looked at Hatch and laughed. "Sorry. But you get the idea."

Now he could reach for the coffee pot.

"I kept on visiting the church. Sometimes we talked; sometimes he was absent. The next Sunday I attended morning service. It was hard going because I have next to no German. But I went again the

following week. When we talked I expected him to use my attendances to sell me Christianity. But he didn't; in fact we talked about
Thomas Mann.

"By the end he knew most of what there was to know. On the
last day he was waiting. Said I could perhaps help him. Said he
needed to know more about divorce. In his rural parish it's almost
unknown. Not condemned; it's just that farming couples tend to
stick together. He said he could see why I might want to leave a
husband whose temperament I didn't share. Realised there might
well be legal reasons for divorce. But did divorce work?

"I thought I'd misunderstood. No, no, he said. The physical
separation obviously works. But you (meaning me), he said, were
married for more than ten years. Had divorce freed me for a new
form of life? Had it been a 'clean break'.

"It seemed too theoretical for me to take seriously. I stumbled a
bit, trying to provide an answer and it became clear he was intent.
My answer mattered.

"Why? In the end I had to ask him just that. He smiled. 'Simply
this, Mrs Kepler. You talk freely and honestly about yourself. And
about your husband. I suspect that clean break has not occurred.
Not that you wish to re-marry him. Only that your husband is still
part of you and that may need resolving.

"Resolving? I said. He nodded and smiled much more broadly.
'You ask me how. I have no talent for advising you.'

"I thanked him and said I was relieved he hadn't proselytised.
He doubted his English was good enough which was nonsense.
However he hoped I'd find a church in England where I could 'sit
quietly'."

"But you do attend church services."

"Out of habit. Because I like the routine. The wrong way round,
obviously."

"So - you'll resume your solitary attendances?"

"I think so."

"Expecting what?"

"Who knows? I'll try and think constructively about myself. And about you."

"And the need for resolution?"

"Does that sound far-fetched?"

"It sounds like an obligation. I don't buy that," said Hatch. "Marriage is mutual and so's divorce. At least ours was."

"Ah but is divorce mutual? The cant thing is to say that blame should be shared. The only thing you can be blamed for is being Andrew Hatch. I was the one who broke up the marriage."

Her expression had remained thoughtful, tranquil; there was no suggestion this was a devious way of gaining his sympathy. He said, "But that's in the past. The pain is over."

"But the pain was very real at the time. And the question I have to ask is: was I justified?"

Hatch's coffee cup rested on the table, neglected. "You were entitled to bail out."

"Was I? My reasons seem trivial. Boredom. Irritation. You on the other hand struggled to meet the contract. You were good to me then and now."

"Driving you home from the airport?"

Her face showed affection. "Is that typical of ex-husbands? But of course you're leaving a lot out. Think of the way you agreed to sell the house – our only asset. No complaints. Phoning me when I was hardly good company. Even now your instinct is to play yourself down."

"But - "

She raised a blue-veined hand and he was reminded of a moment years ago when it had rested on her thigh and he'd thought: Wedgwood. "This is the situation. We're apart and that's how it must stay. But there is something – something gentle – remaining. I treasure that, it's more valuable than I realised. If I can, and if it means anything to you, I'd like to nourish it. It would mean a great deal if I were able to do something useful. Through friendship, through attentiveness. Do you think that's possible?"

"Of course. Speaking, meeting. And I need more opportunities to explain why I cannot blame you. But you have your own life. This duty you feel – which I dispute – must not interfere with that."

She smiled. "That duty is important. I would like to work off some of what I feel. As to the rest, I take it you're hinting at some-one else. That for me isn't a priority. However we must make sure we do not mislead your… friend? lover?"

Suddenly Hatch felt coy. "I'll manage that."

They both stood up. "Are you happy?" she asked. "I care about that."

"Yes I am. I always wondered if I was capable of change. That my roots might be too deep. But I am enjoying myself. I'd be even happier when you're through this rearrangement."

Driving to the airport he was impatient to rid himself of the fee-ble car he had hired and feel the Kawasaki's effortless acceleration again. He considered phoning Celia, spending the night there. It would be unexpected and it would please her. But he would be coming directly from his ex-wife and Celia knew where he'd been. Might this, as Prudence had said, be misread?

In his sparsely furnished flat he lolled on the couch reading Gravity's Rainbow (with some difficulty – an insistent recommenda-tion by Ericsson), delaying a bath which he could nevertheless look forward to, which didn't involve walking half-clothed along a land-ing and down a half-flight of stairs. He was well into a largish whisky and kept on breaking off from Pynchon to consider the ab-stractions of Prudence's new life. Wondering whether he too was capable of abiding such stern duties. His phone rang and an un-known woman's voice said: "Mr Hatch, Andrew Hatch?".

It could well have been the first incoming call he'd taken on this phone and his etiquette was rusty. "Speaking."

"It's Clare Kepler. Of Garton. Sorry for calling you so late. And at home."

A pleasant surprise. "No problem. I'm reading Thomas Pyn-chon; I welcome interruptions."

"Gravity's Rainbow? It sounded like a book for physicists. I tried. But it was beyond this physicist."

"I like the rockets but the rest is mysterious. This is what comes of changing jobs. Nobody at Tempest would have forced this book down my throat. Never mind. What can I do for you?"

"I feel so feeble," said Clare. "I want to get this boffin business right. For myself and for Garton. I've memorised the words in your fax. But I'm missing something. I don't really understand – what can I call it? – the acting."

"The aim is to get rid of words, to keep the script to a minimum. I've only just learned that lesson myself."

"Give me an example."

"When you say 'Gears link up.' you turn one gear and the others move. It's all there, nothing more needs to be said. Another saving is when there's repetition. Instead of saying, 'Gear two turns this way, Gear three turns that way…' you say 'Each turns the opposite way' Your hand does half-circles and the viewer has a picture."

"I see that. But there's the timing. The hand must fit the words."

"Whoever's supervising the test will help."

Clare laughed. "I want to cheat."

"You're looking for a tutor?"

"Specifically, you. I don't mind falling on my face with a fellow professional. But I'd hate to have a BA Media Studies giggling at me."

"I'm no expert."

"All the better. You'll be technical, not emotional."

"What exactly are you asking for, Mrs Kepler?"

"Clare, for a start. After that a little rehearsal."

"At a place other than Gamester, of course."

"Pretty please."

There were arguments against this proposal but he knew he would agree. "There isn't much time. And I can't sneak out during the day. I did that this afternoon.

"I'll book an Edgbaston hotel with a small conference room and drive up tomorrow. We'll have an evening; that would be enough."

"I can't promise great skills. But I'll make sure you don't fall on your face."

"It's not really cheating, is it?"

"Most employers would approve."

"Bless you."

Hatch started to run the bath, topped up his whisky glass and took it in with him. He stepped into the water sensing that life was getting away from him.

Not that there weren't problems. Even if he could have carried it on the bike there was no way he could have borrowed the gear-train mock-up. And yet their rehearsal depended on having some-thing material to work with. The only portable solution was a large roll of paper and some coloured felt-tips to create drawings of the equipment.

The evening's work proved remarkably strenuous since Hatch was, in effect, teaching himself. They started immediately and there was vague talk of dinner. By ten exhaustion forced a quick order of sandwiches. Relating the script to the "acting" was not the only consideration. Clare needed to face a notional camera then briefly swing into profile. A sequence emerged but by then their goal of perfection had been distorted.

"That's enough," Hatch insisted. "If we go on you'll be knack-ered."

"I never thought anything so simple could be so wearying."

"You'll be facing the biggest single audience of your life. The way you look and behave on camera shouldn't affect your status at Garton, but it's an unfair world. Such things can happen."

It was Hatch's clarity that hit Clare. As if he knew or had guessed her recent history. "Is this why I'm taking it so seriously? Dragging you out when it isn't your burden. Perhaps it is serious."

Hatched sucked the last flat dregs of beer from a bottle. "You didn't drag me out. I came to learn."

"I dragged you out."

Their eyes met. "No," he said. At which both busied themselves gathering up felt-tips and collecting torn strips of scribbled paper.

Hatch looked at his watch. "At least you'll have time for a lie-in. You're due at ten-thirty. Ask for Celia when you arrive."

"Any surname?"

"Telly is a first-names business."

"Celia, then."

HATCH was at his desk – made sure he was at his desk – when Clare was escorted to Celia's office. Having met at Basingstoke they were entitled to greet each other, after which Clare passed on leaving the impression of a slightly disdainful, uptilted face.

Half an hour later Celia sat uncomfortably on the corner of Hatch's desk. "They're doing her make-up. You kind of under-sold her when I asked for a description."

"But what were your standards? If I'd over-sold her you'd have said it was Science Solidarity speaking. Anyway Zach tipped the balance."

"Pooh. I wouldn't trust him. All he cares about are face-planes."

"So she'll do?"

"Perfect. A bit haughty. Composed. Jargon-free. Just what we want. I suspect she should be one of the competitors." Celia paused. "What was your reaction?"

"Clever but not heartless. A high-ranker but she doesn't pull rank. I thought she even looked glamorous but then I put that down to her clothes and – do you say it these days? – her grooming. But perhaps that is glamour."

"Do you fancy her?"

A question Hatch had wondered about. "Yeah. I suppose I do."

It seemed the safest response. He asked, "Who gets to watch the screen test? Am I supposed to help in any way?"

"Al will contact you if the script isn't right."

Half an hour later Hatch was asked to sit in on one of Gamester's newest projects, a social services panel show which had a poor prognosis. Poor or not, judges and judged fought it out to the death ("Everyone thinks they understand welfare," shouted the embattled director, "This proves they don't."). By the time Hatch returned to his desk Clare's screen test was over and she had left the building.

Celia finally reported - reluctantly it seemed – mid-afternoon. "She was, of course, superb. Three takes and it was done. Al and I took her to lunch, then she drove off to Basingstoke. Asked to be remembered to you for giving her 'her start.' Hopes to be in touch."

"You sound as if you resent her," he said.

"I suppose it's envy. Wealthy parents, breezed through Oxbridge, not pretty but a striking face. Can't quarrel with her success, though. Most of it in a man's world. I expected she'd be too stiff for the camera but she has a good easy style. Married to a golf pro of all things."

Hatch, wriggling in his chair, said jerkily. "Tonight, why don't we try that new Indian just down the road."

Celia looked surprised. He'd changed the subject too quickly

That night, after the Indian, he knew he was forcing the love-making, behaving out of character. But there were no complaints.

"How was Prudence?" Celia asked, naked, sitting on the side of the bed, sipping cold water. The Christian name jarred but it was a relief to steer away from Clare.

"Contrite. She feels she treated me badly. Hopes to rescue part of what we had. May be turning towards the church."

He'd allowed Celia to dislike Prudence. This piece of news appeared to counter that. "Does she want you back?"

He said, "She says we're not compatible and I agree. She's more reflective. Told me she was less frightened of death than of coming back into the world as someone else. Again, not surprising."

Celia shuddered. "We cling to our average personalities, terrified bits will break off. We always assume it will be for the worse."

"In the end I don't want to be better."

She looked at him, willing him to keep going. Deliberately he buried his face between her breasts.

Next morning he rode the bike into work and she the Land Rover. When he got home in the evening the answerphone light blinked. "Clare here. We missed each other at Gamester. The test went well. Because of you, of course. I'm so grateful. Can we meet?" He played the message a second time.

Wanting to hear her voice yet again he forced himself to switch off Playback. This was in preparation for the awkwardness he expected when she returned to Gamester to record her scenes..

THAT MEETING never happened. Al, the T-Woman director, wrote Clare's scripts himself and asked Hatch simply to check the technology. In any case Hatch had other things on his mind. With the techno-test hardware now complete he needed to find another justification for extending his contract.

A month earlier he'd proposed a three-part documentary about Formula Ford mechanics. When he got Celia to jog Ericsson's elbow he was abruptly given a week to cost the work. This required a monumental series of bike rides between the more extreme British race circuits – Croft in North Yorkshire and Thruxton in Hampshire. While he was away Clare arrived at Edgbaston early one morning and proved sufficiently accomplished to lock up six ninety-second recordings in a single day.

As if trying to break him, Ericsson gave him a further week to come up with an outline for a one-hour pilot, approved during a Sunday afternoon meeting. Endowed with a tiny sum of money, a cameraman rumoured to be alcoholic, a sound man and an assistant director aged nineteen on his first assignment, Hatch had three weekends to bring in the programme.

Rain on all three weekends was his saviour. At each event he managed unerringly to choose a team whose driver crashed in practice and mid-race. The accidents generated tension and angst among the mechanics, all well caught on the camera. Finally some hurried standard footage was shot to rebut the impression that Formula Ford races all ended in disaster.

Hatch did the interviews and asked informed questions which the work-racked mechanics responded to with a minimum of irritation. Since there was no money left Hatch had no alternative but to do the voice-over. This led to a minor triumph. His flat Midlandstinged voice proved an apt commentary on this deliberately low-key view of sport. Ericsson roared with laughter at the rough cut and allocated more money to re-record the narration using a sharper script even better suited to Hatch's voice.

In the viewing theatre Ericsson remained seated. "You've done well, Andy my old Brummie. You're not just a spannerman."

"I've got you to thank."

Ericsson waved a dismissive hand. "It wasn't that hard. You weren't put off by being interviewed in the car. Your ideas came rat-a-tat-tat. You knew what you were talking about. And you had one other thing going for you. You were out of work and yet you didn't have that air of desperation that goes with being unemployed. That's what I remember."

Hatch laughed. "A window on an unreal world. Now washing machines seem distant."

"Perhaps you're better away from them. What am I saying? You've profited! You got to sleep with Seel."

Keeping the affair a secret would have been unrealistic yet it was a shock to hear it referred to so openly. Hatch nodded slightly.

But Ericsson wasn't finished. "And you could be moving into the championship," he said slyly.

Dimly aware, then horrified, Hatch stared straight ahead at the theatre's blank screen.

"Oh, come on Brummie. You're way past teenage shyness. In any case it's another triumph. You picked her out and Al says she's a natural. I'm sure she's grateful. Time for you to cash in."

"You gave the go-ahead," Hatch mumbled.

"But you did the scouting. Saw the talent." Ericsson looked at Hatch speculatively. "In fact, there's more isn't there? She was good during the recordings but what really impressed Al was the screen test. As if she'd been rehearsed. Did you rehearse her?"

"What do I know about facing the camera?" Hatch tried to snarl the reply but his voice slid up a fifth into a whine.

Ericsson shrugged. "Hell, I don't care if you did or you didn't. You saved us time and we got a result. That was professional.

You're entitled to her pants. But let Seel down lightly if you can. And stop looking so bloody self-righteous." Annoyed now, Ericsson got up clumsily and barged his way out of the theatre.

At home that evening Hatch played the weeks-old message a final time. Then deleted it.

PRUDENCE now visited regularly. Effortlessly she had gained a well-paid job with a major charity and insisted he cut his maintenance payments. He looked forward to these visits, creating elaborate meals, luxuriating as she listened to his daily tittle-tattle.

"So your job is secure?" she asked. "Or as secure as anything in your madcap world?"

"It adds up to another one-year contract," Hatch shouted from the kitchen, preparing a paella. "Ericsson has agreed to my three-part series on FF mechanics. Being Ericsson he spotted a point which deserves emphasising and I agree. All motor racing is expensive and with FF there are no financial rewards. So he wants figures. He's chosen a working title 'The high cost hobby' and he's promised a full production team. I got such good value from the drunk and the lad I've asked to work with them again."

"But only one more year?"

"Yes, but after that I'll have a real track record. I've proved I can work to insane deadlines and my voice is OK for commentaries. There'll be opportunities during the year. And if not I'll make them."

"So commanding, Mr Hatch."

"Are you surprised?"

"Not really. Tempest was your one moment of bad luck. If they'd survived you would be on the board."

Prudence called out again. "You've bought a television. After all these years. What on earth do you watch?"

"Very little. I felt it went with the territory. I'm not often tempted though I will watch one programme."

"T-Woman, I suppose. The change of life event." She looked at him more closely. "No? Something else?"

He'd held back so long. By now the need to confess was irresistible and Prudence was his natural confessor.

"I became involved – somewhat. Then disappointed."

Slowly he told her, astonished how the bare bones added up to so little, even without Ericsson's sardonic conclusions. A mere three meetings, the first merely a business negotiation. His low voice and his vain attempts to be casual gave him away immediately and he had her full attention. When she gently asked him to describe Clare he revealed things about her he hardly recognised. At the denouement she shook her head. "The two parts don't go together. Could your friend have been wrong about the marriage?"

"I checked in Who's Who in Industry. There's a child too."

"Tell me again - everything." This time he uncovered even more. Her professionalism across the table at Garton. The way she listened to his instructions during the tutorial. Her intelligence. The intimacy of her voice on the deleted answerphone message.

Prudence listened silently then spoke sharply. "It doesn't add up. Look you're drawn to her, obviously?" He nodded. "Then you need to find out."

"It would be excruciating."

"I know. But you must find out."

But he couldn't. Conceivably Clare's apparent attitude towards him and her marital situation might be explainable. But if so his own behaviour and especially his delays would then seem inexcusable. He returned instead to Celia, somewhat reduced in authority since Hatch's sally into directing.

T-Woman appeared in the autumn. Clare was everything Celia had said. Conversational yet striking. He watched the first programme and told himself he wouldn't watch others. But did. Rapprochement was even more remote. She was a minor celebrity. Beyond his circle.

21. CLARE

Moving on

THESE had to be houses at the upper end, their CVs contained in folders bound in faux leather which looked real. What caught Clare's attention were not the folders but his luxuriously generous shirt cuffs secured with heavy gold links; certainly cuffs of authority. But then the name on his lapel corresponded with that of the estate agency: Prewitt-Clews.

He slid across details of a four-square mansion in Cotswold stone with a lawn of alternating shiny and matt green stripes. She sighed. "That has the hallmarks of 'character' I fear. I have a very characterful house for sale near Sevenoaks. What I'm looking for is something modern with internal wiring, lots of characterless bathrooms, a ten-year NHBC warranty and a double garage."

He laughed fruitily. "Force of habit. I do apologise. You mentioned a price band and I assumed… Which is just as well because Basingstoke doesn't have many houses like that. Do you object to living on an estate."

He assumes I will object, Clare thought. "Is that a factor?"

"Most modern houses, with the features you mention, are on estates. Although most are well below your price band. Modern houses on separate plots may put you off. The architecture tends to be atavistic."

Clare's head rose and her eyes met his. "Not a commonplace word in this field."

He replied urbanely, "Then you won't be surprised to know that none of our properties are deceptively spacious nor do they command views. I own this enterprise and I refuse to hide the fact I've read a book or two."

Clare laughed. "You may be misjudging me. How's your science?"

"Not as good as yours. I might have used your name straightaway but I draw the line at American familiarity. However I do read the local newspaper."

"Let's start again," said Clare holding out her hand. "Clare Kepler. I work at Garton."

Gravely he shook her hand for the second time. "Where you are technical director. I am Trevor Prewitt-Clews and I ask you to forgive the hyphen. Clews is an awkward name and I don't respond well to Pink Panther allusions."

Her eyes slid back to his shirt cuffs, then away. "If I read between the lines it seems you may not have the sort of house I'm looking for."

"I'm enough of an estate agent to say *au contraire*. I merely - " One of the phones on his desk started to ring. "Don't worry, it will stop in a few seconds."

It didn't and Prewitt-Clews sighed. "Man proposes... Please excuse me." he picked up the phone. "I thought I said no more... ah, I see. Thank you for persisting, Julia. Mrs Kepler, it's for you. Your mother. Please stay here, I'll go and investigate the coffee."

Her mother sounded unusually tense. "I hope I'm not fussing. But you did leave a message – two messages – with Consuelo and that's not like you. We've been in Switzerland for three weeks and I had no way of knowing how urgent it was."

"Not too urgent, dear. More in the nature of a courtesy call. But you first. Three weeks? That's unusual."

"I was promised unimaginable luxury and that was the case. After a while I worried whether even your father could dig so deep. But it all revolves round a very modest Fuseli – not my cup of tea, I can tell you – and your father looking terribly smug. An acquaintance dined us out one evening and ordered Petrus. Now that's vulgar, surely."

"What's your verdict?"

"I've had better Lafite. At a third the price."

"Bargain basement, in fact."

"Oh, you're in a teasing mood. Now tell me your news."

"It's Jerry. His young paramour has tired of him, it seems. He's living in a squalid flat in Dartford and making noises about 'regularising things'. By which he means a divorce and a settlement."

"I'm so sorry, dear. Do you need…?" Mrs Morgan's hope, never forceful, faded.

"Not that sort of help. Rather your permission. The house was your gift and I've loved living there. I've hung on even though it's really too small. There are two major factors. One, it's quite a long way from where I work. Two, it appears to be worth a huge amount of money. But I felt I had to ask you first. It seemed so ungracious just to put up a For Sale sign. May I sell your very generous present?"

"My dear, it's yours. I don't need to speak to your father about this. So that's why I'm calling you at an estate agent's."

"I needed to look around and there are financial advantages in moving from Sevenoaks. Oh mother, I'm so grateful for your understanding. But look, I'm using someone else's phone. I'll call tonight."

"Goodbye dear."

Prewitt-Clews must have seen a light go out on the phone system and he appeared with coffee. "I've used the time profitably. There are three houses I'd like you to see." He paused diplomatically. "I don't want to pry; you must shoot me down if you feel I am. But will you be making this purchase on your own behalf?"

The phrasing was so deft Clare had to ponder. "Behalf? Yes, I see. My husband and I are living apart."

He was deliberately brisk. "When is convenient? You have a young son I believe."

"Those newspapers again. I'd prefer it wasn't at the weekend. Would it be possible to fit them into a single afternoon?"

"Almost certainly. But before we discuss these houses I'd like to go over my initial questions again. When we started you were in a puckish mood but that's all right, I'm here for that. I need to know whether you really disdain the status bricks and mortar can confer."

"Mr Prewitt-Clews, you see straight through me," said Clare, laughing. "You have my permission to puncture my vanity. Although I'd appreciate a little skill, a little delicacy and many more adverbs."

Two days later, after they had inspected the last of the three houses, he asked her if she would dine with him. It seemed just a little too opportunistic though she knew he would be an entertaining companion. "Only if you'll let me pay."

He rubbed his chin. "An interesting tactic."

"I know."

"Then I accept."

He proved to be just as entertaining as she'd imagined but after an hour he began to lose her through no fault of his own.

As she unlocked the door of the Jaguar he said, "Your mind was elsewhere. I'm sorry. Just think of me as an estate agent."

BACK from a visit to a potential client the two of them sat among his model ships at Mike Gardner's conference table. Clare said, "I don't have to tell you how much they need us. That collection of chicken hutches and Portakabins belongs in the forties. It's astonishing they've managed to work up a national distribution network. But that's not all. Wearing my two hats definitely has its advantages. The sales department is at daggers drawn with production and it's sales that are driving the company at the moment."

Mike said, "The old story. A twenty-year-old company run by an elderly design engineer. Marvellous products – well, let's say sellable products – but a light hand on everything else. How do you think we appeared to him?"

"A bit like death and taxes," said Clare. "I think he was relieved we didn't browbeat him."

"But how long will he be at the helm? He didn't look entirely well."

"Is your touch subtle enough to raise that point in a draft proposal?"

Mike said, "It would have to be. We'd need bank money to get this off the ground. Minimum contract of five years, should really be seven."

"What about an incremental approach? We have about a thousand metres spare at the moment?" Clare snapped her fingers. "No forget that. If they come to us it's got to be all or nothing. Doing it piecemeal wouldn't get rid of the poisonous situation back at the ranch."

He tilted back in his chair, smiling reminiscently. "It's as if I've been hunting with what the Americans call a bird dog. While I was talking to the boss you sniffed away elsewhere. That sales manager and his deputy looked like schoolboys caught smoking in the bog. Putty in your hands."

"Barbara was so far-sighted. Proof of the power of telly. I'd been seen on the evening news spouting about skilled immigrants. For them I was a guru, a celebrity."

"And there was a photographer in your office yesterday afternoon."

"A woman's magazine. What to wear at board meetings."

Mike asked, "And are you still comfortable with all this?"

"Sometimes I worry. I remember our interview and why I was given the job. To improve efficiency, wrestle with new technology, scout out new areas of interest. When I'm poncing in front of the cameras I'm not doing any of that. But on a wider front I'm here to make Garton more profitable. It's just possible we were invited to the chicken-hutch merchants because my poncing caught someone's eye. There's potentially a hell of a lot more profit there than in rearranging a couple of assembly lines."

"I remember that interview," he said. "A Damascene moment. What impressed me was your seriousness – and I mean that in the best possible way. I admire your pragmatism but let's hope it's not at the expense of that special quality."

"We have to be realistic. My so-called career in the media isn't going to last for ever. Afterwards I can go back to being serious. But for the moment I agree with Barbara, poncing pays off."

"Don't use that word again," he said with mock anger. "One other point. These chicken-hutch merchants as you call them. Kitchen appliances. How does that sit among our mainly high-tech range of clients."

"Probably a higher level of expertise. Lots of cost engineering." She looked out of the window and spoke without thinking. "A world on its own, cost engineering. I knew a production manager at a washing machine manufacturer. He specialised. It's a tight, tough world. There are no contractual contingencies to fall back on there."

"Do I know him?"

"No."

He was disconcerted by her short answer. "There's something else, while we're together. This divorce. Have you got a lawyer?"

"I've used one in the past. But he's in Sevenoaks and that's a pain. I hate taking off any more time than I should."

"Why not use my guy? Get your husband to do the travelling?" Mike had never had any time for Jerry.

Jerry's reaction to Basingstoke was predictable but he calmed down when Clare explained about the escrow account to hold half the value of the Sevenoaks house prior to the divorce settlement. The meeting with the solicitor lasted less than an hour after which Clare hurried back, closed her office door and burst into tears. Her secretary, forcing her way in and finding her normally confident, otherwise adorable boss in this state, sympathetically burst into tears too without knowing why. This at least jolted Clare back to being a manager, offering paper towels moistened *ad hoc* with fizzy water chilled in her office refrigerator.

"He's a shit," Clare said, "and neither of us should cry over a shit."

"Did he… behave badly?"

"No more than usual. It was an accumulation of misbehaviour that hit me."

"You, of all people…"

"Even hardened battle-axes have their limits," Clare said, stopping when more wailing ensued

She handed over freezing wet pulp. "It was more or less a formality. Questions put, Jerry grunting approval. Then the solicitor asked: 'And what are you both looking for regarding custody of your son, Nicholas?' The shit simply turned to me and shrugged his shoulder. His own son! I told Jerry he could whistle for his escrow. I suppose I'd better phone the solicitor and tell him I acted in haste."

Calmed by the solicitor's expert and no doubt expensive counsel she then picked up a call from the Sevenoaks estate agent with a schedule of house inspections starting that evening and trickling on through the weekend. The emotional visit to MacDonalds, now one of Nick's regular requests, would have to wait. Driving home through heavy Friday traffic she found – to her fury – she was crying again. A brief period of reckless driving produced a chorus of car horns, mainly from male BMW drivers.

Since she had never sold a house she was ill-prepared to handle blank-faced, carping buyers breaking into time normally devoted to Nick. Initially she amused herself with presentations of what was, in effect, her past life but this light entertainment quickly evaporated in the face of utterly irrelevant behaviour. Couples whispering disapprovingly about a shade of wall-paper, about flowers that had died in an outdoor planter, a worn patch on the back lawn, hinges squeaking on the garage door. Beyond that, repetitive questions – again censorious – about visible wiring required to pass round rather than through four-hundred-year-old beams half a metre thick. The ingenious office won from space beneath the stairs was seen as an oddity. And then there was the genteel silence when entourages entered her bedroom.

Clare learned what things not to say, to hover rather than point out, to observe while being observed. From the visitors' cars it was obvious all were comfortably off. More than that, their ability to pay for this ridiculously over-priced house seemed to have endowed them with an ugly superiority.

The cavalcade ended midway through Sunday afternoon when an exceptionally pretty woman knocked on the door, said she'd been visiting friends in the area, now faced with a longish drive home and had insufficient time to fix up an appointment with the estate agent. The house, she said, was gorgeous and was it possible for Clare to forgo the "Appointment obligatory" stricture and allow her the quickest of tours. "Five minutes, not a second more," she said winningly.

It was only because the woman was alone that Clare agreed. But her energy for selling was now exhausted and her guidance reduced to monosyllables. Unlike her predecessors, the woman expressed intelligent appreciation of the house's antique beauties and laughed in delight at the office. "Turn the lights on, please. Oh yes, it's been beautifully planned."

But the biggest difference occurred on the landing when Clare opened the door to her bedroom.

"No," said the woman gently. "I assume this is yours. I'm always uneasy about entering a bedroom that's in use. Even when you're selling a house you're entitled to some privacy."

Clare looked surprised. "That's rather sweet. But if the house interests you it would be a shame not to inspect the main bedroom."

"I'd rather not."

"I assure you the contents are perfectly chaste." A memory of the solicitor's office, never far away throughout the weekend, bore in on her. "I am its only occupant."

The woman engaged Clare's eyes. "Let's pass on."

Downstairs again Clare said, "You said something about a long drive. Can I give you a coffee?"

The woman's face lit up. "I've taken more than my promised five minutes."

"If all potential buyers were like you selling wouldn't be the ordeal I've found it. I'm Clare Kepler, by the way."

"And I'm Mrs – no, I mustn't abide by that fiction. Call me Miss Carolson. And if that sounds formal or gauche it's because I need to get used to the mademoiselle state again."

"Then perhaps you should call me Miss Morgan. I'm on the verge of divorce. Mind you," she said, trying to speak lightly, "it's been a rather lengthy verge."

"Let's not talk about it, dear."

Gravel crunched on the driveway. Clare said, "We have the perfect diversion. That sounds like the au pair with my son. The estate agent told me that no child – however well-behaved – represents an asset when showing off a house."

Nick, rosy-cheeked, announced noisily he wanted to play football on the lawn. Clare asked, "Would you mind having your coffee outside? It's not too cold and I seem to have seen so little of him these last two days."

Miss Carolson's agreement was obvious. At the garden table she said little, watching Clare watch Nick.

"He plays well on his own," she said.

"I'd never thought of it that way. Is it a good thing?"

"Good heavens, I'm no expert. At a guess it suggests he's independent. Much better than sulking and kicking his heels, saying he's bored. Meaning, of course, that he needs company."

"You sound more expert than me. I can't pretend I've instinctively known anything about Nick. I take it…?"

"No. I'm not sure why. Perhaps as well in my case. But not in yours. Sorry, that's presumptuous."

Clare turned. "Not at all. You're quite right, at this present moment he's vital. Something I've retrieved. Especially since his father was never… Oh hell. This must be terribly embarrassing."

"Miss Morgan, no I can't say that. Clare. I'm touched beyond words. Crying's not a weakness, it's a strength."

Nick didn't think so. He abandoned his ball, walked over and stared disapprovingly at his mother.

"Look at him," Clare said, laughing, wiping her eyes on her sleeve having failed to find a handkerchief. "How conservative he is. Mothers don't cry."

Uncharacteristically Nick addressed the calmer of the two women. "Has mummy been bad?"

"Never. She was happy to watch you play football. Sometimes people are so happy they cry."

"That's silly. She's like Tamsin at nursery. She cries a lot. Because she's bad." Having passed this judgement he slurred his feet across the grass back to the ball.

Clare accepted a proffered handkerchief. "He's one reason why I'm selling this house and moving closer to where I work. I have a senior job and sometimes I haven't given him the attention I should. Birgitta has been an angel but I must find more time. He must be the compensation."

Her visitor said, "At worst, think of it as a joint failure. You blame yourself. I used to blame my husband. My faults were less obvious but I recognise them now." She stood up. "I must leave you to Nick. This was an impulse visit and I'm a bit of a fraud. I doubt I could find the money for your beautiful house. But I've enjoyed the tour. And…" the sentence remained incomplete.

Clare stood up and tentatively offered back the handkerchief. "Keep it. Don't see me out. Sit down again and watch your wonderful son."

When Nick eventually tired he flopped on the grass and Clare, giggling, took his hand and hauled him up. At the garden table she picked up her own cup and that of her recent guest, noting a faint tinge of Coral Pink on the rim. Proof that there'd been someone there to sustain the dialogue which now seemed eerily distant.

22. HATCH

The Anna K. Lesson

CELIA laid the folder on Hatch's desk. "From Zach with love."

"What do I know about industrial architecture?"

"Nothing, my sweet. That's the point."

Looking up he found her smiling remotely. He said, "So it's a coded message. I doubt I've been here long enough."

"You're no longer an apprentice. This is a proposal for a three-part documentary. Zach gets dozens a week. Most go straight into the bin but he's taken a fancy to this one and he'd like your opinion."

"My opinion!"

"You realise what this means? You're not *such* an innocent?"

"Do I qualify for another ridiculous job title?"

"You do indeed. At a guess: deputy production editor."

"More cash?"

Celia said, "This is like A-levels. Do well and you can go in and haggle."

"Suppose I don't like it?"

"Tell him why in two hundred words."

"And lose a chance of getting rich?"

"The surest way of being fired is to recommend it without liking it," said Celia harshly. "Seriously: read it through, pick out the good points, pick out the bad, list the changes you'd make. Do a bit of research to provide back-up. End up with a yes or no. But think visually. You're lucky, this is a visual subject. It's not psychiatry or monetarism."

Hatch spent the afternoon testing the proposals against images in his own mind, pouncing on weak transitions, and turning the uninspired commentary into something more stirring. Finally he faced the decision: for or against? He got up from his desk and stared out unseeingly through the window. Came back and scribbled "Limited scope. Needs European if not international angle." As he wrote Jean-Claude Lemazaire's preposterous office building swam into his memory. "French buildings more fun, perhaps even comic. Not recommended as proposed."

He dropped down into Celia's visitor chair. "Do you want to see my notes?"

"Do you need me to see them?"

He shook his head. "I'm confident enough. I'll get them typed."

"In that case give them to me."

The ragged blonde wings swung forward as she bent over the folder. Hatch reflected on the benefits of being familiar with a woman. Being able to appreciate the shape of Celia's neat ears. She handed the notes back. "You've come a long way. I could have given you a hint. Told you this was almost certainly a thumbs-down. But I didn't think you needed that. And you didn't."

"Suppose I'd got it wrong.?

Again that slightly dreamy look. "I'd have jogged your elbow."

"Ah."

He stood up. "Let's go somewhere expensive. It's time I wore a tie again."

"Would you like to do me a real favour?"

"Of course."

"Take me to North Wales on the back of the Kwacker. On Saturday, even if it's raining."

"Specifically?"

"A layby on the A5."

"With echoes of your youth?"

HE WAS pulling on his waterproofs when Ericsson made a rare foray into the main office. "Christ, all that dressing-up palaver. How can you stand it? Time you bought a car."

"Not until I'm fifty."

"It doesn't have to be a Vauxhall Vectra. It could be something with more pizazz: a TVR or an Elite."

"Not fast enough."

"One TVR does 160."

"Only on a straight open road. A bike would suck its doors off in town."

Ericsson laughed. "Where did you pick up that? We sure as hell have corrupted you."

"I was willing bait."

Ericsson edged his broad bottom on to the corner of Hatch's desk. "What's this about French buildings?"

"Just a thought. Medium-sized French companies are often housed in truly weird structures. Shaped like cathedrals but detailed in aluminium. Roofs sloping down to the ground at one end. Grotesque windows. I can't pretend I have any figures, it's merely an impression. But there's proof some architects think alike. In northern France at least."

"A jeer-at-the Frog documentary?"

"That would be too easy. It deserves explanation on the French side. And reaction on this. But there could be a comic element. Perfect for Jonathan Meades."

"Suppose I gave you a couple of days in France on your door-sucking bike? Purely to take photographs. Enough visuals to form an opinion."

Hatch said, "And if you give the go-ahead...?"

"Nah. Not you in front. I have in mind a cool woman in a black cocktail dress - an Oxbridge graduate who looks as out of place as the buildings."

"Jonathan Meades in drag!"

"You're getting the hang of it."

"But it's my idea."

"But it's not how I see you. You're too straight, straight with added value. I'd use you shooting war graves. Or people who'd been screwed by the government."

"Is that a compliment?"

"No, it isn't," said Ericsson. "You don't get brownie points for being who you are."

"I'll take the photos next week."

THEY left the Shrewsbury ring-road and swung left on the A5 towards Llangollen. It was their first ride on non-urban roads and Celia had adopted the perfect position – legs in a parallel zig-zag with his, torso inclined forward, helmeted head helping to form an aerodynamic bubble round their northern extremities. For Hatch their interlocking bodies came as close as possible to riding solo. In tweaking the bike to the right to overtake a delivery van he faced an open sports car hard-driven towards him. Braking hard, feeling Celia's weight press against him, he slipped back behind the van – a violent manoeuvre but with no hint of fear from her.

Parked in the destination layby, the rock shoulders of Tryfan to the left, chilly Lyn Ogwen to the right, Hatch took off his helmet. "You're a bloody good pillion passenger."

She had turned away and was looking up at Tryfan. "One of my rare talents."

They threaded their way uphill between boulders, found one with a surface that tilted out from the slope, allowing them to lie down and watch climbers on the first pitch of the route immediately above. Although the road was a mere 150 metres below, the altitude was sufficient for a wind-rustled tranquillity, underlined by the slowness of the climbers' movements.

"I take it this place means something?" Hatch asked.

"I was younger and more foolish."

"Why not more innocent?"

"Oh shit, I'm already starting to tell lies. You're right. More innocent. This is Milestone Buttress. The way up to the left is called

Direct Route. It's the only rock climb I've ever done. But there's more to it than that."

"A man, for instance."

Celia sighed. "In the end all our moving experiences boil down into clichés. Yes, a man."

"Life itself. Birth, growth, death. What could be more repetitive? All clichés. Tell me. I won't interrupt."

"There's an even bigger cliché. Love. Except I can't be sure it happened, and never will be. So there's irony too."

Hatch said nothing. Celia turned to face him across the lichen-covered rock. "I want you to hear this. I want your reactions. I don't want you silent."

"Go ahead."

"I was in my third year at Aston and I met him at a union meeting. He looked so healthy with his tanned face and sun-bleached hair. Doing some kind of agricultural degree. I can't remember what got us started but, when we talked, he had this way of looking at me that shut everything else out. No one has ever gathered me in like that. No one else has *cared* to that degree. Even now I can't use his name. I'll call him Rex – a horrible name, not his. Just a label."

"Good choice. No one's called Rex."

Celia smiled fleetingly. "We saw each other a lot. But never at weekends. I asked him why. 'I climb,' he said, as if that explained everything. Clearly it meant a lot to him. I've never done sports and it sounded laddish. I didn't pursue it."

Hatch reached over and touched Celia's fingers which closed on his.

"We became closer. Very close. He seemed surprised I didn't nag him about weekends. But he was just too precious for that. I didn't want to nag him about anything. One evening I did mention I was going to some gig or other the following Saturday. 'Alone?' he asked, pretty disturbed. 'Of course,' I said. It didn't satisfy him. I could see him frowning, trying to decide whether he should break his unbreakable habit. In the end he didn't; I went to the gig – alone – and he did what he usually did on Saturdays."

Celia paused and they both watched the climbers as the second started out on what looked like a tricky traverse. Tried, went back. Tried, went back again.

"I take it you've never climbed?" Celia asked.

"Too true. And for exactly the same reason that guy up there is presently coming to terms with."

Celia laughed lightly. "Each week he worried we weren't together on Saturdays and Sundays. I insisted I didn't mind, but I did. And he suspected. There was of course only one solution. Timidly he asked me if I'd like to try my hand. I'd have followed him to the fiery furnace and I said yes. So we came here and did this very climb. Scared my tits off but – strange isn't it? – it turned out I liked having my tits in a tizzy. And not just because he was there at the other end of the rope, protecting me. I felt the buzz."

"I take it he was pleased?"

"Not exactly."

"Eh?"

"Tell you later. Not now, though. We've got some more sun. I need to take photos."

Mainly of Hatch. Hatch propping up his chin, Hatch facing out into the valley with the Buttress behind him, Hatch in profile against the sky. Finally, using the timer, Hatch with his arm round Celia. Then it was back to the road and a quick blast down to a Capel Curig tea room offering all-day breakfast with Celia taking full advantage and Hatch limiting himself to buttered toast and Nescafé

Scraping noisily at her baked beans Celia spoke briskly now in well-defined sentences as if what she said were memorised. "I expected congratulations, perhaps a hug. Instead I got interrogation. Rex wanted an exact account of my feelings, a description of how I handled myself on the narrow crack two-thirds the way up where I was out of his sight. Also how I felt when I stepped out on to a foothold that overhung the face.

"I admitted some moves were very hard. A hand seemed to hold me to the rock. At one point I hadn't the bottle to step up to a foothold that was near to vertical. I shouted up and he shouted

down: 'I'll give you a tight rope.' I was able to make the move because the rope supported most of my weight. When I told him this
he stared at me, unsmilingly. 'You're saying you needed that tight
rope?' he asked. I said I did.

"He appeared to be computing my replies. 'And at the top?' he
asked. Thrilling, a new sense of release, a new sense of being with
him. Then he seemed almost to stammer, 'Would you… do you
think you could do more of this?' It was important to him and so it
was important to me. I wanted him. I said yes. Provided he was
there too, provided – I tried a little joke but it didn't reach him – he
could give me a tight rope when I needed it.

"For almost five minutes it was as if he went away from me. His
face was expressionless and he looked out across the lake. It wasn't
a comfortable silence but I had the good sense not to break in."

Celia's attitude towards her breakfast betrayed these memories
and she ate jam and toast with gusto.

"Finally, he came back from where he'd gone to. He smiled and
my legs went to jelly. 'Sorry about that,' he said. 'You must have
guessed - climbing's a big thing. But then so are you. I missed you at
the weekends. It's the first time I've had second thoughts about
what I do. Normally I climb with friends. But if you can stand it – if
you like it – I'll climb with you. Only with you.'

"He grinned and it was more jelly. He went on. 'But you see the
problem don't you. There's a big, big question coming up. Suppose
in the end you can't stand climbing. How'm I going to react? All I
can say, give me time. I've climbed since I was six, my dad taught
me. It's taken up all my spare time. But that was… before. Could
you be patient?' I said I could. He drove me back to Birmingham in
his terrible old van, kissed me goodbye, and that was the last I saw
of him. An HGV sideswiped the van on the M6 two days later and
he was killed."

Hatch, detached from these emotions, said nothing and fiddled
mechanically with his teaspoon, heard the hiss of the espresso machine, saw Celia's jam-smeared plate. There was more. And some-

thing told him to pay attention because there were things in this for him.

Celia inspected him quizzically, seemed satisfied. "If it had ended there I suppose it would have been perfect, in the way that good tragedy is supposed to be perfect. But there was an aftermath. I didn't want to go to the funeral, didn't want to find myself staring at a coffin that contained his healthy, muscular body. But I had no option. I got a letter from his mother – his parents were quite wealthy and lived out in the Marches – saying she hoped to meet me, to talk about Rex. 'Because I suspect you are suffering as much as I am.' We had a long talk but that isn't the conversation that matters.

"I haven't been to many funerals but I suppose the congregation tends to be different when it's someone in their twenties. There were about a dozen of them and they stood out. They shared that healthy look as well as his youth. They were awkward about getting up and sitting down during the service. Afterwards, outside the church, they looked embarrassed, muttering among themselves, trying to decide how soon they could leave. Since his parents were shaking hands and keeping their faces blank I was on my own, linked to no one. One of the healthy ones walked over. 'You must be his girl,' he said in a strong Birmingham accent.

"Somehow I'd assumed his friends were students at Aston. I said as much. Crass of me and he resented it. 'Oh, fuck no. I'm a sparks. A subbie with Barratts. None of your smart-arse college kids.' He was out to be unpleasant and I tried to turn away but he held my arm. 'Just one question. That last Sunday he wasn't at Lliewedd. He was with you wasn't he?' I nodded. 'Doing what?' I could have said it was none of his business but given what I had been doing I decided to punish him, show him he wasn't the only pebble on the beach. 'Climbing, as a matter of fact.' Insolently he looked at my hands, at my arms, summing me up. 'You're not a climber.' I agreed. His face looked awful. 'So tell me – oh fuck – tell me what climb you did.' I told him and in some respects I had punished him. 'Oh, fuck, fuck. His last fucking climb. An arsing V. Diff on Milestone. Fuck me. What a memorial.' And he walked away.

"With him went the rest of the ruddy-faced alpinists and I was glad to see them go. Only one stayed behind. He wore a suit and was waiting near the parents to offer commiserations from Rex's friends. He didn't look like a Barratt subbie. So I introduced myself and made some middle-class observations about shared grief and that possibly his friend had overstepped the mark. He sighed. 'That was Bud. Almost as good as Rex. As Rex was, I mean. I take it you aren't really au fait with Rex's climbing. What he's been up to these last two years?' I shrugged, it seemed obvious: he'd climbed. He sighed again. 'Yes, Rex was a rock climber. But he was special.'

"It took me time to put things together. More time to appreciate what they meant. Do you know anything about rock-climbing?"

Hatch said, "Only that fashions seem to have changed. Once they wore anoraks and clumping boots. Now it's tights and bedroom slippers."

"Rex wore tights, though not on Tryfan. I've seen photographs. He had an angel's body."

Hatch waited.

Celia drew in a deep breath. "Let's go outside so we can see the mountains." The sun had gone in leaving a dull pewter sky against which the greens and the greys stood out. Celia said, "It starts getting technical. But it's the technicalities that tell the tale, the emotional tale. In Britain rock-climbs are graded and that's how climbers measure their competence. Once they used words: easy, moderate, all the way up to extremely severe. Now there are figures as well, E1, E2 and so on. Every so often climbers agree that a new climb rates a new grade and one is added. They're up to E10 now."

"And Rex was E10?"

"Better than that, in fact. It's one thing to climb an E10, it's quite another to climb it for the first time. To pioneer it. That's what he and his group were doing when I met him. Concentrating on a mountain not far from here called Lliewedd, pioneering what they called the New Regime routes. Rex did most of the first ascents. He was famous for it, famous in other countries. I've seen photographs of him and reports in German, French and Scandinavian magazines."

Hatch shifted himself on the low wall they occupied. "A hero, then. But more than that, given the offer he made. A real lover."

"I'll never know, will I? Did he mean it? Would I have held him? Would I have wanted to hold him? How many times would he have been content to do that 'arsing V Diff on Milestone'?"

Hatch looked out at the rolling green waves of the Carneddau. "How many promises are kept? Who knows? However, if you don't mind the blasphemy there's a Catholic side to this. It's fair to say he died in a state of grace. His offer - the intention - was everything. Also, you saw the struggle that took, and you were there for the verdict. A judgement to comfort yourself with."

He delivered her back to her house, knowing there was a coda, sitting astride the bike, waiting as she took off her helmet. She said, "Soon after we met you said you hoped you'd never hurt me. I suppose that always depended on how I felt about you. Two or three months ago I had a chance to find out. Your mind went elsewhere."

"I know. But it's not significant."

"What it did prove is you have the capacity to go elsewhere."

"How many promises are kept?" Hatch asked harshly. "Was it a promise? It doesn't matter. I did what I didn't want to do."

"Should we never have made love? Of course we should. For the record you didn't hurt me. I think I was prepared."

Hatch said, "To be betrayed?"

"You didn't betray me. You were hungry and I'm thirty-four. I never imagined I was the be-all and end-all. I like you still, if that means anything. But I needed to tell you my story. Perhaps to make you the tiniest bit jealous, perhaps simply to complete the image." And she turned round and walked down the path to her front door.

THERE were twenty minutes to go before the library closed. An elemental figure in his rustling, open Barbour jacket, bearing his helmet, Hatch went straight to the Newly Returned Books shelves.

Once the library had been a lottery with disappointing prizes. Now the book spines were the key to members of a wider family.

Against his instincts he had accepted Hester's recommendation and taken out an Anne Tyler. An American? A woman? The doubts evaporated as he slipped into a straightforward story that began without evasions, literary references or an expert view of a long-dead society. He asked: why Baltimore? Then answered his own question: it wasn't New York, London or Paris with their arrogant familiarity. Nor was he invited to interest himself in some writer who couldn't write and who hated his mistress. The characters in Anne Tyler worked in shops and factories, had been married for a dozen years, were worried about who would re-paint the house.

He passed on his reactions to Hester knowing it would please her, that they were still linked in some way. He worried she might see this development as over-poignant, arriving too late, and was relieved by her applause.

"Leopards can change their spots," she said.

"And it didn't take Somerset Maugham," said Tom.

Hatch recalled the byplay between them about this unfamiliar name. He asked Tom, "What was so down-market about Maugham?"

Tom laughed. "Tell him Hes."

"Snobbism, really. He wrote short stories that were, perhaps, just a little too neat. That fitted together too well. Writing's not carpentry; irregularities are a better reflection of life. His novels were simply written, rather like Anne Tyler's, but there was a certain predictability. Whereas she leaves things open to doubt. I must be honest in his defence; Maugham suited me when I was teenager. I particularly liked his novel, The Narrow Corner, which looked at mysticism in a fairly clear-sighted way. But time passed and other authors told me more."

"Should I read him to get that perspective?"

"Only if you decide to go the full eng-lit route," said Tom. "I think you might find him just a touch faded."

"There are other women you may enjoy. Not the Hampstead lot. Try Anita Brookner, Penelope Lively, Carol Shields, Alison Lurie."

All of whom he absorbed, pleased by their brevity, their distaste for wilful mystery, their stories which accorded women natural sexual equality. And when he started to read other authors, some male, some he'd been jokily warned about, it was often the women in them that most caught his attention. Creating antipathies as well as enthusiasm. Even now, as his eye ran over the titles on the library shelves, he noted Amis and passed on. An early Amis novel had entertained him and he'd even remembered one of its observations during that dinner with Linda: male reluctance to discuss women with other women. But Amis's misogyny now distressed him and he looked elsewhere. Having been memorably disturbed a month ago by Graham Greene he took out Loser Takes All, attracted by its shortness and its author's modest views about its significance.

His culinary habits had changed too and in his own properly defined kitchen he created Bolognese sauce from the ground up before adding it to pasta and finishing off with a peach for dessert. As ever he washed up immediately and put everything away. Then ignored his neglected television and opened Loser Takes All - to find it was a comic novel. He laughed aloud at the jokes but felt cheated. When he closed the last page, near midnight, his mind reverted to The End of the Affair and a subject that had never left his consciousness since he'd read it.

Not so much love, as the products of love. How that potentially enriching abstraction turned in on itself and gave birth to the quid and the quo, emergent responsibilities and the nightmare of moral entrapment. In particular, how the woman who loved the deliberately unlovable Bendrix, imagining him to have died, made a pact with God: have him live and I will give him up.

What a cruel situation for her but how much more cruel for me, the reader, Andrew Hatch. God was merely a device; love had that frightening quality for believers and non-believers alike. Thus as Celia unfolded her story, close to the mountain where that reality had occurred, Hatch sensed its ambiguity before the end. Love required a subject and an object and their roles were as immiscible in life as in grammar. For the first time Hatch contemplated ambiguity as a word outside the world of books: exquisite ambiguity.

Prudence was due the following day. Hatch wondered if he might broach the matter.

EXCEPT Prudence phoned first to change the arrangements. "Lots to say. A minor celebration. A minor announcement. Time we dined out. Book somewhere flash and let me pay."

Le Grenier was the flashest restaurant Hatch had ever visited - chosen after much consideration for the dinner with Linda and never revisited. Smoothed by the passage of time that evening had taken on a disturbing sense of perfection, separated from reality. Perhaps dining there with Prudence would change things, causing the memory to disintegrate or turning it into something more believable. Le Grenier, then.

Prudence was not impressed by, perhaps did not even notice, the orchid in the single-stem vase. But then she outshone the restaurant's attempts to glamourise itself. Her blonde hair had outgrown the hospital curls and reverted to an organic bob; her confidence, eroded by surgery, was in full flow. She leant across the table to kiss Hatch – a public first since their divorce – and the insistent French waiters, conscious of the theatre, held back in discreet recognition.

A moment for champagne and a careless disregard of the prices. Fortunately lobster was unavailable.

"A minor celebration?" Hatch enquired.

"It could be seen as treachery. I no longer attend church and the helpful Swiss pastor would be disappointed by that. It was inevitable, I suppose. Revealed Christianity never survived any of my examinations. Nor is the hideous symbol that represents its so-called truth anything other than disgusting. I attended services to share time with people whose thoughts were directed to some kind of altruistic goal. But that was when I was ill and mildly terrified."

"So you're stronger, now? Capable of meditating alone?"

She laughed and pretended to slap his arm. "Describing what I do as meditation is over-dignifying it. In the long-term I'm looking like most of us – at self-reliance but I have no plan. In the short term I'd like to be less silly."

"Start by avoiding silly statements. I don't ever remember silliness being a failing."

"How about lacking purpose?"

"Perhaps. But not lacking goodness. Come on, Pru. You're an adult."

A ravishing French waiter, slender as a bread-stick, contorted himself visibly to avoid looking at Prudence as he served the *amuse bouche*.

"And now the minor announcement," said Hatch.

"Ah, yes. I have a friend. A male friend. Older, older even than you. Gentle. Urges me towards chamber music. A constitutional lawyer, which is something I need to find out about. At the moment he's best defined - "

" – you don't have to tell me anything. I'm just happy there is someone."

"That's very noble but I do intend to mention him from time to time. One reason being I've discussed you very generally with him. He's a widower and still in mourning for his wife. He envies my ability to reach out to a departed spouse. Offers his blessing."

"Thank him for that but tell him to concentrate on you."

Prudence lifted the delicate pastry case and bit into it seductively. "Mmm. Girolles and a hint of oregano. How have you been occupying yourself?"

"Reading, mainly." He had intended merely to list the titles, some of which she already knew. But he found himself elaborating his unexpected interest in the fictional treatment of women. ("Women authors are often quite harsh. Men would hardly dare...")

The champagne worked on him as he spoke and his passion grew. Abruptly he saw the climax of The End of the Affair in stark clarity. Talked of its implications, of its horrors. Felt he had gone too far. Tried to return to normal with an unpersuasive shrug. "A dangerous business, love."

Her face had stepped back in time, reminding him of the early, untesting days of their marriage. He said, "I've come to this reading game too late in life. Perhaps I should stick to biographies

"Sheer nonsense. We're supposed to suffer – providing the writing's good enough. Why don't you try Anna Karenina? It left me in the same state. It's not hard to read." She twiddled her flute. "Now, am I allowed to tackle an awkward subject?"

"Be my guest."

"We were childless by intent. Correct?"

Hatch nodded. "In your case damage limitation for a failing marriage. I on the other hand misread what you wanted but the effect was the same."

"Have you ever wondered - ?"

"I think we would have remained together."

"I'm glad we agree," said Prudence. "And do you also agree it would have been hell?"

"Oh yes." Hatch paused, then his expression changed. "However…"

"Ah, you see that too. Like as not we'd have passed through hell and arrived at who we are today. Battered but – I hope – still capable of compromise. Seeing each other differently. As we do now. But still a couple."

Hatch said, "It's a long shot of imagination. But not out of this world. What do you have in mind?"

"Nothing for us, my dear," said Prudence, smiling. "Our divorce was absolute. But I had a touching experience recently. A commercial matter which, alas, came to nought. I met a woman facing divorce and the reasons for that rift were very much on her mind. She has one young child; describes herself as caring but not an instinctive mother. Holds down a responsible job which has kept her apart from the child though she's worked hard to prevent this. Her husband's the other way round; for him the child might as well not exist. The divorce proceedings have highlighted his attitude and she's horrified. It's emphasised her duty towards the child. She foresaw the divorce for years and feels it may be a good thing."

"She's probably right."

"What she didn't say, what I have guessed, is that divorce will be a larger matter than she expects. She's very successful in what she does and this has shaped her life. Now, being a mother – or rather, more aware of being a mother – may alter that definition."

"I see."

"So I compare her to the two of us. Are we lucky we avoided being redefined?"

Hatch's face cleared. "I get the point. You're saying the whole process may have changed her for the better. Whereas we missed that opportunity."

Prudence's turbot cooled on her plate, untouched. "Are either of us capable of great change?"

"Your tone sounds… apocalyptic. In my case, perhaps not. One of my defects."

"Oh, I hope not."

Hatch, too, lowered his knife and fork. "What's this all about, Pru?"

"I suppose you might say it's about resolution."

"Resolution? Oh, the Swiss cleric. He thinks you owe me a debt. It's not true. But I still don't understand."

"I fear I have re-entered your life, my dear."

The last two words, uttered for the second time this evening, contained something alien.

"That sounds like an apology. I still don't understand but there's nothing you need apologise for. I trust you as much as I trust myself." Hatch tried to lighten the mood, knowing he would fail. "Not that that's a great guarantee."

"You know the woman."

Hatch looked from side to side around the room. Anywhere other than at her face.

Prudence said, "Look, it's not irreversible. She doesn't know who I am. I was discreet. I met her legitimately."

Now he looked down, noticed cream sauce round the veal beginning to dry, withdrawing at the edges.

"You may back away without her knowing anything."

He picked up his fork then put it down noisily.

"But you shouldn't."

Again he inspected his plate then turned his face away. Finishing the meal was impossible. Nor could he comfortably remain seated at the table confusing waiters. Prudence intervened, waved away the plates and the second recently opened bottle of champagne. Produced a credit card and ordered coffee as rent for two easy chairs in the lounge.

Pushing the coffee tray to one side she leant forward to speak in low, precise words. It took no more than three minutes. Then she leant back. "I can now order a couple of taxis and we can go our separate ways. Or you can take time to put your thoughts in order and we can discuss this."

Hatch breathed deeply several times. He too sat up. "Two days ago a friend of mine – a woman – told me something personal. She began with a cliché. And I, God forgive me, pointed it out. Back there, at the table, my throat tightened. Just as it does in thrillers. And women's magazines. A cliché to mark the moment."

"And now?"

"I'm relieved. But it's not pleasant. The sort of relief you feel when you've been deciding to jump. And then you jump."

"Take your time."

Hatch shook his head. "No need. It's all fairly clear. I was misinformed. Made a decision. Seems I got it wrong. But there isn't any way back. Easy enough to explain being misinformed. But drawing away said other things about me. Remaining silent added to these things."

"What things?"

"A sort of Old Testament inflexibility. At a stroke, she ceased to have value. Worse, it must seem I wanted her for one thing alone. And when I couldn't have that she didn't exist."

Prudence smiled to herself. "It does fit, of course. Old-fashioned honour – a horrible hindrance in the year of Our Lord 1992. Now I could make a guess about your feelings but I won't. I'd be risking another cliché. Disregarding this morass how do you regard her?"

"I could be the victim of yet more banality: something positive happened the first time I saw her, standing at the lectern, talking about women in industry. A strange kind of parallelism. Yearning. Don't force me to say that hackneyed phrase. Beyond that we've only met a handful of times."

"Stop temporising."

"She's physically and intellectually desirable. We share things – our professions, our way of life, for instance. She sees something in me. I desperately want to be in her company."

"Well said! Write her a letter, a very short letter. Letters come with a wonderful option, they can be ignored. Give her that option. But keep it short, that's vital."

"But the problems remain."

She took his hand. "No they don't. Those are assumptions on your part. Reasonable enough if I accept your old-fashioned logic. But they don't have to happen, even if you guessed her initial reaction. The letter gives her a chance to change her mind."

"But the hurt, and my delay?"

"The letter, Andrew, the letter. Do it for me, if you like. Allow me to win my absolution. In any case, you're forgetting. I've seen Clare, more recently than you. This isn't a shot in the dark."

"You can… tell?"

"Of course," said Prudence, over-acting the casualness. "But keep the letter short."

In the shared taxi she held his hand.

"You never asked why I went there."

"I think I know."

"And, of course, there is no guarantee."

"I know."

"I'm betting on what I know of her."

"So am I."

Drafting the latter took two hours but the post-midnight silence helped. Afterwards, using a fountain pen, he re-wrote the few sentences several times to get the line-breaks right, wondering if this was evidence of shallowness. He added Personal to the envelope and tried to imagine how a third party – say, her secretary – might read what he had written. Exhausted, he slept badly but found comfort here and there.

> Dear Clare,
> I bitterly regret I never answered you.
> My reasons were trivial and misguided.
> I added to them by imagining passing
> time made it more difficult – perhaps
> impossible – to get in touch with you.
> Without my knowledge my former wife
> Prudence (Miss Carolson) met you and now
> suggests I write this short letter. The time for
> stupidity is over and I agree.
> It's possible for you to ignore a letter without
> embarrassment. I hope you won't do that but
> you're entitled to that choice.
> I need your presence.
> Please telephone or write.
> Andrew.

23. CLARE/HATCH

Movement on foot

SHE ARRIVED early, wanting to re-discover the rendezvous, to inhabit it alone. A chill rose from the grey-brown Thames and she buttoned her new coat – an ankle-length sheepskin either two decades out of fashion or simply beyond fashion. The wind teased at the rainbowed slant of hair but she had faith in Kylie, knowing it would separate then cohere. On the bridge above, heads of people crossing the river bobbed up briefly and disappeared. There were still twenty minutes to go and she had a paperback in her handbag but she preferred to look casually at the south bank skyline, to flirt with her tensions.

She expected the first sighting to be far down the Embankment. But he emerged from Carpenter Street, quite near, at the other side of the main road. Comically the underpass forced him to walk west, away from her, before he could cross over Even at this distance he seemed alert. When he saw her she wondered if he would continue to look in her direction or downwards, sideways. His gaze never altered.

"Clare," he said.

"Andrew."

"Why here?"

"It's a corner of London. Not absolutely well-known but unmistakable. Blackfriars Bridge is as Victorian as the old queen. The river runs west-east and the afternoon sun turns it into bronze. Once when I was crossing the bridge a deranged man stepped out of one of the recesses – see up there, designed as pulpits - and dropped into the river. I was near enough to see his face. He was having a fit. I've wondered if I should have reached out and taken his hand."

Hatch looked at her severely. "No."

"Perhaps not. But here we're safe on the Embankment. There's a thick wall to prevent us joining other deranged men. The wall's crowned with huge black slabs. Feel them, they're dimpled and have a very shallow arch. London is a dirty place but the slabs always feel clean. Welcome to London, Andrew."

Gravely he ran his hand over the dimples. "I'm pleased to be here. I wish I knew about these slabs – your slabs - but it would be no more than a guess. How about basalt?"

"A word I've always liked. Let's be unprofessional and call them basalt."

They were silent without awkwardness, inspecting each other. Clare saw again the face shaped like a pre-war child's top, found it familiar. "I feel I must say something about - "

He interrupted. "Prudence. I want to say a lot about her. Can we delay that? She deserves my…" He frowned. "I was going to say eloquence but will I be eloquent? I promise I'll explain. Later. What did you have in mind generally?"

It was clear he had an idea. "Suggest something."

"Could we walk and talk?"

"I come prepared." She indicated calf-length boots.

"Let's go west." And she slipped her arm under his.

"Who made 'Let's start at the beginning.' famous?"

"It's a song from The Sound of Music."

"Disappointing. I hoped some literary type said it. Samuel Taylor Coleridge, say."

Clare said, "If you want to pass for eng-lit it's better to drop the Samuel Taylor."

"OK. Let's switch to GCE chemistry. Remember when all experiments started with 'Object.' Let's use that."

"You start."

Hatch pointed at Festival Hall. "My father visited the Festival of Britain. Saw the Skylon. 'Elegant but pointless.' he said."

"Perfectly true. I like his spare judgement. Start with your father."

"A lathe operator working on gearboxes in the Black Country. Company long since bagged up. In those days he was a craftsman, now the word means basket weaving. Then lathes were nowhere near as precise. But a good operator could play with the tolerances. I have absolutely no idea how."

That last admission pleased her.

"He died," Hatch coughed, "of testicular cancer. He wasn't alone in that. Machine tool operators wiped down work surfaces then stuffed the cotton waste back in their trouser pockets. When it was far too late they found that cutting fluid is carcinogenic."

He was silent, turning his face away, towards the tomblike front of the Shell Building. "He was stoic, of course. His sort were. But I've only recently wondered how stoic. It was a man's world and he had the surgery. Do you know the procedure?"

Clare said, "It's either a joke or a terrible euphemism."

"Orchidectomy! Afterwards he went back to work for a time and I wondered how he coped with the sniggering. At home he was distant but then he'd always been like that. He was on his last legs when I was picking my subjects for sixth form. He refused to guide me: 'You'll only do the opposite.' Grudgingly he recommended manufacturing 'because things'll always have to be made'. And just before he went into hospital for the second time, knowing it was the end, he said, 'Stay off the shop floor'."

"Which you did."

Hatch continued. "Manufacturing seemed inevitable. It was what my friends did, what I did. It was a general environment. I suppose there was one magic moment, one little push. A bit vague, though."

She jiggled him via their linked arms. "Spit it out, you great anti-romantic."

"A measure of my naiveté I suppose. He used to bring home spoiled or torn engineering drawings for me to scribble on. Perversely I looked on the used side and asked him to explain. The legend had been ripped away and he took a scale out of his breast pocket. Ever seen a scale? A precision wooden ruler with ivory edging. He measured some dimension or other. 'I mean it's a layshaft as any fool, even you, could tell,' he said. 'But I needed to check. This is the one we use in the – I can't now recall – the XYZ box.' None of that mattered. What struck me was he measured the paper, he didn't need the component. There was a connection between paper and metal."

"Are you a good engineer?" The answer wasn't important; his reaction to the question was.

Hatch frowned and looked straight ahead as if avoiding the influence of her face. "Dogged."

"A good engineer, then." And he laughed at the neatness.

She said, "You were talking about that little push. Listening to you I've had one myself. Not as beguiling as yours. More a moment of clarity. When I'm asked what I do for a living I tend to say I'm a physicist. Being a manager is boring, too vague. I prefer to be a physicist. There's more zing to it. But it's not true."

Again, that attentive look.

"I was good at school. Did well in most subjects. When the time came for a decision I chose physics simply because it was supposed to be hard. Doing it set me aside. But I was never a physicist. I know this because I never had any interest in any of physics' big questions. Didn't fancy a post-graduate degree. Or research."

She looked directly at him. "I can tell you this now. You are an engineer through and through. It's what makes you who you are. You became a manager quite naturally, the result of your technical discipline. In effect I simply became a manager."

He didn't like this, she could tell. What she was saying appeared to diminish her and he didn't want her diminished. Oh my goodness.

She went on. "I'm not apologising. I've had wide experience and I've contributed. I've got a senior position and I've made an impact already at Garton. But I'm not a physicist and I must stop making this claim. It's like harping on about my eleven-plus."

He was thinking hard. Had she been guilty of special pleading? she asked herself. Had she deliberately put herself down so he could rehabilitate her?

"You're not a physicist, OK. But you have a physicist's nature. Beating physics academically was worthwhile because it's hard. Too hard for me. It's hard because of what it explores. But sixth form and university weren't just a series of hoops; the process moulded you." His face was contorted with the effort of getting things straight. "I'm running out of profound reasons. OK, you're a manager. But to me you're an undercover physicist."

They were now almost in the shadow of Big Ben. Hatch gestured at the seat of government, "All this confessional stuff, all these truths. Uncommon activity in this area." As they reached the bridge and were able to see Parliament Square he pointed to one of the exits. "Just beyond there is Birdcage Walk. Very swank. It's where the Institute of Mechanical Engineers had their headquarters. Imagine the wealth and the confidence they must have had to take up residence. Alas, no longer. Some years ago they moved out into East Anglia. A sign of the times."

"For those who couldn't handle a changing world," said Clare briskly. "Look at you. From swarf to telly glamour."

He wriggled. "Ah, don't. The guilt, the fraudulence. What would my dad say?"

"That crusty pragmatist? That you were off the shop floor. A flibbertigibbet but safe from cutting fluid."

Crossing the square halted conversation. Finally they were on the river side of Millbank and Clare said, "There's a seat empty in those gardens. Let's sit down and you can talk about Prudence."

She felt him start. Then he said, "Yes, you must have that. I'm the one dragging my heels. But then I'm not exactly covered in glory. Let's sit down."

And she knew it was wrong. "Never mind. Later. Over a drink."

They'd stopped and were face to face, their arms disengaged. People were brushing past on either side. "No, you're right. I should," he said.

She took his arm again and said gently, "Later, Andrew. I'm rushing things. I'm sorry."

"Sorry? I don't want you sorry."

She squeezed his arm. "I know you don't. But there are things I must say first." She had considered telling him about the bank interview but wasn't sure she was up to it. Instead she explained Barbara's scheme to reinvent her as a spokesman for the company and the world in general. He immediately recognised doubts she'd hidden from both Barbara and Mike.

There were events he was unaware of and their telling took them past Vauxhall Bridge as the undistinguished skyline unscrolled to her left. She tried to remember when she had last been the centre of such concerned attention.

"Your problem is it's all been a success." He said it straightfaced and made her laugh. "I know, I know," she said. "How should I react to that?"

"Deep down you think it's not your job. That it's not you. Luckily you're speaking to someone who asks that question every day. I think you're wrong. You're a manager: you spend your life asking, advising, telling, disciplining. You've attended those cant seminars on communication, haven't you? Well this is more of the same."

It was the first disagreement, even if it was a minor one. They looked at each other and she expected him to be smiling, to soften the rift. But there was only intensity. "You didn't want me to tell you that."

She said, "Not that part. There is another. But it can wait. Let's nip into the Tate, sit down and look at a Turner."

"Am I allowed to behave stupidly?"

"You've heard of Turner?"

"The light man? Yes. But I have no opinion about him."

"I have enough for both."

They threaded their way through German and Scandinavian teenagers untidily scattered over the front steps and found an upholstered bench in front of Snow Storm: Steam-Boat off a Harbour's Mouth. Deliberately she remained silent, knowing he was staring hard at the painting.

He said, "He's feeling it: the danger, I mean. Usually I struggle, I want things to be real, to be explicable. The failings of my trade. But how do you paint danger? This is how."

"Would you like to own it?"

"Provided I could hang it where I saw it every day. Do you know all about Turner?"

"My father is a specialist in paintings. He regards it as the great tragedy of his life that none of his dealings, none of his advice, have ever concerned a Turner. I know about painters, admire them, but I never inherited his feel. Mind you I wouldn't mind this one."

He continued to look, unhurriedly, at peace with the task. It was she who stood up first. "This is how you're supposed to use galleries. Look at one painting, not shuffle around. Yet this must be the first time I've ever done exactly that."

Outside, in Grosvenor Road, she pointed across the river. "There's an artefact that explains itself. Somebody loves it, it's got a preservation order. Is it worth preserving?"

Self-consciously he looped his arm as an invitation to hers. She felt herself smile as she linked up. Why?

"I'm wary about industrial buildings. Hag-ridden by function. Does it work? That one, over there, is a shell so it's simply architecture. Power stations are big and beauty has to be a factor as long as it doesn't interfere with the job. That one's restrained enough and somebody designed it. But I'd knock it down."

"Son of the crusty pragmatist."

"That's me."

She realised he never tailored his views to what he imagined hers might be. Perhaps he was the only person who could usefully drive away her self-doubts.

"Could you stand the risk of being embarrassed," she asked.

"About something you're going to tell me? Of course. I'd want to."

"Over a year ago something rather horrid happened. My appearance was criticised – not gratuitously, there was a reason, but it happened. Before then I'd never paid a great deal of attention to myself. I don't mean I went around in rags, didn't wash my hair. But being presentable didn't interest me. In a sense I didn't have to bother. I'd done well professionally."

There were parts of this that needed editing. Her looks impinged on other aspects of her life but this wasn't the time to widen her brief. As she considered this she felt increased tension in his arm.

Clare continued. "For various reasons I took advice. Clothes, make-up, that sort of thing." Vanity stopped her short of mentioning the orthodontist. "Soon after I interviewed for my present job. I had the qualifications and I flatter myself – in fact my boss confirms it – they would have been sufficient. But the new me had an effect on Mike, my boss. He'd never taken women seriously and our interview nudged him. But would he have made that confession to the old me?"

Am I being silly about this? Terribly feminine? Too late now given those round green eyes.

She said, "Mike felt he wanted to take advantage of my appointment. Use it to prove how forward-thinking Garton was. Did I mind? It seemed innocent enough given that women holding jobs like mine are fairly rare. My only reservation I've just mentioned. Would he have boasted about the old me?"

Her words suggested there was more and he waited.

"Very quickly all these vague policies became concrete. Barbara understands the way to the heart of the media. She proposed turning me into something of a media figure. A spokesman for the company and, later, for much else. Lo and behold I even found myself part of a television programme."

A tight expression on his face.

She said, "Now don't get me wrong. I haven't become Cinderella. But I'm certainly no longer just a manager. For what the words are worth, I have presence. In some respects I embrace it. It's fun and I enjoy the give and take. And exposure has benefited Garton.

But who am I? It's a question I need to answer. This puffball stuff isn't going to last and I may end up a retired semi-celebrity."

He sighed as he grappled with the conflicting elements. She added, "I'm able to ask you because of your new life. You admit feeling a fraud although I'm sure you're over-egging."

Hatch said, "With me it's an indulgence. I'm used to a world with substance and this new one seems to lack just that. But that's not strictly true. Both worlds involve hard work and real goals. And I still trade on my competence. What's more I've added a few skills and that's allowed me to extend my contract. But your feelings aren't indulgent. There's this matter of exploitation, although I think you can handle that."

He looked at her shyly. "Am I right? What worries you is self-exploitation."

She pretended not to understand. But did. "Explain that."

"I'm not inclined to. The problem is internal. You say you aren't a physicist but I say you're the product of understanding physics. Of being able to explain the material world. Your concerns are serious. You see these changes at Garton as non-serious. But are they even changes? You are you - with or without make-up. The camera doesn't just dwell on your face, it records what you say. Journalists aren't struck dumb, they write down your answers."

He stopped to gather his thoughts. "I never knew this old you. But I'd have taken this walk with her just as willingly. I'm sure of that"

"I'm worrying about nothing, then?"

He shrugged. "Worry away, along with all of us. None of us is satisfied. Get over this and there'll be something else. Why were you so certain a PhD wasn't for you? Meanwhile I'll be worrying about – What are they called? The plastic arts? But save all that for wet Sundays. Revel in your intelligence, in your 'presence'."

"And in present company."

"Hey, I don't need flattery." Though of course he did. "I'm like one of my dad's gearboxes. Over-engineered."

They'd walked the length of Grosvenor Road, avoided turning into Chelsea Bridge Road and were now halfway along Chelsea Embankment. Clare said, "What's this next right turn? Flood Street. Let's take that up to the King's Road. We'll have a drink at a chintzy little caff. Alien territory for both of us."

"Where people eat cake with a fork?"

"Just so."

The tables were wrought iron with tops no larger than a tea-tray. In sitting down they were so close they bumped heads. He said, "I am out of place, and clumsy with it."

They were early enough to order a glass of wine without committing themselves to lunch. He sipped, rested his forearms on the cramped space hardly a foot away. "Tell me, back there near the river," he said, "were you in effect complaining about your looks?"

"How could you possibly think that?"

"It's one interpretation. Guilt, angst and make-up."

A joke with an ounce of truth. "Once how I looked didn't matter. Now it seems to. And it's expensive. You wouldn't credit how much the salon costs."

"Money well spent," he said. "One of life's mysteries to men. To this man at least. Can women assess their own looks? I don't mean by results. In absolute terms."

"They try but they usually get it wrong. They veer away from, say, Marilyn Monroe in favour of greater dignity. The English actress Valerie Hobson used to be the yardstick."

He said, "John Profumo's wife. Appeared in Kind Hearts and Coronets. Prudence was – is – beautiful; somewhere between Marilyn and Valerie. I was surprised she married me. Crucially I never really asked why."

Clare remained still and silent.

"It was an unsuccessful marriage and I wasn't equipped to know why. After we divorced she was diagnosed with a brain tumour and for various reasons she preferred Switzerland. This needed discussing and I used the opportunity to ask why she left me. She didn't want to say but I more or less forced her. What she said was painful and I pretended it was all a big surprise. But it sounded likely."

He said, "When Prudence proved my solid virtues were also vices and defects – that was hard. Even worse when I discovered that lack of imagination kept me from realising this."

"You're being too self-critical."

"Because I wasn't critical enough a decade ago. But never mind. As you know this story has an upbeat ending. Prudence convalesced in Switzerland and admitted she'd had time for meditation. Not just about herself but about me. She asked if we could be friends, if I minded her taking an interest. She'd changed a lot, much more focused. And she's a good listener. I chatted."

His head bowed. "This is the difficult bit."

She wanted to touch his hand even though she knew it would be filmic. "We're not in any rush. Tell me later."

"Was I a Jane Austen character or just a fearful twat? I still can't answer that. I enjoyed meeting you at Garton; thought you deserved your success, admired your professionalism, liked you of course. The tutoring session drew me closer. Too close. I was busy the following day, convinced I'd see you again. Knew I'd enjoy that, too." He raised his head. "I was told you were married."

"By Celia, of course."

Hatch refused to acknowledge this. "I was away that evening. Got home the next. Listened to your message. Played it a second time. Later, my boss made an observation about me I still can't bear to dwell on. I deleted the message."

He sighed and drank a huge mouthful of wine. "And there things stood. I was desperately occupied at Gamester, working on my contract. Weeks went by. Prudence came for dinner. I talked about you and she did what she's good at – she listened. She was dissatisfied by the logic and asked me to go over it all again. I did so, remembering more. She was still dissatisfied. The rest you know. It was her initiative. If I'd known I'd have discouraged her. I am not entitled to pry."

Clare said, "My strange yet beautiful visitor. My God Andrew, you're lucky to have an ex-wife like that. Did you try to check up on me? Did you want to?"

He was hangdog. "There was a Who's Who. Other than that, no. Each passing day made it more difficult. Boorishness is cumulative. Prudence recognised that."

"But it was a mistake. You were misinformed. Why so wretched?"

"In not replying – there was… What? A presumption."

It took Clare time to work out this coy admission. "Let's turn this into a discussion between grown-ups. You dreamt of sleeping with me but all bets were off when you discovered I had a husband."

Now he was sheepish. "Slightly worse. Being married meant you ceased to exist. Or you'd become a leper. I suppose that's how I saw it. That you would conclude I had only one aim. Not just boorishness, juvenile boorishness"

"Oh Andrew, juvenile is right." But now a teenage waiter in a maroon apron and with an Australian accent stood beside them. Having asked a question and got no answer he was listening intently. "I just said, were you going to order? We need the table for lunches."

Hatch said, "Here's as good as anywhere else. Bowl of pasta?"

"Perhaps we could rent a couple," said Clare, giggling.

"Two spag bols?" asked the waiter and they both nodded.

Clare opened her mouth to resume but Hatch was ahead of her. "I've done a lot of agonising on my own behalf."

She ignored this and continued – firmly. "I was disappointed. Very disappointed. I'm not given to agonising. More than that I was surprised. It didn't fit what I knew of you."

"Prudence's reaction. Even so…"

"Let's take it at face value. A worst case assessment. I can't complain that you daydreamed – in an impossibly gentlemanly manner – of sleeping with me. That does happen from time to time in the twentieth century. I'm more disturbed that you drew back, like a Victorian curate, on finding me spoken for. Not because I'm keen to sleep around. Rather that being married automatically cut me off from you."

Hatch looked at his glass, found it empty, raised his eyebrows at Clare. "But I have form on this. Prudence sees it as an excess of honour. For me it was an acute attack of social awkwardness. I'm relieved it's in the open but…"

Clare's mouth opened in astonishment. "You're not thinking of pulling out, surely? Not after what Prudence did for you. Not after telling me about your gruff old Dad?"

"But I'm no longer the dependable, slightly thick Andrew Hatch. A bent if not broken reed."

"Mercifully you don't know about my bent reed. That horridness I talked about. I'll tell you if you like."

He leant back in his rickety chair, his expression neutral, his eyes roving over her face. Time for her to measure the straightness of his nose, his short-cut hair, the tiny beads of perspiration that glistened in his eyebrows. Feature by feature took away the certainties: she saw vulnerability instead of confidence, some fallibility. Qualities that fitted the gaps in her. Steady on, Clare.

"I'd rather you didn't." He didn't want her reduced too.

Food and wine made them more relaxed. "Prudence liked your boy. Found it hard to leave."

"She and I had this intermediary. I was in a bad mood showing off the house to buyers. I should have been irritated with her and yet I wasn't."

"She likes you. I wouldn't be here otherwise."

"What should we do this afternoon? How do you relax?"

He said, "Doing humdrum things. DIY work round the house. Volunteering as a racing mechanic. Reading books others have recommended."

"Suppose you were on your own in London?"

"Science Museum."

"Let's do that."

"No. That isn't taking advantage of being with you. Like looking at the Turner."

"Music?"

He sighed. "I'm stick in the mud. Never got beyond Bach."

"You don't have to apologise for that." And, after a pause, "Or anything else."

"Perhaps we could find a church. Not for the God stuff. Sometimes there are choral services."

It seemed a long shot with more walking than anything else. But they found what they wanted in a richly endowed high Anglican church in Kensington. The liturgy was sung by a treble choir and within minutes Clare was affected. I'm not going to cry. I'm not going to cry. But the need was irresistible. A different form of tears this time; like being washed. He noticed and held her hand. When she had the composure to turn she saw him stone-faced. No tears for Andrew but only because he was better at controlling himself.

Outside she repaired the damage using her compact. "My time to be juvenile," she said feebly. This time he took her arm unequivocally.

At Hungerford Bridge they boarded a near-deserted boat downstream and back. There was less need to fill the afternoon with talk and the silences had their own appeal. Hatch was moved to speak at the Barrier: "I don't know how that thing works and it annoys me."

"Do you *need* to know?"

"It's a personal obligation. It's my world. I don't know bestsellers, politics, popular television programmes and team sport but I can usually claim the made world. Here's a small vacuum. I take it you don't suffer such failings."

The wine had made her lazy. "I cover up with dishonesty. River barriers don't worry me. Faced with an LED or a non-stick frying pan I tell myself I could work them out. Notice the huge gulf between us."

"Is that why you're a better manager?"

"That remains to be seen."

"Why do I want you to be better?"

On the wide open Thames the boat was scoured by the wind but neither wanted to go below, to share the boat with others. "I have this idea," said Hatch, "but no one understands. It's American. I see myself as a working stiff. It means working class and probably dates back to the Depression. But I like its unpretentiousness."

"It won't do," said Clare.

"Why not? Because stiffs are corpses?"

"Because it's dishonest. Once you were a working stiff. But not for ages. You were in charge at Tempest. These days you do creative work. No dirt under your finger-nails."

"Dishonest?"

"Don't look so hurt," she said, smiling. "If dishonesty pains you, how about sentimental?"

"A rotten choice."

"Never mind rotten, is it true?"

He rested his chin in his cupped hand, looking back down towards the Barrier. "It's true. But why didn't I see that?"

"Because you're guessing at what's on my mind. It's not one of your talents. Also trying to undersell yourself so there's not the tiniest hint of boasting."

Now he was rueful. "It gets worse."

"Andrew. Why do you think I'm here?"

"How can I answer that?"

"Because you have to. Because you're courting my forgiveness."

This alarmed him. "I suppose… because you know I'd tell you if you were wrong."

"Wow, Andrew. You're even shrewder than I thought. What a darling answer." This time she laughed wholeheartedly. "Though I hope there's just a bit more. My legs aren't bad."

"It's that slant of hair. When I imagine your face I think: asymmetry! I'm not supposed to go for imbalance. But you've persuaded me. Against my instincts."

"My dear Andrew. Your instincts are wider than you know."

Back on the Embankment she looked at him questioningly. He said, "I'll walk you back to Waterloo."

"Are we finished?" she asked, surprised.

"Nick needs you. It's my treat and I can't think of anything that costs me more."

He knew Nick's name.

On the platform, he said, "I'll cock things up now."

"I work in IT. I can decode cock-ups."

"I must avoid adjectives, that's what they say, isn't it? So I'll say your name: Clare. There, I'm warmed. Doesn't scan does it? Scan me, see the warmth. You understand infra-red don't you? What the hell am I talking about? Clare."

"I don't cry much but I cried when my husband ignored my son. I was mad. I cried again today but for different happier reasons. I can't improve on you: I'm warmed too. Andrew."

They embraced and kissed lightly, lips only just parted, as if in rehearsal.